THE STARS WE HOLD

THE STARS WE HOLD

MELISSA ARMSTRONG

This is a work of fiction. All the names, characters, businesses, places, events and incidents in this book are either the product of the author's imagination or used in a fictitious manner. Any resemblance to actual persons, living or dead, or actual events is purely coincidental.

THE STARS WE HOLD
Advanced Reader Copy

www.melissaarmstrong.com

Published by Green Gables Press LLC

All art and designs by Rena Violet
Editing by Maria Tureaud
Proofreading by Diane Telgen

ISBN (paperback): 979-8-9906157-2-4

For Tata.
Because of your stories, my dream came true.

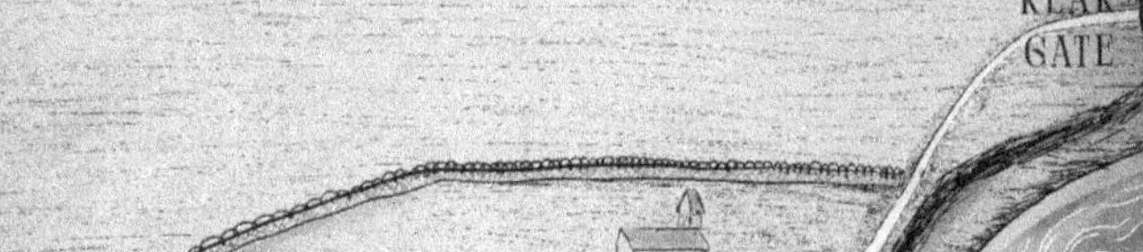
REAR GATE
ARMORY
SAVA RIVER
BARRACKS
HOSPITAL
BRICK PIT
EXCAVATION PIT
BRICKWORKS
GUARD HOUSE
TRAIN TUNNEL
BRICK KILN
SOUTHERN GATE
CAMP ADMINISTRATION
WAREHOUSE
GUARD HOUSE
MAIN GATE
JASENOVAC

SERBO-CROATIAN

PRONUNCIATION & TRANSLATION GUIDE

Name/Word/Phrase	Phonetic Pronunciation	Name/Word/Phrase
Ester	Es-tair	
Henrik	Hen-rik	
Nada	Nah-duh	
Vinko	Vin-ko	
Ante Pavelič	Uhn-teh Puh-vel-ich	Leader of the Ustaše
Baka	Bah-kuh	Grandmother
Crnobog	Tsur-no-bog	"Black god" – a Slavic deity
Deda (Serbian)	Deh-duh	Grandfather
Djed (Croatian)	Dyed	Grandfather
Hvala	Hfah-luh	Thank you
Ja Sam Sirota	Yuh Suhm Si-ro-tuh	"I Am Poor" – a children's song
Jasenovac	Juh-sen-o-vuts	The Ustaše's infamous death camp
Jugoslavenske	Yoo-go-sluh-ven-skeh	Yugoslavian
Jugoslavija	Yoo-go-sluh-vee-yuh	Yugoslavia
Kobasica	Koh-buh-sits-uh	Air-dried sausage
Kumova Slama	Koom-ov-uh Slah-muh	Godfather's Straw
Mama	Muh-muh	Mom
Miš	Mish	Mouse
Moj mali miš	Moi mah-lee mish	My little mouse
Ništa	Nish-tuh	Nothing
O Bože	O Bo-zheh	Oh God
Orahovica	O-ruh-hov-its-uh	A village in the countryside
Osijek	O-see-yek	Nada's home city
Partizan	Pahr-ti-zahn	Partisan

Partizani (Plural)	Pahr-ti-zahn-ee	Partisans
Partizanka	Pahr-ti-zahn-kuh	Female partisan
Poglavnik	Po-gluhv-nik	Chief / "supreme leader"
Pršut	Pur-shoot	Dry-cured ham
Puška Puca	Poosh-kuh Poots-uh	"The Gun Fires" – Ustaše anthem
Rakija	Ruhk-ee-yah	Brandy
Retfala	Ret-fuh-luh	A district in the city of Osijek
Sarma	Sahr-muh	Stuffed cabbage rolls
Sestra (Singular)	Sest-ruh	Sister
Sestre (Plural)	Sest-reh	Sisters
Slatko	Sluht-ko	Sweet
Slavuj	Slahv-ooi	Nightingale
Srbosjek	Sur-bos-yek	Serb-cutter
Srce moj	Sur-tseh moi	My heart
Svinje	Svin-yeh	Pigs
Tata	Tuh-tuh	Dad
Tito	Tee-to	Leader of the Partizani
Titovka	Tee-tov-kuh	Partizan cap named after Tito
Ubica	Oo-bits-uh	Assassin / killer
Ustaša (Singular)	Oo-stuh-shuh	A member of the Croatian regime
Ustaše (Plural)	Oo-stuh-sheh	A fascist Croatian regime
Vila Rebar	Vil-uh Reh-bahr	Name of Pavelič's mansion
Vino	Vee-no	Wine
Vrag! Ubit ču te!	Vrahg! Oo-bit choo teh	Devil! I'll kill you!
Za dom – spremni	Zuh dom – sprem-nee	For homeland – ready

CHAPTER 1

Yugoslavia, April 1945

THERE WERE NO DEMONS AS RELENTLESS AND CRUEL as hunger, loss, and war. Though the three fell hand in hand, hunger demanded Nada's attention, circling her thoughts with wicked whispers while burrowing its way into her stomach. She sank deeper into her seat, trying to let the lingering scent of burning coal and the rattling and chugging of the train ride drown out the maddening ache. But she knew all too well the devil could never be ignored.

As the carriage rocked and teetered around a bend, Nada swayed into her little brother's shoulder. She squeezed Filip's hand, small and light in hers, and glanced at him. His free arm snaked around his middle. His dull eyes reflected in the window amid a backdrop of hazed green and gray.

Nada's brows drew together. When was the last time he ate? Perhaps she shouldn't have let him come on this journey. It would only drain him. Then again, maybe it would prove a better distraction for Filip than for Nada.

"It won't be long till we're there," she murmured in his ear, a feeble attempt to comfort him.

Filip nodded, though he kept his gaze on the passing fields.

Rubbing away the tension in her temple, Nada looked at the drawstring bag sitting empty at her feet—a pool of fabric waiting to be filled with food once they reached the countryside. There, in a small village near Orahovica, her grandparents would greet her with the fruits of their farm, enough to feed her family back in Retfala for a month. Retfala, a district in the outskirts of Osijek, was a wasteland where food was concerned. Every store in the city had been cleaned out long ago, except for one local butcher who continued to sell only horse meat. Like Nada, all of Osijek would rather starve than stoop to such revolting measures.

Occupying the row in front of them, Nada's best friend since childhood spun to lean over her chair. Ester's green eyes glowed bright as she rapped the back of it. "That soldier looks like Henrik," she whispered.

Nada's heartbeat tripped and stuttered. *Henrik.* She shifted forward in her seat, holding her breath, as her eyes darted over the carriage in search of him. She skimmed past the older gentlemen dressed in worn coats and hats to hunt down a lean frame, olive skin, and light brown hair. Where was he? She couldn't find him. Nada's gaze landed on a young German soldier seated a few rows down with a machine gun propped between his knees, bearing a passable likeness. That's what Ester meant. Nada's breath broke free as she slumped back. A heaviness surged within her. Of course it wasn't him. Why would it be?

Nada's chin lowered, and she stroked the wooden button threaded with a string of leather tied to her wrist. Was Henrik all right, wherever he was? Would he come home soon?

"He's handsome," said Ester. "I'd bet an entire loaf of bread Henrik looks like that now."

Her words reminded Nada of the soldier's presence and her eyes turned to Ester's neck, checking that her friend's necklace remained hidden beneath her simple ivory blouse. Why was Ester adamant about wearing her Star of David pendant at times like these? At least Nada's Serbian heritage wasn't such a visible beacon, at risk of being seen. Not that she needed to fear a German.

Nada cleared her throat. "Do you even remember what Henrik looks like?"

"Don't *you*? It's only been two years, Nada."

On a sigh, Nada cast her gaze out the window. "It feels like a lifetime ago."

The war had slithered and coiled its way into their world over the last four years. Living with such a sinister shadow forced time to crawl by.

With a knowing grin, Ester reached over to give Nada's knee a playful whack. "Admit it. If that was Henrik, you would swoon."

Nada's lips parted and her brows lifted. "Swoon over the boy who hid a frog in my desk and stole my shoe to sail down the river like it was a toy boat?"

Ester chuckled. "*No.* The boy who left to join the resistance and looked at you one last time like you were all the stars in the heavens."

Nada looked away, swallowing hard. If that were the case, he wouldn't have left in the first place. Wouldn't have left when she needed him most. "He did no such thing."

"He adored you."

Warmth bloomed in her chest. "I was a skin-and-bone fifteen-year-old. There was nothing to adore."

"I liked Henrik," Filip piped up. "He taught me how to tie knots."

Nada couldn't help the grin lighting her face. Filip had been seven last time they saw Henrik. Clearly his lessons made an impact.

"We *all* liked him," said Ester. "Your sestra more so, though she won't admit it."

Nada gave her a leveling stare. "He's family."

Filip's chin swung up, and his nose scrunched. "Henrik's not family."

Her lips itched to smile at him. She nudged his leg with the back of her hand, still joined with his. "Family is more than blood."

"That's right," said Ester. "Nada isn't only my closest friend. She's my sestra."

A solid bump against Nada's shoe had her glancing down. Her mouth watered and the pit in her stomach deepened. A smoked kobasica had rolled to her feet.

Across the aisle, a wisp-haired boy with a drooling smile fished into his mother's basket-weaved bag as she gazed out her window. It would have been so easy to take the air-dried sausage and slide it into her bag without anyone noticing.

Nada picked it up and stifled a grimace. "Excuse me."

The boy's mother turned.

"You dropped this."

The woman's jaw dropped, and she placed a hand against her chest. "Hvala," she said, expressing her thanks as Nada handed the meat back to her.

With a tight smile, Nada settled back into her seat. The woman's grateful reaction didn't ease the pain of having to surrender the kobasica. But if it were Nada in her place, she would have raged if someone stole her family's food. With a widowed mother and another two younger siblings at home, Nada understood the importance of holding on to every morsel.

A thunderous boom shook the carriage, shuddering the floor beneath her. Nada gasped and gripped the seat in front of her as her body flew forward with force. Her knuckles turned white as the train screeched and whined and jolted to a stop. The baby next to her screamed with a fit of tears.

Filip grabbed her arm, his breath heaving. "What's happening?"

Frenzied passengers launched to their feet, all crying out with fear. Without a second thought, Nada tugged on Filip's hand and pushed her way into the rush of bodies fighting to escape the carriage. She was jostled in the melee but kept a firm grip on her brother. Figures pressed close near the exit, surrounding Nada and Filip. She scanned the faces and profiles around her. None of them were familiar. None of them had blond hair.

Her heart raced. "Ester?" Nada twisted, glancing back, eyes flitting to every face. "*Ester!*"

"I'm here!"

Nada spun the other way. Ester shoved her way to them, face pale as chalk. She clasped Filip's other hand, keeping the three of them connected.

They stumbled out of the front carriage, pushing through the crowd and into a vast, grassy field flanked by forest. The train continued to hiss, its steam rising in a cloudy plume, as gray smoke wafted around them. The acrid scent of coal melded with hints of oil and metal and a strange, burning bitterness. Through the chaos, Nada managed to catch a glimpse of the nose of the train. It had run off the tracks and wedged itself into the earth. The long stretch of flat wagons trailing behind the two passenger cars remained intact—both its heavy artillery cargo and the German soldiers perched atop them.

The thrum of a plane's engine retreated in the distance.

"How long until the train is running again?" asked Ester. "Surely they can repair it."

"Raus! Raus!" shouted the soldiers, gesturing for the passengers to back up.

Ester turned to Nada. "What are they saying?"

"They're ordering us to get out of here."

Nada studied the soldiers as they dashed about on the wagons, setting up hefty weapons. They propped MG 34s on large stacks of canvas-covered boxes as other soldiers swooped in to attach ammunition belts in a hurry.

"The plane," said Nada. "It must have bombed the tracks. We have to run. Now!"

She grabbed Filip by the arm and bolted for the forest ahead. Ester sprinted alongside them, her blue floral skirt fluttering behind her. The passengers and crew scattered and shouted in a panic. Too fast for her brother to keep up, Nada released Filip's arm, freeing him to run unhindered as she slowed to keep pace with him.

A humming drone swelled around them. Nada looked back, turning her eyes skyward. Flying low, the plane headed straight toward them. Adrenaline spiked in Nada's chest as it opened fire, jackhammering through the air.

Ester dropped to the ground and Nada followed, but Filip kept running out of sheer terror.

"Filip, get down!"

Her brother dove for the grass and Nada wrapped her arms over her head. Soil hissed as large bullets thudded the ground, flinging grass and dirt that stung Nada's cheeks and trembling hands. She gritted her teeth, rapid breaths bursting as she braced herself.

A new source of gunfire pounded away to her left, and Nada peeked out from under her arm. The young soldier from the train lay on his back nearby, firing at the plane. Ferocity flared in his eyes as he kept his sight trained on the aircraft, bullets flying one after another. He jerked and grunted as the plane's ammunition pierced his thigh, but he never once lost aim as the plane passed overhead.

When the aircraft's assault ended abruptly and the Germans ceased firing back, Nada peered up to catch sight of the tail-end of the plane.

"*Russians,*" someone muttered.

Nada sat up. Turned to her brother, chest tight. "Filip! Are you okay?"

His pale face lifted from the dirt to nod. He grimaced with the effort of holding back his tears.

Panting, Nada surveyed the field. Passengers rose around her, glancing about them to see if anyone had been hurt. But where was her best friend? Her sestra?

"Ester?"

"Here, Nada!" Ester was crawling across the grass toward the young soldier. "He's hurt!"

"We need to get out of here!"

But Ester ignored her. She leaned over him, applying pressure against the man's bloodied leg while he propped himself up with one arm, wincing through the pain.

Nada scrambled over to them, her instincts shouting at her to run.

"He's bleeding too much." Ester reached for the belt closed around his coat.

He pushed her hand back. "Was machen sie?"

"Nada, I need his belt to use as a tourniquet."

Nada pressed a hand to her head, trying to ease her swimming mind. "Gib ihr den Gürtel!" Nada told him. "Sie wurde von einer Krankenschwester ausgebildet." *Give her your belt! She's been trained by a nurse.*

Nada cringed as soon as the words flew out of her mouth. Had she used formal or informal language with him? She couldn't think through the swirl of her anxiousness. Nada watched the man for his reaction, but he gave none.

The German soldier unbuckled his belt and pulled it free. Ester wasted no time circling it around his thigh, above the wound, and cinching it tight.

The soldier didn't flinch, his focus transfixed on Ester. Nada looked at her—a pretty picture in her ivory blouse, knitted cardigan, and blond tendrils. Even stained with dirt, and hands slick with blood. No wonder the soldier stared.

Then Nada froze, heart thrumming faster than the bullets that had rained down on them.

It wasn't Ester's striking features holding his interest as she fumbled for his fallen cap to press against his injury. It was the Star of David necklace, swinging free of her blouse and glinting in the daylight.

"Ester," she whispered in horror.

Her best friend looked up to find Nada staring at her collar. With dread, Ester's eyes dropped to the pendant dangling beneath her chin, and her busy hands stilled.

Afraid to move, to run, Ester's eyes crept up to meet his.

Their gazes locked. A breeze rippled the grass around them, tickling Nada's ankles.

"Gehen," he murmured. "Bevor sie zu helfen kommen." *Go. Before they come to help.*

Breath escaped Nada in a rush as her eyes widened. "He said we can go."

Clasping Ester's arm, she drew her away from the soldier. A glance toward the train confirmed it. German soldiers bustled about, tending to their wounded.

"We need to run." Nada whirled in search of her brother, but Filip waited behind her, panting from fright. She took his hand, readying to leave. "Quickly. Let's head back to Retfala. We're closer to home than the farm."

"Did you say Retfala?" the German asked in his native tongue.

Nada spun to look at him. At his wrinkled brow, his steady gaze. "Yes."

His eyes went to Ester's throat, where her dainty necklace dangled, and back to Nada. He studied her face a moment. Took in her waves of dark brunette hair and brown eyes. "You're Serbian?"

She could only nod.

He glanced away on an exhale. "Don't go to Retfala right now."

"Why?"

He shook his head, lips curling into a scowl as he swallowed. "I heard Ustaše are raiding that district this afternoon."

Nada's blood ran cold. The ground shifted beneath her.

Ester tugged on her sleeve. "What is it, Nada?"

She blurted a quick translation and Ester's eyes widened, her lips parting with a tremble. Nada turned back to the German. "Why are you telling me this?"

"I couldn't in good conscience let you walk into whatever horrors those animals are committing. Those people make me sick."

For all the evil the Germans waged throughout Europe, it

spoke volumes that a Nazi was repulsed and horrified by the Ustaše.

"Don't go home. Save yourselves." He jerked his chin toward Filip. "Save the boy."

"Thank you," Nada breathed.

He gave her a nod.

Nada gathered Ester's arm, latched onto Filip's hand, and turned them toward the forest.

"What else did he say?" Ester asked as they stumbled forward into a run.

With feet rushing through grass, not one of them spared a glance back at the derailed train or its passengers.

"He told us not to go home. To save ourselves."

Ester's silence had Nada turning to meet her sestra's eyes. They burned with the same determination firing through her own body. Nada set her jaw.

No, they weren't going to run. They needed to get to Retfala to warn their families.

CHAPTER 2

NADA'S LUNGS BURNED COLD IN HER CHEST AS THE evening chill bit her skin. Her relentless, punishing pace had slowed to a jog, and each gulping breath prodded the sharp stitch in her side. Ester and Filip straggled behind, but she refused to stop, to rest. She needed to get home before it was too late, and prayed to God that they would make it before the Ustaše arrived.

How many more times would the Croatian regime invade Serbian neighborhoods, taking droves of people away with a crazed desire to keep Croatia "pure" and strictly Catholic? Nausea roiled in Nada's stomach, and her face pinched. A cold sweat crept over her, stirring the memory etched into her soul. Her father's desperate shouts, the savage grip and strikes of strange hands, the helplessness that crippled her. Nada's gasps quivered and she shook the thought from her mind. She needed to get home and hide her mother and sisters. Or, if time allowed, she would gather them to run.

The golden hues of sunset were beginning to fade, giving way to a full moon on the horizon—painted a dusty crimson from distant fires of some war-ravaged place—when they finally reached the clustered terracotta rooftops and simple, white-bricked houses of Retfala. A reflection of its former self, their beloved village bore its own war-torn scars in its lifeless flesh. Bullet holes pockmarked brick walls. Weathered boards covered shattered windows. Once-thriving and well-tended gardens now sat haggard and forgotten. Nada's toe kicked a stray bullet shell, sending it scooting across the asphalt. Such crumbs left from past skirmishes were as common as falling leaves.

Filip and Ester caught up alongside Nada, their breaths heaving. Their street lay ahead within easy reach.

"Nada, please!" whined Filip. "Can't we take a break?"

"We're almost there," Nada puffed. "We need to keep going."

"But my feet *hurt*. These shoes are too small."

She frowned, jerking a quick glance at him. "Mama bought you new shoes. You should have worn them."

"They were girl's shoes!"

Nada scrubbed the crawling itch on her face. "And I bet you're sorry you didn't wear them now."

"They were all she could find, Filip," said Ester, her words faint. Even breathless, Ester had more patience and compassion than Nada could muster. "There aren't many choices these days."

Nada's gaze roamed their surroundings. From the moment they stepped through the outskirts of Retfala, she'd kept her eyes peeled for any sign of Ustaše.

Her footfalls slowed as her skin prickled. Something wasn't right. "It's quiet. It's never this quiet."

She took in the houses around her, dark and silent. Where was the clacking of skipping ropes against pavement? Or the hum of a radio straying from someone's living room? The smell of sarma cooking in an oven?

Frantic screams pierced the quiet, curling around the corner to meet them.

No, no, no, no. Heart in her throat, Nada flew down the road, feet thundering against the street. Her clothing rippled and her hair whipped behind her. Ester's voice trailed through the panic, but her words melted to watery mumbles in Nada's ears.

Nada rounded the corner and stumbled to a stop. All color drained from her face as she wavered on her feet. Ester and Filip staggered to her side a moment later.

A tide of dark gray uniforms crowded the road—machine guns slung across their backs, blades swinging at their hips, and the distinct metallic "U" pinned to their caps.

Nada's knees weakened as her stomach dropped. They didn't make it in time.

Before the Ustaše could see them, Nada grabbed Ester and Filip and pushed them toward the nearest house, forcing them behind it for cover. Tucked close against the brick, she peered around it. One Ustaša barked orders while at least twenty Ustaše shoved her Serbian neighbors into an idling, canvas-covered truck. Children cried and screamed, clinging to their mothers' dresses as the women begged the Ustaše for mercy. An Ustaša struck a man's face with the butt of his gun, shouting at him to get on the truck. Other men tried to shield their families by urging them to do as commanded. The old Croat lady who lived up the road stood to the side, gripping her son's arm, watching the chaos with trembling lips and furrowed brows. Both Croat mother and son remained untouched as Ustaše corralled the rest of the neighbors like unruly livestock.

The Ustaše knew. They knew who the Croats were, and who weren't, which meant there were local informants.

Filip lurched forward. "Ma—!"

Nada snatched him back, clamping her hand over his mouth. "No, Filip," she whispered sharply in his ear. "Be quiet."

Her heart hammered in her chest. She needed to think. What could she possibly do? How could she make her way farther down the road, to her house, without being seen?

A sharp pain shot through Nada's finger as Filip bit her, and she yelped, letting him go.

He whirled on her, gasping. "I saw Mama in the back of the truck!"

Nada's veins laced with ice. Her breaths steepened. It was happening again. Hand to her forehead, Nada staggered backward until her shoulders bumped into the wall. She couldn't help her father last time. Couldn't help herself. How could she help her mother and sisters now? Powerless against so many Ustaše, a deep, consuming quake ignited inside her.

Ester let out a strangled cry. "They have my parents!"

Ester moved to rush for the street, but Nada grappled her arm. "Don't!" she hissed. "If we go out there, they'll take us too."

Face ashen and chin quivering, Ester's wide, glistening eyes stared at Nada.

While the Ustaša regime had their own resolute agenda—the slaughtering of Serbians, no matter their age—they also worked with the Germans toward the extermination of Jews. And for a pair of seventeen-year-old girls, one Serbian and one Jewish Croat, Nada couldn't bear to think of their fates in such a situation. She wouldn't allow Ester to charge toward certain death.

"We have to do something, Nada."

"Do what?" Nada demanded. "We're outnumbered. There's nothing we can do here."

"*Please*," Filip cried, clutching at her sleeves. "We have to get Mama."

Nada shook her head. "We can't," she choked.

He yanked at her sleeves. "What about Ana and Maša?"

Those names wrapped around her throat, tightening. Nada kneaded the button tied around her wrist and pictured her little sisters—so innocent, so small—bawling within the rough grip of Ustaše. Tears blurred her vision as she looked around her, desperate to think of a solution. But only the pained cries of her father played over and over in her mind.

"Maybe we can cause a distraction," said Ester.

But no distraction would be enough to draw away every Ustaša. It wouldn't work.

Nada couldn't move. Couldn't breathe. Each second that

ticked by hammered a nail into her nerves. A lone slavuj twittered in the boughs above as though life carried on as normal, mocking her.

Filip began to cry. "We have to help Mama!" He pushed her, slapped her arms, bringing Nada to her senses.

She grabbed hold of him. "Ssh! You're being too loud. Calm down."

She peeked around the corner. An Ustaša glanced over his shoulder toward their end of the street. Nada's heart stopped. She ducked back further, squeezing Filip's shoulders in warning. And then the man turned back around.

Nada's eyes dipped closed. She pressed a hand to her stomach. "We need to stay quiet or they'll find us here."

A guttural keening cut through the air, drawing their attention back to the street. A young woman wrenched against an Ustaša's hold, her bare feet scraping against the pavement. He slammed her into the side of the truck with a sickening thump and drew his fist back to hit her.

"No!" The Croat lady's son threw himself into the street, holding out shaking palms. "Please! Stop this. You don't need to do this. Let them go. I beg of you."

The Ustaša shoved the woman free. She curled in on herself, sobbing, as he turned to glare at the Croat man. His chin lifted as he straightened his shoulders. "What did you say to me?"

The Croat man froze. His mouth parted to speak, but no sound came from his lips.

The Ustaša tilted forward and gestured toward his ear with two fingers, beckoning for an answer.

The Croat swallowed. Licked his lips. His words came out in a rasp. "I asked you to stop."

The Ustaša slowly nodded, his stare unwavering. "You asked me to let them go. Begged me, even. You're siding with Serbs? With *svinje?*"

The Croat man's lips flattened as his eyes lowered, breaking contact with the soldier's. His fingers curled into fists. "They're *people.*"

The Ustaša sneered and wrenched the dagger from his belt. With vicious accuracy, he slit the Croat's throat.

Nada flinched. Closed her eyes. Shudders wracked through her body, and she sagged against the house as everything seemed to tilt. Whispers peppered her ears, but she failed to catch them. A hand clasped her shoulder. Small arms wrapped her middle, fingers bunching at the back of her blouse. A face buried against her waist. Nada's skin crawled. Her throat closed up. She wanted to fling them off. Slap them away. As her teeth clenched and the heel of her palm hooked against the limb at her side, ready to shove against it, the scent of blood reached her nose, and the ghost of a memory slid through. Nada forced her eyes open, refusing to slip away. *I'm not there. I'm not there.*

She was here, with her brother holding onto her. With her sestra watching over her, brows creased. She wasn't there again, even though her body told her otherwise. *Feared* otherwise. Grasping hard to her present reality, Nada kept her focus on them, letting their presence ground her.

The groan of a vehicle accelerating seized all thought. Trembling, Nada whirled to peer around the house. The canvas-covered truck that held her mother—her sisters—drove away. Her stomach turned to stone. Not a soul remained in the street except the old Croat lady, moaning into her hands. A fresh pool of blood seeped into the pavement at her feet, smeared into a short trail to one side. A single, worn shoe lay forgotten nearby.

Silence rang loud in Nada's ears. The evening's shadows crept closer, turning the world black around the edges, inviting her to fall apart. To tumble into its darkness. But Nada resisted. She clenched her eyes shut, pressing tears free as she struggled to contain the hysteria fighting to come tearing from her lungs.

With rasping, peaked breaths, Nada staggered out into the street.

"They killed my boy. They killed my boy," the Croat woman cried over and over, grasping her chest and pulling at her collar.

Nada continued forward as her world threatened to cave in. She had failed them. Didn't even try to save them. "Where did they go?" she asked through her tears. "Where did they take them?"

The Croat turned to her, tears streaming down her reddened face. Wet patches blotted the lines of her headscarf where it tied beneath her chin. "Ustaše. O Bože, o Bože." *Oh God, oh God.* "They took so many. They forced them on the truck and took them away. My boy tried to stop them." The woman clasped at her heart again and yanked her clothing, wailing her next words. "They cut his throat. O Bože."

Nada grasped her arm. "Where did they take them?"

"I don't know. I don't know where."

Nada stared ahead, wading in hazy but overwhelming grief. Arms wrapped around her. *Ester.* Nada clutched onto her sestra as a wave of heartache lashed at her, sending her legs buckling beneath her, and Ester followed. The two of them wept, huddled on the road beneath a bleeding moon, holding each other's fracturing souls together. And as darkness crept over them, shrouding them in the finality of nightfall, only one word could be heard in the stillness.

Bože. Bože. Bože.

CHAPTER 3

That same evening

Dusk had fallen over the forest, spilling swathes of gray shadow and buttery light between the trees. Though night was fast descending, with April's full moon the color of scarlet flame hovering on the horizon, it wasn't too dark for Henrik to see the three practice targets in the distance, held up by his fellow Partizani. The volunteers crouched behind a natural rocky embankment, holding the wooden stems of targets above ducked heads—a crude sheet of card bearing the outline of a man's upper body.

Henrik let out a weighty sigh. The last thing he wanted was to join the boys in their training and risk the possibility of bonding with them, but they demanded it, and Henrik could have used the practice anyway. He didn't want his unique set of skills to grow rusty, and that included gun wielding.

Henrik shifted and lined up his sight guard to the middle target in stern silence. Letting out a slow, steady breath and then holding it, he gently pulled the trigger of his Schmeisser. The bullet smacked through the target's head. Henrik lowered the machine gun, but the volunteer continued to hold up the target.

Henrik frowned. "Why isn't he putting it down?"

"Maybe you didn't hit it," said Vinko beside him, peering through the sight guard of his own machine gun while a lit cigarette hung from his lips. He fired, hitting the dirt in front of the embankment. He muttered a curse under his breath.

"I got it dead between the eyes." Henrik readjusted his tilted titovka— a green-brown cap with a red star stitched to the front. Raising his gun once more, his solid-built frame stilled, shoulders tensing. He shot the figure through the chest. Again, he waited for the target to fall forward, but it didn't move. He shook his head, tapping a finger against the metal of his gun.

On Henrik's other side, the ever-quiet Matej lined up his weapon. His shot echoed around them and hit the figure's neck, prompting his volunteer to lower the target.

Jerking his head back, Henrik spread out his hand and looked to Matej and Vinko for answers. Why was his target still standing?

Matej kept his gaze on the two remaining posts. "Maybe he's too afraid to move."

Vinko took aim again and struck the tree beside his volunteer. "Fuck," he muttered, smoke waggling between his lips. "This gun is defective."

Matej chuckled as Vinko took his cigarette between his fingers and inspected the machine gun. His disheveled, dark curls fell into his eyes, matching his rumpled, untucked shirt and its few loosened buttons.

Henrik smirked, adding a bite to his words. "Your *aim* is defective. No wonder my volunteer is pissing his pants."

Vinko's brows arced as he grinned. "Are you poking fun at my weaponry skills, Henrik? Who knew you had a little humor rattling around in that intense brain of yours?"

Vinko drew a mouthful of tobacco smoke and propped the butt of his gun on his hip. With a sweeping gesture of his hand — cigarette still between his fingers—Vinko fired off a volley that strayed high into the tree canopy. "Freedom to the people!" he shouted.

Matej chuckled, coaxing a rare but subdued half-laugh from Henrik. He stopped it, composing his features as he silently chastised himself for letting it slip.

Henrik hardened himself. "At least until the people get accidentally shot by Vinko."

"Shut your mouth, Vinko!" Farther behind them, one of the Partizan men stood at the fringe of their camp, silhouetted against the firelight. "Do you want the Ustaše to find us all?"

"Forgive me, comrade!" Vinko raised his hand in surrender. "I was swept up in the moment of my victory. Do you see the target I hit twice, right through the head and heart?"

Henrik narrowed his eyes at Vinko, who returned the look with his typical slanted grin. Taking a drag of his cigarette, he winked at him.

In response, Henrik whipped up his gun and with a nimble pull of the trigger, struck Vinko's target, dead center. The Partizan volunteer let the figure drop forward.

But still, Henrik's twice-hit target remained standing.

With a huff and a glint of defiance in his blue-gray eyes, Henrik aimed at the stem of his target. Squeezing the trigger, a series of bullets hit the wood, splitting it across the middle. The target toppled forward, landing in the dirt.

Having witnessed the display from camp, a handful of Partizani erupted into laughter and applause. Their delight in Henrik made him want to cringe.

"If only the girls could see you now, Henrik!" Jakov bellowed. The leader of their troop was known to carry banter and jest on the tip of his tongue.

Unbidden, Nada flooded Henrik's thoughts.

She had stared from the hallway in her house, hand gripping the door frame to keep herself steady. Her beautiful brown eyes—bruised black and swollen from a beating that made his stomach curdle—took in Henrik's neatly pressed uniform and the red star on his cap. When they snagged on the packed bag by his feet, she had paled, and her chest rose with a deep breath. Beside her, Ester's glance had moved from

Henrik to Nada as she settled a light hand on her friend's shoulder.

The only instinct he'd had in that moment, the only thing he had wanted, was to kiss her, just once, before he left. He ached for it like a drowning man ached for air. But it wasn't the right time for that.

Nada's sharp gaze had lifted to his, glistening with the whisper of tears. But before Henrik could open his mouth to speak, she had turned and padded down the hallway without a word.

Henrik caught himself. He closed his eyes and shoved the memory away. Yes, Henrik once believed the sun rose and fell with her. But he had seen too many horrors that fueled his Partizan heart, which in turn ironed out such fanciful notions. For that reason, he made himself let go of Nada a long time ago.

War had that effect. It forced you to grow up.

With a sigh, Henrik rubbed the raised burn mark on his forearm. No matter what, he'd never forget why he was there. Why he fought for an end to the war and the Ustaša regime.

"Play time is over, boys," Jakov called out. "It's your turn to keep watch."

"It's just as well." Vinko put out his cigarette with his boot. "I was beginning to make you two look bad."

Henrik and Matej shared a look, prompting Matej to grin as they trudged deeper into the surrounding woods.

The three of them took their posts amongst the trees. Henrik stood not far from Matej, sleeves rolled up, weapon in hand, with his eyes keen and focused. Vinko sauntered farther into the woods, no longer visible from where they kept watch. It was probably for the best. No doubt his comedic antics would distract them from the task at hand.

Silence consumed them for a time, and as dusk gave way to nightfall, pouring fire-tainted moonlight through the forest, Henrik's mind wandered. Tiptoed toward Nada and those fathomless brown eyes.

Footsteps crunched in the undergrowth, slapping Henrik

awake. Tension rippled through him. With squared shoulders he whipped up his weapon and pointed it at three approaching men.

Matej appeared by his side, his own machine gun trained on them. "Stop where you are!"

Henrik widened his stance, heart thumping deep in his chest as he surveyed the men dressed in civilian clothing. They halted, raising their hands.

One of the men jerked his chin toward the bag hanging from his shoulder. "We've come to bring food in aid of the cause."

It happened often enough. Wherever they traveled, villagers would bring food or supplies or intel they collected on the whereabouts of German or Ustaša troops. Civilians would even track down the resistance to join in their efforts—most half-starved, bringing nothing but the clothes on their back and a stubborn desire to make a difference. It was guerilla warfare at its finest. Only a few of Jakov's ragtag troop wore the official Partizan uniforms, including Henrik. The rest went without and were only handed a weapon with a shoulder slap of welcome.

Matej lifted his chin. "You came from Niza?"

It made sense. Niza was the village nearest to their location in the woods, and Henrik's troop had passed through only yesterday. Villagers would have likely expected to find the Partizani nearby.

"I did," said the man.

Even so, Henrik proceeded with caution. "You must know Dragica then," he said, mentioning the woman who had welcomed the soldiers into her home, feeding them both food and information. Not only was she considered head of the village, she was a Partizan spy. "Her daughter is a real beauty, isn't she?"

The man with the bag grinned. "The prettiest girl in Niza."

Wrong answer. Dragica only had a son.

Matej's eyes flicked to Henrik, catching the mistake.

A black heat writhed in Henrik's core, followed by the rush

of adrenaline, while he maintained a straight face. He clenched his jaw as Matej gestured for the men to come forward.

As the strangers passed between them to head into the camp, Henrik and Matej moved in unison to attack.

Matej wrenched the nearest man's bag away and kicked his legs out from under him. Henrik lifted the barrel of his Schmeisser at another and pulled the trigger. Gunshots rang out in time with the lurches of the spy's body, and he collapsed in a heap before Matej managed to plant his foot on his opponent's back, pinning him to the ground. Matej pressed the barrel of his gun to the head of the stranger, whose bag now lay tossed aside and out of reach.

Nostrils flaring, the final man standing spun and aimed a pistol at Henrik. Quick and fierce, Henrik fired a series of bullets at the spy's hand. The pistol fell from his bloodied, mangled grip, and the man growled through his teeth, straining the tendons in his neck.

Clutching his wrist, the spy panted in feverish bursts, then glowered at Henrik. Not ready to give up, the spy reached back with his good hand and withdrew a dagger from beneath his coat.

A dark smirk spread across Henrik's face. More than willing to face the attacker on his level—gun free—Henrik pushed his machine gun back behind him, still hanging from its strap. Henrik leaned forward, hungering for the fight with deadly calm.

The spy charged Henrik and a primitive desire to tear him apart took over. The man swiped with his blade and managed to slash Henrik's bicep before he snatched the spy's hand, dagger pinned within. In a flash, Henrik twisted the spy's arm out to the side, forcing the man's body to turn, and slammed the back of his upper arm with a solid hit. With a muted pop, the spy's shoulder jerked from its socket. His scream pierced the quiet night as he doubled over.

"Fuck you and your Serbian mother!" he spat through gritted teeth.

With methodical ease, Henrik took the dagger from the spy's crippled fingers and hauled him upright by the collar. He steeled his features as he held the spy's gaze, seeing nothing there but the cruel faces of men that haunted him.

With a powerful thrust, Henrik stabbed him beneath the ribs. "I'm not a Serb, Ustaša filth."

Agony glittered in the man's cold eyes. Still he bared his teeth, lips curling back with a twitch. Henrik twisted the blade before rending it sideways, and the man choked and gagged as blood spurted from his lips. Henrik yanked the blade out and pushed the dead spy, toppling him over.

He then looked at Matej, expressionless, and noted the intruder beneath Matej's boot was still alive. "You know we can't let him live."

They stared at the Ustaša spy heaving under the press of Matej's weight. If they freed him, he would run to his comrades and report their position. It would risk the lives of the entire camp.

Henrik glanced up at Matej, at his tight jaw and knotted brow. He recognized the unease, the hesitation in the way Matej's throat bobbed. Henrik had once hated to do it too—making tough choices—but somewhere along the way the hesitation had dulled. Despite Matej's reluctance, Henrik knew he understood what needed to be done.

Matej pulled the trigger. A single crack echoed through the woods.

Armed and on high alert from the sounds of the attack, Jakov and his men hastened toward them, with Vinko flanking the group.

A burning throb in Henrik's arm reminded him of his injury, and he spared a glance at the cut bleeding through his shirt.

Matej raised his hand. "It's all right. We've taken care of it."

Jakov took one look at the bodies. "Ustaše?"

"Pretending to be Partizan sympathizers," said Henrik. "Someone in Niza sold us out."

Jakov scratched at his graying beard. "We've gained a lot of ground in this war. They're getting desperate."

Henrik helped himself to the Ustaša's bag nearby, opening it. Along with a tin of food, a pistol, and extra ammunition, he found blocks of C-4 and two detonators. Henrik retrieved a block and tossed it to Jakov. "I don't know how they got their hands on it, but it looks like they had big plans for us."

Their leader clicked his tongue while he examined the C-4. "I should thank them for their kind donation." He reached out for the bag and Henrik passed it to him. "We should pack up camp. Move away from here before more of these assholes come looking for them." Jakov tapped the dead Ustaša beside him with his foot. "We'll head for Topoline now instead of in the morning. It should only take us a couple of hours to get there, maybe two-and-a-half in the dark, and then we can all get some sleep. You boys did well. You've earned the rest of the night off. I'll have some others keep watch while we pack up."

Vinko clapped his hands together and rubbed them, his gleeful smile shining brighter than the moon.

Jakov barked a short laugh at him. "*You* did nothing."

He sputtered, hands on hips. Then he settled, lifting his brows as he gestured at Henrik. "My friend is going to need my help bandaging his injury."

Friend. Henrik hated the word.

The Partizan leader's eyes rolled back. "Go, before I change my mind."

Vinko flashed a smile. "Your kindness is appreciated, Sir."

As the Partizani filtered back into the camp, the three boys approached their own dying campfire, set apart from the others. Jakov called out orders to the rest of the soldiers, spurring them into motion, and they began gathering their meager supplies.

Vinko, whistling an old Croatian tune, perched himself on the fallen log by their fire. He fished about on the ground through his scattered mess of personal belongings and lifted his coat to check beneath it.

Henrik scoffed and flung a hand toward Vinko's possessions. "If you kept your things in order, like I've told you to a thousand times, you would be packed by now."

"Possibly. But then we'd miss out on these moments together. I do it for you, Henrik, only so we can continue our rapport of witty banter."

Finally finding strips of an old shirt in his satchel, Vinko sauntered toward Henrik, who stiffened in reaction. Bandages. He had been looking for bandages.

Henrik swiped a hand over his face. It was his own stupid fault. He had made the mistake of laughing at Vinko's antics earlier. Of joining him and Matej at target practice in the first place. Such actions lulled them into a false sense of friendship—something Henrik couldn't allow to happen. Matej was easier to keep at arm's length, respecting the distance Henrik placed between them. But Vinko? Vinko was reckless and far too thick-headed to take a hint. He was like a cockroach you couldn't squash.

Henrik would have to push him away harder.

"I don't want your help, Vinko."

Matej sighed, lifting his eyes skyward before he crouched to collect his things.

"You're bleeding," said Vinko.

"I've bled before."

Vinko squinted, drawing his head back. "Even a pain-in-the-ass brute like you needs first aid from time to time."

Henrik pumped his jaw and reached out for the makeshift bandages. "I'll do it myself."

"With one hand?" Vinko quirked his brows, leveling him with a flat look. "I'm sure you're adept at certain *other* one-handed activities, Henrik, but this isn't one of them."

Matej snorted but Henrik clamped down on any urge to laugh.

"Let him do it," moaned Matej, shaking his head as he slipped the satchel over his shoulder.

Vinko folded his arms and stared him down. "Even Tito himself would insist."

Henrik wanted to roll his eyes. As if Josip Broz Tito, head of the Jugoslav Communist Party and leader of the resistance, would be concerned if one, solitary soldier of his didn't bind their inconsequential injury.

Vinko unraveled the clumped ball of cloth strips. "You won't be any good to us if your arm gets infected, Ubica. Besides, I need the practice. If I'm all you can rely on when your life hangs in the balance, wouldn't you feel better knowing I can at least wrap a fucking wound?"

Henrik released a heavy exhale through his nose. "Fine." Anything to make Vinko leave him be.

With a serene grin, Vinko wrapped Henrik's arm, sending a sting through Henrik's bicep each time Vinko pulled the cloth strips taut with unnecessary flourish. As he tended to Henrik's arm, Vinko smirked, but Henrik only glared into the glowing embers of the fire.

Once Vinko tied a knot, he clasped a hand over Henrik's shoulder and gave it a squeeze. "Good as new."

"Now get lost," Henrik growled with a wave of his hand.

Vinko flinched away from him—a knee-jerk reaction. He stilled as a flush crept into his cheeks, then forced a smile, cleared his throat, and resumed his earlier whistling as he sauntered back to his log.

While Vinko feigned ease, Henrik hadn't missed it. Vinko's recoil caught him off guard. Did he think Henrik would hit him? A weight pressed on his chest, and he dropped his gaze to avoid catching Vinko's eyes. Henrik might do all in his power to make people dislike him, but he would never physically hurt them. Had his harshness toward others made more of an impact than he thought?

As Vinko settled in front of the fire to pack up his pile of mess, Henrik squatted to gather his own belongings, shoulders tense. An uncomfortable silence descended.

While Henrik let the moment lie stagnant between them, unattended and thorn-like, he took the jacket he'd set aside earlier, folded it into a neat square, and tucked it into his orderly satchel.

CHAPTER 4

NIGHT BREATHED THROUGH THE HOUSE, SHIFTING and surging like Crnobog himself lurked in the hall, as Nada lay awake. With deadened eyes she watched the inky depths taunt her. Not only did the black god shroud their world in darkness, he bled shadows into the husk of Nada's home, into Ester's across the street. The distant rumbling of gunfire and explosions marred the quiet—an ever-familiar backdrop in their lives—echoing against the emptiness within the walls.

Nada had stopped sobbing an hour ago, when she could no longer take the intense, throbbing headache it brought on. Ester's steady breaths brushed the back of her neck as Nada remained curled up on her side. Behind Ester, Filip stirred. They had decided to share the bed for the night as none of them wanted to be alone. Thankfully, Filip fell asleep with ease, his tears lulling him to slumber, but Ester tossed and turned, often shaking the mattress with her delicate sobs.

The bed creaked as someone climbed off, and small feet padded around the room as Filip walked to the doorway and paused, looking over the living room beyond it. He went to the far corner beside a cabinet and relieved himself. Nada's heart ached and a tear escaped, veering across the bridge of her nose.

Filip was too afraid to go outside and use the outhouse. After all he'd been through that day, she couldn't blame him.

Nada closed her eyes and pretended to sleep as he made his way back to bed and settled in once more.

Time meandered on until gray light filtered through the window and the faraway battle faded to silence. The change in sound disrupted Ester's sleep and her even breaths turned to a deep and slow sigh. She was awake. When your best friend was like a sister to you, you knew how to read every nuance.

Ester whispered into the dim morning, "Do you think they're okay?"

Nada took a moment to answer, swallowing back the thickness in her throat. "If they are, I doubt they will be for long."

A grave exhale ruffled the back of her hair. "Maybe they'll escape. Or maybe they'll be released."

"Don't be so naïve, Ester. They're not coming back." Nada understood the reality of this better than anyone.

Silence fell, layering them both in a blanket of hopelessness. Ester's parents were all she had in the world, apart from Nada and her family. And they were gone too. If Nada was quietly losing her mind, Ester had to be utterly heartbroken.

The humming of numerous planes drifted toward them in the quiet. Drained and tired of staring into space, Nada crept out of the bed, careful not to wake Filip, and went to the window. She pushed the lace curtain aside and gazed up into the clear sky. Fading stars glittered against a wash of dreamy gray blue, but her eyes focused on the dozen planes flying west in the distance. Miniature parachutes descended toward the earth, weighted with crates and swinging like pendulous bells.

"Ester." A spark of life, the hint of an idea, lifted Nada's demeanor. "Come look."

Her sestra slipped out of the covers and joined her, looking out into the breaking dawn.

"The British are dropping food and supplies."

Ester tilted her head, brows drawing together.

A restless flutter in her stomach sent Nada's fingers to play with the button at her wrist. "They only ever do that over the forests, and, judging by their direction, they might be somewhere near Topoline. What do you think?"

"What are you talking about?"

"It means there are Partizani in that forest."

Ester held her gaze, eyes widening as Nada's words seeped in. Her back straightened. "You want to go to them."

A frantic energy bubbled through Nada, and her thumb circled the button, around and around. Every day Nada lived with the haunting ghost of loss, of the pain of being left behind —a fact she couldn't change—but she refused to lose any more loved ones by sitting back and doing nothing. Not while her family were in indescribable danger. Not while there was a chance they could come out of it alive.

"If anyone can help us get our families back, it's the Partizani," said Nada.

"Are you really certain they can help?"

"What other choice do we have?"

Ester studied her, brows heavy and creased from a night of sadness and suffering.

Nada doubled down. "Do you want to sit here in these vacant houses, day after day, reliving last night? How much time will pass before we stop wondering what happened to them? How many weeks will we sit here in despair? I'm telling you, Ester, I can't stand the thought of it. I'll go completely mad."

Madness already clung to her like a demon of torture, hand-feeding her nightmares until she woke drenched in sweat, whispering fear into her mind until her body quaked, touching her with blackened fingers until apprehension skittered along her skin. Adding even more to that unstable heft on her shoulders sounded like a fate worse than death.

"The whole thing could be positively perilous," Ester murmured.

"Staying here, being helpless and fraught with agony, is not an option for me. I can't do it." *Not again.* "We should be fighting for them, Ester. We need to kick and scream and claw till our fingers bleed if it means saving them. If I have to give my last breath to find them, I will. I swear it. I'll do whatever it takes."

"I know you will." Ester revealed a slight but resolute grin. Her eyes glinted with promise and hope and need. She gathered Nada's hands, holding tight. "That's why I'm coming with you."

Nada reflected the resounding agreement in her best friend's face. Still, she needed to say it out loud. Needed it to be more real than the horror their lives had become. "We're going to join the resistance."

Nada's veins buzzed with excitement as she said the words, but quickly dampened when Filip rolled over in his sleep, drawing her attention. Deep slumber would be a balm to his grief, and as Nada watched him, she envied him. But then it struck her. Filip could be all Nada had left in the world. She rubbed a hand against her chest. If her mother and sisters were—

She closed her eyes and didn't allow herself to finish that thought. Casting her gaze back on Filip, she bit her lip. Nada would rather die than lose him too. But this hateful world was too dangerous. Too quick to take and take and take. Nada pulled back her shoulders, vowing to never let him out of her sight again.

Ester read the look in her eyes. "You know he can't come with us."

Nada blinked at her. "Where else would he be? Of course he's coming. He's my responsibility."

"Yes, he is. And that's why I'm asking you to please see some sense," she said, her words gentle. "I know ever since you lost your father, and since the day Henrik left, you've been ... struggling, but—"

"Why do you always insist that Henrik had any kind of effect on me? I was fine then, and I'm fine now."

"Whether you'll admit it or not, they both triggered something in you. I know my sestra. I know you've been holding on tighter to everyone. And that's okay. But you need to think clearly now. You might hate to let Filip go, but you can't put him in danger just to bring you comfort. Put him ahead of your fears."

Nada stood motionless, trapped in the painful truth before her. Her throat ached. "But I'm all he has right now."

Ester's gaze softened as she brushed her hand down Nada's arm. "What about your grandparents?"

"They live so far away. We'd lose too much time. We can't risk the Partizani moving on elsewhere. We'd never find them."

"The baka down the street, then."

"The Croat lady from yesterday?"

"Have her take care of him. Or better yet, she could take him to Orahovica. Your grandparents have food. I'm sure she'd take that as payment for helping."

The idea turned sour in Nada's stomach, and yet she couldn't ignore the fact that it was the only way. Her features turned blank as she nodded. "We should start packing. A small bag each, with only what we need. Then we'll go talk to the baka before Filip wakes up."

If I have to give my last breath to find them, I will. I swear it.

She would do whatever it took. Even if it meant letting Filip go.

When Nada lost her father, it ripped open a jagged hole inside her. When Henrik left, that hole wrenched wider. It became a chasm that nothing—not even the passage of time—could fill or heal. Ester was right. Nada was terrified of losing someone she loved again. But that was exactly why she had to go.

With her little brother's slight hand clasped in hers, they met with the old Croat lady outside her house—a sad picture of two broken girls about to hand over a weeping boy.

Though the baka's headscarf was now dry of tears, a heaviness dulled her eyes. She held her hand out to Filip with a muted smile and said in a soothing tone, "Come with Baka Zora."

Ester and Nada were thankful that Zora was willing to help when they asked in the early hours of morning. But now, with the sun cresting the mountains, shedding light on the harrowing reality of what was to come, Nada wished she'd made a different decision.

"I don't want to go," Filip whimpered, gazing up at Nada with watery eyes. "Let me come with you. Kids my age help the Partizani too. Tata used to tell me stories about them."

Nada pressed her lips together, fighting to still their quiver as she crouched before him. "I know, Filip, but I won't allow it. It's much too dangerous."

His chin wobbled as his eyes continued to plead with her. Those same brown eyes she'd gazed into when he was a baby, rocking him to sleep in the dead of night. With her mother unwell at the time, Nada had taken it upon herself to settle a wailing Filip so her mother could rest. When his cries tapered off and his eyes drifted closed, Nada had beamed. Stood a little taller. She had always taken care of her siblings alongside her parents and took pride in it.

Nada's heart shrank. She hadn't taken care of her baby sisters yesterday. Didn't protect them like she should have. Ana—seven years old and obsessed with collecting dried flowers—covered every surface in her room with her botanical finds. And Maša, her arm forever glued around the floppy neck of her stuffed bear, had worn it to flimsiness after five years of steadfast love.

The bear that now lay forgotten and alone in an empty bedroom, in an empty house.

Setting her jaw, Nada blinked back tears and took hold of Filip's shoulders. "Be a good boy for Zora. She'll take you to Baka and Deda. They have food waiting for you, remember? And Deda will teach you how to milk cows and chop wood and all those fun things. You'll have such a good time, you'll forget all about wanting to come with me."

Filip threw his arms around her, latching tight to her neck. "Don't go. *Please*. Don't go, Nada."

Her heart sank and burned all the way down as she hugged him back, just as fiercely.

Filip sobbed in her arms, and Nada rubbed his back. "I need you to be brave. I'll be back soon. I promise. You want me to bring Mama and our sisters home, don't you?"

He nodded into her neck.

"Then you have to let me go so I can find them, okay?"

Moving slowly, Filip drew back, his face wet and splotchy and red. Nada stood, wiping away the dampness from her own tears before fishing into her pocket for a folded piece of paper.

She handed it to Zora. "I wrote a letter for my grandparents, explaining everything."

Zora wound the letter into her wrinkled palm. "I'll make sure they get it."

"Hvala. For everything."

Ester swooped in to give Filip a hug while whispering words of comfort in his ear.

"Be careful, you two," said Zora. "I'm sure I don't need to remind you of what you may find out there."

Nada worried her lip and steadied herself for a goodbye. With a quick and vehement kiss to her brother's cheek, Nada turned and walked away.

As Filip called out for her, begging her to come back, Nada split in two—her heart tugged from behind, while determination propelled her forward.

CHAPTER 5

Before

It had been six months since the war began, since that first day when Nada watched an army of German soldiers march through Osijek, carrying a formidable aura unlike any she had ever seen. Crowds gathered in the streets, many of them of German heritage, cheering and clapping while brandishing red armbands adorned with a symbol she had no understanding of. Nada was almost thirteen, but even so young, she could sense the oppressive lick of shadows that swept along with their boots and writhed around their weapons. While other children stood agape, captivated and piqued by the fanfare, dread anchored heavy as a stone in Nada's stomach. She may not have known the meaning of the symbols the soldiers wore, but she did understand nothing good could come from such a calculated display of power and weaponry.

Then the war began to wage around them. Skirmishes and assaults broke out without notice, cropping up anywhere and everywhere. The day of Nada's first experience with warfare, a regiment of German tanks took over her family's land as if it belonged to them. They cut down her father's fruit trees in the field behind her home and used them to take cover, firing their weapons at some unseeable opposition in the encroaching woods.

Now, it was simply the way of life. Unpredictable but constant. They all stood on shaky ground, and yet people carried on with their days as much as possible.

Henrik and Nada were no exception, using their circumstances to find whatever joy they could.

The stream babbled an endless tune beside Nada as she knelt in the grass, fashioning a thick pile of kindling beneath a small, rustic bridge before setting a lit match to it. Though the bridge was a simple construction of loose planks, settled and fused into the earth after years of cattle crossings, it provided enough shield from the wind. While the fire began to crackle and glow, Henrik dropped down from a nearby tree branch, landing light on his feet.

"I found some eggs!"

Sure enough, he cradled three bird's eggs within his palm and offered them to her. The pit in her stomach hollowed. Too hungry to think too much about it, she took one, poking her fingers through the thin shell to part it, and tossed the slimy contents back into her mouth. She grimaced as she swallowed.

"Have another," said Henrik.

Nada shook her head as she fed some sticks to her fire. "You're bigger than me. You should have two."

Henrik crouched beside her, took her hand, and dropped another into it. "Eat it. You're starving."

She watched him pierce and eat his own egg before she finally caved and ate her second. "Pass me the pillowcase?"

Henrik picked up the makeshift bag, its bulging contents jingling as he handed it over. She poured out the treasures she'd gathered. Bullets and shell casings toppled onto the ground—remnants of battles past. Thanks to the war, you could always find them lying around, scattered throughout the woods and in the village streets.

"Is there any particular reason why we're targeting Miroslav?" he asked, his lips twitching with the itch to grin.

Nada glanced up at the farmhouse that stood some distance away, visible through the slender trees. She narrowed her eyes. The old Croat man had it coming. She suspected he was the one who set fire to the little garden in her backyard. The one she tended to with care and commitment. Having no proof wasn't going to stop her, though.

She had sobbed when she discovered the blackened earth and charred remains—her beautiful flowers turned to ash, shrubs singed to nothing more than protruding twigs.

Her father had tugged her into his arms, comforting her as she had wept into his chest. "Don't cry, srce moj. It'll grow back."

Her inhale had shuddered as she looked up at him. "How, Tata? Everything is dead."

"You will see," he had said, eyes crinkling with his gentle, knowing grin. His rough palms wiped the tears from her cheeks. "The fire will make them grow back stronger than before. But you must give it time. That's the wonder of nature. Of life. With destruction comes renewal."

Nada would make Miroslav pay for what he had done, regardless. Frowning, she tossed more sticks onto the flames.

"It's because you have a crush on him, isn't it?" said Henrik.

Nada's head snapped up, mouth falling open to stare at him.

"You like him, so you want to tease him. Isn't that the way these things work?"

Nada laughed and shoved his shoulder. "Stop it!"

"Listen, I know it might be hard for you to voice your feelings, but this isn't the right way to go about it. It'll get lost in translation."

Face bright with a smile, Nada shooed him with her hand. "Be quiet and keep the fire going while I do this."

Henrik's gaze, sparkling with mirth, remained on her as she set to work. Nada used pliers to stretch out the openings of two 30 mm cannon shells—the large ammunition fired from planes for ground attacks—and poured gunpowder into one of them from a handful of unused bullets. Then, using a rock from the waterside, she pounded the two cannon shells together, end to end, so they were wedged in place.

"Sometimes I wonder what must go through your mind to come up with such ideas," said Henrik, shaking his head. Then his brows lifted, and he flattened his lips to suppress a grin. "I suppose you got inspired by one very lucky old man with a round gut and a balding hairline."

Nada set her jaw. "You better be careful, Henrik, or you just might become my next victim."

Henrik simply smiled wide.

It stole her breath, that smile, and woke a flutter in her belly, so Nada looked away. She turned the makeshift bomb over in her hands, inspecting her work. Sometimes she wished she could express her feelings to Henrik. She wished she could tell him she adored him without sounding ridiculous, without making herself vulnerable.

"Do you think we'll ever be forced to fight in the war?" she asked.

Henrik's expression grew serious. "I don't know."

"If we did, I'd want to fight beside you."

Henrik nodded. "I promise I'd keep you safe."

"That's not why I'd want you there. If anything, I'd keep *you* safe."

His grin returned. "Is that so?"

"Clearly, I'd make a better soldier than you." She waggled the homemade incendiary device in her hand as proof.

"Clearly."

She lowered her eyes to stare at the metal between her fingers. "No, I'd want you beside me because, well, you're *always* beside me. There's no Nada without Henrik." At least, sometimes it felt that way.

Henrik's brow furrowed. "Of course there is."

Nada wasn't sure what she was trying to say, but she let the words fumble out of her anyway. "I suppose what I mean is, if something bad was headed our way today, I'd choose to save you first, before anyone else."

"No, Nada. You'd choose your family."

She looked at him.

He shrugged. "That's okay. It's how it's supposed to be."

Nada broke away from his gaze with a weak smile. Her heart withered. She shouldn't have opened her stupid mouth. As Henrik had joked earlier, her efforts got lost in translation.

She cleared her throat and stood. "Let's do this. The fire is hot enough now."

Henrik straightened to his feet while studying her, trying to read something he might have missed.

Nada pretended not to notice and dropped the makeshift bomb into the fire. "Run."

They bolted away together and skidded to duck behind a broad oak tree. Hands against the ridged bark, Nada peered around its trunk as the fire continued to flicker with a steady blaze.

They waited. And waited.

"Why isn't it working? Did it roll away?" Nada stepped out from behind the tree.

"Nada, wait—"

A resounding boom shattered the silence. Her mini bomb exploded, sending the bridge planks swinging up and over, splashing into the water, and tumbling to the ground. Dust and smoke drifted on the air. The once-blazing fire had scattered about in a ray of misting embers, and littered leaves still flamed like candles.

Henrik chuckled as Nada whooped, raising her arms in the air. She couldn't contain her smile. It worked.

"No turning back now, Nada," said Henrik. "Miroslav will have gotten your love message loud and clear."

As if conjured, the heavy-set man stumbled out of the house, shouting and waving his fist. "Vrag! Ubit ču te!" A plethora of profanities followed.

"Go, go, go, go, go!" Henrik took off at full speed with her, both laughing as they ran.

Nada flew ahead, hair flailing wild, her skinny arms pumping. The wind on her face and the rush of the escape energized her. When she glanced at Henrik, he beamed with eagerness, and she grinned with revelry.

Once they retreated far enough, Nada slowed in a grove of trees, bracing her hands on her thighs as she caught her breath. Henrik leaned against a tree beside her, his chest heaving. They smiled at each other through puffs of air, high on their mischief, on who they were together—what they could achieve.

Henrik glanced away a moment, rubbing the back of his neck as his smile waned to sincerity. "Just so you know, Nada, I'd choose you first too."

Blushing, Nada didn't think it was possible to adore him more.

CHAPTER 6

THE WHOLE WORLD NARROWED AND SHRANK TO A single dark point before Nada. The business end of a rifle.

Her heart thumped in her chest. Pulsed in her temples. The boy wielding it had to be around Nada's age, but his large brown eyes were weighted with jaded experience—an all too familiar mark of war. He stood over Ester and Nada, rifle trained where he had ordered them to sit. The damp, leaf-littered ground itched at Nada's thighs through the fabric of her slacks, but she didn't dare move. Not even to wipe her sweaty hands.

Though certain they neared the Partizan camp they had hoped to find—scattered supply crates paving the way—Nada couldn't determine which army the boy was loyal to from his crumpled, nondescript clothing. While she had often caught sight of Partizani, recognizable by the absence of uniforms, moving through the forest behind her home, for all Nada knew the boy could be an Ustaša sympathizer. Nerves wound tight, she kept her eyes on him, on the finger resting on the trigger.

"I found more of them!" he shouted into the surrounding woods, and Nada flinched. "More fucking spies!"

Nada's heart raced faster.

"We're not spies," Ester told him, her voice small. "I assure you we're not spies."

"Quiet." He raised the rifle a touch, and a muted notch of sunlight glinted off the barrel.

Nada closed her eyes and reached for the comforting presence of her makeshift button bracelet. She worried its smooth surface with her thumb as the fresh air and lush green scent of the forest filled her lungs. She'd promised Filip she'd find their mama and sisters. She couldn't fail him before she'd even begun.

Nada looked up at the boy and his rifle. *Was* he a Partizan? She couldn't come right out and ask which side he was on. Questions like that were suspicious, and the conversation that followed would be like walking the edge of a knife. Words were precarious.

Frowning, he grunted through his teeth. "Someone, get down here! I have them fucking cornered!"

Quick footsteps skittered through the forest floor, hidden from view by the boy with the rifle. Then a male figure swooped in to flank their captor, swinging his pistol up at them with both hands.

Nada's heart stopped. His aim faltered.

"Nada." The mumbled word fell from his lips.

The world expanded and began to spiral. The tempo of her heartbeat shifted. *Henrik.*

His breaths deepened, and his gun lowered. Those blue-gray eyes, as emblazoned in her mind as a tattoo on skin, were glued to her, mirroring her stillness ... her parted lips. He was taller. Shoulders broader. Older. The young man before her conflicted with the image she had carried of him for so long. But he was here. He was whole.

A warm pressure settled on her chest as she stared at the boy who had starred in all her childhood exploits. Her precious memories. How many times had they skipped school together, or spent sun-bright days with Ester by the Drava River? How often had they counted stars and whispered secrets, laughed at their mischief, and raced each other to see who was fastest?

Every aching, vacant part of her that had burst into being when he left two years ago would finally be refilled again. She finally had her Henrik back. The warmth in Nada's chest radiated through her. Her eyes shined. Her cheeks flushed.

Henrik broke away from her gaze and noted Ester's presence while reaching for his comrade's arm. "Put the rifle down, Vinko. They're not spies."

"We tried to tell him." There was a touch of awe in Ester's smile, and she shook her head.

"How do you know they aren't spies?" asked Vinko. "That's the whole point of being a spy. No one knows they *are* one."

"I know these girls." Henrik nudged his arm down. "Let them up."

Ester and Nada rose to their feet. While Ester eyed Vinko and the weapon he slung back over his shoulder, Nada drank in the sight of Henrik and his artfully positioned Partizan cap—a sharp red star at its center. Even war and life in the forest couldn't contend with his compulsive neatness. The only item out of place was the haphazard bandage wrapped around his sleeve.

A smile blossomed across Nada's face, and she rushed forward to throw her arms around him. He smelled of sweat and campfire smoke, but she didn't care. A delayed hand came up to touch her back. Not a hug, exactly, but an absent-minded acknowledgement that she was there. She hugged him tighter.

"You're okay." With a half laugh, tears sprung to her eyes. "You're alive."

"I am."

Ester grinned. "Like I told you, Nada, Henrik's far too stubborn to die."

Nada drew back to let her oldest friends greet each other, and as Ester stepped in for a hug, Nada turned so she could blink away her watery eyes before anyone could see them.

"We've missed you terribly," said Ester.

Certain the moisture was gone, Nada faced him again.

Henrik's tight gaze pinned her in place. "Why are you here, Nada?"

The coldness in his tone gave her pause. She studied him. The lack of warmth in his eyes and the harsh set of his jaw made her stomach drop. Her glowing expression faded, replaced with a crease in her brow. Why wasn't he happy to see her?

"Please excuse his poor manners. I'm his good friend, Vinko," said the boy next to him. "I'm sorry I held you at gunpoint, but we're a bit on edge this morning." He brought a cigarette to his lips and lit it. "I promise I'll make up for it with my comedic flair and delightful disposition. Everyone loves Vinko."

He sent a goading grin Henrik's way, but he might as well have been invisible.

Henrik's face remained like stone. "What are you doing here? We have to be at least half a day's walk from Retfala."

Which was why the girls had stolen their neighbor's vehicle to get here. Not that the neighbor was around to see it go or to catch them taking the keys from the vacant house.

Nada swallowed, but her voice cracked anyway. "We came looking for Partizani." She and Ester glanced at each other. "We want to join."

Henrik's body turned rigid. His chilled stare froze on her.

"Girls for soldiers." Vinko blew a stream of smoke. "Finally, we'll have some comrades that smell infinitely better."

Henrik shook his head. "No."

"Of course they will. Honestly, Henrik, if you can't tell they smell fresh as daisies from here, there's something wrong with your nose."

"*No,* they aren't *joining*," he clarified, shards of ice in his voice.

Nada narrowed her eyes. The way he spoke, the way he looked at her, was so ... wrong. She averted her focus to the forest and folded her arms. A tight heat stirred in her gut.

Ester tilted her head. "Many girls have joined before us."

Women weren't only welcomed to fight in the resistance, but the Partizani were known for praising the valor and strength of their female soldiers, championing their equality with men.

"And far be it from us to deny a woman a weapon," agreed Vinko.

Henrik turned his head slightly, toward Vinko. "I said they're not joining."

Nada huffed, shaking her head. "We're not asking permission."

Henrik's stern gaze met hers. "This isn't some childish game we played as kids, Nada. This isn't an adventure."

She glared at him. His words scratched her inside, teasing at the edges of her temper. She wasn't a child. She knew perfectly well what becoming a Partizanka meant. How dare he imply she didn't?

Ester's jaw hung open. "I don't know who you think you are, Henrik, or what gives you the right to refuse us, but I promise we're not leaving."

"What's the big deal?" Vinko asked Henrik.

He ignored him. "Turn around and go back home."

"Back home to what?" Nada flung her arms out, her open palms trembling. Her hitching breaths carried in the muffled quiet of the woods. "To an empty house?"

A crease formed in Henrik's brow. "Empty?"

Nada teetered on the brink of tears. She wrenched her gaze away, staring hard into the distance, unable to say it. The shadows of the forest stirred and deepened, awakened by the memory of their return home the previous night.

"Ustaše came to our street yesterday." Ester's quiet, flat tone said more than words.

Henrik's chest sagged as breath left him.

Tears flooded Nada's eyes, and her words came out thick and heavy. "Ester and I were out with Filip, running errands. When we returned home, there were Ustaše everywhere. They forced everyone onto a truck and took them away. Ester's parents. My family. Almost the whole street."

She turned to him again as he clenched his fist and stumbled back a step. Brow creased, he trained his eyes on the ground while the muscles in his neck corded.

Though he tempered his reaction, Nada knew him well enough to see the news pained him. Her family, Ester's parents —these were people he grew up with. They were his family too.

"My mother?"

He didn't know. Of course he didn't. "She went to be with your father in Osijek right after you left. She's fine."

"Where's Filip now?"

"A neighbor is taking him to Orahovica to live with our grandparents."

Henrik's furrowed brow deepened. "They took them all? Even little Maša?"

Nada's face crumpled. The fact he still thought of her as "little Maša" made her heart ache. The three-year-old girl he remembered loved him to death. Would reach for him with chubby hands, squealing "*Hennik! Hennik!*" Where was she now? Was she frightened? Was she—

Nada shoved the thoughts away before she could fall apart. She stepped up to Henrik and held his gaze as she planted her feet. "We're not leaving."

"I don't want you here."

The sting of his words lashed hard.

Vinko studied Henrik, brows knitted together as he tugged on his ear. "Maybe it would help Henrik change his mind if you have some useful skills to bring to the table."

"I speak fluent German," said Nada, her cutting glance going to Henrik. "I certainly know Henrik doesn't."

Henrik's father had taught Nada the language as a child. Mostly, she used it as an excuse to be around Henrik, who couldn't care less about learning his grandparents' mother tongue. Who knew it would be a commodity someday?

"She's also wily and can't be trusted," countered Henrik. "She masterminded all of our antics growing up."

Even though the delivery was harsh, his words hinted at the

way he used to tease her. "I seem to recall *you* being the one behind our mischief," Nada said, attempting to get a playful rise out of him. "I never had any desire to steal the neighbor's chickens so we could race them."

He remained silent, eyes burning a hole through her.

"I have some medical training," offered Ester. "My mother's a nurse. She taught me everything she knows."

Vinko perked up. "Can you stitch a wound?" When she affirmed it, he jerked his head toward the forest behind him. "Come with me. I'll get you some supplies. At the very least, Henrik, you should let them stay long enough to fix your damn arm."

"Of course. Anything to help." Ester hurried alongside Vinko, and they made their way deeper into the forest.

Henrik glared at their backs as they left, giving Nada a moment to really look at him. No longer lean and wiry, his arms and shoulders now filled out the long sleeves of his green shirt, pulling the fabric taut in places they never had before. Nada's focus lingered, causing her breaths to shallow. While the deep olive tone of his skin and his light brown hair remained familiar, Henrik's jaw and features had grown more defined. Angular. He was all hard lines and rigidness, and not just in appearance.

It made Nada think of the automobile she and Ester had just stolen. The very same one where a happy, boyish Henrik had spent hours bent over the hood, learning the art of mechanical repairs from their neighbor, while Nada sat on the work bench, swinging her legs and making daisy chains. That memory, threadbare from overuse, accentuated the difference.

Henrik caught her gaze again.

Nada's chest rose and fell. Despite the hardness she found in him, he made her breathless. He had become more handsome than he had any right to be, and any steadiness Nada maintained inside wavered. Her gaze shifted away, only to flit back. "I can't believe I found you here." Once again, the surprise of finding him washed over her.

"Once Ester's done stitching me up, you're both leaving." He turned and walked toward the camp.

Nada wrapped her arms around herself and lowered her head. Had she done something unforgiveable to upset him two years ago? Was that why he had left for the resistance without explanation?

"I'll *leave* once I get them back," she said.

He stopped. Stilled. "Get them back?"

"It's why we came here. Who better to help us rescue them than the Partizani?"

He whirled back around. "It's not what we do, Nada. We don't go on rescue missions. If that's what you came here looking for, you won't find it."

"I can't abandon them." *Not the way you abandoned me.*

"Do you know where the Ustaše took them?"

Her gaze fell in answer.

"They could be anywhere," he said. "If they're alive at all."

A rush of pained breath escaped her. "I *have* to find them, Henrik," she said, shaking out her hands, needing to move. To not stand still, to not do *nothing*. She shifted from one foot to the other. "And if the Partizani won't help, then Ester and I will find them on our own."

"You'll get yourselves killed."

"Then help me convince your troop to come with us."

"The Partizani would never agree to walk into a slaughter like that. Wherever your families are, you can guarantee they're surrounded by a lot of heavily armed men."

Nada's mouth slackened. "So you would just let them die?"

"If we're outnumbered, then *everyone* dies. What good are we then?"

Mind reeling, she stepped back, chest constricting. "You won't help us?"

"I *am* helping you. I'm stopping you from making a stupid mistake."

Nada's skin tightened and itched. She rubbed her face with both hands. "I don't want that kind of help."

"The whole point is void anyway. You don't know where they are."

"We could figure it out. The Henrik I remember wouldn't have thought twice about going after his friends. His *family.*"

He held her gaze in hard earnest. "I'm not the Henrik you remember."

Her heart sank. All this time she had anticipated seeing him again, but she never expected to find someone so cold. So different. What a waste that had been. What a useless, pointless waste. Her nails dug into her palms as she closed the space between them and glared up at him.

"No, you're not," she said, her words icy. He wasn't the boy she'd cried over, night after night, after he'd left. He wasn't the boy she'd worried for, wondering if he would ever make it home. "You're nothing like him."

"That's because I grew up. When you're in the thick of war, you learn to be practical."

Stunned, Nada took one more good look at him. "Apparently, you learn to be heartless too."

With one foot in front of the other, Nada followed Ester's trail between the trees, while Henrik remained rooted in place. Just as he had once done to her, she left him behind—a young, cruel man siphoning the boy she once knew into a fading mist.

CHAPTER 7

HENRIK'S BLOOD SIMMERED AS HE GLARED AT THE remains of the campfire at his feet. Rubbing the back of his neck, he tried to squeeze the tension out of the muscles there, but the tightness coiled deep. What was Nada thinking coming here? Demanding to join the Partizani! How could she be so reckless? He scoffed at himself and wrenched his hand away from his neck. Who was he kidding? This was Nada—bullheaded and impulsive.

She could ruin everything by being there.

Henrik clenched his fists at his sides. He couldn't believe it. Nada was here. The one person in this godless world he wanted to remain safe and alive had come barreling into his camp to throw herself at the feet of danger.

So of course he had no choice but to lie to her.

He *could* have rounded up his comrades to orchestrate a mission to liberate her family. Under different circumstances, he wouldn't have hesitated. But Henrik knew Nada better than anyone. If the Partizani started packing up camp and sweeping up their weapons to go on a rescue, Nada would insist on going with them. There'd be no stopping her.

Henrik's best chance of keeping her safe was to kill all hope.

To lie and tell her the Partizani don't operate in that way, so she'd give up and go home. Besides, they had no intel to go on anyway.

Henrik drew a heavy breath and swiped a hand over his face. Nada. Nada was here.

The moment he saw her his heart had stopped. Everything in his being responded to her as if no time had passed. He missed her. More than he cared to admit to himself. And when she threw her arms around his neck, it took every ounce of strength he had to resist returning the embrace.

He needed her gone. And the sooner the better.

"You shouldn't bandage your arm over your shirt." Ester dragged him from his thoughts, unwinding the scrap of cloth Vinko had tied to his bicep. "You need to tend to your wounds properly. Take off your shirt for me."

Henrik darkened and unbuttoned his shirt. Vinko was being overly cautious in enlisting Ester's help. The cut would heal, in time, like any other. Surface wounds were a part of life for Henrik. Nothing to get worked up about. At least they were the kinds of wounds that *could* heal.

When Henrik pulled his sleeve off his left arm, peeling the fabric back, blood pooled along the cut and a drop trickled down his skin. She inspected the slice across the hill of his arm. "It's deep. You certainly need stitches."

There was no need for her to fuss. Gunpowder and a match would do just as well.

Ester pressed the stained bandage to his bicep. "Hold this down and take a seat."

He did as she asked and sat on the log by the campfire remains. She joined him there and riffled through the first-aid kit Vinko had given her.

"How did it happen?" she asked. "Your injury."

Henrik didn't want to engage in conversation with her, but he settled on grinding out his words. "Spies came into the camp."

She glanced at him as she prepared a needle and thread.

"That would explain why your friend Vinko held us at gunpoint."

There was that word again. Friend. Vinko was no friend of his.

"Do you have something you can take for the pain?"

He gave a terse shake of his head.

Doe-eyed, Ester tipped up her chin and held his gaze. "Nothing?"

He waved at his arm. "Just do it."

Ester pressed her lips together and brought her needle to his skin. "Try to hold still for me."

A sharp burn shot through his arm and Henrik drew a breath, clenching his jaw, eyes firmly fixed on the ground. It hurt, but he had been through worse.

"You're different now," she murmured, gaze shifting to his face, searching.

Henrik had nothing to say to that. He turned away from her as she continued stitching him up, letting his eyes roam toward Nada. She spoke to Vinko by the collection of crates, tucking her hair behind her ear after a gust of wind tossed it into her face. Vinko grinned at her like a fool.

Though still too thin from lack of food, Nada didn't resemble the scrappy girl Henrik had left behind in Retfala. While her face had lost its youthful roundness, her deep brown eyes had grown even more piercing, more captivating ... if that were even possible. Fuller and softer around the edges, she no longer looked like a small, feisty girl, but a fiery young *woman*. She was beautiful. More beautiful than he remembered.

"I see you've been hurt before," said Ester.

Ester was bound to see the scars on his torso with his shirt hanging from one shoulder, leaving him half exposed.

Jakov wandered over to Vinko and Nada, stealing Henrik's full attention. His thumb drummed against his knee. Would Nada ask Jakov for his help? Tell him what happened to her family? His heart rate picked up. Vinko sauntered away from Nada and Jakov and headed toward Henrik and Ester.

Tired of the one-sided conversation, Ester sighed. "I'm so glad to see you're okay, Henrik."

"Is he beyond saving?" Vinko's eyes skirted Henrik while a crease formed between his brows.

Ester smiled, bright and soft. "He'll survive. Though I'm not sure there's much I can do about his chattiness. He's been talking my ear off over here." Cloaked in lightness and wearing a teasing grin, she glanced sideways at Henrik.

He didn't give her the reaction she was searching for. He didn't want her thinking that things were the way they used to be.

Unruffled, Ester continued her work.

"That's our Ubica for you." Vinko grinned with a glint in his eye. "Always itching for a good conversation."

Ester's back straightened. "Ubica?" *Assassin.* Her eyes fell on Henrik, but he didn't meet them.

Did it frighten her to know what he had become? Disappoint her, even?

"Oh yeah," said Vinko. "Henrik's the one who takes on our more ... *delicate* jobs, should I say?" He leaned in closer to inspect Ester's work. "Speaking of jobs, I have to say I'm impressed. Your mother taught you well. Did your father also happen to teach you something we could use to our advantage?"

She grinned. "Unless you count shoveling coal as an advantage, then no. But even then, that's as much as I know about driving a train."

As Ester finished tying off the final stitch, Nada approached them and Henrik stiffened. She had pilfered supplies from the crates and now wore a holstered pistol around her waist, and a machine gun hung from her shoulder. She carried that flinty air about her that only Nada could. The vision of a true Partizanka.

Henrik gripped his knee, knuckles turning white, and remained frozen as his heart seized.

Vinko took one look at Nada and whistled, suggesting he was impressed. He flicked a finger against the magazine pouch at

Nada's hip. "Don't you look prepared? And damn intimidating."

"Good." She held a straight face. "Maybe the Ustaše will shit themselves when they see me coming."

Vinko's eyes widened as he burst into laughter. "Oh, I'm going to *love* you. There's nothing better than a Partizanka with bite."

Ester reached for fresh bandages, but Henrik barely noticed thanks to his hammering heart. The thought of Nada going anywhere near Ustaše made his blood run cold.

"You look ridiculous," Henrik spat, his tone harsh because it *needed* to be. "Like you're playing dress-up."

Nada glared at him in response.

"I told you to leave," he said.

"And I told you, I won't."

Henrik gritted his teeth, locking his own stubborn gaze with hers, both caught in a battle of wills.

Vinko cleared his throat and scratched his head. "So, have you girls known Henrik a long time then?"

When Ester realized no one else was going to answer, she stepped in. "Yes. Since we were little."

"Tell me, was he always so annoyingly tidy?"

Henrik wanted to scoff. The two of them were complete opposites in that regard. Vinko's mess and clutter drove Henrik crazy.

Ester smiled. "For as long as I've known him."

Nada smirked with harsh mockery. "When we were children, he couldn't stand to get dirty."

When Nada was angry, everyone knew about it. And damn it, Henrik felt a surge of fondness toward her for it. For the familiarity of it all. He tore his focus away from her, tamping down that warmth inside him.

He needed Nada to go home. Now.

Ester finished tying up Henrik's clean bandage, then packed up the medical kit as he slid his aching arm back into his sleeve and buttoned his shirt. If Nada wasn't going to listen to him, there was only one thing he could do. Without a word, Henrik got up and stalked toward Jakov. They held mutual respect for each other. Jakov would hear him out.

"Henrik," he greeted.

"What did Nada say to you? Did she ask you anything?"

Jerking back at Henrik's abruptness, Jakov took a second to reply. "Only if we had been near any roads yesterday and seen a truck pass by. I told her we've been camped in the woods for two days. Nothing to see but birds and trees and Vinko's tomfoolery."

"Anything else? What did you talk about?"

"I told her that we're headed to Našice to meet another troop. She seemed eager for that. Said she wanted to join us." He shrugged, rubbing fingers against his beard. "Why do you ask?"

If Henrik's attempts to send Nada home weren't working, he needed Jakov's help. So he used the only tactic he could think of to convince him to turn Nada and Ester away. "They're not cut out for this, Jakov. Those girls know nothing of combat."

"They'll learn."

Henrik shook his head. "They don't belong here."

"Is this because they're women? I'm surprised you feel that way, considering your time with Katarina. You know what a fierce Partizanka she was. And she was only seventeen."

Henrik's nostrils flared and his chest heaved faster. The reminder of her stirred poison in his stomach. "Katarina *died*," he spat.

"Men die too, Henrik."

"Please, send them home."

"It's not my place to do that."

"Of course it is. You're the one with authority here."

"If someone wants to fight, that choice is theirs. The resistance can use as many people as we can get. I won't turn anyone away."

"You're not *listening* to me," Henrik snapped. He needed to make Jakov believe they were better off without them. "You don't want them to stay. I know these girls better than anyone. Ester's too soft. She doesn't have a single aggressive bone in her body. She can't even bring herself to end a dying bird's suffering. You think she'll be of any use to you in a war? And Nada! She's impulsive and temperamental to a fault. She's not going to take orders from you. She always does what she wants, and that'll only put the others' lives in danger. It's not smart to let them stay. They're nothing more than a hindrance."

"No one joins the Partizani unless they have a hunger for it. A reason. If they have that drive to be here, they'll work hard for it. Like you did, remember? In fact, I'd never seen such dedication."

Henrik gritted his teeth. Squeezed the back of his neck. Why not toss Nada into the hands of the enemy and call it a day? Either way, it would end with the same outcome. Henrik would have to take matters into his own hands and find a way to trample their hope and determination. Henrik turned, done with the fruitless conversation, and stopped short.

Nada stood before him, arms folded as her eyes glistened. She'd heard everything. Heard him call her a hindrance. Witnessed his attempt at getting rid of her.

Good. Maybe if she hated him enough, she'd finally leave and forget this dangerous plan of hers.

Nothing more than a hindrance. That's what she was to Henrik. A nuisance. A thorn in his side.

How many times had she daydreamed of their reunion? Envisioned the way he would pull her close in a bear hug, his soft chuckle tickling her ear? He would tease her about how she no longer looked awkward and spindly, and then he'd hook his arm around her shoulders as they walked down the street together to his house. Because, naturally, Henrik would come to her doorstep before his own.

Not once had she pictured him being cold and harsh. She never imagined him calling her a *hindrance* with such contempt.

Yet here he stood before her—caught red-handed in his cruel sabotage—holding her gaze with deadened eyes. She barely recognized him.

Fighting to keep the sting in her eyes from welling, Nada spun on her heel and stormed back to Ester, where she waited for her on the log.

Ester's brows pinched as Nada neared. She stood. "What happened?"

Nada pressed a hand to her forehead. "I don't know who he is anymore," she said on a breath, fighting back tears. She swallowed hard. "We made a mistake coming here."

"What's going on, Nada?"

"We were wrong. The Partizani don't go on rescue missions. Henrik said they won't even consider helping us. We wasted our time coming here and now our families are getting farther and farther away from us." Nada clutched her stomach as panic taunted her, circled her, trying to find its way into her body. Her chest began to heave.

"All right, let's take a breath and think about this," said Ester.

Nada drew in a shuddering breath and looked away to find composure. Her eyes found Vinko, who watched her with a frown. No doubt, he'd listened in on their conversation and was now witnessing her on the brink of falling apart.

"Everyone, get ready!" Jakov called out from the center of camp. "It's time to move out!"

"They're going somewhere?" Ester asked.

Nada's heart thundered. What would she do now? The Partizani couldn't help her, and Henrik was intent on forcing her home. She had no choice but to carry on with this rescue on her own, with Ester.

"Change of plans," said Nada. "We're going to Našice with them."

"We are?"

"They're going to meet more Partizani there. They've been traveling. Maybe some of them have seen something. Heard something. All we need is a good lead on where our families might be, and then we can figure out what to do next."

"Okay. That sounds like a good idea."

The plan of action settled her. Able to breathe again, Nada picked up her bag from beside the ashen firepit as Partizani ambled from their camp around her. Henrik forged past, moving ahead of them as Ester and Nada began to follow. She glowered at the back of his broad shoulders.

"Even if we get answers in Našice, we should find a quiet moment to sit with the Partizani," said Ester. "Maybe we can convince them to help. Beg them if we have to. There's no way we can go up against the Ustaše alone."

"I know. But if it comes to it, you should know, I'll do it anyway. I'll always choose them. I'll choose my family."

Ester met her eyes and nodded. "And as I promised, I'll be right there beside you."

"Let's hope we can convince them to help."

"If not, maybe Henrik will come with us."

Nada scoffed, glaring in Henrik's direction. He marched farther ahead of them now, as though he couldn't get away from her fast enough. "There's not a chance he'd do that."

"Surely he would."

"He's changed. Tell me you don't see that."

Ester nodded, subdued. "I do."

"He said rescuing our families would be impractical. And he told Jakov we'd be nothing but a nuisance for the Partizani. He has no interest in helping us. I don't think he even cares our families are in danger."

"I don't understand. Henrik would never talk like that. *Behave* like that. He certainly wouldn't turn you away."

"Well, he did." An ache flared in Nada's chest. "He told me himself, he's not the same Henrik anymore. And he meant it."

"I wonder what happened to make him change this way?" Ester murmured.

Nada wished she knew.

Vinko sidled up alongside Nada, staring at the ground as he walked. "Looking forward to your first adventure, ladies?" Vinko withdrew a cigarette from his breast pocket, then changed his mind and tucked it behind his ear. When he caught Nada watching the move, he shrugged. "I'm running low."

"Maybe *you* could shed some light on why Henrik is the way he is," said Nada, having no doubt Vinko overheard their conversation.

He let out a sigh. "Henrik's a mystery to us all. He rarely interacts with anyone unless he has to. So he's not exactly a fountain of information when it comes to his life."

As though recalling something, Ester reached out to clasp Nada's arm. "They call him *Ubica*."

A cold sensation rushed through Nada's body at the word. Made everything around her spin and tilt. That did *not* sound like Henrik.

"Maybe that has something to do with it," said Ester.

Nada turned to Vinko with a pained expression. "Is that why he's so cruel now?"

"I couldn't say. I joined only a year ago, so I haven't known him as long as the others." His brows drew together in thought. "All I know about Henrik is what others have told me. When he arrived, he trained differently to the rest of us. He learned his skills from a beast of a man before an enemy bullet took him down. By then, Henrik had already gained himself an impressive reputation. But I do remember Matej once saying something about a girl who died. Henrik failed to save her or was too late. Something like that. And Henrik loved her. I suppose that could be responsible."

Nada turned pale as snow. Her breaths grew shallow.

Katarina died.

Henrik's darkened voice replayed in her head, over and over.

Katarina died.

"Nada, are you all right?" asked Ester.

She lifted her chin. "I'm fine." Her words were sharp.

A weight pressed on her lungs as her thoughts swirled. Henrik had loved someone, and it wasn't her.

All those times Ester had teased her, insisted that Henrik adored her, loved her, Nada had batted the notion away. But despite her constant denial, a secret part of her always hoped Ester was right. Because there was no Nada without Henrik.

But now everything was so painfully clear. Nada was no longer Henrik's whole world. And she hadn't been for a long time. She was separate. Past. Abandoned on an entirely new level.

Trying to hide her emotions, she dropped her gaze to her button bracelet, rubbing her thumb over it as she blinked back tears.

How stupid she was. How humiliating to know he never loved her after all. And she had waited for him, prayed for him, cried for him.

Ester slipped her hand around Nada's and squeezed. "Even though he's changed, it doesn't mean what he felt for you has."

Ester might as well have pierced Nada's chest with a knife.

Nada huffed, yanking her hand away as a flush rose to her cheeks. "When are you going to let go of these silly, romantic perceptions of yours? Henrik has never cared for me that way. I wish you would stop talking about it."

"You cared for him too."

Nada whirled on her. "For the last time, Ester, I don't have any feelings for him, and his leaving didn't affect me in any way. I *hate* him. Do you hear me? After today, I'll hate him for the rest of my life. So stop trying to conjure fairytales from nothing."

Ester held Nada's watery gaze, and when she finally spoke, her voice was soft. "All right, Nada. I'll stop. I'm sorry."

Nada swallowed down the tightness in her throat and continued walking, scrambling to gather the breaking pieces of herself. Because just as there was a trace of hurt veiled by Nada's anger, there was a trace of empathy hidden in Ester's apology. Ester saw right through her.

If her sestra could see the truth, could others? Nada would rather die than let Henrik ever see what she really felt for him.

And so she wouldn't.

Nada didn't need him. Not to love, and certainly not to rescue her family.

CHAPTER 8

SHE FOLLOWED THEM. TREKKED THROUGH THE WOODS with his fellow soldiers as though she belonged, talking with Vinko most of the way. As though *they* had been friends for years.

Henrik spent the whole time grinding his teeth, inventing arguments in his mind, studying every angle he could possibly use to send Nada home. He couldn't afford to have her here. Henrik had his convictions—made his choices long ago—and she was messing with them, putting everything he fought for at risk. So tense he could snap, Henrik kept his glare on the ground ahead of him and tried to ease his stewing by flexing his hands.

When they met with the other Partizan troop—a pride-swelling display of the uprising's devotion to fighting for freedom—their number increased to sixty-two men and women. With the meeting came the reputable intel that a German convoy would be traveling outside the nearby town of Gazije that evening, and Jakov decided it would be the perfect opportunity for an ambush. Which meant the Partizani wouldn't be staying in Našice for long.

With many soldiers welcomed into their village, a trio of bakas set up pits of burning coals out in the open air, over which they busied themselves, stirring cumbersome pots that stewed with soups and potatoes and beans to feed the resistance. The beauty of passing through farmlands meant there was more food to go around.

The Partizani congregated by the main road—groups gathering in conversation and lounging in the grass to rest. But Henrik sat by himself on a gently sloping hillside, separate from the crowd, eating his bowl of soup. From his vantage point, he watched as Ester and Nada continued to move from Partizan to Partizan, group cluster to group cluster. He had questioned a few of them earlier as to what the girls were asking them. It's how he knew they were still searching for leads on the Ustaše that took their families, and how he knew they weren't going to give up so easily.

"How's your arm?"

Vinko's shadow crept over him, and Henrik wanted to groan. He frowned at his presence, at the fact he brought attention to the constant ache in his arm.

What did Henrik have to do to make Vinko stop caring? He had flinched away from him the night before. Would violence make it end once and for all? Henrik finished his soup and placed the bowl in the grass, ignoring Vinko.

The boy nodded, not surprised by Henrik's silence. "So I overheard your girlfriends talking back at our camp. They said something that made me curious."

Vinko paused, slipping his hands in his pockets, likely hoping that Henrik would prompt him for more. But Henrik kept his gaze on the gathered soldiers.

"Nada said you told her the Partizani wouldn't help save her family."

Henrik's shoulders stiffened, but he didn't react. Didn't give Vinko any body language to read.

"Why did you lie to her?"

Henrik launched to his feet and stood over him, fists clenched, jaw set, unbottling every drop of intimidation he possessed. Vinko needed to back down. To leave the subject alone.

"Some Partizani liberated a train full of Serbs headed to slaughter last week," Vinko said. "You damn well know this. You *know* we help people when the opportunity presents itself."

"This is none of your concern."

Vinko shook his head, running a hand through his messy hair. "Why would you make her suffer like that?"

His words burned. Scalded him. Henrik snatched at Vinko's collar, fisting the cloth of his jacket, and drew him in close. Henrik glared. "If you so much as breathe a word of that liberation to Nada, I will make your sorry life more miserable than it already is. Do you understand?"

Vinko raised his hands in surrender, throat bobbing.

Henrik released him with a shove and stalked down the hill.

His nerves rattled in his chest. Had the girls mentioned their plans to anyone else? Could he trust Vinko, a boy so reckless and glib, to keep his mouth shut?

Jakov spotted Henrik across the crowd and approached him with purpose. With a quick glance, Henrik checked for Vinko's whereabouts. He ambled toward Ester and Nada—the girls no longer questioning soldiers but wrapped up in close conversation together.

"I have a job for you, Henrik," said Jakov, almost at his side.

But Henrik barely paid attention, distracted by the scene unfolding across the way. Vinko joined the girls. Started talking. Henrik clenched his fist, trying to remain calm.

"I've set up a practice shooting range in the woods behind that house over there."

Vinko made the girls laugh, giving Henrik some modicum of relief. And then Vinko took off his Partizan jacket and swung it around Nada's shoulders. He stepped back and made some grand comment with his arms open. Had Vinko taken a liking to her? Was that why he concerned himself with her business?

"Henrik?"

"Huh?" He turned to face Jakov.

"I need you to teach those new girls how to shoot."

"What for?"

"To prepare them for the ambush."

Henrik froze. "They've never even held a weapon, and you're going to throw them into the deep end?"

"Of course not. That's why I'm having you teach them first. You're the best shooter we have."

Henrik's pulse raced. "Jakov, they should hide far away in the woods until the ambush is over. One lesson isn't enough."

"With you as their teacher, it's more than enough. And there's no faster way to learn than under pressure."

"Jakov—"

"That's an order, Ubica." Jakov's hard stare warned there was no room for argument. "Prepare them well, and you'll have nothing to worry about." The man strode away to carry on with whatever preparations he had in the works.

Nothing to worry about? Henrik had *everything* to worry about.

Pressing his lips together, Henrik helped himself to the supply crates and took a rifle and ammunition. At the very least he could start small, with a less frightening weapon than a machine gun. He headed over to where the girls had been, but only Nada and Vinko remained, deep in conversation.

"Where's Ester?" Henrik asked.

Their talk deadened. She turned a flat gaze on him and took a moment before she answered. "She went somewhere with Matej."

Henrik began loading the rifle with bullets, one by one, focusing on it to avoid the indifferent look in her eyes. "I've been ordered to teach you both to shoot."

"Right now?"

"Right now. You can be first. I'll find Ester later."

Nada picked up her Schmeisser from where she had set it down. Henrik gritted his teeth.

Vinko plucked the cigarette from behind his ear and lit it, shooting a crooked grin in Nada's direction. "When you're done learning from that amateur, come find me. I'll show you how to really wield a weapon."

"Ignore him." Henrik closed the bolt and lowered the rifle. "He couldn't strike a donkey if his ass was sitting on it."

Vinko chuckled and winked at Nada. "Good luck." He sauntered back toward the gathered Partizani.

Henrik led the way without a word, passing the house Jakov had pointed out. With Nada following a step behind, he pushed through the encroaching woods and up the slope until they came upon a clearing. Sure enough, Jakov had set up a row of old tin cans along the ridge of a fallen tree.

Henrik turned to Nada and slid the Schmeisser off her shoulder. Off Vinko's jacket. The muted green fabric hung loose on her slender frame.

Nada noticed him staring at it. "Vinko gave it to me. He said it completes the look."

He placed her Schmeisser off to the side, leaning it against a small boulder.

"Aren't we here so you can teach me how to use that?" she asked.

"We're starting with something easier."

"Easier?"

"The Schmeisser's heavy. Deadlier."

Her eyes narrowed as she crossed her arms. "Isn't that the whole point? Teaching me to be deadly?"

Henrik never wanted to see such a weapon in her hands. The thought alone made his knees weaken and his pulse unsteady. Carrying a weapon invited danger and made her a target. The rifle was more palatable.

"Walk first. Then run," he said.

Nada drew a deep sigh and took the rifle he offered. It looked awkward in her slender hands as she held it straight across her middle, testing its weight and feel.

"First rule," said Henrik. "Don't carry your weapon like that. Always keep the barrel pointed at the ground or toward the sky. Never horizontal. Accidents happen."

She dropped the barrel and waited for his next instruction.

"Now, put the butt against your shoulder and line up your aim through the front sight. That's the small ring at the end of the barrel."

Nada complied, squinting as she steadied the weapon. "Got it," she mumbled.

"The gun will kick up a little when you shoot, so be ready for that. Once you've lined it up, hold your breath to keep yourself still, and gently pull the trigger."

She fired. A loud crack assaulted his ears as the rifle's barrel lifted from the force. A spray of bark hissed as her bullet skimmed the trunk, far to the left of her target. Nada's breaths quickened from the rush of firing her first weapon.

"Try again. Be more patient this time. There's no hurry."

Her tone grew sarcastic. "There's no hurry when an enemy's running straight for me?"

Henrik frowned at the idea. "To reload, lift the bolt here, slide it back, and then snap it back into place."

She did as instructed, sending a bullet shell flinging out of the chamber. Raising the weapon again, Nada aimed and focused on her target. With a slow exhale, she hooked her finger around the trigger and squeezed.

Dirt and bark puffed out beside the can, causing it to tremble.

Her face brightened as she lowered her gun. "Surely that would have at least been a limb. Or a torso. What do you think?"

"Depends on what result you were aiming for."

"A kill-shot, of course."

Henrik's jaw tensed. "You say that now. But moments like that leave a dark aftertaste in their wake. Taking someone's life can break you."

She let out a mirthless laugh. "I break and break all the time. It's part of life." Nada slid the bolt of her rifle back. A shell tumbled out, tinkling against the rocky earth. "With destruction comes renewal."

Henrik beheld her, truly devoured the sight of her up close, for the first time since she had arrived. Dappled light danced against her long, rich brown hair as a whispering breeze lifted strands of it to tickle her cheek. The shadows she carried in her eyes, the press of her lips, both tugged at something deep inside him. Something he had locked away a long time ago. His heartbeat slowed. The urge to step closer, to shield her from the cause of those shadows, floated to the surface.

Henrik wrenched his thoughts away with a grit of his teeth. "Why are you still here, Nada?"

She met his gaze. "Because I haven't gotten what I need yet."

"You've been asking around all day and no one knows where your family went. You're out of options."

A crease formed between her brows. "There's always a plan B."

"Enlighten me."

"Ester and I are going to talk to Jakov. We have a convincing—"

"Go *home*, Nada." Henrik growled and scrubbed at his face. "I already told you, they'll never help you."

She set her jaw and lifted her rifle, lining up another target. A shot rang out, and the tin can hurtled back into the grass and rocks. A clear hit. She let the shell loose from the chamber.

Nada held the rifle out to him. "Stop wasting my time. I want to run."

He held those fathomless brown eyes as the biting mineral scent of gunpowder drifted between them. Then he hung his head, took the rifle, and swapped it for the Schmeisser. "What happens when Jakov says no? Are you waiting for *me* to swoop in and save you?"

She quirked her brows and laughed at him. "I don't need you, Henrik. I haven't needed you for two years. You think I came here expecting to find you? Hoping you'd be here to save me?" She smirked and rolled her eyes. "Please. I came here looking for Partizani. Finding you was just bad luck. Because if you weren't here, everything would be a lot easier."

Her words stung like the lash of a whip. Their impact

surprised him. He wanted her to hate him. Had been harsh toward her so she'd keep her distance. But still, her indifferent attitude caught him off guard. Hit him hard in the chest.

And the part that dug deepest? If she'd found a different troop in the woods that morning, no one would have stopped her from joining them. No one would have tried to protect her or keep her from embarking on a suicide mission.

Nada called it bad luck. Henrik called it a blessing. The fact she stumbled upon *his* camp meant Henrik had the advantage to do whatever it took to keep her alive.

He knew what her next step was going to be. He just needed to buy himself some time to figure out a countermove. A new way to block her.

"If the ambush goes well," he said, sighing, "Jakov will be in a good mood tonight. He likes to celebrate his wins. That's the best time to ask him for favors."

Her nonchalance slipped a little, softening. "Okay. I'll wait till then."

And that was all he needed. For her to wait. And for Vinko to stay quiet.

Henrik carried on with his lesson, teaching Nada how to use the Schmeisser. Frighteningly adept, she picked it up fast, her aim impressive. But firing at a target that remained still was no true comparison to combat. It wasn't the same as when chaos whirled around you, heart pounding in your chest, adrenaline screaming through your body while enemies closed in, trying to kill you.

A quiet clearing, filled with birdsong and warm sunlight, was no preparation for that.

When Henrik deemed her lesson as thorough as it could get, they went back into the village to find Ester. She and Matej had joined Vinko, who watched Henrik and Nada approach, his gaze going from one to the other.

Vinko shook his head at Nada. "There's still something missing."

"What do you mean?" she asked.

Vinko's mouth tilted in a crooked grin. "Henrik, give me that." He snatched the titovka from Henrik's head and slapped the red-starred cap onto Nada's. "Much better."

Matej smiled and gave her a nod. "Looks like we have ourselves a new Katarina."

Henrik's stomach plummeted. Eyes wide, he looked at Nada —at the Partizan hat and jacket, the pistol at her waist, the Schmeisser she'd just learned to use. A slight tremble crept into his hands.

Nada's gaze flitted to him, and he slammed down any emotion that might have appeared across his face.

But dread still ran its icy fingers along his skin. Because Henrik was no longer confident she'd walk away from all this, no matter what he did to try and stop her.

CHAPTER 9

Before

HENRIK TRIED TO IGNORE THE RUMBLE OF HIS stomach as he scanned the pages, flicking through the book on hunting and trapping that he'd taken from his father's collection. With food being as scarce as it was, Henrik wanted to find a way to help provide for his family. If he learned how to, he could start capturing rabbits for them to eat. Maybe, if he became skilled at it, he could even share them with his friends too. And so, he searched the book for instructions that would teach him.

Spring sunlight poured over the pages and the blossoming flowers in the garden behind Henrik's house. The days were growing longer, thawing all reminders of the harsh winter. Wanting to feel the warmth of the sun and fresh air in their lungs, Nada and Ester had dragged Henrik outside with them to sit in the grass. The girls did each other's hair as Henrik sat tucked against a tree to read his father's book.

"I'm bored," Ester announced the moment she finished braiding Nada's hair into a rope-like crown. "Let's play a game."

"What kind of game?" asked Nada, rolling onto her knees to face them both.

"Any. There's so many we haven't played in a long time."

While the girls were likely intrigued with the idea to distract themselves from hunger, Henrik was fifteen and far too old to play childish games anymore. Henrik sighed and refocused on his book. He had more important things to do, like learning how to hunt.

"How about"—Nada's wicked gaze went to Henrik—"we dress up Henrik."

They hadn't done that to him since he was ten, and he wasn't about to let them reintroduce it. "Don't even think about it."

"Oh, I know." Ester leapt to her feet, prompting Nada to join her. "We could play my most favorite of all time."

Nada tilted her head. "Which one's that?"

Ester hunched forward, fingers curling into claws, and growled. "I'm a bear!"

Nada threw her head back with laughter and trotted away as Ester advanced, trying to catch her. Nada squealed as she dashed about the yard, dodging Ester's attempts to grab her.

When Nada yelped, Henrik looked up. Ester had caught her from behind, arms locked around her in a bear hug.

Smiling wide, Nada laughed. "Help me, Henrik!"

Despite the ridiculousness of their childhood game, Henrik's lips twitched. They were having fun, and part of him itched to join them. "Help yourself. You're more than capable of escaping Ester's clutches."

"But how? She has me pinned!"

With feigned impatience, he threw out the first thing that came to mind. "Drop to the ground using your body weight."

She did. She broke free and slammed butt-first onto the grass.

"Ow!" she cried through pained laughter, tipping over onto her side. "I hurt my tailbone!" She curled inward, writhing from the impact and chuckling at the same time. "That's the worst advice anyone could give!"

Henrik smiled and shook his head before turning his attention back to his book. "Better to hurt your tailbone than get eaten by a bear."

"I vote for a new game." She got up, dusting herself off.

"Hide and seek, then," said Ester. "You both hide. I'll seek."

"I'm not playing," said Henrik.

"Oh, come on, Henrik." Nada clasped her hands together and unleashed those brown eyes on him. "Please?"

He wanted to say yes. That look could always get him to say yes.

"I'll count to one hundred. Starting now." Ester whirled, and shielding her face with her hands, she pressed herself against the wall of the house.

Rhythmic numbers carried through her fingers.

Nada hurried over to Henrik. Planting her hands on his shoulders, she leaned in close to whisper in his ear. "I'll race you for the best hiding spot." With a wild grin, she bolted toward the field.

Henrik slapped the book closed and tossed it aside, unable to resist. He launched himself after her, closing the distance between them. She ran for the barn across the field, nestled against the enveloping woods. Blades of tall grass pattered against his shoes and shins as he flew, trying to beat her there. But she was always so fast.

Rapid gunfire sounded, and the dirt at their feet sprayed into the air. Henrik jolted, ducking his head, and he and Nada dropped flat to the ground by instinct. Pulse racing, Henrik panted into the grass as silence fell around them. Shaking fingers clawing at the soil, he watched an ant meander in the dirt as wavering blades tickled his face. Nada's fast breaths rasped nearby. Who fired at them? Would it be safe to get up and look?

Approaching footfalls stirred the grass, and Henrik's gut turned to stone as a tingling coldness washed over him. Bracing himself, muscles tightening, Henrik peered up. At least thirty

Ustaše surrounded them, machine gun barrels pointed at their faces.

"Are you running because you're going to warn the Partizani we're here?" one asked.

Henrik looked at Nada to check she was all right. Pale and wide-eyed, she still gasped from her run.

Henrik shook his head as he eased to his feet. "We don't know where any Partizani are. We were going to the barn." Nada stood and stepped close to Henrik's side, eyeing their weapons. The move only awakened his protectiveness of her. "I was just playing with my little sister."

"Do you have any Partizani living in your village?"

He knew if he told the truth, those people would die. "No. None."

The Ustaša studied Henrik, squinting against the sun's glare. "Is your father home?"

Henrik shook his head again. "He's in the city."

"Is he in the army?" the Ustaša asked.

"No, he works there."

The man continued to stare at Henrik, then shifted his gaze to Nada. Henrik's nerves lit up like a live wire.

"Do you know who the head of your village is?" the man asked her.

Henrik jumped in before Nada could speak. "I do." The man they spoke of was a Partizan sympathizer, and if they knew this, the man would be dead by day's end. But with the Ustaša's attention on Nada, Henrik would do anything to take it off her again. "Dmitar lives about a kilometer away."

"You'll take us to him then."

He didn't hesitate. "Okay."

"Henrik—" Nada started.

"Go home, sestra. I'll be back soon." He held her pained gaze with steadiness, hoping she read the veiled sternness in him. "You promised to help Mama with dinner after we played. So, go. And don't forget to take your bear inside with you."

Her nod came slow as her brow wrinkled. With a visible

swallow she stepped back, eyes flitting toward the Ustaše, then back to him. Henrik was a Croat. As long as he remained smart, he'd be safe. Nada knew this. She treaded toward the house, looking over her shoulder at Henrik, before he finally turned and led the Ustaše away from her.

They barraged him with nonstop questions on the way. Wanting to know every little detail of his life and who in the village lived where. They asked if he had ever seen Partizani around before. He shrugged and lied that he didn't know.

When they arrived at Dmitar's house, flecked in light and shade from the towering beech trees nearby, Henrik pointed to it, and they let him go home. As his feet carried him back to the corner of the street, a single gunshot fired.

Henrik flinched and his stomach roiled. He had no doubt in his mind what it meant.

Forcing himself not to think of it, to detach from the tragedy, he latched onto one good thing: that he had caved and decided to play with Nada.

Because if Henrik hadn't done as Nada wanted, she would have faced those Ustaše alone.

CHAPTER 10

THE EFFORTLESS COMMAND HENRIK HAD AMONG HIS fellow soldiers, the way they deferred to him with respect, drew Nada in. There was a fierce confidence in his stride, in the straight set of his strong shoulders, that had her sinking into relaxed observation. She leaned against a moss-covered cluster of boulders and, brushing a finger over her bottom lip, trailed his every move. Studied the differences in him, yet searched for the familiar.

All that time Henrik was gone, this was who he'd been. Who he became without her. Capable. Intense. Skilled. Important. The hair on her nape lifted, and her chest swelled with a deep, slow breath.

The sun, making its descent toward the horizon, trailed long streams of slanting light through the trees. Lashings of it moved across Henrik's form as he trudged back up the quiet mountainside after he and Jakov prepared C-4 for their ambush. He glanced up, catching her gaze, and looked away again. As though he caught sight of nothing more than a tree stump. Or an insignificant leaf drifting on the wind.

Nada's chest tightened and her eyes prickled. With a swallow, she wrapped her arms around her torso. Closed her eyes. How was it possible to have Henrik so close within reach and still miss him? To still ache for him as though he wasn't there at all?

Are you waiting for me *to swoop in and save you?*

Nada frowned, casting her gaze to the dirt beneath her. He had said it as though he knew she was waiting for an offer of help. Because really, the Henrik she used to know would have. The detestation in his voice had made Nada recoil. Made her pretend it didn't hurt and put up a wall that hid her feelings from him.

Down through the valley below snaked a narrow road, solitary and silent. No vehicles had passed since they had arrived in the area. Many of the soldiers now lurked behind the trees on the hillside across the way, waiting for the German convoy that was supposed to pass through before long.

If the ambush goes well, Jakov will be in a good mood tonight. That's the best time to ask him for favors.

Nada needed this ambush to succeed. She depended on it for the sake of her family. Her palms turned clammy as her pulse beat harder. Every minute they delayed rescue was a minute in which she could lose her family. Nada braced her hands against the rock behind her and inhaled deeply.

The nature around her radiated peace, and yet for Nada, panic was but a breath away. She clutched her desperation close to her chest. Stoked it like a fire so the embers of urgency and determination would remain smoldering. To burn away her disappointment in Henrik and fade her heartache into the background.

Henrik approached her, carrying a hell box detonator. He'd rolled his sleeves up earlier to work, giving Nada a glimpse of the definition in his forearms as he set the detonator on the ground beside him. "Orahovica is close by. Take the weapons with you and go home to Filip and your grandparents. You can make it there in two, maybe three, hours."

She huffed, narrowing her eyes at him. What ever happened to the advice he gave her, to wait until tonight to ask Jakov for his help? She'd thought he had finally come around, if only a little.

Nada yanked his titovka from her head and slapped it against his chest. "I forgot to give this back."

He took it, jaw clenching after her non-answer. She wouldn't give him what he asked for.

Ester wandered to Nada's side, unaware of the tension between them. She inhaled the forest air, eyelids dipping, luxuriating in her surroundings. "Isn't it wondrous out here? Even though I'm nervous, I want to soak it all in." She turned to Henrik with an expectant smile.

He didn't so much as glance in her direction.

"Perhaps that's why you're silent." There was a glimmer of teasing in her tone. "The beauty has rendered you speechless."

Still nothing.

What happened to Nada's Henrik? Was he not even in there anymore? Frowning, Nada crossed her arms. She made a mental note to ask Matej if he had any insight later. He'd known Henrik for longer. And while she was at it, she would ask about Katarina. Because, apparently, Nada was a glutton for punishment.

A trill whistle sounded to their left, sending an electric charge through Nada's body.

"Get behind the rock," Henrik told them.

Ester's eyes widened as she dropped to a crouch and shuffled around the outcrop as ordered. Henrik and Nada did the same, meeting her behind the boulders. As Henrik peered beyond the rock, waiting, Nada readied her Schmeisser. Her pulse pounded in her temples.

She would fight hard now. Fight with all her might for the chance to get help in rescuing her family.

Moments later the convoy came. The rumbling of engines marred the quiet as the Partizani drew a collective breath. Nada's stomach roiled. Tank after tank cruised along the road, their sides marked with a black and white cross—a compact trail of machinery and symbolic hatred. Canvas-covered trucks and jeeps flanked them, along with helmeted Germans driving three-wheeled motorcycles complete with armed sidecars.

Henrik took up the detonator and stayed his hand. A second passed. Then another—each second marked by the beat of Nada's heart. The first tank approached a hefty log by the road —Jakov's makeshift signpost—and Henrik plunged the handle.

The explosion boomed through the woods and shook the ground, flipping the tank onto its side in a blowout of thick smoke and fire. Another blast went off at the rear of the convoy —Jakov's doing—blocking the Germans in. They were trapped in the valley.

From all around her and across the way, Partizani swung their weapons out from their hiding places and opened fire. Nada braced herself and followed suit, unleashing bottled desperation as her pulse thrashed in her chest. Bullets rained down from all sides at the Germans, though it didn't stop them from shooting back. The thunderous pounding of warfare made Nada's ears ring, but she didn't falter. A satisfying release could be found in the shuddering of the weapon in her hands and the brute force of fighting back. Of not being powerless.

As Nada trained her sight guard from soldier to soldier, firing at each one, sidecar machine guns arced up and across the mountainside, peppering the dirt and igniting sprays of earth. The tanks still standing aimed and launched their ammunition in a steady stream. Pebbles and rock dust spattered from the outcrop. With a gasp, Nada inched lower behind the stone. Her heart thumped so hard her body throbbed, and Nada's hands grew slick against the metal of her Schmeisser. But still she fired through the dust wafting in the air.

From the other mountain, hand grenades flew at the remaining tanks, causing more shrapnel-inducing explosions, disabling them all together. The gunfire lessened.

Gritting her teeth, Nada held down her trigger, the Schmeisser vibrating her arms with the onslaught of bullets. Shells tumbled to the ground like tiny bells around her as she targeted every German left standing in her sights. But one of the soldiers zeroed in on them behind the rocky outcrop and took aim. Bullets struck Henrik's side of the boulder and he ducked back, shoulders pressing to the rough rock as Nada dove for cover alongside him. Her breaths heaved through her open mouth.

Henrik, gaze darting toward Ester, did a double take. His brow creased.

Ester sat huddled, hiding behind the outcrop with her star pendant sparkling in the waning sunlight. Her weapon still hung from her shoulder as she clutched her drawn-up knees. Nada's mouth turned dry and a heaviness cloaked her. She wished she could comfort Ester and ease her fear.

But then Nada studied her sestra's face and her pity faded. While Ester's skin had drained of color and her fingers trembled, she also stared ahead with steadiness, alertness. Her limbs held firm. Ester was *choosing* not to fire back.

Nada glared at her, her face turning red. What the hell was Ester doing? They needed to win this ambush to gain favor with the Partizani! Why wasn't she doing her part? Nada wanted to shout at her. Shove her into action. What if Jakov found out Ester didn't pull her weight during the ambush? They could lose all chance of the soldiers' help.

An itching heat coursed through Nada's body. This was what they came here for. To fight back and save their families. They were only at the beginning of their journey and Ester was failing her.

Whatever Henrik made of the situation, it had him throwing himself back into the fight with vigor. Within seconds, he took out the soldier targeting them, and with the onslaught of bullets slowing, Nada could ease out over the boulder again.

Breaths shaking, she lined up her sight guard, bringing a soldier into its circle as he fired from his sidecar. She pulled the trigger, and her ammunition hammered away. A trail of holes sprung along the motorcycle until the soldier flung backward and splayed over the vehicle. She continued her rain of fire until her Schmeisser clicked empty.

Nada whirled back against the rock and, with a trembling hand, switched out her magazine for a new one before launching herself back into position. She carried on fighting, relishing the distraction from her constant, rising grief and frustration. When you were fighting to survive, there was no time for heartache.

The gunfire of the ambush continued for an eternity, and yet it ended so soon. The barrage dwindled away, and as silence descended, a caustic, metallic scent hovered in the air. Movement in the valley caught her eye and Nada's focus went to the single soldier below who raised his hands in surrender.

Panting, she lowered her Schmeisser and stepped out from the outcrop, eyes trained on the young German in the valley. He couldn't have been much older than her seventeen years. His hands quivered in the air, and his pale face screamed fear. Helmet missing, the soldier exposed short-cropped blond hair that dulled in the setting sunlight. And then a pack of Partizani swept him up, taking him away.

Her expression souring, Nada turned to Ester where she remained tucked behind the rock. Hadn't they come on this journey together? Didn't they swear to fight tooth and nail, to do whatever it took to get their families back?

Her eyes watered. "*Why?*" Nada demanded.

The girl's gaze dropped to the ground as she swallowed.

Nada couldn't understand it. Couldn't even form the words or collect her thoughts, so they scratched under her skin like sandpaper. She stepped back, needing to pace, to scream. *Something.*

"This isn't the place for her," said Henrik.

Nada's audible breaths deepened. She needed to get away from them both before she lost her mind. She wrenched the strap off her shoulder and clunked her Schmeisser down on the boulder. Turning her back on them, she stalked off.

It was then a figure darted out from behind a tree. The figure snatched Nada, grabbing her from behind, and Nada's heart flew into her throat.

CHAPTER 11

The man snarled in German to all who would listen, threatening to kill her if they didn't hand over the boy they took prisoner. But no one could understand him except for Nada.

She screamed, trying to wrench free, but her strength was no match for his. His arms circled her front, fingers digging into her bicep and waist, scraping against her as she fought and writhed. Nada shuddered, heartbeat bursting against her ribs. *Not again. Please, not again.* A darkness wrapped its hand tight around her throat. Started to squeeze as the German swung her around, her back pressed to him.

Henrik came into view. He glared down the sight of his Schmeisser and aimed right at her. "Nada, he's a bear!"

His words clicked into place in an instant. Nada let her legs give way and dropped her entire body weight. She broke from the man's arms, and Henrik pulled the trigger. The German soldier flew back in a spray of violent ink.

Gasps quaking, Nada scooted away from the German, hands and heels grappling against grass and stone in her haste. Her focus froze on the man. On his motionless form and the vicious bullet wound in the center of his forehead.

Henrik stalked over to the body, gravel crunching beneath his boots, and peered down at it, his steely eyes laced with fervor. He lifted his Schmeisser to empty a few more rounds into the lifeless man, and shots echoed through the silence of the valley. Henrik took a moment to glare at him, his chest rising and falling fast. The line of his throat bobbed as he swayed back a step, finally turning to look over at Nada.

His expression seared through her. Brows pulled low over glassy eyes. Muscles in his jaw feathering. He shook his head at her and glanced away, as though searching the forest for some patience far out of reach, then turned to her again.

Henrik's voice rasped deep. "Are you ready to go home yet?"

It shivered through her, that voice, that look. Tied knots in her stomach. Without another word, Henrik strode away, carrying his Schmeisser in a white-knuckled grip.

Ester rushed over, sweeping Nada into her arms. "Oh, sestra! Are you okay?"

She could only nod, absently hugging Ester back as her gaze followed Henrik.

Her frantic breaths slid into a new, steady rhythm. Because not only did she witness the Ubica in action—frightening and proficient—she caught a glimpse of the old Henrik too. In the way he called on their past in a moment of need. In the fact he saved her.

Perhaps her Henrik wasn't lost to her after all.

Aching to uncover more, Nada slipped from Ester's hold and got up. She trailed him between the trees, unable to take her eyes off his purposeful gait and the tension in his shoulders. Nada didn't know what she'd say to him. What excuse she'd conjure for following. Maybe she could start by thanking him.

Henrik neared Jakov, jerking his chin toward the German soldier who had surrendered, now tied up and surrounded by members of the resistance. "What are we going to do with him?"

Nada hung back. She'd wait for them to finish their conversation.

"I have plans for that one," said Jakov with a faint grin,

puffing out his chest. "The Partizani we joined with today received information about a huge shipment of supplies on its way to our enemy. I want to intercept it. It would cripple them, and with victory so close, I can taste it."

"When do we head out?"

"I want every one of these soldiers fed well tonight and ready to set off tomorrow. I'm going to let the German sit and sweat a little before we interrogate him in the morning for the locations and routes of the supplies."

"I can see it on your face," said Henrik. "You won't relinquish this for anything." Something about the way he said it seemed more like a hopeful question.

"You know I can't be derailed once I smell blood in the water."

Henrik nodded, his shoulders relaxing, the tightness in his face easing.

Nada shrank, letting her gaze slip away. Her hopes for the Partizani's help collapsed before her, and a heaviness settled in her ribs.

She couldn't count on Jakov any longer. She definitely couldn't count on Henrik. And apparently, she couldn't count on Ester either.

The only person Nada could rely on to do what needed to be done was herself.

So be it.

HER BREATHS DROWNED OUT ANY OTHER SOUND IN the night, and her heartbeat pulsed at the ends of her fingertips. The button hanging at her wrist weighed heavy, its leather string itching her skin. The acute sensations amplified her apprehension with every careful step she took through the undergrowth. With the momentary flickers of lightning to light her way and a pistol at her hip to keep her safe, Nada ventured farther from the sleeping camp.

The sheathed blade in her pocket made her insides quake, deep and shifting. Flexing her hands to try and shake off heightened nerves, Nada cursed at her inability to make it stop. It was exhausting, the way certain things rattled her, and she hated the complete absence of control over it. Would the demon ever leave her be? Would she ever function like a normal person again? As always, Nada kept moving forward despite it.

She spared a glance over her shoulder. Henrik still slept by the smoldering embers of the fire. Good. If he was going to continue blocking her every move, her every hope of finding her family, then she would go behind his back. There once was a time Nada could trust Henrik with her dreams, her hopes. Trust him to cradle them as if they were his own, not crush them. But, like he said, he wasn't the Henrik she remembered.

"Where are you going?" a voice murmured.

Nada whirled with a gasp.

Vinko stood behind her, dark curls flashing blue in a throb of lightning. Nada released a breath, bringing a hand to her chest. Her pulse raced as she looked over at the camp again. No movement.

"You're going to question the soldier, aren't you?"

The Germans worked together with the Ustaše, and Nada hoped the boy knew something. *Needed* him to know something.

She studied Vinko and his impassive face a moment. "Are you going to try and stop me?"

"No." The whisper of a crooked smile crept in. "I'm going to help you."

Nada grinned in response. She had no objections to that.

She walked ahead, her steps soundless. "First, we'll need to take him farther from camp so we won't be heard. The two men guarding him left to relieve themselves, so now is our chance."

"That won't be enough time."

Nada glanced over her shoulder at him. "I slipped croton oil in their dinner."

It was an effective laxative if you had it on hand. So when

Nada learned which two soldiers would stand guard over their German prisoner for the night, she poured a significant amount of the oil into those men's steaming meals and served it to them both with a smile.

"They'll be a while, if not all night," she said.

A twinkle sparked in Vinko's eyes as he raised his brows, catching the slight grin on Nada's face before she turned back around.

The boy hurried to Nada's side. "Well, aren't you a tricky little devil. Where did you get the oil from?"

"I noticed one of the Partizani was looking particularly bloated and uncomfortable this morning. I watched him sip the oil in Našice before he stored the bottle in his satchel." Nada's mouth twitched. "Needless to say, by the time we made it to Gazije, he was looking rather serene."

Vinko erupted into a fit of hushed chuckles. "It all makes sense now, why you volunteered to serve everyone's food tonight." He shook his head, grinning. "You're like a mouse, sneaking through the house at night, conspiring to steal cheese. I should call you Miš from now on."

"I'd like to think I could cause more damage than a mouse."

"Oh, don't you worry. They cause damage. They just go fucking undetected while they do it."

As they approached the German soldier's silhouette, lightning flashed. Darkness doused them again, but a clear image burned behind Nada's eyes. Arms tied behind him to a tree, the soldier rested his chin on his chest. His body's shadow fell deeper around him than the night, stretching and reaching toward Nada.

The Partizani had decided to keep him there, separate from the camp, with the plan to "make him sweat" before interrogating him. But would he be difficult to crack at all? He looked so young. Vulnerable. Not that she'd let it deter her. She couldn't.

Nada reached for her dagger and hesitated, fingers hovering over the hilt. She swallowed hard, remembering her baby sisters were counting on her, and managed to withdraw it. She looked at it in her hand, the blade sharp and sparking in a throb of light. Her heartbeat knocked hard against her ribs and the air around her thinned. Her hold on the dagger trembled. Her skin grew clammy. Nada closed her eyes and tried to gather herself. Tried to slow her breathing. *You can do this. You're okay.* But a taunting poison swirled through her.

Vinko touched her shoulder, and she looked up at him. Brows drawn together, he held out his hand. "Why don't I take that while you do the talking?"

She nodded fast and released a shaky breath.

When Vinko took the dagger, she wiped her hands against her pants and grappled to regain her calm. She could only imagine what perception Vinko had of her right now. The Partizanka who couldn't even hold a knife.

Nada fought for composure and crouched before the soldier. The moment her hand clamped over his mouth he startled awake, eyes darting from her to Vinko.

Nada spoke to him in German, managing to keep her words steady and sure. "If you make a sound, we'll kill you."

The boy nodded—assurance he would cooperate.

Nada took her pistol in one hand and untied the rope holding him to the tree with the other. Grabbing his still-tethered hands, she dragged him to his feet.

"Gehen." She continued in German, pressing her pistol to his back. "If you cooperate, we'll let you live."

Vinko and Nada marched him through the woods, farther and farther until Nada finally halted. They were far enough away from camp.

"Sit." Nada stepped back and aimed her gun at him as he sank to his knees. She tried to ignore the way her hand still trembled. "I'm looking for a truck full of civilians that left Osijek yesterday, taken by Ustaše. Do you know anything about that?"

"No," he replied in his native tongue. "I haven't been anywhere near Osijek."

"Maybe you've heard something. In passing conversation or rumblings amongst your men."

"I told you, I know nothing."

"Is he giving you information?" Vinko rotated the unsheathed dagger between his fingers.

"No. He says he doesn't know anything."

Vinko spotted the rag Nada had brought spilling out of her coat pocket. Without a word, he took it and squatted in front of the soldier, then shoved the cloth against his mouth. The boy resisted, jerking away from his force, but Vinko managed to stuff it between his lips.

Vinko lifted the blade and drove the dagger hard into the German's thigh.

Nada cringed as the soldier lurched and cried out with a guttural scream, muffled and muted by the cloth. His cries peaked like breaths as Vinko rose, straight-faced.

"Try now."

Nada inhaled and refocused. She ripped the cloth from his lips. "What do you know about the Ustaše?"

"Fucking Ustaše," he spat through gasps. "They're all raging mad. Taking pleasure in their bestial torture. We gave them their power, and they squander it. I've no loyalty to them. So when I say I haven't been to Osijek, it's the truth."

"Then do you know where the Ustaše would take a truck full of Serbs?"

The German panted and glared at her. "If they're lucky enough to live that long? Jasenovac. It's where they've been sending them all these days."

"Jasenovac?" A crease formed between Nada's brows. *Why there?*

"He means the death camp," said Vinko.

"The what?" Ester's voice made Nada jolt.

There she stood in the night's shadows, silent and still with her mouth agape. But Nada wasn't focused on her presence. Nada's entire world condensed to those two words—*death camp.*

"You've heard of it?" Nada asked Vinko.

He gave her a gentle nod.

Nada whirled on the German, urgency threading her veins as the lightning surged to match it. "How do we get into Jasenovac?"

He laughed—a tired, hoarse sound. "By being captured."

Heat flushed through her. She jabbed her pistol to his temple, lowering to level her eyes with his. "How do I get my family out of Jasenovac?"

"You don't. The place is a fortress and a graveyard. No one escapes."

"What is he saying?" asked Vinko.

Nada kept her fierce gaze on the man as she answered, trying not to let her heart sag within her. "He says no one escapes Jasenovac. That it's a fortress." She ignored his other choice of word.

"There's always a way. You just need a plan."

"You need a *map,*" said Ester.

Nada turned her eyes to Ester as a fire lit inside her. "A map would show us all points of entry. Which buildings are situated where."

"Guard towers. Blind spots," added Vinko. "Knowledge is everything, Miš."

Pressing her lips together, Nada glared into the German's eyes. "Where can I find a map of Jasenovac?"

He scoffed. "You'll die if you set foot in that place. And if you don't, you'll wish they killed you. One of my comrades visited there once. He didn't last ten minutes before he threw up."

She firmly nudged the gun against his skull. "*Where?*"

He gritted his teeth. "If I had to guess, I would say with Ustaša officials. Most likely with Ante Pavelič."

"Did he say Pavelič?" asked Ester. "Leader of the Ustaše?"

Nada forged on. "Do you know where I can find Pavelič?"

"He has a mansion in Zagreb, called Vila Rebar," said the German. "I know this because some of my comrades are heading there for a party on the twenty-first of this month—for his Ustaše and Nazi friends."

Nada stood, holstered her weapon, and looked at Ester. "He said Pavelič is throwing a party in a few days."

"Well then," she said. "Obviously we're going to invite ourselves."

A twig snapped, and Nada spun toward it.

Henrik stepped into the circle and her heart quickened. He glared at her. In a flash of lightning, the star on his titovka blazed red before dying out.

How long had he been lurking out there? Listening in?

"A party would be the perfect cover to sneak in and steal his documents. He must have a map," said Ester as if Henrik wasn't standing right there.

Never had Nada been more grateful for her sestra than she was right then. They were in this together. For better or worse. Whether she had fought in the ambush or not.

"You'll need help," said Vinko.

Nada shook her head. "We don't have anyone. But we can do this ourselves."

"I'm saying I'm willing to volunteer, Miš."

Ester's eyes widened. "But you have nothing to gain from helping us."

"Actually, I think we all have something to gain from it."

Nada couldn't believe her ears. After Henrik's insistence that the Partizani would refuse such a task, Vinko was certainly eager to jump in.

Henrik stood off to the side, arms folded tight, waiting to meet Nada's gaze. She finally gave it to him. Full of defiance.

His furious eyes narrowed. "What were you going to do? Get your information and then disappear into the night? Go on your suicide mission alone?"

"Something like that."

He nodded, looking away into the darkness. "I should've known you would pull something like this."

"You didn't leave me much choice."

His jaw ticked. "There's no stopping you from doing this, is there?"

She shook her head.

He huffed. Scrubbed his face as if exhausted. "Okay. You win, Nada."

What?

"I'll help you find them."

Nada's jaw slackened. She stared at him. "You're coming with us?"

"Like Vinko said. We all have something to gain."

Nada didn't know whether to laugh, cry, or kick him in the shins.

Vinko re-stuffed the German's mouth with the rag and yanked his dagger back out. Ester flinched as the boy groaned, tilting forward.

"If we're going to do this, we need to go tonight, and go quietly," said Henrik. "No one can know we've left."

"We'll need weapons," Vinko said to him. "Are we really going to resort to stealing them?"

The two of them exchanged an unreadable look.

"We have no other option, Vinko," said Henrik, his tone pointed. He sighed, eyes roaming the ground as he thought it through. "It won't be easy. Jakov's a light sleeper, and he's right beside the crates holding all the new weapons."

A low and strangled moan drifted in the quiet, causing Henrik's focus to dart in every direction of the forest to find it. Nada's lips twitched at the sound, fighting back a grin, while Vinko doubled over, chuckling. Henrik watched them, trying to decipher what was happening between them.

"It's too fucking bad you didn't slip croton oil in *everyone's* dinner, Miš," said Vinko. "It would have made stealing the weapons a lot easier."

Henrik looked closely at Nada. "Croton oil?"

Did she detect the faintest hint of a grin there? Did he remember? Nada's chest squeezed in reaction.

"It worked for us in the past, didn't it?" She couldn't help trying to evoke her Henrik, to see another glimpse of him, no matter how small. "At least our notorious mischief can be put to real use now. We were always a good team."

The change was so slight, but Henrik's face returned to stone. "Reminiscing won't help us steal the weapons we need."

"Do we set up a big distraction?" Ester asked. "Try to draw them away from camp?"

Nada shook her head. "Too risky. Sleep is the safest distraction right now. There's less chance of eyes on us."

"We'll need to be as quiet as possible and take our time," said Henrik. "When you rush, you make mistakes. You make noise."

Vinko eyed Henrik. "And we're definitely going ahead with this plan?"

Henrik's neck tensed. "I suppose you would ask Jakov to spare them out of the kindness of his heart."

"I think he would."

"Haven't you heard? The Partizani are going on an important mission tomorrow. Jakov will want every weapon he has at his disposal. Soldiers included. You know how he gets." He locked eyes with Vinko. "So we might as well *keep* our mouths *shut*."

Vinko frowned and looked away. He let the subject rest.

"Okay, let's go then," said Ester. "There's no time to waste."

"When we leave, we'll be seen as deserters," Vinko said to Henrik, a strange gravity in his voice.

Nada looked back and forth between the boys, a tingle crawling up the back of her neck as Henrik glanced at the German soldier. It clicked into place for her. If the German told the Partizani where they were heading, Jakov would spare a few of his men to pursue them. Nada and Ester couldn't afford that.

Silent and fluid as a wraith, Henrik approached Vinko, took his blade, and in a swift move—so quick it was almost insignificant—he slit the German's throat.

Nada squeezed her eyes shut and jerked away. A sharp, electric jolt shot through her chest. Nausea followed, rippling its waves through her while her body rattled. Her chest heaved up and down, fighting to keep from being sick.

Ester shuddered a gasp, bringing both hands to her mouth. Breaths, bordering on sobs, escaped through her fingers.

As a rapid pulsing of light crossed the sky, Henrik stared hard at Nada, his cap's star gleaming red. Tremors took a firm hold of Nada as she stared back at him. He didn't recoil, didn't flinch, as though he wanted her to see him this way. Ruthless and cold. Intimidating. Her chin shuddered despite her desperate desire for it to stop.

Heat crept into Nada's cheeks and her eyes welled at the loss of control over her body. She dropped her face to hide it all. Turned away and stepped in front of her sestra. She took Ester's hands from her mouth and clutched them to get her attention. Waited for her sad, green eyes to fall on her. "This is how it needs to be now." Nada's eyes burned as her hands shook. "If we want to find our families, we let nothing get in our way."

When that German soldier had grabbed Nada after the ambush, Henrik's whole world hovered on a precipice, waiting for the tiniest nudge to bring it crashing down. He'd been trying so hard to send her away, to keep her safe, and in that instant, Henrik's worst fear snatched him by the throat. Leered into his face.

And still Nada didn't turn back for home.

So when Henrik discovered that Nada had slipped away from the camp while he slept, he wasn't surprised. She always had a will of her own. But it also terrified him to learn exactly how close she came to leaving camp for good without his knowledge. Which was why he realized he needed to give up on his plans to derail her. Sure, maybe he could have figured out another way to stop her. But how long would it be before she snuck away again? And maybe that time Henrik wouldn't be so lucky, and she'd be gone. Nada was going to do what Nada was going to do. It was better he took the chance he had in his hands right then, to go with her and do everything in his power to keep her alive.

"Take the Schmeissers you left by your beds first," Henrik murmured to the others. "That'll be the easiest part."

They stood clustered in the forest, watching the sleeping camp from some distance away as Henrik gave them instructions.

"Then we'll need to make our way to the crates. Stick to the ones already sitting open. Only take what you can carry, and don't overload yourself. You don't want to drop something and wake Jakov."

"So much as fart and that man's eyes will open," said Vinko, his tone more of a warning to Henrik. Yet another of his not-so-subtle hints.

Vinko had tiptoed too close to being obvious earlier. To having Nada figure out the truth. Yes, Henrik had lied. He had told her the Partizani would never help. But he did it to keep her safe. Because the moment she asked, the Partizani would have swept her away on a rescue mission. It would be dangerous and risky and Nada would be right in the middle of it.

But that was all moot now anyway. The circumstances had changed. It wasn't a lie anymore. Because now that Jakov had set his sights on intercepting that supply shipment, there wasn't a hope he'd say yes to a rescue. There was no stopping Jakov when he was focused on a mission of this magnitude. Henrik knew the man well. In Jakov's mind, if he could end the war, the Serbs would be freed by default—and therefore Nada's family. The supply shipment would take priority.

Which still brought them right back to the necessity of deserting the Partizani and stealing their weapons.

"Take items that make as little sound as possible," Henrik continued. "No loose bullets. Magazines and clips only. We'll need the hand grenades. Daggers. A pistol each, at least. And if you can manage, take a second Schmeisser."

Ester let out a heavy breath and a light, mocking tone. "That's all?"

"Do what you can."

They crept back to their campfire easily enough, gathering their bags and satchels and Schmeissers. Henrik finished first—his belongings always in neat order—and turned for the weapons. Thankful the camp had settled for the night on such soft and grassy ground that it muffled his footsteps, he inched toward the crates stacked between a snoring Jakov and a handful of solidly built but sleeping Partizani.

Jakov's bag sat rumpled next to him. Henrik leaned in and carefully lifted its flap, keeping his eye on the man. His heart palpitated and his senses tuned in to every slight sound and movement around him. Jakov's folded road map sat tucked inside, and Henrik tugged on it, slow and steady until it pulled free, then slipped it into his satchel.

Nada joined him then, looking over the crates in her reach. Henrik jerked his chin toward the daggers, piled in neat rows in the box. She glanced at them, swallowed, then inspected the other crates. But they only held loose ammunition and first aid kits. Henrik frowned, unsure what she was doing. Ester headed over as Henrik reached for a pistol.

"He's dead!" a man shouted from deep in the woods. "Someone killed the German prisoner! Everyone up!"

Jakov's eyes opened.

CHAPTER 12

FOR A SPLIT-SECOND HENRIK CONSIDERED LYING TO Jakov. He considered pretending they were all awake and reaching for weapons because they were on alert after their prisoner was discovered dead. But if he did, it would mean they'd lose their only chance of escaping the camp.

But none of it mattered when Jakov's gaze went to his only map, poking out of Henrik's satchel. There was no explaining that away.

Heart lurching in his chest, Henrik snatched Nada's arm and yanked her away. They bolted together, having no other choice. When Ester saw them running, she flew toward the woods too, Vinko following close behind. They slipped between the slender but close-knit trees, barreling through shrubs and grappling branches.

They didn't get the weapons. Henrik wanted to curse.

"Where's Ubica going?" someone called far behind them. "Is he chasing the killer?"

It wouldn't take them long to figure out he wasn't. And then they'd be hot on their trail.

Nada sped ahead of them, always the fastest, but Ester lagged. Henrik took her hand to help pull her along. Farther and farther away they escaped from camp. Harder and harder his heart pounded.

"After them!" drifted a faint shout.

"Shit," panted Vinko to his left.

Henrik needed to find a way to shake them loose. He dug into his satchel—slapping against his hip as he ran—and grabbed his flashlight. Dead and useless to him anyway, he tossed it to the ground—a breadcrumb for the Partizani to find.

"Nada, head left. Higher up the mountain."

She angled off and they followed, chests heaving and arms pumping. Henrik clenched his teeth as he ran, frowning at their blunder. Their escape couldn't have gone any worse. So much for slipping away quietly. They clambered over boulders and shoved aside branches as they made their ascent, with nothing but lightning flashes to light their way.

"There's an outcrop somewhere ahead," he said between breaths. He'd spotted it after the ambush—its massive clusters of rock the perfect place to hide. Or to at least take a minute to rest.

"I see it," said Nada. She burst forward with renewed energy.

"Oh hell," Vinko puffed, growing tired.

Ester gasped for air behind Henrik. He reached for her hand again, helping her to climb up ahead of him.

When they reached the outcrop, Ester collapsed into its shadows.

"Now what?" asked Vinko, leaning his shoulder into the rock.

"Everyone be quiet," said Nada.

Her eyes roamed the forest below. They all stilled and listened.

Henrik caught a muttering in the distance. "There." He pointed to where it came from. "That's about where I dropped my flashlight for them."

"Do you think they'll keep moving in that direction?"

"I certainly hope so."

She nodded. "Better have a plan B in case."

Vinko braced hands on his hips, still struggling to catch his breath. Even so, he managed to send a pinched look Henrik's way before turning to Nada. "What do you propose, Miš?"

"Ester, do you still have that first-aid kit?"

"Yes." Ester fetched it out of her bag.

"I need the thread you used to stitch Henrik's wound."

"What's your plan?" Henrik asked.

"I want to set up another distraction in case they start heading this way. You all should go on ahead along the mountainside and find a new place to hide. I'll catch up."

Henrik's muscles stiffened. *She'll catch up?* As if he'd leave her here undefended. "Not a chance."

Bright light strobed around them, bringing Nada's probing, dark eyes into view. Henrik jerked his face away before she could clearly read the knot between his brows, the tension in his neck and shoulders. He came with them to keep her safe. He wouldn't let her get in the way of that.

"It'll be quieter if only one of us is moving through the forest to get away," said Nada.

Shaking his head, Henrik stepped away, then back again, unable to keep still. "That's not happening. Vinko, you take Ester ahead of us. I'll stay with Nada."

Ester stood and handed Nada her spool of thread. "Be careful."

"Make sure you don't go higher up the mountain," Nada told her. "Try to stay at this level."

Vinko heaved himself off the rock, gave Henrik one last glare, then trotted off with Ester into the darkness.

"What do you need me to do?" Henrik asked Nada.

"I need rocks. Five or six of them, about this big," she said, indicating the size of her head.

As Henrik set to work collecting rocks for her, Nada searched the forest floor. She picked up a fallen leafy branch and wrapped her thread around it, below the end of its break. She looked at the different grooves and shapes of the boulders under her feet, and when she decided on the right one, placed the branch—angled on its precarious slope—leaves down. Nada took Henrik's stones and carefully placed them on top of the branch.

"Okay," she whispered. "Now we need to go higher up and hide."

She unspooled the thread as they crept between the crags and rounded edges of the outcrop, until they tucked themselves behind a natural embankment. Side by side, they lay flat on the rock, peering over the edge. Though it remained too dark to see anyone in the woods, they had a great vantage point from up there.

They waited. All was quiet. All was still.

Nada shifted beside him, her arm brushing solid against his. Henrik's chest expanded on an inhale as all of his senses turned toward her. He let his eyes drift to her delicate hand and the way it pinched the thread between her fingers. And then he clamped his eyes shut and refocused his attention on the woods below.

Lightning pulsed, illuminating the world around them. Partizani flashed into view far down below.

Henrik cursed. "They're coming this way."

Nada nodded, having seen them herself. "Plan B." She pulled on the thread.

It only took the slightest nudge for the stones to tumble off the branch and down the outcrop. The longer they rolled, the more rocks they knocked loose to join them. With any luck, they'd draw the Partizani's attention toward a point much farther downhill.

"Stay low," Nada murmured, turning in the direction Ester and Vinko had gone. "I don't want that lightning to give us away like it did them."

They stuck to the shadows as they moved along the hillside, slow and quiet, careful not to kick any stones on the way. When their feet met soft leaves and tufts of grass, they quickened their pace until they heard a whistling bird call. Vinko waved from a thick-woven grove of trees. Henrik and Nada hurried over, and together they all continued to make an angled descent down the mountain, while the Partizani—they hoped—made their way in the opposite direction.

They sprinted and then jogged through the woods for an hour before they reached a vast open field, where they finally dared to pause and catch their breath. Lightning continued to pulse in the churning clouds above as dampness hung in the air.

Henrik studied them, all flushed, doubled over, and breathless from their escape. There was no going back now. They'd gone rogue. Any chain of command they had with the Partizani had disappeared the moment they stepped into Nada's small army. Henrik couldn't afford for them to falter in this mission. For Nada to barrel her way into danger and put her life at risk. So, he seized his opportunity to take control of the situation. To steer the group in a safe direction.

He planted his feet, pulling his shoulders back. "I want to make something clear, before we go one step farther."

They all turned to him, waiting.

"There's only four of us. We don't have the numbers, and we certainly don't have the might. If we're going to do this, we need to use our heads." His focus turned toward Nada. "No rushing into anything, no getting caught up in emotions. We do this with caution. We need to be smart about it to stay alive."

"Agreed," said Nada, back straightening. She gave him a nod. "We'll do whatever you say. We'll follow your lead."

Though he kept his expression in check, Henrik drew his head back. His lungs filled with a deep, slow breath. She trusted him. Believed him worthy of guiding them. A faint pull stirred in his chest.

Vinko snorted, looking at Henrik. "Why should *you* be in charge?"

He leveled Vinko with a cold stare. "Do you really need to ask that?"

He crossed his arms. "Okay then, Commander Use-Our-Heads. How exactly are we supposed to rescue anyone without a large supply of ammunition? We can't rely on your glare alone to bring an army to its knees."

"How much do we have between us?" asked Nada. "I only have what's in my pistol."

Henrik knew that to be true. Her Schmeisser had nothing left in it after their battle with the German convoy, and she hadn't replenished her magazine pouch. He knew because his eyes had strayed toward her most of the evening. He couldn't help himself. Weak as it was.

"My gun was never loaded," said Ester, inviting a tight glance from Nada.

"I used my last on the ambush." Vinko scrubbed his head, rough and fast. "My weapon is as good as fucking decoration."

"No one restocked when we returned to camp?" Henrik pulled out the magazine from his Schmeisser to look at it. "One bullet."

Vinko huffed. "We should have asked Jakov."

"I already told you that wasn't an option." Henrik slammed the magazine back into his gun. "He never would have allowed us to leave."

Vinko scoffed and turned away.

"We'll find what we need ourselves," said Nada. "I imagine farmers are likely to own weapons and ammunition."

Ester's brows quirked together. "Do you think they'd be willing to give them to us?"

"Doubtful," said Henrik. "We're going to have to steal them."

"Well, isn't that perfect," muttered Vinko. "We can repeat that unnecessary disaster all over again."

Henrik's jaw clenched as his fingers curled and flexed open again.

"But, hey," Vinko continued. "At least Ester still has the first-aid kit. So when the Ustaše riddle us with bullets, she can slap a bandage or two on us."

"Stop it, Vinko. Please." Nada gently grasped his arm to get his attention. "It wasn't his fault the plan fell apart."

"Wasn't it, Miš?" His sharp, heated gaze locked with Henrik's in challenge.

Henrik narrowed his eyes in return, a simmer building beneath his skin. "Why do you call her Miš all the time?"

"It's a term of endearment."

"Comparing her to a pest? You must really like her."

"Enough, you two," said Ester. "The *Ustaše* are your enemies. Not each other."

"Of course not," said Henrik. "Vinko's nowhere near as threatening."

"No, and I'm far more handsome than one," said Vinko.

"Even your Ustaša brother?"

Lightning flickered. The girls stared agape.

All color drained from Vinko's face. His breaths deepened, eyes cold and frozen on Henrik, who showed no inkling of remorse. That information wasn't common knowledge, and Henrik knew that. Used it to hit him where it hurt.

Nada's forehead furrowed. "Your brother is an Ustaša?"

He swallowed, hard. "Yes. And your Henrik is a fucking liar."

Henrik's heart stuttered and he kept still, afraid to draw attention.

"What do you mean?"

"Nothing," Henrik interjected. "Vinko's running his pathetic mouth, as usual."

Vinko scoffed. "It's your need to control Nada that's pathetic. I just don't know why you did it."

Her gaze crept to Henrik, a hand coming up to brace her stomach. She spoke quietly. "What is he talking about?"

Henrik's pulse throbbed in his temples. He didn't reply. He couldn't. Words evaded him.

Vinko didn't have the same problem. "The Partizani wouldn't have turned you away, Nada."

She stiffened, eyelids fluttering. "What?"

"If you asked, we all would have set off right away to liberate your families. Henrik lied to you."

She winced, glancing away, then exhaled a broken half-sob

before she faced Henrik again, eyes welling. Her unguarded hurt pummeled him where he stood. He wilted inside.

"Why?" she demanded, her voice cracking. She moved closer. "Why would you do that?"

Henrik could do nothing but watch the train wreck unfold.

"You *lied* to me?" she cried through gritted teeth, shoving him. He stumbled back a step. "Who *are* you?" She hit him in the chest with both fists. Once. Twice.

Her slight hands packed a world of fury, jarring him as she struck his chest over and over. He held her anguished gaze, his own unyielding and glassy, taking her punishment as it came. Embracing the sting. When her hits weakened with the eruption of tears, Henrik caught her fist, clasping it steady against his heart. He pinned her there as her breaths heaved, an attempt at comforting her, while also needing to bask in her hate for him. He deserved it. And he wanted to feel every shard and twist and squeeze of pain it brought him.

Nada sagged, all out of strength, and her head fell forward as she sobbed.

I'm sorry. I'm so sorry, Nada. Henrik bled and burned with an apology, but he couldn't say it out loud. He needed to keep her at arm's length, and his cruelty would do that.

With a shuddering inhale, Nada ripped her hand from his grip, and lifted her tear-stained face. "Now it's my turn to tell you to leave. Go home to your Partizani. I want nothing to do with you."

"He can't go back after what he did," Ester reminded her. "He looks like a traitor now."

No. He *was* a traitor now. And he did it for her.

"I hate to say it," said Vinko. "But we'll need him. They don't call him *Ubica* for nothing. You should use it to your advantage."

"How can I trust him?" Nada asked. "He's nothing more than a stranger wearing Henrik's skin."

Pain lanced beneath Henrik's ribs and lingered like poison. He gave it free rein.

"He's still here, Nada," came Ester's quiet voice of reason. "He still came with us to help."

Nada half-laughed, her shoulders drooping. Wiped her face. "Fine," she murmured to Ester. "Just remember, he didn't only let *me* down with his actions. He let *you* down. He let down our parents, and Ana and Maša too."

Her words punched Henrik in the gut and winded him. He lowered his gaze, unable to look her in the eye anymore.

Nada turned toward Henrik again, eyes rimmed red. "For that I will never forgive you."

Good. She shouldn't forgive him. Now that she hated him, it would make it easier to be around her. She'd keep her distance.

Thunder rumbled, waking them all from the intensity.

"We should keep moving and try find cover under the trees," said Ester, attempting to change the subject. "Before it rains."

As the words left her mouth, sporadic drops spattered from the sky. Nada turned and stalked through the forest, leaving Henrik and the others to trail her.

They weren't too deep into the woods again before the subtle glow of lit windowpanes appeared between the trees. The four of them stopped to peer through the darkness. A house sat nestled in a grove, within a clearing. A rickety fence wrapped its perimeter while a barn—dark as night—contrasted with the flickering light of lanterns inside the house. While the cities still had working electricity, houses in the countryside did not.

"Do you think they might have weapons?" asked Ester.

"Maybe," said Vinko. "But I think we should spend the night in that barn before the rain really comes down. There's nothing more miserable than traveling in the woods after you're soaked to the bone. It takes days for your clothes to dry."

"And what if the owner doesn't allow it?"

"Who says we're asking?" said Nada. Heading for the barn, she glanced over her shoulder. "Coming, Ubica?"

Her dig hit him the way she intended—a quick jab in the chest—and Henrik's conviction faltered.

He had vowed a long time ago to never put himself in the position to feel heartache again. And yet here he was, drowning in it. A slow torture of his own making.

CHAPTER 13

Before

With the Nazi invasion came the takeover of Jugoslavenske schools. Now that they were run by the Germans, Nada and Henrik refused to go. Not that their parents knew about it, of course. And Nada ensured their obliviousness by cleverly enlisting Ester—who didn't have the gumption to skip school herself—to bring Henrik and Nada evidence of their attendance.

"Are you two *ever* going to go back to school again?" Ester swished her way through ribbons of grass over to the water's edge.

Nada startled, having not heard her best friend approach. She looked to Henrik, who grinned at her as he bobbed his string of fishing line in the Drava River. They had spent a good half of the day fishing, to no avail, and the first half occupied in the woods playing tag and setting rabbit traps.

"Never." Henrik raised his empty hook. Sighing, he let it plop back in. "As long as the Germans occupy the school, I won't set foot in that place."

And knowing Henrik—stubborn and inflexible to a fault—he would follow through.

"Well, I brought your homework *again*." Ester waved papers at them before slotting them back into her leather school satchel.

"Hvala, Ester. I wish we'd caught something for you in return."

"I don't mind." She sank onto the bank on Henrik's other side. "You can pay me back with interest later."

Nada grinned. "*Two* fish?"

"A whole *basket* full."

Nada laughed. "What on Earth would you do with that many fish?"

Ester shrugged while scrunching her nose. "Set them free?"

Nada smiled while Henrik chuckled and said, "Typical Ester."

He began winding up his line and hook to pack away, and Nada couldn't help watching him. He neared sixteen now; his body growing wirier every day, and his eyes carrying more gravity than they used to. As Ester hummed a quiet tune along with the hush of the river, Nada's eyes skimmed over his deep olive skin and drifted up to stare at the way the sunlight burnished his light brown hair. She marveled at the golden strands peeking through. Blue-gray eyes met hers mid-observation—a pair of ice chips floating in a winter sea. Nada's cheeks warmed, prompting her to avert her gaze.

Henrik's mouth inched up on one side. "We should get home," he said to both girls, putting his neat spool of fishing line in his bag.

Once on his feet, he slung the bag over his shoulder. Lips twitching, his gaze fell on Nada, glinting with mischief. "I'll race you there." And off he went like a shot, sprinting toward Retfala.

"Henrik, that's cheating!" Nada launched off the ground to bolt after him.

Her legs flew beneath her as she raced across the open field, soul soaring from the thrill and excitement. Henrik glanced over his shoulder and laughed. With a determined grit of her teeth, Nada pushed herself faster, all her energy surging outward to her limbs.

Ester's voice reached her from far behind. "Hey, wait for me!"

But she wouldn't relinquish the race for anyone. She was going to beat Henrik at his game. Again.

Nada beamed as she closed in on Henrik—no match for her speed—but as she was about to fly past, Henrik's eyes flicked to her.

"No!" His brows lifted in good humor as he grabbed her arm to stop her from shooting by, and Nada squealed.

But the move caused his stride to falter, and Henrik went down, skidding and tumbling into the grass.

"Henrik!" Nada backtracked and kneeled beside him. Her hand hovered toward him.

The boy chuckled between labored breaths as he lay sprawled on his back. "How are you so fast?"

His joy eased Nada's concern. With a slow smile, she sank back to lean on her hands, breaths heaving in time with his.

Rapid footfalls pounded toward them as Ester caught up. "I hate it when you two do that." She bent over, hands on her knees. "You both run like the devil is chasing, and there's cake waiting for you at home."

"Only if it's chocolate," said Nada. "I only run for chocolate."

"Or Henrik." Ester pressed her lips together tightly to keep from giggling.

Nada turned bright red, glaring at Ester. She opened her mouth to retort—

But the popping of gunfire shattered their conversation to pieces.

All eyes went to their hometown in the distance. Retfala was nothing more than a cluster of terracotta rooftops visible over the enveloping trees. The sharp sounds of war rang out from within. *Pop. Pop. Pop.*

Waves of ice crashed over Nada. Gasping for air, she leapt to her feet and ran for home as fast as she could.

"Nada, stop!" Henrik scrambled to chase after her. "Stay here!"

But her family was at home, right in the middle of all that gunfire. She needed to reach them.

"*Nada!*" Henrik's cry bled with panic as she headed straight toward danger.

She barely registered her body moving as it plummeted and weaved through the trees. She slowed and caught herself against the back corner of the nearest house. With chest heaving and fear rattling her bones, Nada surveyed the street beyond, her gaze touching every conceivable hiding place for soldiers.

Hands gripped her and spun her away from the edge, planting her back against the whitewashed brick. Blue-gray irises flared in her line of sight as hands cradled her face.

"Are you crazy?" Henrik's voice rasped. "Do you want to get yourself killed?"

Ester stumbled up alongside him, brow creased and hands trembling as she tucked herself out of view beside Nada.

Shouting in the street reclaimed her attention. Nada peered around the wall to see what was happening. An Ustaša soldier fretted at someone's door, rattling at the locked handle in a frenzied attempt to get inside. It was then a Partizan swooped in from behind, taking his chance. He raised his weapon and the resounding crack of a bullet pierced Nada's nerves.

The Ustaša slumped to the ground. Blood pooled beneath him like a spreading shadow—a darkness reaching to touch and stain all in its path.

Nada's knees weakened, and the chaotic din turned to watery muffles in her ears. Yet, immobilized in the moment of horror, she couldn't look away. Nada had never seen a man killed before.

Something pulled at Nada's shoulders as words spoken around her began sifting through, washed clearer by the second.

"Nada. Come here. Don't look."

Henrik's hands. Familiar. Gentle. They clasped her arms and drew her back behind the house.

Nada's lips trembled and her body shuddered. He enfolded her in his arms, taking her farther from the scene now seared into her memory.

"Home," Nada whispered. "We have to go home."

Tears tracked crystalline pathways down Ester's cheeks, her eyes wide and glassy and dilated. Ester would want to go home too. Henrik gazed at Nada with a pinched brow. While the fight was between the Partizani and Ustaše, there was still danger of being caught in the crossfire.

"Okay." He guided the girls back against the brick wall. "Wait here." He slunk away around the corner.

A minute passed before he appeared again, his hand waving at them to follow. "Let's go."

Together, they crept between two houses and paused to check the street for more soldiers. Shots continued to echo elsewhere, but their road remained vacant. Nada's heart thumped in her ears as the three of them darted across the pavement toward the cover of a house across the street.

They picked their way through backyard after backyard, climbing fence after fence, while taking care to stay shielded from the gunfire.

When they made it to Ester's yard, Henrik turned to her. "Go on inside. I'll make sure Nada gets home safe."

Ester stole a quick hug from Nada and trotted up the steps to her back door.

Henrik and Nada snuck along the side wall of Ester's house to face the street. Nada's home waited for them on the other side.

The moment Nada set foot on the pavement, glancing to the right, she spotted a sniper down the road. Her stomach dropped. A shot fired and she lowered herself by instinct. She didn't notice the Ustaša soldier to her left until he collapsed with a thud. Scarlet bloomed from the center of the man's torso. His breaths hitched as he curled upward to check his middle.

Nada's limbs turned to water as she stared.

"Hurry." Henrik guided her upright to run for home.

Legs heavy, she raced and threw herself through the front door, Henrik right behind. Her father, Petar—pacing the floor of the living room—looked up. A weighted breath left him as moisture shined in his eyes. He rushed forward and scooped his daughter to him, pressing her close. Maša's cries filled the room as Nada's mother, Teodora, entered with Maša on her hip. Her hand went to her chest at the sight of Nada and she closed her eyes.

"Tata, there's a man outside," Nada said into her father's shoulder. "He was shot."

"He's still alive," said Henrik.

"Are you certain?" Petar hurried over to the window and pulled back the curtain. Without a word, he darted for their short hallway.

"Petar, don't," pleaded Teodora, watching him pass.

Nada stumbled after him to his bedroom, her eyes big and round. "Where are you going?"

"We need to take him to the hospital." He tore the blankets from his bed, bundling them up in his arms.

"But, Tata, he's an Ustaša." And her father was Serbian.

Oil and water. Hunter and prey.

Her father paused long enough in the doorway to brush her cheek. "Srce moj, he'll die if we don't help him."

He stormed for the front door and her stomach churned when he went out into the street. Nada and her mother watched from the window as Ester's father, Ivan, met Petar beside the Ustaša. They spread out the blankets on the pavement and together they shifted the soldier onto it. Grabbing each corner of the makeshift stretcher, they lifted him and hastened down the road.

Teodora pressed her lips together and turned her attention to bouncing Maša, trying to quieten her.

"Where are Filip and Ana?" Nada asked.

"They're playing in the other room. I have music playing in there to cover the noise and keep them from being afraid."

Teodora went into the kitchen by the front room and stirred the soup simmering away on the stove. "Your tata will be okay," she said, reassuring herself as well as Nada.

Nada's eyes prickled as she stood there, unsteady on her feet. Henrik's hand came over Nada's shoulder, a silent reminder of his friendship. He was always there when she needed him—without fail.

A gunshot cracked and a loud ping sounded in the kitchen. Teodora startled. A bullet had struck the metal stove right beside Nada's mother and the baby. A hole pierced the front door, letting in a pencil of light.

Teodora's wooden spoon clattered to the floor. Her hands shook. "Get to the back of the house. Both of you!"

As Henrik snatched Nada's hand and swept her toward her bedroom, Teodora scurried down the hall with Maša in her arms, then plunged into the room with Nada's other siblings.

"Under the bed."

She did as Henrik said. Sinking onto the cool floorboards, she shuffled backward to the wall so he could slide in next to her. Henrik's arm came around her and he covered her with his body to shield her from any stray bullets. Nada's breaths shuddered and she clutched his old coat while pressing her face to his collarbone. No matter how hard she tried, Nada couldn't stop shaking.

The clapping of gunfire continued to strike outside.

Henrik swallowed, the movement brushing her temple.

"I'm scared," she whimpered.

"You're safe here, Nada."

His heart raced against her jaw, throbbed in her ears. If only the sound could have drowned out the shooting beyond the walls of her home.

The image of the Ustaša gunned down on the stoop flashed through her mind. She pictured the one gasping for life in the street. So much horror in such a short time. And her father was out there.

"I don't want Tata to die like that man on the doorstep." Her whisper filled the space around them.

"He won't." The sensation of Henrik's voice buzzed against her cheek. "He'll come home soon."

Nada closed her eyes. "Don't go home yet, Henrik. I don't want you to die either."

He let out a shaking, breathy laugh. "I wouldn't leave you behind like that."

"Do you promise?"

"I promise. I won't *ever* leave you." Because Henrik was always there for her, unwavering in his loyalty.

"Do you think—"

A boom trembled the floor beneath them and shook the windows.

Nada flinched and clutched Henrik's coat so tight, so desperately, that a loose button snapped off in her hand. She squeezed it, held onto it for life like it was a part of Henrik, like it could save her too, for as long as the battle raged outside.

When nightfall crept in with its haunting shadows and the echoes of war dissipated, Nada finally eased her hold on Henrik. Fingers bleached white and stiff, she stared as she tried to uncurl them. Henrik took her hand and slipped his warm, comforting fingers into her palm. His button broke loose and clattered to the floor, lost between them. But it was Nada's gaze Henrik held as his fingertips brushed over the circular imprint burrowed into her skin.

He promised he would never leave her, and Nada would hold onto that forever. Hold onto *him.*

Henrik was her safe place. He was home.

CHAPTER 14

THEY MADE IT INSIDE AS RAIN BEGAN TO PELT DOWN, pattering against the barn walls. They latched the door closed behind them, but not before Nada spotted an oil lantern on a small table during a flash of lightning. She fumbled in the dark for the matches beside it, and then lifted the globe to light the wick. Delicate radiance flared around them.

With light to see by, they passed two dozing horses in their stalls and climbed the ladder to the loft. Though far warmer in the confines of the barn, Nada tugged Vinko's jacket snug around her as she stepped over waves of loose hay blanketing the upper level. The dusty, earthen smell, familiar like home and childhood play, eased the tension in her body. Drew her into its comfort.

Vinko headed for the far end, where a set of bolted doors adorned the barn wall, and Ester accompanied him, rummaging through her satchel. Nada found a nail on the wall and hung the lantern. Silent and in shadow, Henrik made himself comfortable against the wall by the loft entrance. He didn't speak, and he didn't look Nada's way, as if he hoped she wouldn't notice his presence. But she did. Of course she did. And with it, the blow of his lies resurfaced.

Her lungs constricted and a knot formed in her throat. Henrik wasn't the boy she used to know. He'd betrayed her. Jeopardized her chance to save her family. Nada's grip tightened on her jacket as her chest hitched, and she averted her gaze. Her Henrik was gone.

Vinko shuffled about in the hay, smoothing himself a bed, when his hand bumped against something hidden underneath it. He brushed away the straw to reveal a huge glass vessel full of dark amber liquid.

He uncorked the bottle and sniffed it. "Rakija," he sang, and swigged three big mouthfuls in a row.

Ester neared Nada's side, carrying some first-aid supplies, and looked over to Henrik. "When was the last time you checked your injury?" she asked him.

He stayed silent.

"That's what I thought. You don't want to get an infection, Henrik."

"I'm fine," came his somber answer.

"Here," Ester plopped her supplies into Nada's hands. "He needs a fresh bandage and iodine."

"Why are you giving it to me?"

"I need to see to Vinko. He hurt himself when we escaped. You take care of Henrik."

"Ester," she shook her head vehemently. "No. There's nothing wrong with Vinko."

Her sestra stepped in close, murmuring so only Nada could hear. "Take this opportunity to mend your fences."

Nada frowned. "I don't want to."

"It's *Henrik.* And he killed a man for you tonight. Walked away from his fellow soldiers. Yes, he lied. But he's still Henrik."

"I'm not so sure after what he did."

"Have you even stopped to wonder *why* he lied?" she asked. "I mean *really* thought about it?"

No, she hadn't, too blinded by hurt and anger in the moment to see anything else.

"For as long as I've known the two of you, Henrik has never done anything he didn't believe to be in your best interest."

Nada's heart twisted at the thought. "Even so, I'm the last person he'll want helping him." Nada held out the supplies for Ester to take. "He hates me. He can't even stand to be near me."

Ester pushed her full hands back. "If he's intent on battling with you, then let softness be your weapon." With that, she walked over to Vinko, who promptly offered her his bottle.

Nada turned and took in Henrik's shadowed form. Head down, sleeves rolled up, bare forearms resting on his drawn-up knees. Could Ester be right? Was he still her beloved Henrik?

She approached him, hay rustling as she went, and kneeled at his side in the straw—sharp and itching against her legs. "Take off your sleeve."

His voice drifted, quiet and subdued, between them. "I don't need tending to."

Where had his hardness gone? Where was the stone and ice she expected?

Ester said to let softness be her weapon, but softness wasn't a trait that came naturally to Nada. She was all abruptness and temper, willful and wild. She could be warm, of course. Playful. And she loved deeply. Fiercely. But she wasn't sweet or heartfelt or thoughtful like Ester. Maybe that's what Henrik needed to get through that hard exterior of his.

Had Katarina been like that?

Nada shoved the thought away as quickly as it came. "Ester asked me to do it. If I don't, I'll never hear the end of it."

Which wasn't true, but she had no tactful way to convince him otherwise.

He exhaled through his nose and unbuttoned his shirt. Straightening to pull off his sleeve, he then stretched his legs out as he leaned back against the wall. Nada untied his bandage, trying to keep her fingers steady as they brushed against the bare swell of his arm. Henrik took off his titovka, resting it on his lap rather than letting it touch the dusty straw, and ran a hand through his hair to smooth it out.

Nada hadn't seen Henrik's injury up close. An angry, red slash ran across his bicep—a little swollen but stitched to perfection. It had to be aching.

"Does it hurt?" she murmured.

He finally looked at her, everything about him sedate. Timid curiosity swarmed within those tempestuous eyes. "No."

As she bundled the old bandage, her eyes skimmed over him. Half his shirt draped loose over a solid chest of curves and ridges; the other half exposed an arm corded with muscle. Her hands slowed, kneading at the gathered cloth. Nada could only imagine the power behind them, and the force this ubica possessed in his impressive form.

Her breath stilled as she caught a scar on his shoulder. Then another beneath his ribs. Another by his hip. How many times had he been hurt like this? Her chest squeezed tight. All those nights she spent praying he was all right. Did any of it do any good?

Nada swallowed and refocused on her task, trying to ignore the way his body made her heart skitter.

Though his brows were knotted together, Henrik couldn't keep his eyes away from Nada as she tended to his arm with care, gently dabbing iodine onto his wound. Was he feeling remorse for what he'd done? Was that why his mood had sobered?

Her eyes flitted up to meet his and slipped back down again.

"Why did you do it?" she whispered. "Why did you keep me from saving them?"

He sighed and dropped his head back against the wall. "I don't want to argue with you, Nada."

Her words remained quiet. "We never used to argue."

The two of them had always been in sync. One of them a reflection of the other. Two parts of a whole. Now they were so ... disjointed. Distant.

When he didn't answer, she tried again. "I don't want to fight either. I want to understand."

"There's nothing to understand."

"Why can't you give me a straight answer?"

He stared ahead, giving her nothing.

Nada groaned through her teeth. "Stubborn as always. I see *that* part of you hasn't changed."

"*Impulsive* as always," he threw back at her. "I see that part of *you* hasn't changed."

She threw the cotton wad to the side and snatched up the clean bandage. "What did I do that was impulsive?"

"You threw yourself into the Partizan camp out of fear and panic. You had no plan, no direction, nothing. You didn't think it through. You never do. You shouldn't make decisions based on emotion."

"Not all of us can be as unfeeling as you, Henrik."

She stopped the moment the words came out. They were arguing again. So much for softness.

Nada wrapped the fresh bandage around his arm, annoyed with herself for letting anger take over. She didn't want this. She didn't want to fight and squabble all the time. She wanted her beloved Henrik back. Close and permanent.

Nada tied the bandage in place. Maybe she could remind him of who he used to be.

"Filip remembers how you taught him to tie knots. He talked about it recently." It brought a slight curve to her lips, lightening her face. "He said he liked you."

Henrik lifted his gaze to her. "Is he still as blunt as he was then?"

Nada smiled wider, picturing the quiet, dark-haired boy who would often tell Henrik with a blank face that his jokes weren't funny. "Always."

He met Nada's faint smile with a hint of warmth in his eyes.

"He was confused when Ester and I said you were family. He thought we meant you were related."

Henrik turned to stare at the red star on his cap. "I thought I was a stranger."

Heaviness flooded her, sagging her shoulders. "You'll always be family." Then, with a trace of humor in the lift of her brows, she said, "Whether I want to tear you to pieces or not."

Henrik's lips twitched. That slight movement made Nada's heart soar.

"What are you two whispering about?" Vinko wandered over to them, bottle in hand.

Henrik sat up to slip his arm back into his shirt, buttoning away his scars. Nada looked down at the other end of the loft. Ester lay curled up in the hay, already fast asleep. It had to be at least two or three in the morning.

Nada settled into the straw beside Henrik, leaning against the wall. Vinko offered the bottle to them. Henrik shook his head, but Nada reached for it. Handing her his rakija, Vinko sat in front of them, stumbling as he did. She looked at the liquor, the bottle nowhere near full. He'd had a fair amount. Nada tipped the bottle to her mouth and grimaced as she swallowed. The liquid burned as it settled in her stomach, warming her from the inside out.

She stared at the bottle for a second before giving it back to Vinko. "Is it true, what Henrik said? About your brother?"

Vinko downed more of the rakija, then looked away with a crease in his brow. He ran his fingers through the mess of his curls, then clutched the back of his head. "Yes."

"How does that happen? Two brothers, fighting on opposite sides."

Vinko let out a heavy breath—a potent woody, fruity blend—and dropped his hand to his thigh.

"We had our own fucking opinions about things," he shrugged, the move sluggish. "We used to argue over it. Stipe was adamant Serbia were the oppressors and the Croats were chosen by God to defend Catholicism against *the invasion of their Communists and orthodoxy*," he quoted in a mocking tone. "He believed in a racially pure Croatia, and I didn't. Eventually, the Ustaše indoctrination bled from the brother I once knew, and he left home to join their damn ranks."

"And you?"

"*I* had no fucking choice but to find my way to the Partizani. Stipe knew where I stood. It would have only been a matter of time before my brother and his new comrades came for me."

Nada frowned. "Surely he wouldn't have. You're his flesh and blood."

Vinko yanked aside his collar, revealing the skin over his heart. There, a scar in the rough and puckered shape of a star marred him. "He cut it into me while my father pinned me down. Trust me. Blood means nothing to him anymore. He's one of them now. And the Ustaše are empty shells of humans. They have no souls."

Nada's eyes lowered as her forehead creased. "I won't argue with that."

"But I still have hope." The liquor made his mind and mouth slippery, sending slurring words from his lips. "All we can do is believe that things will get better. No matter how we find a way to fight for it. I need to save my brother from them. That's why I'm coming with you. I have to find him. If I don't, his soul could be lost forever. I refuse to let go of the hope that Stipe can be saved. That there's goodness deep inside him."

"If he's anything like you," said Nada, "I'm sure there is."

Vinko grinned in his drunken stupor and lifted his brows at Henrik. "Everyone loves Vinko."

Nada laughed, but Henrik pressed his lips together, unimpressed with Vinko's inebriated jokes.

"Oh, come on, Henrik," she said. "Don't you remember, early on in the war, your grandfather had us sneak into his neighbor's barn to steal the vino hidden there?"

Henrik nodded. "Stole some of it ourselves too."

"We were so drunk our bare feet were shredded and bleeding from the straw by the time we made it home."

"We're different people now," he said. "Our lives changed. We grew up."

And just like that he made her chest cave. Reminding her nothing was the same.

"Never mind him." Vinko swished the bottle in her

direction in salutation, liquor sloshing out of the bottle. "You have me now." He winked at her.

Smiling, Nada crawled over to him. "I think you've had enough." She grabbed for his bottle, but Vinko swung it out of her reach. She lurched forward for it, chuckling, the move tugging back her coat sleeve. "Vinko, stop!" She managed to pluck it from his hand. "The last thing I need is a Partizan with a hangover."

"It might be a little late for that," he slurred.

Nada sat back down and placed the bottle between her and Henrik. She noticed his stillness then.

Henrik's eyes were on her wrist. On the wooden button tied around it. *His* button. Henrik's breath shallowed as his face altered with intense gravity—an emotion she couldn't decipher. Nada drew her sleeve back over it, her nerves alight. What did that treasured button declare to him? Henrik lifted his gaze. The way he looked at her, with the faintest furrow in his brow, Nada found it harder to breathe. He knew. He knew why she wore it.

Vinko began to whistle, shattering the moment. Nada's heart raced. She unlocked her gaze from Henrik's as Vinko stumbled to his feet, the cheerful song of the Partizani forming through his lips. He swayed as he stood, whistling away with rising feeling, arms conducting an invisible orchestra. A moment later, melodic lyrics erupted from his mouth, rough and off-pitch in his drunken state. He laughed between verses, putting on a show and spreading out his arms, singing louder and louder. "We raise our heads, we walk boldly, and we cleeeench our fists haaaard!"

Henrik launched to his feet. "Be quiet!" he hissed, fists shaking, the veins in his forearms straining against his skin. His nostrils flared beneath a set of furious eyes.

Nada leapt up and grabbed Vinko's arms to quiet him. But Vinko had already paused, his grin wide on a half laugh as he looked at Henrik.

"This isn't some circus act." Henrik's voice reverberated through Nada, though he didn't yell. "Are you a clown or a soldier? Make a decision, because there are people in the house out there. They could hear you and come find us. You're putting us at risk."

Vinko sobered, smile dimming.

"Let's sit down, Vinko," Nada murmured. "You can teach me the words to that song. Quietly."

She guided him over to the wall, so he could sit slumped against it, and joined him there.

Vinko's glazed focus slid to her. "Moj mali Miš," he said with a conspiratorial grin, one eyelid dipping in a failed wink. He threw his arm around her neck, pulling her close. "She's going to steal Ante Pavelič's cheese." He brought his finger to his lips. "Sshhh."

He chuckled, and Nada couldn't help her laugh. He was a ridiculous drunk.

Still on his feet, Henrik watched them, emotionless and stone-like. Then he went back to his place in the straw. Gone was the look in his eyes from when he saw her wearing his button. Or the twitch of his lips when she made a joke about her temper.

But that didn't matter. Between the harshness and the indifference, Henrik was still in there. Nada was convinced of it now.

And she wouldn't stop reminding him of it until she pried him free.

CHAPTER 15

HENRIK RESTED HIS ARMS ON HIS KNEES, WATCHING over the others as they slept. The storm that battered the barn walls all night had faded away to lulled peace. With the lantern long since doused, the gray glow of morning filtered through a gap in the barn wall, offering little light. But it was enough to let him see the crease in Nada's brow as she continued her fitful sleep.

Henrik had jolted awake at her gasping cries, heart thundering, only to find her asleep and dreaming. Safe, at least in the real world. He couldn't get back to sleep after that. Especially not when she whimpered a single name. *Nedelko.*

Unfamiliar with the name, Henrik's mind stirred. Who was haunting her dreams? What had he done to her, to ignite echoes of him in her sleep? Then he caught himself. Caring about her in such a way would lead to a slippery slope. But hardening his heart toward her wasn't easy. It certainly hadn't been easy the night before. He'd let her get too close, talking of the past, of home. The soothing balm of her gentleness and care after she lashed out at him pulled him right into her gravity, and he'd foolishly allowed it.

The fun and ease she had with Vinko didn't help. She

laughed with him, playful and radiant, the way she used to with Henrik. An itchy heat had writhed beneath his ribs as he watched them.

But Nada's biggest snare of all was a hook she hadn't even thrown on purpose. The moment he saw that button tied to her wrist, he couldn't stop his wretched heart from twisting. She had been holding on to him all this time. Holding on to any remnant of him she could while Henrik had let her go. He'd turned his back on the past, on the memories he had with her, and dove deep into another life. Became someone new.

And that was just it. The button she held on to belonged to the boy he no longer was. She was holding on to a memory.

Henrik ran his thumb along the burn mark on the inside of his forearm. He'd never be that boy again.

"Nedelko. *Please. NO!*"

Nada shrieked and thrashed in the hay. Henrik lunged forward to grab her arm, shaking her. "Nada, wake up."

A garbled scream caught in her throat as she flinched awake. Her chest heaved as though she'd been running. The hair by her face clung to her skin with dampness.

Henrik's grip on her loosened. "You were having a nightmare."

Nada's sigh shuddered as she sat upright, unable to meet Henrik's eyes. She inched backward to lean against the wall, swallowing hard and closing her eyes as she eased her breath. As if of their own will, her fingers went to her button bracelet.

"Who's Nedelko?" Henrik asked.

Brown eyes flashed at him in the dimness. "No one." She rubbed at her face. "What time is it?" She scooted to peer through the weathered hole in the wall where steady gray light poured through.

"Early."

Nada stiffened. "Henrik. Partizani."

Alert and on his feet in an instant, he hurried over to crouch and look through the hole himself. He cursed under his breath. A handful of them shifted among the shadows between trees, trudging a fair way off. Henrik recognized them. "They're still looking for us."

"Then we need to go."

"Maybe we should stay hidden. They'll see us if we go. And then it'll become a race to see who tires out first."

"Not if we're much faster," said Nada. "We can take the horses."

Henrik gave her a nod before turning to jostle Vinko's arm. The boy startled awake, squinting at him.

"Partizani are coming," Henrik murmured. "Wake Ester and tell her to get ready. Nada and I are going to prepare the horses. We need to make a fast getaway."

Vinko bolted upright and clasped his head with a quiet groan. Henrik frowned. The idiot's hangover better not cost them their escape.

Nada clambered down the ladder. Feeding off her urgency, Henrik climbed down after her. She made a beeline for the saddles resting on a bench outside the horses' stalls. Tack jangled as she scooped up a saddle. A small leather satchel dropped to the floor, its unbuckled flap falling open to reveal a protruding, gray cap. A tingle crept down his spine. Henrik snatched it up and yanked it out. His heart stopped. A silver *U*, pinned to the front, gleamed in the low light. Nada gasped in the stillness.

A muffling of voices carried close outside. Henrik's gaze snapped up to Nada's, matching her wide eyes.

Ustaše were in their midst.

CHAPTER 16

Tension rippled through Henrik. With smooth, practiced steps, he crossed the barn with the barest of sound to peer through the small, dusty window high on the wall. Nada appeared at his side—the saddle abandoned. Two young Ustaše stood at the back door of the house, talking with someone still inside, their faces wrinkled from deep sleep. One of them carried a lump-filled sack, his arm cradling it underneath.

"They must have been here to visit family," Henrik whispered. "I don't know if we can saddle the horses in time. They could come over at any second. I'll need to kill them quietly before the Partizani get too close. Then we saddle the horses and go."

"We can't kill them. If you're right and they were visiting family, they'll be heading back to their camp. They'll have weapons there. We need to follow them."

"How? With the Partizani breathing down our necks?"

Her eyes darted about the barn, the wheels of her mind turning. Henrik knew that look well.

Nada whistled softly up at the loft and Vinko and Ester's heads popped into view. "Ester, keep an eye on the Partizani," she whispered, loud. "Vinko, mound the hay so we can hide behind it."

"What are you planning?" Henrik asked as the two in the loft disappeared.

"I want to use the Ustaše to divert the Partizani's attention from us. If we can get them to fight each other, neither of them will even notice we're here." Nada trotted to a tall and rickety wooden shelf against the far wall.

With a quick glance to check the Ustaše hadn't moved, Henrik followed her. "There's only two of them. The odds are in the Partizani's favor."

But Nada didn't respond, her eyes and hands grappling over the various items on the worn shelves. Thick dust coated the tools, broken lanterns, and bicycle parts.

"Nada, like you said, if the Ustaše die, they can't lead us to their camp." Her plan wasn't foolproof, and all Henrik cared about was keeping Nada alive. He rubbed the back of his neck.

She shifted a metal bucket aside. "Do you remember how your djed used to get blind drunk at the local tavern?"

His hand dropped in a fist at his side. "Is this really the time to stroll down memory lane?" he hissed.

"Every time, the patrons would carry him outside after he'd pass out, then throw him onto the wagon hitched to his horse." She grabbed a tin of paint and pried the lid open with a screwdriver.

Henrik nodded fast, focus flitting to the window. "The horse always brought him home to Baka."

"Exactly." She poured some of the white paint into the metal bucket. "Horses know how to go back where they came from." She snagged two stiff paint brushes and slapped one to his chest. Henrik clasped it. "Help me paint their hooves."

His breaths grew heavier. "This is too risky, Nada."

She carried the paint tin and bucket to a stall and unlatched the gate. "It's better than wandering the forest for days in search of a farm. For what? One rifle and a handful of bullets? We need those weapons."

He sighed and took the bucket from her, stepping into the stall with the horse. It whickered at his presence.

Nada hastened to check on the Ustaše as Henrik dipped his brush in the white paint, then whispered up to Ester. "How far away are they?"

"Getting closer," she whispered back. "We have maybe five minutes before they reach us."

Running his hand down the horse's leg, Henrik clutched its fetlock to pick up its hoof. He slopped the paint on liberally.

"Make sure you get the whole hoof, not just underneath it," said Nada. "We need a lot of paint to drip off." She hurried to the next stall, dipping her own brush into the paint tin.

Once finished, they let the horses out of their stalls, their slick white shoes clip-clopping on the cement.

"How far now?" Nada hissed up at Ester.

"We're in easy sight. Whatever you're doing, hurry."

As Ester and Vinko ducked into the hay, Nada darted to the barn door. The latch moaned, making her wince as she opened it. And then she left the door ajar—enough for the horses to pass through.

"Help me push the shelf over," she told Henrik, hurrying back. Together, they nudged the wonky shelves, tipping them forward. They crashed to the ground, scattering tools and broken glass.

Horseshoes clattered as the beasts startled and reared into a bolt for the forest, the tumbling sound of their hooves retreating.

"Hey!" the men shouted outside. "Hey! Come back!"

Nada tossed the rest of the paint onto the floor, covering the source of the horses' tracks, and dropped the tin to make it appear part of the accident. The men outside continued to gripe and bellow curses after their horses. In a matter of seconds, Nada and Henrik were up in the loft again.

Gunfire cracked and popped far behind the barn. Nada jerked her sharp gaze toward Henrik, standing firm, her chest rising and falling faster. He dipped his chin at her, his nerves spiking. With a determined press of her lips, Nada dropped behind the trench of straw Vinko had made and ducked low. Responding gun-blasts rang out by the barn door as Henrik swept up his Schmeisser. He joined her in the hay. Shuffled deep. He lay in wait, weapon at the ready with his one remaining bullet, should anything go wrong. A fierce readiness hummed through his body.

Shouts and bullets continued to thunder outside between the Ustaše and Partizani. The metallic, sulfuric scent of war permeated the slats of the barn walls, seeping through its cracks to burn Henrik's nose, until finally the barrage ended.

Everyone stilled, holding their breath as they listened. Footsteps and muttering drifted in from outside. Someone exclaimed with victory. The barn door creaked, and pale light washed inside. Henrik trained his sight guard at the top of the ladder as footsteps crossed the ground below. His heartbeat pounded but he stayed calm. Stayed steady. The ladder shook in rhythmic pulses. A head peered over, meeting the barrel of Henrik's Schmeisser.

With a start, Henrik recognized him.

Matej took in each of their faces staring back at him. Henrik's heartbeat hammered in his temples. A weight pressed on his chest, knowing what he'd need to do.

"All clear!" Matej called out, and then grinned.

Henrik's muscles loosened. He gave Matej a single nod, his heart rate slowing.

Matej winked at Ester before he climbed back down the ladder, disappearing from view. "There's no one in there!" he continued. "Let's keep moving!"

The sounds of boots dispersing and fading followed.

Letting out a breath, Henrik shifted to his knees, only to slump back against the wall. He looked at Nada, who already had her bright eyes on him, sitting up with a smug grin on her face. Nothing less than playful vaunting. An expression so familiar it threw him right back to the time she blew up Miroslav's bridge.

"I knew it would work," she said.

He itched to smile back at her. "You got lucky."

"Lucky I was here to save your ass, more like it."

If anything, I'd keep you *safe.*

Unnerved, Henrik shook his head at her, averting his gaze. He needed to watch himself. Nada was wily. Crafty. Not only when it came to outwitting their enemies, but at worming her way through Henrik's defenses. He needed to stop her before she reached his heart.

LIKE SPECTERS IN THE EARLY MORNING LIGHT, THEY vanished into the rain-freshened woods. Trudging through the undergrowth and weaving between dense trees, they followed the white-painted hoofprints and sprayed droplets. The farther they went, the paint spatter lessened, until the markings became little more than a smear on a shrub's leaf or a scrape of alabaster on stone. Even so, the trail led them to a weatherworn house in a clearing.

Abandoned houses were common when many fled to avoid war. Cities and the countryside were littered with them, so it wasn't unusual to find that Croat soldiers had set up a temporary camp in one. Three young Ustaše lazed against the outside wall of the house, smoking and chatting, laughing every so often. Only one of them bothered to carry a weapon. The two horses, snoozing after their escape, were tied up next to a hut, its door hung wide open. Visible among stacks of firewood sat a sizeable collection of weapons and ammunition.

Nada and the others lurked in the woods bordering the house, keeping to the shadows behind the trees. A musty carpet of damp earth and leaves absorbed their low voices and kept their footsteps hushed.

"Why are there so few of them?" murmured Nada.

"Well, we had two of them killed this morning," said Vinko.

"Surely there'd still be more."

"Maybe the rest went somewhere to fight in battle," said Henrik. "They could have left the incompetent ones behind to watch over their weapon supply."

"Let's *hope* they're incompetent," said Vinko. "How the fuck are we supposed to get our hands on those weapons with one bullet between the four of us?"

"Don't forget, Nada has her pistol," said Ester.

"Like that will make much difference."

Nada inspected the scene in front of her, taking in the details to formulate a plan.

Henrik scoffed at her. "We don't need to overcomplicate things with your distractions and fancy ideas."

At his condescending tone, she looked at him, unsure of how to respond. Since leaving the barn, he'd returned to his icy demeanor. As though he hadn't thawed the slightest bit last night as she tended to his injury.

"What do you suggest then?" asked Ester.

"We bluff. If we act like we have bullets, they'll respond like we have bullets."

"You hope."

"Well, it could be our one chance to get what we need," said Vinko. "We can't damn well go traipsing into Jasenovac with nothing but our wits and wiles."

He was right. Nada took the unloaded machine gun off her shoulder. "Better make it convincing, then."

After a quick discussion of the plan, one by one they spread out and crept closer to the house before huddling behind every natural shield they could find. Everyone waited for Henrik's signal through the tall, feathered leaves of undergrowth, inhaling the green scent of the woods with tense breaths. Nada's hands grew clammy holding her Schmeisser.

With a glance toward the house—and the unaware Ustaše—Henrik raised two fingers from the greenery and waved them in the direction of the camp.

Nada's gut fluttered as all four of them stepped out of the

forest, machine guns aimed at the unsuspecting Ustaše as they swept toward them.

"Put down your weapons!" Henrik ordered.

The Ustaše startled and whirled. Seeing the futile situation they were in, the soldier carrying a weapon dropped it to the ground while the rest raised their hands. Vinko swooped in and kicked the machine gun away from the Ustaša's reach.

"Line up against the wall. All of you," said Henrik, an imposing picture with his feet wide and shoulders back. "As long as you follow our orders, no one gets hurt."

The three Ustaša boys shuffled across, spreading out to stand along the house's brick wall. They stared back with pale faces, eyeing the Partizani cornering them.

Vinko chuckled and let his Schmeisser fall to hang at his side. He wrapped an arm around Nada's shoulders and tugged her to him. "You see, Miš? That's how it's done."

Nada slid her wide, glowing eyes and incredulous grin to Henrik. "He says this like he accomplished it all on his own."

Vinko shook his head, wincing. "True genius often goes unnoticed."

Nada turned away and laughed.

"How about we get a move on?" Henrik snapped. "Vinko, make yourself useful and collect some weapons."

Vinko's light mood sobered, and he released Nada from his side.

"I'll come with you," said Ester, lowering her weapon.

Vinko sauntered over to the hut, and Ester followed to help collect from the treasure chest of ammunition.

"Please don't kill us," one of the three boys whimpered, his face crumpling.

Henrik stepped toward them, lined up against the wall, his weapon trained and steady. His physique and stern expression made it clear to the Ustaše that Henrik wasn't someone to mess with. He paced the dirt in front of them, looking them each in the eye. Taunting them. He thrust his gun toward the face of the whimpering boy, and the boy broke down in tears.

Nada cringed at the ruthless Ubica.

By the time Henrik shifted back beside her, Vinko had emerged from the hut, carrying a canvas bag loaded with weapons. He dumped it at Henrik's feet, some of its contents tumbling out. Henrik's glower at him said more than words could have.

Nada studied the Ustaša soldiers. "We should take their uniforms. We could use them."

With what they had coming, the ability to blend in was paramount.

In answer, Henrik surged forward, raising his gun. "Take off your clothes."

At his intimidating approach, the crying boy flinched and trembled. A dark patch bloomed across the crotch of his pants and trailed down his leg.

Henrik scoffed with a curled lip and moved to tower over him. "Not so brave without your weapons, are you?"

The frightened boy cast his gaze downward as the barrel of Henrik's Schmeisser dropped to aim between his legs. "Keep your pants, coward. No one wants to smell your piss."

The boy chugged with shaky sobs.

While Nada had no compassion for any Ustaše after what she'd been through, she didn't care to watch this callous version of Henrik any longer. While his attention remained on barking orders at the soldiers and Vinko's back was turned, she slipped away.

Nada rounded the house and made her way to the back door. She thought of the sack of food the Ustaša had carried outside the barn. She prayed his fellow soldiers weren't depending on that sack making its way back to camp. Prayed they still had some supplies inside for Nada to help herself to.

The screen door groaned when she opened it. Inside, Nada stepped into a kitchen—a little dusty and bare but showing enough signs of use for her to have a spark of hope. Used dishes sat on the dining table, smeared with remnants of their breakfast. Clutching her middle, Nada darted across the room to the pantry and flung the doors open. A thrill went through her. Three cans of beans, a tattered cardboard box of eggs, and a loaf of bread lined the shelf. She set aside her Schmeisser and wrenched Vinko's jacket off. Grinning, Nada placed the items on it before bundling the lot up and shouldering her weapon again. They would eat well tonight.

As Nada turned, taking another glance at the dining table, a crisp rectangle of card caught her eye, tucked under a plate. She stepped closer. Moved the plate. Nada's body jolted with the find. She couldn't believe her luck. Breathless, Nada slipped it into her pocket and left for the door.

A creak sounded behind her, and then a clammy hand clamped over her mouth.

CHAPTER 17

PLAYING THE PART OF "CRUEL HENRIK" HAD BECOME second nature. A new extension of himself that took on a life of its own. Sometimes, unintentionally, coldness spilled from his mouth like grimy water, and Henrik would wonder if he was even playing a part anymore. If he had instead *become* what he pretended to be. But this wasn't one of those times. Henrik needed to stand firm in his convictions and keep Nada at arm's length. And he could only do that by showing her that Cruel Henrik was someone to stay away from. A brute. A heartless beast.

He bared his teeth at the Ustaše who hesitated to remove their uniforms. "*Now*. Clothes off."

As the soldiers undressed, he ordered Vinko to tie up the Ustaše and collect their uniforms while he kept his weapon trained on them. Using makeshift bandages, Vinko began fastening the soldiers' hands behind their backs. They quivered in their undergarments, either from the cold or from fear.

"We have at least one more bagful left in there," said Ester as she emerged from the hut, arms straining with the hefty weight of the weapons she carried. "Although I think we have more than we'll need."

An Ustaša stepped out from behind the hut. Before Henrik could take a breath to shout, the soldier raised a lump of firewood to strike her.

Henrik's body became a live wire, and he swung up his Schmeisser and shot the Ustaša approaching her, striking the center of his chest. The man fell back and hit the ground, firewood rolling aside.

Ester flinched from the gunfire. Her shaky hands dropped the bag. She gasped as she whirled to see the dead soldier on the ground.

"Are you okay?" Henrik asked her.

She nodded, face pale.

With the last of the soldiers bound, Vinko laughed. He tapped a palm to the Ustaša's cheek. "And to think this was a bluff. Henrik just used his last fucking bullet."

The soldier turned red as he glared at Vinko. Vinko only winked back.

"There could be more of them in hiding," said Henrik. "We should—"

A scream ripped the air. Henrik's stomach lurched toward the sound.

"Nada!" Ester shouted.

Henrik met Ester's eyes for a split second, bulging like his own, before they both sprinted for the back of the house. Dropping his worthless Schmeisser, Henrik barreled around the corner.

His nostrils flared. His pulse rushed in his ears.

An Ustaša had pinned Nada to the ground while she thrashed and punched and slapped at him. Blood trickled from her collarbone as the soldier reached for his knife in the dirt. Nada threw her hand out to the cans of food scattered about on the ground. Grasping a tin can, she cracked the soldier over the head with it.

The Ustaša growled and seized his blade, raising the knife over her sternum.

And Henrik plummeted into him, wrenching the man away.

With clenched jaw, Henrik followed his force, thrusting the man backward. The soldier stumbled across the grass. Powerful tension surged through Henrik's muscles as he struck and hammered him. No match for his skill and fury, the Ustaša lost his weapon as Henrik rammed him against the wall, pressing the soldier's own knife to his throat.

"Henrik, don't!" Nada cried. "Don't kill him."

Her words gave him pause. His breaths heaved while he still glared at the soldier. No, he would definitely kill him. He shoved the man harder against the wall, then lifted his elbow to take the killing blow.

"Don't! Not with the knife." Her voice fell quieter, pleading, "Not the knife. Please, Henrik."

Her plea took the wind out of him. When Henrik had cut the German soldier's throat under a sky pulsating with lightning, Nada had stared at him in utter terror while her body shook and her chin trembled in fear. She was afraid of him in that moment. As much as he needed her to see a monster, he hated it. It made him sick to his stomach, knowing how well he'd accomplished it. And despite his need to push her away now, Henrik didn't want her to look at him that way again.

He worked the muscles in his jaw and dipped his head. In one swift move, he grasped the Ustaša's head and smacked it into the brick. The soldier's eyes rolled back before he sank to the ground in an unconscious heap.

Henrik met Nada's dazed eyes and her open mouth. She couldn't believe he listened. Neither could he.

As she sat there, Henrik's gaze slid to the blood smeared on her collar. To the bruise blooming across her jaw. A raw pressure settled on his chest. He should have killed the Ustaša. The next time someone dared to touch her, he'd kill them, whether she begged him to walk away or not.

Ester fluttered around Nada in a whirlwind. "Are you hurt badly?" She bunched up a handkerchief from her coat pocket and held it against the cut from the Ustaša's blade. "Are you hurt anywhere else?"

"I'm okay." Holding her side, Nada winced as she tried to get up.

Ester took her arm. "Wait, we'll help you."

Henrik stepped in to grasp Nada's other hand. When she rose with them, her gaze flitted to Henrik, but he skirted his away from her, growing still. What was she doing back here on her own? Had she forgotten what he'd said about using their heads? He drew in a deep, pained breath. He could question what she did all he wanted, but it was his fault this happened to her. His throat bobbed as he swallowed, and he loosened his hold on her. Her own fingers slipped away, slowly.

Beneath Nada's feet, squashed into the earth, laid the crumbled remains of a loaf of bread. A smashed carton of eggs. She looked down. "Oh no!" she breathed, shoulders sagging.

"Never mind that," said Ester.

"Miš! What happened?" Vinko bolted over to them, skidding to a stop in front of Nada. "I tried to come right away but one of the Ustaše decided to fight back after I mentioned we had no bullets. He somehow slipped out of his bindings. At first, I thought he was enamored with my pretty face when he tried to grab me and bring me close. I figured it out fast, though."

She half-laughed, lighting up in his presence.

Henrik's mood curdled. He stepped away, silent, and crouched to tie up the unconscious Ustaša.

"I know why there are so few Ustaše here," said Nada, lifting her chin. She pulled out a rectangular piece of card from her pocket. "It's because the rest of them are making their way to Pavelič's party."

Vinko took the card to read it. "It's an invitation." He looked up at Ester, his mouth agape. "With Vila Rebar's fucking address on it."

Henrik straightened and took it to see for himself. The curving script confirmed it.

"There's nothing to stop us now," said Nada. "We can go to the party, we can steal the map, and we can free our families. It's all falling into place."

Henrik kept his eyes on the card, his focus blurring.

Vinko glanced down at the broken eggs soaking into the ground and gave her a crooked grin. "I'm relieved you're all right, Miš. But you're not much of a cook, are you? Most people like to scramble their eggs in a pan, not in the dirt."

But Nada didn't laugh. Henrik swung his face up to find her staring ahead at the fringe of the encroaching forest, fingertips resting against her sternum.

Henrik, Ester, and Vinko followed her line of sight.

Tied to the trunk of a tree sat a boy, motionless and gray-skinned. He couldn't have been older than fourteen. Purplish bruises ringed his neck, and dried blood streaked into sightless eyes and down his face. Into his forehead, someone had carved the crude shape of a star. Red, from his own blood.

Ester paled, and her hand flew to her mouth. Vinko moved closer to the boy, brow creasing as he studied him.

Henrik paled with a haunted look. What if Nada had ended up like that boy? If Henrik hadn't heard her scream? He'd been too busy trying to prove to Nada he wasn't the old Henrik anymore to even notice she'd left. He failed to keep her safe.

No matter how hard he tried, Henrik still had limits—both when it came to keeping Nada alive, and when it came to stifling his feelings for her.

CHAPTER 18

THE ICE-COLD WATER OF THE CREEK SPARKED LIFE back into Henrik's weary body. Washing the sweat and dirt off himself soothed his muscles a little. His arms and back still ached from digging the boy's grave. Henrik paused and stared at the babbling water. A waning moon wavered on the surface while the white noise of a distant fight boomed away. How did the world get to this point? When would it end?

Henrik plunged his hands into the creek for one last splash over his face and combed them back through his already wet hair. He straightened from his crouch, and rivulets of creek water ran down his damp body before soaking into the waist of his pants. Retrieving his sopping shirt from the rock nearby—washed clean of dirt to the best of his ability—he hung it over a low branch.

Meandering footsteps crunched on the gravel. "How is your arm feeling?" asked Ester. "You must have put some strain on it today when you saved Nada."

Henrik shook his head in response as he seated himself on a boulder. "I'm fine."

After they had raided the Ustaša safehouse and buried the Partizan boy, the four had walked and walked until nightfall, desperate to cover as much ground as possible, until finally stopping to make camp for the evening. They devoured what little food had survived Nada's attack as soon as they settled—barely enough to silence their hunger.

Henrik had slipped away from the others to clear his head. To find a moment of peace. Ester didn't pick up on that. She sat on the boulder beside him and drew her knees up to wrap her arms around them. They stared at the water together.

"I didn't expect to find fear in their eyes today," murmured Ester, speaking of the Ustaše. "In creatures of turbulent hate and unimaginable violence, no less."

Henrik set his hard eyes on her, brow furrowed, and she met them.

"I suppose it doesn't matter who you are inside," said Ester. "When facing death, everyone is the same."

Except some deserved it when others didn't.

Ester sighed. "It wasn't your fault, Henrik. Nada got hurt because she wandered off alone. That's not on you."

Henrik frowned. "What makes you think I take any blame for what happened?"

"You're withdrawn. Quiet. And I recognize the guilt."

The crawling heat under his skin chased away any patience he had. "What do you know of guilt?" he asked, a condescending lilt to his question.

Her eyes snapped to him. "What makes *you* the expert?"

"Experience. No one is more familiar with guilt than I am."

"Your experience doesn't diminish mine."

"What could you possibly feel guilty for, Ester?" He looked at her, his face tightening. "You couldn't hurt a fly."

"Not intentionally, no." Her eyes grew glassy, and she turned her head away. "A man was killed because of me."

Though Henrik wanted to be viewed as cruel and cold as ice, succeeding at it always chipped away a small piece of himself. Remorse was unavoidable.

"I heard their boots first. There were only a dozen of them, but the Ustaše marched as though they headed toward battle and not down a quiet street in Retfala," she explained, though he hadn't asked for it.

"I'd been outside, clipping roses in the front garden. I didn't dare hurry back inside and draw attention to myself. But they approached me anyway. They asked me where to find Lav Babič."

Henrik recognized the name of their neighbor.

"I wasn't sure what to say at first, but then I remembered Lav was a Croat. I thought he would be safe from them because of that. So I pointed them to his house, and they went to his door. They let themselves inside while many of our neighbors watched in the street.

"It was then my mother came outside and said, 'God help him.' I couldn't understand why. Then she told me Lav was a spy for the Partizani and someone must have given up his name to the Ustaše. I had no idea that it didn't matter what your ethnicity was as a Partizan sympathizer. I didn't know anyone who went against them is considered the enemy.

"Then I saw Lav stumble out of his door surrounded by the Ustaše, carrying a red accordion in his arms. The commander ordered him to play their anthem and march with them. They shoved him toward the road and he started to play. They circled him, singing along as they made their way back up the street.

"I remember thinking the upbeat melody, coming from such a festive instrument, was so at odds with the scene in front of me."

Puška Puca. Henrik knew the anthem. He'd heard it before. And he could hear it now, playing in his memory.

As rifles shoot and guns roar, banging like thunder,
The young Ustaša Army fights for their Croatian homeland.
Rifles shoot, blood is spilled, the cursed enemy runs,
And the brave Ustaša Army fulfils their holy oath.
Oh, Croatia, my dear land, your dawn is coming,
For the brave Ustaša Army is fighting for you.

"I'll never forget how Lav's brow beaded with sweat as he played his accordion while he and the soldiers passed me. When they were no longer in view, I could still hear them singing. It cut through the silence of the entire neighborhood."

Ester closed her eyes. "I found his body days later. On the side of the road, with his throat slit and flies crawling all over him." She wiped away a stray tear. "I made a fatal mistake that led directly to his death. It was fitting I found him. I deserved to see the repercussions of what I'd done. And not a day has gone by since when I'm not burdened with guilt. It's why I didn't fire my weapon during the ambush. I don't want to compound that guilt and make it any worse. It's already unbearable."

She turned to look at him, eyes wet and shining. He could see the heaviness there now, as though she pulled back a curtain for him. "I've never told Nada about it. That's why she was furious with me at the ambush."

"Why haven't you?" he asked.

Ester shrugged. "At the time, she was mourning the loss of her father. And grieving your absence. Worrying about you. She had enough to deal with."

Ester's words punched Henrik in the chest. She worried for him? He had no idea his leaving could have impacted Nada that way.

"You know, she's never spoken of what happened to her that day. Not to me. Not to her mother. No one."

He tensed and looked away into the darkness of the woods.

"It still affects her. Sometimes she can't get out of bed for days. Or she gets overwhelmed with panic. Or she starts trembling out of nowhere. She has nightmares too."

Henrik lowered his head. Rubbed his thumb into his palm, as he swallowed back the ache in his throat. "I heard her shout someone's name."

Ester nodded. "Nedelko Tomič. But I have no idea who that is."

Henrik didn't want to hear all this. Couldn't bear to learn of the way Nada had suffered.

He watched the ripple of the water and ran a hand into his hair, clutching it there for a moment. "You would think she'd avoid situations like this. Going on a dangerous journey to save her family."

"We all cling to something. Revenge. Compassion. Hope. Family. We need to. How else do we make it through days like this?" She turned her steady green eyes on him. "What do *you* cling to, Henrik?"

Her words tremored through him. He knew the answer. Henrik clung to his desperate need to keep others at arm's length. To never be hurt by loss again.

Ester slid off the rock and brushed her hand over Henrik's shoulder. "Sometimes we cling to the wrong things."

With that, she faded into the woods, heading back to their camp.

Was she right? He had failed Nada today because he was so focused on pushing her away. But did that make it wrong? Henrik wasn't sure how long he sat there with his thoughts mingling with the far-off rumbling of a battle. Eventually, he gathered himself and strolled back to camp, his hair damp and his shirt dripping in his hand.

Hanging his shirt over a branch near the heat of the campfire, Henrik glanced over the group. They were asleep, making good use of the few blankets they had stolen from the Ustaša safehouse. Vinko lay wrapped from head to toe, facing away from the fire. Ester slept soundly, using her bag as a pillow. But where was Nada?

Before he had a chance to worry, twigs and dried leaves crackled beyond the verge of light and Henrik straightened. Nada wandered out of the darkness, and her steps faltered when she saw Henrik. Her eyes skirted away and came back. They skimmed over him so fast he wasn't sure if it really happened, and then she slipped the Schmeisser off her shoulder to set it against their growing pile of belongings.

Faint, thunderous gunfire filled the silence between them.

Henrik picked up the folded blanket by his satchel, warm from the fire, and held it out to her. "Here. It's the last one."

Nada's brows pinched. "Henrik, you'll freeze. You should have it."

"I'll be fine."

She worried her lip. "We can share it, if you want."

Henrik's gaze meandered over her face. The flame's light pulsed amber against her skin. In answer, he sat in front of a broad tree trunk and wrapped the blanket behind his shoulders, holding one side open for her. His heartbeat quickened. Nada settled into the space beside him, cringing as she did.

Henrik frowned. "Are you all right?"

She took the corner of the blanket from him to gather around herself. "I got a little bruised today. That's all."

Henrik pulled his edge of the blanket tighter around him, and their arms pressed up against the other's. A spike of nerves raced through his veins, and Henrik drew a deep breath to center himself, to push the feeling away.

"Henrik," Nada gasped. "What happened?" Her cool fingertips went to the mark on his bare forearm.

She looked at him, and he found himself trapped in her gaze. "It's a long story."

Her eyes fell to her knees. "I don't know any of your stories," she murmured. "At least none of your new ones."

Henrik hesitated, chest rising and falling faster. His first instinct was to brush her off, to give her nothing but silence. But Ester's damned words played over in his mind. *Sometimes we cling to the wrong things.*

"We were traveling through Vaška one night," he said, his voice low. "The townspeople there took us all in, two to a household, to join them for their evening meal."

Henrik shifted on the ground and stared into the burning licks of the fire. "Matej and I were in the home of a young Croatian couple. We barely spoke to them as we ate, wary they could be spies for the Ustaše. I didn't even know their names.

"Right when we finished our meal, someone pounded at the door and shouted to open up. The couple hurried out of their chairs. The wife took our dishes and put them in the sink while the husband ushered us to hide in their bedroom and stay quiet.

"We were confused, but we didn't fight it. Instead, we listened with our ears to the bedroom door."

Henrik paused to rub a hand behind his neck. "Two Ustaše came into the house. And they were angry. From what I could hear, earlier that day they had asked the husband for directions to a nearby town they were searching for, and he told them how to get there. What the husband didn't know was there were Partizan troops lying in wait for them. The Ustaše were attacked, and those men returned to accuse the husband of setting them up."

Her focus glued to Henrik, Nada's brow furrowed as she listened.

"While one Ustaša was shouting, I cracked the door open a little to see what was happening. He said traitorous Croats needed to die. And then his comrade handed the wife a big, heavy mallet. They ordered her to beat her husband to death."

Nada's eyes dipped closed. Henrik took the moment to steady himself. To throw some wood onto the fire. Glowing speckles of ash flew into the sky, twisting among the stars.

"It wasn't until then I realized we left our weapons in the other room. Otherwise, we would have gunned the Ustaše down. But we did nothing because one of the soldiers was armed." Henrik drew a slow inhale. "The wife cried and begged, trying to explain her husband didn't set them up, that it was a coincidence. But the men wouldn't hear it. When the husband realized there was no way out, he told her it was okay. He told her to do it.

"When she refused again, one of the Ustaše threatened to kill her if she didn't. The husband panicked and begged her to kill him. Begged her to just do it. He'd rather die in place of her. And then the wife spat in the Ustaša's face. They slit her throat.

"Matej and I charged at them. We didn't care about anything but ending those soldiers. We caught them off guard and, together with the husband, we managed to get the upper hand.

But not without a fight. I was struggling with one of them on the ground, and he pressed my arm against the hot grate of the fireplace before Matej was able to put a bullet in each of them."

Henrik would never forget the keening in the room that followed—the way a man shattered, gathering his wife to him, to cradle the other half of his soul and beg it not to drift away. In that moment, Henrik had burned with him. Recognized and understood his anguish intimately. A pain so visceral even time stood still to make room for it.

If Henrik was smart, he would leave Nada with the blanket and walk away. But her hand slid over his wrist—an act of comfort—pinning him to the ground with a stronger force than gravity itself.

"I have no words," she whispered.

"Neither did I."

Her hand slipped away, leaving him cold. "I would have spat in that Ustaša's face too."

Henrik tensed. "She should have done as the Ustaše ordered."

Nada's face swiveled toward him, her eyes narrowed in disbelief.

"Her husband wanted her to. He wanted to save her. Instead, she let her emotions get in the way and it got her killed."

"You can't possibly believe that."

"I do. Completely. If it were us, I'd want you—" He caught himself. His choice of words implied too much.

Nada's mouth hung open. "You would want me to beat you to death?"

He looked her square in the eye. "Yes, I would."

She scoffed and sank back against the tree, glaring at the flames in front of them. "You know I wouldn't even consider it."

"Are you certain?" His lips twitched with tired humor. "With the way we argue these days, I would think you'd be the first to volunteer."

Nada chuckled and lurched forward with a wince, clutching her side. "Ow. Don't make me laugh."

But it felt so good to make her laugh. Heroic, even.

She unleashed her brown eyes on him, lightened with laughter and as familiar as his own heartbeat. Warmth curled through him, hushed and dreamlike. He wanted to hold onto it, to capture it in his hands and never let go.

Hissing through her teeth, Nada grimaced and held her breath for a moment. She clutched her side, making it clear she had suffered an injury far worse than she'd let on.

Henrik's brow wrinkled as he sat forward and turned into her. "Let me see it, Nada."

"I'm okay. It comes in waves."

"*Show me.*" He held her eyes in earnest. "Please."

She leaned back into the tree and lifted her shirt over her ribs. "See? It's not so bad."

A purple bruise the size of her fist adorned her side. He clenched his jaw, trying to draw slow, steady breaths. But hatred simmered in his gut, directed toward the man who had done this to her.

The blanket dropped further down Henrik's shoulders as he tried to get a closer look in the firelight. "I don't think anything is broken. It looks like he missed your ribs. But it might ease the pain if we put something cold on it."

He lifted his eyes to hers and found her own darting over his chest. Was he making her uncomfortable? Or was it something else?

Though his heart thrummed, Henrik didn't move an inch. "My hands are still cold from the creek, if you ..."

Her nod came fast.

Pulse racing, Henrik pressed a light hand to the hot skin of her waist, covering her bruise.

Nada closed her eyes as she sighed. "That helps."

"Good." His voice scratched.

Tilting close to her like that, his hand on her bare skin, their faces a breath apart, he couldn't help it. Everything in him softened. Softened and burned with protectiveness.

He should have been watching over her when they were

raiding the safehouse. He should have stayed by her side so no Ustaše could hurt her. Offering all he had to relieve her pain did little to alleviate his guilt.

His old coat button peeked out from under Nada's sleeve, a wavering glow from the firelight dancing on its surface. A heady fluttering stirred beneath his ribs—overwhelming tenderness tangled with apprehension. Did the button really mean what he thought it did? He was desperate to know.

"Hey, Henrik?" Nada's eyes remained shut. "What's your favorite memory? From when we were kids."

Every second I was with you. While she remained unaware, he gazed at her, drinking her in. "When you were shouting at the stars."

At the time, a seven-year-old Nada had been caught stealing and had been taught a moral lesson about the Kumova Slama—the Serbian myth of the Milky Way. It was said a man once stole another's straw, and as he fled with it, he left a trail of straw behind him. God took the straw and placed it in the sky, creating the path of scattered stars across the heavens as a constant reminder that all thieves would be punished.

Nada grinned as Henrik spoke. "You were calling out to the sisters in the sky, telling them to clean up the straw so you wouldn't get in trouble ever again."

"It seemed logical." Her smile brightened. "My favorite is when you stole Baka Rozika's underpants."

Henrik laughed deep in his throat, prompting Nada to laugh with him.

"We were quite a pair of thieves," he said.

"*We?*" Her eyes flew open. "That one was on you! You were the one who made a flag out of them and used it to wave your surrender when she started yelling at you."

Henrik caught himself smiling and reined it in. How easy his smiles and laughter slipped out of their own accord. Perhaps he was growing weary of the mask. Or maybe, after all Nada had been through, Henrik's cruelty only piled more pain onto what she already carried, and his subconscious didn't want to dig the knife deeper. To tear the cuts wider. One thing was for certain. Hurting Nada was hurting him too.

Henrik's hand remained on her waist, even though it had thawed from the contact with her skin. "It's a good thing we grew out of it."

"Who knows? Maybe those days of mischief were leading us to this point. Preparing us to steal from Pavelič."

He met her eyes and gave her a restrained grin. "Let's hope we learned from our mistakes of getting caught."

CHAPTER 19

"I'M BEGINNING TO WONDER IF WE'LL EVER FIND ANY signs of life," said Ester.

After they had spent two days traversing the forested hills in search of anyone who might provide food to a handful of starving Partizani, hunger had a firm grip on them all. They wandered through the woods all morning, but as the day wore on, the likelihood thinned. Nada hoped they hadn't become turned around at some point, traveling away from Zagreb instead of toward it. With Henrik and Vinko in the lead and Ester and Nada following, they hadn't crossed paths with a single house, let alone a single soul. According to Henrik's map, they should have reached a village by now.

"We could always hunt," said Vinko, a lit cigarette hanging between his lips.

"Sure." Henrik held his hand out. "Why don't you hand me your things and go pounce on a bunny."

Vinko waved him off. "I could catch a rabbit. Easy."

"Good. Then when you come bounding back with something dead between your teeth, I'll be sure to give you a pat."

Ester and Nada lagged behind, but not so far that they

couldn't hear the constant bickering between them. Henrik glanced over his shoulder at Nada, as though checking she was still there.

"He's been less cruel these last few days," Ester murmured to her.

She was right. He'd been distant, but not cruel. Since the night they shared a blanket by the fireside, the strain between them had eased. They'd laughed that night, connecting for the first time since reuniting, and it left her buoyant. But even so, the true Henrik remained out of reach.

"I wonder what changed."

Nada kept quiet. She hadn't told Ester about that night by the fire. She didn't want to. That moment with Henrik had been a gift. A breath of air. One she wanted to keep close to her heart.

"I spoke to him the other night, after the raid," said Ester. "He worries for you. Still has *feelings* for you."

Nada rolled her eyes. "This old story again."

"He loves you, Nada. I saw it. If you paid attention, you'd see it too."

"I do pay attention. Yes, he's been less cruel, but now he's someone who barely talks to me. Who walks away when I come near. That's not love."

Ester donned a smug grin, as if she knew something Nada didn't. "He gets jealous when you and Vinko laugh and carry on together."

"Vinko's a friend. Nothing more." Judging by the way Nada had caught him looking at one of the undressed Ustaše during the raid, she'd say Vinko felt the same way about her.

"Henrik doesn't know that."

She sighed. "Is there a point to this conversation?"

"You think your Henrik is lost to you, that he's not there anymore. But he is. And it's the part of him that still holds on to *you*."

Nada's skin itched hot. She stared ahead.

Ester grabbed her arm to get her attention. "Maybe if you pull on that thread, you'll find him again."

Nada stopped to face her. "He's not holding on to me, Ester." She had proof of that. And its name was Katarina.

"He's always loved you. That doesn't just go away."

She shook her head, but Nada's lungs ached, making her eyes glisten. "How much could he have loved me if he left without explanation and then fell for another girl?"

"He came to your house to give you an explanation. You turned your back on him before he could give it," said Ester. "And are you talking about the rumor of a girl Vinko mentioned? He barely had any details about her. For all we know, it's not even true."

But Nada did have some details. "It *is* true. She was a Partizanka, and her name was Katarina."

Ester's brows knotted together. "When did you learn this?"

"I overheard him and Jakov talking about her." Heard the way Henrik said her name. Like it hurt to say it out loud. "It's not a rumor."

"Oh."

"Everything okay?" Henrik waited for them farther ahead, while Vinko continued walking.

Nada nodded and forged ahead, Ester following a second later.

"Regardless," murmured Ester behind her. "What I said still stands."

Vinko doubled back at a trot, waving at them all to hurry over. He had found something. And Nada was glad it brought an abrupt end to their discussion.

THEY REMAINED HIDDEN BEHIND THE TREES, PEERING through the forest's lush undergrowth, to observe the quaint house in the distance. Its two-story white walls stood crisp against the backdrop of vivid green. Capped by a terracotta roof, with a dark wood balcony stretching across its front, the house reminded Nada of her grandparents' home. Smoke swirled and wisped from its chimney—a sure sign someone was home.

Henrik shifted in his crouched position between Vinko and Nada. "Asking them outright could be too risky."

"I'm sure I could use my charms to convince them to share their food," said Vinko. "I'm fucking hard to resist. Everyone loves Vinko."

Henrik ignored his jokes. "Forget the fact that for all we know they're Ustaša sympathizers. They could turn us away or lie about what they have to keep for themselves."

"There's not much we can do about that," said Ester.

Vinko turned to look at her where she kept low on his other side. "Actually, there is. We can wait till they leave and damn well help ourselves."

Nada made no move to disagree.

Ester's mouth dropped open. "We can't steal from them."

"How do you think the Partizani have survived this long?" asked Vinko. "It's not only from the donations of others. Sometimes we have to resort to more creative means. Like the time Henrik chased a sheep across a field." He laughed under his breath, keeping his eyes on the house. "Our Ubica was in fine form that day."

Henrik laughed through his nose.

Nada lightened. "I can see it now, and I'm willing to bet the sheep keeled over when it caught sight of Henrik's withering glare."

She glanced at Henrik and found his lips curving up a touch at the corners, his eyes light as he kept focus on the house.

Voices carried through the quiet. Nada ducked low, her eyes sharpening on the house as a woman emerged from the front door carrying a basket full of laundry. She called out over her shoulder, and a man followed with two boys. As the woman made her way to a tub and washboard around the back, the rest of her family collected shovels and hoes by the woodpile and tended to the sparse vegetable garden near her.

"That's a whole fucking family right there," said Vinko. "The house will be empty. Now's our chance."

"So how are we planning to do this?" asked Ester.

"Quietly," said Nada.

Henrik nodded. "Best way to go about this is to sneak in and sneak out."

Ester looked at them, a spark of something dawning on her face. "Then Vinko, you and I should stay here. I'm useless with something like that. This is clearly a job meant for Henrik and Nada."

Nada whipped a narrow gaze toward Ester. What was she up to?

"Speak for yourself," said Vinko. "I'm a man of many skills."

"Yes, but Henrik and Nada used to sneak out late at night all the time and then sneak back in in the early hours of morning. Their parents never knew a thing."

Henrik's eyes skirted the ground by Nada. Was he thinking about it? All those times they whispered laughter, meeting under the cover of darkness simply for the thrill of it? To lay in a field side by side, watching the stars move across the sky while murmuring deep truths to each other? It made Nada's heart ache to remember. Those were the last weeks she'd had with him, and she hadn't even known it.

"Besides," said Ester. "I'll need you here with me, Vinko. For protection."

"Fine. Then they better hurry before that family goes back inside." He fished into his pocket for another cigarette.

The line of Henrik's throat bobbed in a swallow. "If anyone heads toward the house, you'll need to distract them."

"I can fire my gun into the sky."

"Idiot. They'll run inside for cover. We want to draw them *away* from the house."

"Ester, you should call out for help," said Nada. "Pretend you've been hurt. They're more likely to come running to help a young girl. But don't let them find you. Stay hidden."

"We should be able to hear you call out from inside," said

Henrik. "So if it comes to that, let's use it as a signal to meet up by that waterfall we passed a little while ago."

Ester nodded. "We'll wait for them to stop searching for me before we head there."

"And if they *don't* stop searching," said Vinko, waggling his eyebrows at Nada, "*that's* when I can fire my gun into the sky."

Nada snorted her way into a quiet laugh.

Henrik's jaw ticked. "With *your* aim, Ester should duck for cover."

Ester widened her eyes pointedly at Nada. She didn't say a word, but Nada could hear it all the same. *See? I told you.*

Henrik led the way, hunched over as he crept through the edge of the forest. A succession of trees wove out of the wood's perimeter to reach a corner of the house, and he and Nada took cover behind them as they made their way to the front, keeping an eye on the family. Once they hid themselves against the wall, they hurried across to the front door.

Nada opened the unlocked door a crack and peered inside. Finding nothing but silence, they swooped inside and closed the door behind them.

Floral-patterned furniture adorned the small living space, while a doorway in the far wall framed the kitchen beyond it. A simple worn staircase, sandwiched between two walls, divided the rooms. A large Croatian flag hung on the wall to the left, the letter U stitched into its corner.

The unmistakable scent of smoked ham lingering in the air sent Nada's mouth watering. With her stomach ready to cave in with hunger and so close she could taste it on her tongue, Nada tiptoed toward the kitchen, Henrik right beside her.

Footsteps stomped down the stairs and Nada froze, her wide eyes darting to Henrik.

CHAPTER 20

HENRIK GRABBED HER AT THE WAIST, PULLING HER with him into the shadowed corner behind the stairs. They squeezed between the wall and a tall, hefty cabinet. Hands against his chest, Nada felt Henrik's heart pounding beneath her palms in time with her own.

The footsteps tramped down the stairs, ominous with every fall. Drawing closer. Louder. Nada's hands began to sweat. Her core quaked deep and quiet, like they were coming for her again. Like they'd close in on her, just as they'd closed in on her hiding place in that cream-colored church. Henrik's eyes went to the doorway leading into the kitchen, but Nada could only duck her head, wanting to curl into him.

A chair scraped against the floor tile and creaked as someone settled into it. A man sighed and papers rustled.

Henrik's grip on her waist loosened as he slowly moved for the dagger at his hip. He clasped the hilt, withdrawing the blade from its sheath. Nada's breaths quickened and she clasped his wrist, stopping him. She shook her head, eyes pleading with him. Studying her, he slid it back into place.

He mouthed something, but her foggy mind couldn't grasp what he was saying.

Henrik leaned close, barely whispering in her ear. "He's in the kitchen. I can take him."

But Nada shook her head again. The deep quake intensified, churning its poison through her.

Henrik dipped his head so she could reply to him. "Wait him out. Please."

He looked down at her a moment and nodded.

Paper rustled again, and something metallic clattered on the tile floor in the kitchen. Nada startled, hands snatching at the sides of Henrik's shirt. He kept his stern focus on the kitchen, able to see the man from where he stood.

Nada's heartbeat knocked harder against her ribs and the air around her thinned. Her eyes prickled with the threat of tears as her chest began to heave. *No, not now.* She needed to calm down. What was wrong with her? Why did this keep happening? The quake within slithered, coiling up through her lungs to tie a rope around her neck. The room whirled around her. She couldn't breathe. There was no air in that tight corner. She shrank in on herself, back pressing against the wall, wishing she could slide down and lie on the floor. Why couldn't she breathe? Nada's vision blurred in a teary kaleidoscope as tingling waves rippled through her.

Gentle hands caught her face and tipped it up. Words whispered in her ear. "Sshh, Nada. Look at me."

Nada blinked her tears free to find those blue-gray eyes holding hers—his gaze intense, his brow furrowed.

"I'm here," he mouthed. "Focus on me."

But how could she focus when she couldn't breathe? And what if the man could hear her gasping?

Henrik leaned into her ear again. "You're here with me. You're safe. Try to slow your breathing, Nada." He pried her hand from his shirt and placed her palm over his heart. "Feel my breaths and try to match them."

Steady arms slipped around her, scooping her against him, and Nada let herself sag into him so he could hold her upright. Let her forehead fall forward to his chest. She tried to focus on the easy rise and fall of it, fighting hard to do as Henrik suggested.

"Do you remember that last night we sneaked out together?" he asked.

She nodded against him. His hand came up to rest at the nape of her neck, holding her there. Comforting her the way only Henrik could.

"We went down to the river's edge and sat there for hours in silence."

Her eyes fell closed, and she let herself slip back to the hush of the black water, the slight breeze carrying the scent of wildflowers, the way Henrik's eyes turned stormy gray in the night.

"We had no need for words. Content to just be together."

Nada thought about that night often, wondering if something deep inside them knew what was coming. That they'd be apart for a long time. So they'd steeped themselves in each other's presence, soaking up all they could.

On some of Nada's worst days, she returned to that memory. As if that night gave her an overflow of Henrik, and she could absorb a drop of him whenever she needed.

Nada drew a slower, more even breath, her lungs filling with the scent of Henrik. Of campfire and trees.

"Then you finally turned to me. You smiled the sweetest smile, and then shoved me into the water."

Nada grinned against his shirt.

"You always were the devil."

Nada gazed up at him. Humor gleamed in her eyes, and softness colored his. Something profound settled inside her. Quietened. There he was. Her Henrik. And he looked at her like ...

If you paid attention, you'd see it too.

Chest to chest, his arms firmly pressing her into him, Nada melted. He'd never held her like this before. He was warm and solid and so much more *real* up close. The intricate lines of his irises, the distinct scent of his skin, the rapid beat of his pulse at the crook of his throat painted a picture of what life would be like in his arms. Nada's heart swelled. She wanted that. She wanted it so badly it hurt.

Was Ester right after all? Did some part of him care for her? Want her?

Nada's breathing eased at some point, and the bundle of apprehension in her stomach uncoiled, all of it long forgotten as Nada fought the desire to reach up and touch his face. To brush her fingers against his jaw and whisper all the ways she missed him.

Faint feminine cries drifted from somewhere outside. Ester.

Henrik averted his gaze and swallowed as he let his arms loose. All warmth enveloping her fell away as their situation came screaming back in.

A rushed fumble sounded in the kitchen—a chair shifting, followed by hurried footsteps. A door squeaked open and slammed closed.

Henrik peered to the side, getting a better glimpse of the kitchen. "He's gone. Are you ready?"

She nodded, unable to speak.

They stepped into the kitchen and Nada's eyes settled on the sizeable smoked ham sitting out on the counter. Her mouth watered. Baka made the best Pršut. She would have a row of ham legs hanging up on the eaves, swaying in the breeze, while swatting Nada and her father away from touching them. Was Filip with her now, eating his own slices of ham, all thoughts of following Nada long gone from his mind? She hoped so. She tossed her empty satchel on the dining table and shoved the Pršut inside.

Henrik stooped to look out the small, kitchen window. "They're all going into the forest."

Good. Their plan was working. Not that it relieved Nada's unease. Shaky and off-kilter after falling apart by the stairs—and after her close moment with Henrik—Nada flexed her fingers. Refocused on her task.

Henrik opened the pantry cupboard as Nada checked the

refrigerator. With no electricity to keep it running, it made sense she found it empty. At least Henrik fared better. He pulled out a sack of potatoes, setting it aside on the floor, and reached back in for a loaf of bread and a handful of apples.

Nada moved to the corner of the kitchen and searched the cabinets. In them she found a few jars of homemade sauerkraut and pickles and tucked them under her arms. She turned for the table and tripped over the sack of potatoes.

Henrik reacted fast. His strong arms flew out and caught her —glass jars held safe against her middle.

Nada flushed. It wasn't like her to make such a mistake. "Hvala."

He gave her a terse nod and released her. He'd returned to stone. To the emotionless Henrik that starved her of what she wanted.

They wasted no time, packing it all up into their bags and slipping back outside. They hastened into the woods unseen.

As they escaped deeper into the forest, Nada's gaze flicked toward Henrik. A nervous energy hummed in her veins. All this time, she had been convinced Henrik cared nothing for her. Could she have been wrong? After the way he looked at her by the stairs, hope burned a flame inside her, insistent and unwavering.

If Nada pulled on that thread, would it free her Henrik?

CHAPTER 21

Before

NADA WOULD OWE HIM FOR THIS, AND HENRIK couldn't wait to tease her with all the absurd demands he'd concocted. She had forgotten her cousin Milena's book—the book she was instructed to return today upon pain of death—leaving it at Henrik's house by accident when she and her father stopped by on their way to visit extended family in the next village over. They'd been gone for half an hour before Henrik spotted the book sitting on the coffee table. Saint that he was—at least when it came to all things Nada—Henrik took the book and headed straight for Milena's.

Almost there, Henrik grinned as he treaded through the streets, anticipating Nada's reaction. But when a guttural scream ripped him from his thoughts, Henrik looked up. He checked the street around him. Nothing but condensed rows of houses with simple gables, crumbling cement, and trees growing out of squared patches of grass. Another cry carried from some distance away. A young woman bolted around the corner ahead, her face flushed while clutching a bag to her chest.

A man followed, carrying a small boy in his arms. "Hurry," he breathed.

Henrik's lungs tightened. It could only mean one thing. He needed to warn Nada. Squeezing the book in his hand, he sprinted to the center of town, toward the building cacophony of shouting. Turning onto a new street, he stopped short. Henrik's blood ran cold. Ustaše swarmed, pillaging in the street. Not for money or valuables but for Serbs.

Ustaše barked, corralling people, herding them down the road. Women gripped their children close as they screeched and cried at the strange men grappling their mothers. At the weapons pointed at their fathers' faces. Elderly were shoved to the ground and kicked for not moving fast enough toward the end of the road, where more of the monsters gathered.

Henrik clasped the back of his neck, panting as his eyes flitted over the scene. Over the familiar faces of his Croat friends from Retfala, now dressed in Ustaša uniforms.

"Danijel!" Henrik called out to one of them, striding past. "What's going on?"

"What does it look like?" he said, jerking his chin toward the chaos. "We're gathering up the Serbian scum."

His heart thrashed. He needed to find Nada. Now.

Danijel tapped his palm against Henrik's arm. "When are you going to put on a uniform and join us?"

Instinct told Henrik to lie through his teeth. "Soon, my friend," he said. "But right now I'm looking for my father. Have you seen him?"

Danijel shook his head. Henrik waved a quick farewell and jogged away. If Danijel knew Henrik was looking for Nada, a known Serb, Danijel would have followed. He wouldn't hesitate to snatch up the girl he'd gone to school with. Past relationships meant nothing anymore.

Once out of his friend's sight, Henrik flew through the lanes and alleyways of close-knit buildings toward Milena's house. His lungs burned by the time he made it to her street corner, and then his heart rate doubled. *Please, no.* Before they could see him, Henrik ducked behind a dense copse of trees and shrubs, his hand growing tacky against the leather of the book. He watched as at least a dozen Ustaše circulated, bursting through doors, dragging people across the pavement. Eyes darting, Henrik searched the faces of the Serbs.

A gasp cracked from his chest, chased by rapid breaths. *Nada*.

Her growling scream tore through him and his body seized, nostrils flaring. Ustaše forced her and her father, Petar, toward a horse-drawn cart. Henrik's lips trembled as she tried to kick at them, lashing and wrenching in their grip as she fought to get away, but an Ustaša stepped in and backhanded her. Henrik jolted, a moan escaping him. Nada's head lolled to the side, though she remained on her feet, still conscious. Petar cried out, spewing vicious curses at the men.

"Get those last two into the cart!" snarled an Ustaša by the horses. "Take them to the town hall. The church is already full of all the svinje being brought in from other villages."

Shoved onto the cart with a handful of others, Petar pulled his daughter into his arms, shielding her.

Scraping fingers into his hair, Henrik groped around in search of help. He needed to stop them. He needed to get Nada out of that cart. But the empty streets offered no solution. There was only Henrik, armed with nothing more than a worn leather book.

He stumbled a step toward them and hesitated. What could he do? How could he help her? His arm flopped down at his side as the horses moved forward, rolling the cart away. Tears sprung to his eyes and his breaths rasped, tilting toward the pull of sobs. Henrik clenched his fist, fighting against them, and turned to stare in the direction of Retfala. If he could creep away unseen and run for his village, he could make it home to his father in half an hour. Karlo, a trained soldier, was his best chance of helping them.

With careful steps over grass and leaf litter, Henrik made his way beyond the Ustaše's line of visibility, and then he ran.

His chest heaved and his hands shook as he careened through the front door of his home. "Tata! I need your help!"

He swerved into his parents' bedroom, throat dry and burning.

Karlo stood over the bed, packing his clothes into a canvas bag when he looked up in alarm. "What is it?"

Henrik's voice choked, "Nada and Petar were taken by Ustaše. We need to go and stop them."

With a heavy sigh and a hollow gaze, Karlo shook his head. "I can't, Henrik. There's nothing I can do."

"Of course there is!" He pointed out the door. "We need to go. Now."

Karlo had spent years in the army. If anyone could help, it was him.

"These things happen all around us. We can't save everyone. And if we try, we'll only fall into an early grave."

"Everyone?" Henrik's eyes narrowed as he shifted from one foot to the other and angled himself toward the door. "It's *Nada.* There's *only* Nada."

His father ignored him, continuing to place his neatly folded clothing into the bag.

Henrik slammed his fist against the wall. "Why aren't you listening to me?"

"Your mother will be home any moment to see me off."

"*What?*" Henrik frowned as he registered his father packing. "Where are you going?"

"The Germans are looking for soldiers to fight on their side. I have German heritage and I speak the language. If they find me, they could force me into their ranks."

At the cusp of the war, as Germany's forces stirred and whispers of uncertainty circulated, all members of the Jugoslavenske Army had been relieved of their duties and sent home to their families, including Henrik's father. While the world held its breath, Karlo washed his hands of the war. Refusing to be swept up in any fight, he had burned his army uniform and buried his rifle deep in the ground. Karlo would never submit.

Henrik clutched at his hair. "So you're leaving? You won't help me?"

"An old friend of mine has offered to take me in, to hide me in plain sight. He's procured a train worker's uniform for me so it will look as though I work at the Osijek station. As long as I wear it, no one will question my presence in the city."

Because as much as the Germans were hungry for more soldiers, they also needed crews working to keep the trains running.

"Why hide at all?" Henrik asked. "Join the Partizani instead. They need everyone they can get. Fight for freedom."

Karlo exhaled through his nose and zipped his bag shut. He turned to face his son. "If I turn to the Partizani, I will only become a target for the Ustaše. And then they will come for you and your mother. This is what I must do to keep us all safe."

Avoiding sides. That was his solution. The whole idea made Henrik's stomach churn.

"I want you to look after your mother while I'm gone," said Karlo. "I may be in Osijek until the war ends. Whenever that will be."

Henrik stared at him, long and hard. The grandfather clock in the hallway tick-tocked away, marking each second Karlo remained silent. Each second Nada was in danger. A white-hot pang of pain singed beneath Henrik's ribs.

His father was a coward.

"I need to go." Without another word, Henrik turned for the back of the house and barreled for the door.

"Henrik, wait."

But he paid his father no heed, stumbling outside into the waning sunlight. Raging heat boiled and stewed in his gut, in his chest, its agitation surging outward to his arms until they seized the handle of a shovel leaning against the wall. He bludgeoned the corner of the house. Over and over Henrik smashed it against the brick, gritting his teeth to fight back the torment wanting to tear free of his lungs and mouth in a guttural scream. He struck the house with such ferocity that his palms began to burn with the promise of blisters. But he preferred enduring that kind of pain to the agony waging inside him.

He did nothing. He watched those monsters cart Nada away, and he did nothing. Henrik hated himself for it.

He was a coward, like his father.

CHAPTER 22

HENRIK NEVER SHOULD HAVE ALLOWED HIMSELF TO get so close. He was a fool to play with fire like that. But when Nada started trembling, *panicking*, his worry for her shoved aside all common sense. He hated that it felt good to hold her. To have her lean on him, trusting he could soothe her. He became the protector, the comforter he used to be with her, and had slipped into the role with ease. He was stupid. So, so stupid.

The worst part was it had worked. She had calmed down. Felt safe because of him. And it made his damned heart flood with warmth. He desperately needed that to stop. To keep it from happening again.

Still a full day's walk from Zagreb, Henrik trailed close behind the others as they made their way downhill beneath a dense canopy, weaving through rocky ground and gnarled tree roots. They'd finally eaten a decent meal, thanks to the food they had stolen, fueling them with enough energy to continue their journey.

Vinko groaned and scrubbed his messy hair. "I'm bored. All this walking is making me fucking crazy."

"We could always race." Nada gave him a sly grin.

Of course. Nada would leave Vinko in the dust, and she knew it.

Vinko feigned a gasp, dropping his jaw in mock horror. "Ladies don't run."

"That's true. We don't." Her eyes brightened with wicked mischief. "Why run when we can shoot our opponent in the legs?"

"*Much* more ladylike."

"No, ladylike is taking an axe to their ankles."

Vinko slung his arm around her shoulders. "You can be real frightening, you know that, Miš?"

Nada let out a quiet laugh and slipped her own arm around Vinko's waist as they continued downhill. Henrik looked away.

Ester stopped dead, grabbing Vinko's free arm. In reaction, they all halted and listened. Shouting drifted up toward them from the valley ahead.

Henrik crouched and crept to a rocky outcrop nearby, and the others followed suit. They peered over the boulders.

Below them, Ustaše paced back and forth in the sunlight, casting long shadows beneath their boots. With machine guns in hand, they corralled a group of unarmed youths. Some were dressed in civilian clothes; others wore caps bearing a red star. Partizani. Henrik counted sixteen as the Ustaše lined them up at the bottom of the mountain.

Nada drew her Schmeisser from her shoulder and lifted it to aim down the hill.

Henrik shoved her barrel low, frowning. "What are you doing?"

"Let go, Henrik. We have a chance to ambush them."

"Are you crazy? There's at least twenty Ustaše down there and four of us. If you fire, all hell will rain down on us."

"We can't sit by and let the Partizani die."

Henrik didn't want to sit idly by either, but they needed to be pragmatic. "There's nothing we can do."

"There's *always* something we can do," Nada argued. "What kind of person watches and does nothing to try and stop it?"

Henrik stilled. Her words pointed right at him—an arrow aimed true—whether she realized it or not.

Her eyes welled and, though she tried to hide it by clenching her weapon, her hands trembled. "Right now, every one of them is praying to God for someone to help them. They're bleeding with desperation for this moment to change because if it doesn't, it's all over for them. They know what's coming."

Was she speaking from experience? Insides turning raw, Henrik broke away from her gaze, unable to look her in the eye. He had never told her the truth—that he'd watched the Ustaše take her away and done nothing. She was right. What kind of person watched without acting? A coward like Henrik, that's who.

He hated himself for it. *Punished* himself for it.

Multiple gunshots cracked in succession, echoing around them, and Nada flinched.

Her breaths shallowed as her hard, watery stare pinned Henrik in place.

The Ustaše moved away from the devastating scene below, marching through the valley and out of view. It was then that Nada rose with that flinty look in her eyes, lips pressed together, and stalked in their direction.

Pulse spiking, Henrik leapt and stumbled after her. "No! Stop!" He dashed in front of her and skidded on the rocky earth, blocking her path. He held his arms out wide to keep her there.

"Get out of my way," she demanded through gritted teeth.

"You need to think things through, Nada. Stop trying to run headfirst into danger."

"They killed sixteen boys. Not one of them looked much older than us. Doesn't that anger you? Think of the boy you buried the other day! We can't let them get away with it. They should die for what they did. For all they still do every single day."

"It angers me more than you know." His brow wrinkled. "Trust me, I understand."

"If you did, you wouldn't stop me." She tried to push past him, but he grasped her arms.

"Damn it, Nada, I'm doing everything I can to keep you safe!"

"I don't need you to!" She yanked herself from his hold. "You make me so furious I could scream."

"Because I won't let you march off to your death?"

"Because you try to impede the choices I make at every turn. Because I don't know who you are anymore. You never would have treated me this way before."

"What do you *want* from me, Nada?" he growled, ripping his cap off and crushing it in his hand. "Are you waiting for me to be that boy who followed your every whim, no matter how reckless? Who did whatever you wanted just because it was you who asked? I already told you, he's gone."

"Oh, believe me. I'm aware. You're a poor replacement."

"Is that why you keep bringing up the past, trying to get me to reminisce about the good old days? What, do you think a few reminders will make me go back to the old me? Don't think I haven't noticed. I've noticed your obvious disappointment. Your misplaced hope. That damn button you wear that belonged to the old Henrik."

Nada faltered, lips falling open to speak, but nothing came out.

"Let me make it real clear for you. I'll *never* be him again. Ever. He's gone."

Her eyes flared with renewed fire. "What about when we were hiding behind the stairs? Was he gone then?"

The hair on his arms lifted but Henrik clenched his jaw, holding her in his glare.

"I know what I saw." She jabbed her finger to his chest. "*That* was my Henrik."

He tilted his face forward, closer, unveiling all the steel and ice he had inside. "I did what I needed to calm you down. Your hysterics were about to get us caught. If it meant giving you a fantasy to keep you quiet, then I was willing to play the part."

All breath left her body. Her eyes glistened. "I suppose you're right. Because there's not a hint of him in you right now."

"And that bothers you, doesn't it? That I'm not the same anymore." He slammed his fist to his chest. "I'm not what you wanted to find. How disappointing for you."

"Who *would* want to find an ubica? A cruel, heartless monster who doesn't even flinch at taking someone's life? Who would *want* that?"

His heart sank. Withered away inside him. He tried to quieten the shaking in his breaths.

She all but spelled it out for him. Nada didn't want this unworthy Henrik, she wanted the boy from her past. Even though Henrik forced the cruelty and the coldness to keep people at bay, he *had* changed. The boy was gone.

Which meant Henrik wasn't enough for Nada. He never would be.

That was his goal. To keep her away. To not give in to the gravity of her and sever his feelings for her once and for all. If something were to happen to Nada, if he lost her, it would hurt a hell of a lot more than realizing his worthlessness.

Nada dug her knife in deeper. "You're no different than the Ustaše."

The blow clobbered him into silence as searing pain erupted beneath his ribs. Henrik's fist dropped and hung limp at his side. Her words reverberated through him. Worthless. Vile. Shameful. Throat aching, he swallowed hard.

Henrik stepped back, cap still tight in his grip.

Off to the side, Vinko stared at the ground, hands in his pockets. Ester watched on with glassy eyes, arms wrapped around herself. Henrik forgot they had an audience. Did *they* think he was no better than an Ustaša too?

Nada barged past him, jostling him as she went down the hillside. The others followed her in silence, leaving Henrik to lag behind.

Nada approached the bodies in the valley while Henrik and the others gave her room. She made her way from one young

Partizan to the other, closing their eyelids if they remained open, whispering the Orthodox prayers for the dead.

On the last word she breathed, her focus turned to a boy beside her, to the red star, pinned and gleaming on his collar. She gently removed it from his shirt. Closed her fist tight around it. And then her dark gaze lifted to Henrik—a look that demanded the Ubica, the *Ustaša*, stay away from her—before she turned and stalked back up the hill.

All this time Henrik had tried to push her away, he never expected her to push back so violently.

ACCORDING TO HENRIK'S MAP, VILA REBAR WAS within two hour's walking distance from their estimated location in the woods. It brought Nada relief. Ante Pavelič's party was only twenty-four hours away, and they would make it to Zagreb with plenty of time to spare.

With the forest awash in deep blue twilight, Ester's attention turned to glimpsing stars as they peeked between the net of leaves above, then picking wildflowers as they went. How did she do that? While everyone else focused on the next obstacle, their current worries, Ester found time for beauty. For *living*. Nada couldn't remember the last time she looked at the stars like Ester did—for the wonder of it all.

No, she did remember. It was right before Henrik had left.

I did what I needed to calm you down. Nada wanted to crawl into a hole. He had played the part of a fantasy all right, and Nada fell for it willingly. Had he seen what she felt for him in that moment? Could he read the longing in her? She could only imagine what it was like for Henrik. To have such control while a gullible girl turned to butter in his arms. Maybe he found it pathetic. Maybe he pitied her for it. The whole thing made Nada shrivel up inside.

She glanced over at Henrik and caught his eyes already on her. He swung them away.

Ester noticed the exchange and sidled up beside Henrik, breathing in the bundle of flowers in her hands with dreamlike contentment. Henrik acted as though she wasn't there, giving her his typical cold shoulder.

Ester plucked a wildflower from her humble bouquet and held it out for Henrik. Startled, he took it, dazed and staring at her playful grin. She remained at his side, continuing to dive for blooms here and there.

If he's intent on battling with you, then let softness be your weapon.

Was silence as good as softness? Because Nada wielded that with precision. They hadn't spoken to each other all day.

Vinko inched closer to Nada. With his cigarette glowing between his fingers, its smoke rising and undulating in curlicues, he nudged his shoulder into hers. "Hey, Miš."

She looked up at his gentle grin and he winked at her. Nada's cheeks warmed. He felt sorry for her. Perfect. Even Vinko thought she was pathetic.

"I know I was fairly intoxicated that night in the barn, so stop me if I've already told you the story. But did you know my brother tried to kill me once?"

Nada's eyebrows shot up. He had her full attention.

He nodded. "It wasn't long after we went our separate ways. A skirmish broke out in my hometown. I was there with the Partizani, battling it out with the Ustaše. The last person I expected to come across was Stipe, but there he was, a little way down the road, aiming his fucking weapon right at me.

"I called out to him, trying to convince him to walk away from the Ustaše and come with me. I told him I missed my brother. Do you know what he said?"

Nada shook her head, waiting for the answer.

"*I have no brother.*" Vinko snatched his gaze away and took a drag of his cigarette. "Some of our old neighbors saw us and came out of their houses. They started crying out, 'Don't shoot him! He's your brother! Stipe, don't!' But he fired his gun anyway. I was damn lucky he had terrible aim. He got me right here," said Vinko, pointing at the side of his calf. "Of course, I ran to get away from him then. But I could hear Stipe screaming through the village if he ever saw me again, he'd kill me."

"Vinko," Nada breathed, wincing.

"I ran into the forest and hid up in a tree. After the battle ended, I watched the Partizani move out from up there, but I didn't dare follow. I stayed in that fucking tree all night."

"Of course you did. I probably would have done the same."

"The thing is, Nada, even though Stipe threatened to kill me, even if I can never get through to him and he's an Ustaša forever, he's still my brother. I still love him."

She studied him a moment. "Why are you sharing this with me?"

Vinko jerked his chin toward Henrik. "At the end of the day, are you going to love him any less because he's not what you expected?"

Nada slowed to a stop and opened her mouth to speak.

"Psst." Henrik hastened over to them, pulling Ester along with him. He gestured for them to get down. "Hide."

Nada and Vinko obeyed without hesitation, dropping flat to the ground. Henrik and Ester sank down on Nada's other side. All four of them stretched out on their fronts to disappear into the undergrowth.

"What is it?" Nada whispered, peeking her head up through the shrubs to see.

Henrik clasped her arm. "Get down, Nada. Ustaše."

She dipped her head down, heart racing as coldness trickled through her veins.

Vinko cursed, putting out his cigarette in the dirt.

"Relax," breathed Henrik. "If we stay hidden, we'll be fine. They're most likely traveling for Pavelič's party."

Soon the group passed them by, their forms painted in moonlight, oblivious to the Partizani watching them through the leaves and grass.

When they deemed it safe to get up, Henrik realized he still held on to Nada's forearm. He jerked away, as if her skin burned him. On his feet again, he moved away from her, refusing to meet her eyes.

"Let's be on alert the rest of the way," he murmured to the dark forest. "We could bump into more of them."

Vinko patted down his breast pocket for more smokes but found it empty. He slumped and looked at the cigarette he'd stubbed out on the ground, cringing. "Fucking Ustaše."

As they continued in silence, Nada fidgeted with the button at her wrist. She'd held on to that button for so long, she didn't know if she could ever let it go. Perhaps if she had something new to hold on to. Nada reached into her pocket for the red star she'd taken from the Partizan's body and pinned it through the leather string of her bracelet.

It was time to stop looking back. She had to turn her eyes forward. Toward Jasenovac. Toward her family.

"There's a house up ahead," announced Vinko, grounding Nada back in the present.

Sure enough, they found a lonely, rundown home the color of bleached bone in a vast stretch of valley. They crossed the quiet road and made their way across the grass.

"It looks abandoned," said Ester. "I doubt there's food there. Not that we're desperate for any yet."

"No, but look," said Henrik with a tone of disbelief. "There's a vehicle hidden under the trees."

"Then someone must be living there. No one who's fortunate enough to own a car would leave it behind."

Henrik trotted ahead to the dark green automobile while Vinko went to the house and peered through its dusty windows. He saw no point in taking half measures. Vinko slammed his shoulder into the door, breaking its weathered lock, and let himself inside.

Ester and Nada moved to join Henrik by the car. He already sat in the driver's seat, door hanging open, by the time they reached him. He continued to ignore her presence, but Nada busied herself with looking over the car's rounded edges—anything to keep him from noticing her discomfort.

Henrik's brows inched together. "They left the key in the ignition."

Vinko approached, rustling through the tall grass. "There's no food in the cupboards but they left most of everything else behind. Personal belongings. Clothes. It looks like they've been gone for quite some time."

Henrik turned the key, waking the engine with a scraping sputter. He tried again, but the vehicle still didn't turn over. "That explains why they left the car."

Leaving their possessions meant they must have fled in a hurry. Or perhaps they didn't choose to abandon their home but were taken from it.

Ester sighed in defeat. "We could have used this for tomorrow night."

"I could try to fix it. But it's too dark to see the engine."

"Then let's stay here for the night. We can get a good night's rest out of the cold, and you'll have tomorrow to repair it."

"Brilliant plan," said Vinko. "Except, there's only two beds in the house, and I'm not about to bunk with Ubica." He took Nada's hand, threading her arm through his. "How would you like to share with your slatko Vinko?"

Henrik stared at the thin steering wheel in front of him, his hand squeezing the leather.

Nada quirked her brows. "Slatko?" She hip-bumped Vinko with a laugh. He was many things, but she wouldn't exactly call him sweet. "And have your *slatko* cigarette-breath blowing in my face all night? No, thank you."

"How you break my heart, Miš."

Henrik averted his hard gaze to stare out the passenger window, his jaw ticking.

Vinko's eyes flitted to Henrik, noticing. "I suppose you'd prefer to bunk with Henrik then."

Nada's insides jolted and she stiffened. What was Vinko doing?

"And leave me to share with *you?*" Ester feigned complaint, her grin seeping through.

"What the fuck is going on here?" Vinko threw his hands into the air. "Everyone loves Vinko. You girls should be fighting over me, not fighting to get away from me."

"You know we adore you," said Nada, her eyes bright. "We just don't want to cuddle with you."

Vinko slapped a hand to the roof of the car and bent over to look close at Henrik. "Care to weigh in on this one?"

Henrik exhaled through his nose. "No point. I won't be staying here tonight."

"What are you talking about?" asked Ester. "Of course you are."

He shook his head and got out of the car. "I'm going to survey Pavelič's home and grounds. I need to see what we're up against and ensure we're prepared for whatever might be thrown at us. I'll be gone most of the night."

An unsteadiness grew within Nada, like the ground could shift beneath her at any moment. "You can't go by yourself." The first words she'd spoken to him since their fight. "It's too dangerous."

Henrik shoved the door closed, everything about him rigid and tense. "What else is a monster good for?" His eyes flashed to meet hers before he strode away to the abandoned house.

Nada's heart twisted and twisted. Vinko had asked if she would love him any less. No, she wouldn't.

But she *would* stop trying to dig up a boy who lay deep in the ground. Nada was done looking at Henrik through the lens of what he wasn't.

CHAPTER 23

Before

NADA LOST ALL SENSE OF TIME. NO ONE WAS SURE how long they had been waiting in the motionless wagon. Then again, maybe the lack of oxygen muddled their perception. When you had around a hundred and fifty people crammed into a single, coffin-like cattle car, breathing became difficult.

She swallowed, trying to moisten her dry throat. The sound smacked in her ears and set a twinge of shooting pain through her skull. With one eye almost swollen shut and her lip throbbing, the entire left side of her face screamed with pain. Her body, pounding with agony, grew stiff while standing in place for so long.

If only she could have turned the clock backward. If only she and her father hadn't visited her cousins, her aunt and uncle, they wouldn't have been captured by the Ustaše. They wouldn't have been carted away to the town hall, where they were forced to line up in a queue and receive violent beatings, one by one, before moving onto the train going nowhere.

The wagon jolted forward and clanked to a stop.

"They're hooking the carriages together," her father mumbled behind her.

Sure enough, the cattle car soon rolled and rattled along the railway tracks to the steady rhythm of chugging mechanisms. Captives swayed against each other in the darkness, not breathing a word to each other. What was there to say when everyone quaked inside, their heavy hearts beating toward the same shared fate?

After a far too brief journey they slowed to a stop again. Voices gathered outside before the rolling carriage doors were flung wide open, letting in a painful wave of floodlights. Nada jerked away, clamping her eyes closed. Fresh air rushed in, relieving her nose of the hot, oppressive smell of sweat.

"Out! Out!"

"Two and two together! Hold hands!"

She squinted to see what was happening beyond the beaming lights. Outside in the night, Ustaše swarmed—too many to count—on the flat, gravel grounds of a train station. They had been waiting for the cattle cars to arrive.

The passengers filtered out from the train as ordered, stumbling onto the rows of railroad tracks snaking by.

"Do not look anywhere!" shouted an Ustaša, a machine gun in his hands. "Keep your eyes straight ahead!"

With the surging of the crowd around them, Nada and Petar were swept out of the wagon together. Her father caught her hand, his fingers shaking where they locked with hers. Nada couldn't speak, her stomach a queasy, swirling storm.

Each pairing of captives was matched with an Ustaša soldier and directed in an orderly queue past the station house toward a Serbian Orthodox church down the road.

"Look straight ahead!"

A hand shoved against Nada's back, pushing her and Petar forward. Nada's lips trembled, her heart thundering. She didn't dare turn her head to search for her cousins.

"No!" a woman wailed behind them in the cattle car. "I won't go. I won't!"

The crack of a single gunshot rang out.

Nada flinched, her ears ringing as silence fell over the crowd. It drowned out the aches in her body, if only for a moment, before her hands began to sweat.

"Is that Emerik?" Petar whispered to her.

Nada looked at the Ustaša striding in the queue in front of her. Dark hair. Slender shoulders. Sharp jaw. He glanced over the captives, giving her a glimpse of his profile. She'd recognize the face of Henrik's Croat friend anywhere. He grew up in their village and had played in their home many times when they were children, often sitting to dinner with them during his teen years.

Nada nodded in reply, being sure to keep her focus ahead.

"Emerik," Petar called. "Hey, Emerik."

Nada's nerves jumbled and she squeezed his hand in warning.

Emerik turned to glare at her father.

"I'm Petar. Do you remember me? What are we doing here? Where are we going?"

The boy stormed over, whip in hand. Emerik gritted his teeth and struck Petar over the head—once, twice—as Nada cried out, grasping at her father while he tried to curl away from the beating. "I don't know anyone," he spat.

Emerik turned his back and continued forward with the moving line.

Panting, eyes blurring, Nada clutched her father's arm as he slowly straightened. A line of blood crawled out of his hairline. "I'm all right, srce moj. I'm okay."

Ahead of them, a cream-colored church rose from the ground, strange and foreboding for a place of peace. The spire-topped bell tower loomed as they drew closer, and the leafy green trees on either side of its entrance branched out in morbid welcome.

Were they being brought there to be forced into converting? If so, wouldn't they have taken them to a Catholic church instead?

As they marched up the stone stairs and through the

doorway of the church, one soldier said to another, "Go get the key so we can lock these corpses in."

A tremor sprouted deep inside her and, turning pale, she tightened her grip on Petar's hand.

Flickering candelabras splashed buttery light against the colorful and ornate walls. Arched paintings of prophets, archangels, and saints—framed between gilded embellishments —looked down at her as she crossed the tiled floor. A faded carpet runner trailed through the center, toward the elaborately decorated altar. There, a crystal chandelier hung lightless overhead.

Soul after soul, the Ustaše pushed the captives into the church. With the steady pouring of people, Nada and her father had no choice but to filter toward the back, where a small crowd already collected.

"Petar! Nada!" Her aunt broke free of the gathering, her face ashen and beaten.

Nada covered her mouth with her hand, tears springing to her eyes. As her aunt's arms crashed around her in a fierce hug—rousing the pain in her body—her uncle followed behind with her cousins, Milena and Brajan, by his side.

Nada closed her eyes and sagged against her aunt. They were all there. All alive.

An eternity passed as more and more people flooded into the church. Nada's family stayed together, drawing and pressing closer to each other as the Ustaše filled as many souls into the room as they could possibly fit.

Eventually the numbers stopped, and the doors closed with an ominous boom.

Nada glanced around her, heart hammering, as men and women shed muted tears—shoulders jerking, faces buried in hands. The palpable despair made her legs shake.

Nada knew the Orthodox church to be a place that would swell with the most beautiful and haunting chants—intricate melodies emanating an ethereal otherness. Now, it suffocated, weighed with fearful whispers and hopeless cries.

"What's going to happen?" Nada whispered to her family.

None of them answered. They didn't know either.

SOMETIME LATER A GROUP OF USTAŠE ENTERED THE church. They all looked the same—empty, soulless eyes and a callous turn of their mouths. They surveyed the horde, crammed into every corner and every free space in the building. The stillness in the room hung so dense that Nada's blood rushed in her ears.

"Have any of you here converted to Catholicism?" Dressed from head to toe in the dark gray uniform of the Ustaše, the soldier who spoke had one distinguishing feature to tell him apart from the rest. A brown birthmark branded the side of his neck. "We will let you go."

Silence. No one moved. And then, finally, two hands crept up over the sea of faces.

The men who admitted to their conversion wove through the crowd for the entrance and the Ustaše let them leave.

"Does anyone here have money?" the Ustaša continued. "We will buy you things with it, things you need. After that, you will be sent to work in forced labor. Do not fear. Whoever wants to get out is free to do so."

Nada's aunt inched forward, but her husband grasped her arm to keep her still. When he looked at her, a thousand words passed between them. Her uncle didn't buy it for a second.

A man adjacent to them raised his hand. The Ustaša waved him over and the Serb made his way between the captives, toward the soldiers waiting by the door.

The Ustaša with the birthmark gestured at the man when he arrived. "Turn your neck."

The man's hands shook but he did as was asked.

The Ustaša swung a knife, slitting his throat. "Sing!" he demanded.

But the man couldn't sing as his blood sprayed out of him.

The Ustaša leaned over him as he sank to the ground. "Fuck your Serbian mother." He dove forward to cut his throat again.

While the entire gathering of captives watched in horror, bile crept up Nada's throat. She wanted to close her eyes and find herself far, far away.

You will not die today, Nada. You will not.

And then, in unison, the Ustaše swept forward. Blades slashed and cut and sliced, and one by one the Serbs fell. More, and more, and more.

The room spun as sobbing erupted in the church—some of the voices threaded with panic, others with defeat. The crowd thinned near the entrance as the soldiers made their way methodically toward the rear of the building. The other Ustaše dragged bodies outside, but they couldn't keep up with demand.

A metallic tang hung in the air, filling Nada's lungs, and scarlet red flowed over the patterned tiles among a tangle of lost souls. Ustaše stepped through it like they were harvesting wheat, swinging their sickles as if all in a day's work.

Closer and closer, they cornered Nada's family. Fewer and fewer lives remained.

Petar gripped Nada by the arm and leaned into her, meeting her gaze with his pained brown eyes. "Hide, Nada."

She stared at him, unable to move, unable to understand. The world trembled, unstable around her.

Urgency rife in his tone, he jostled her. "*Go.*" It woke her up. "Find somewhere to hide."

Petar shifted his body in front of her to keep her from view. The hair on her nape prickled. With a speeding pulse, and using all the stealth she possessed, Nada slipped away, careful not to draw attention as she made her way to the back of the church. Stepping over the railing there and on to the altar, she squatted low behind the surviving pack of captives. With bodies already strewn across the low-elevated platform, she picked her way between them, afraid to step on any limbs.

An ornate and hefty cabinet stood against the wall, and Nada hastened to duck behind it. There, she laid herself among the slaughtered. Face down on the floor, feet layered over someone's legs, she loosened her muscles and let out a quaking breath. Willed her heart to slow down. She needed to appear dead. Her life depended on it.

Wet warmth soaked into her clothes beneath her, and pooled against her lips, her cheek.

I will not die today. I will not die today.

Keeping her movements minimal, Nada looked toward her family. The Ustaša with the birthmark approached them. He reached out for her aunt, and in one rapid move he took her life. He took Brajan. He took her uncle. When he moved on to Milena, she couldn't watch any longer. Nada's eyes clamped shut.

Dizziness whirled in the darkness there. It mingled with the growing numbness and the spreading abyss in her chest. Nada left her body, floating in some empty space where nothing was real. Where nothing existed.

Before long, it grew quiet in the church. Nada cracked open her eyes to slits. An Ustaša made his way through the building, stabbing each corpse with a knife, making sure they were all dead, while others paired up to carry the slaughtered outside.

Feet crossed into her line of sight, the soles of the boots inches from her face and rimmed with oily red. Nada didn't move, not even as he planted a foot on her back.

Another soldier came along and tap-tapped his boot against her head as if testing an automobile's tire. Pain lanced through her present bruises, but she embraced it. Let it course through her as she kept her body limp.

"Fuck their Serbian mothers. They're all slaughtered. Not one of them is alive."

"I'm still alive."

That voice. Nada's lungs caved, waking her from her numbed state. That voice belonged to her father. Nada's fingers twitched.

"Well, get up, then."

She looked at him as the soldiers turned their back on her.

Getting to his feet, her father flitted his eyes to her, a split-second move that made it clear. He had given himself up to draw them away from her.

The Ustaša with the birthmark joined them. "How do you feel?" he asked her father.

He glanced down at himself, spreading out his trembling hands. "You see how I look."

The Ustaša jerked his chin at his two comrades. "You two, hold him."

Nada could only watch with a quivering chin as the men grasped each of his arms while the other Ustaša claimed one of the flickering candles from a gilded sconce. He brought the flame to her father's moustache and his eyes, burning him till his face coiled with smoke. Nada bit down hard on her lips as her vision blurred with tears. He howled and howled, arcing his back to get away, and Nada could do nothing. She clenched her teeth against the urge to cry out, to sob and scream and writhe.

A man called out from across the building, "Slaughter that corpse already, and throw him among the dead."

The Ustaša blew out the candle, tossed it aside, and withdrew his knife. Nada let her eyes fall closed.

SILENCE WAS AN OCEAN—VAST AND DEPTHLESS. A place to drift weightless as Nada waited for the current to take her away from the blood and the corpses. But it never came.

She lifted her gaze again. Her father's arm laid outstretched against the bodies, his fingers motionless and half curled. A single tear escaped Nada's eye and spilled across the bridge of her nose before dropping into the red lake beneath her. She glanced down as it rippled waves across the surface.

But something small shone there by her own limp fingers, lost on the wet, slick floor of the church. How did it get there? What strange twist of circumstances occurred to bring it to her? Whatever the case, it comforted her to see it.

I'm not going to die today.

Nada shifted her hand and closed it over the polished, wooden button, clutching it tight in her fist.

From some distant recesses of her mind, Nada recalled a game. Ana liked to pinch her big sister's belongings and hide them elsewhere. Beneath her pillow. Between the pages of books. In the pockets of her clothing.

When the Ustaše finally came to carry her out of the church, picking her up by the arms and legs, she kept her eyes closed and her muscles loose as she swayed. Even so, the button remained safe in her hand.

Cool, night air whorled against her skin, and then her body swooped, flying as the soldiers let her go. She tumbled onto a pile of bodies—elbows and faces and knees sticking into her back.

A flaccid and heavy corpse dropped onto her. Followed by another and another. And though hot liquid trickled over Nada, though they encompassed her in death, she refused to make a sound.

"How many trucks have we filled now?"

"I think seven."

An engine rumbled to life, waking vibrations beneath her.

"Hey, wait! Don't just leave. We need to be careful. Go back in the church and make sure there's no one still alive first. And then when you go, make sure you never come back here. No one can ever know what happened."

"Mother fucking Serbs," spat another. "They won't all fit! Throw some of them into the other truck."

Pressure lifted off Nada's body as they removed the dead. Hands grabbed her ankles and dragged her off the truck. Her back and head smacked against the ground. White spots of light danced behind her eyelids and her head seared with agony, but still she kept silent.

I'm not going to die today.

They tossed Nada onto a truck again, and Ustaše climbed in around the dead. One perched himself by her face, another by her feet, and then the truck began to pull away.

THE EARTHEN, GREEN SCENT OF THE DEEP WOODS revived her, bringing acute relief to the overpowering rust-smell of blood drowning her senses. Once again, the Ustaše took Nada from the truck and threw her.

She thumped onto a new layer of corpses and there she remained, listening as body after body, soul after soul, landed in the space around her. Peering through the slits of her eyes, she glanced around. The watery, blurred figures of Ustaše moved above her as Nada discovered she lay in the corner of a sizeable pit, almost filled to the brim with the dead.

More trucks appeared from the veil of darkness and trees, parking alongside the pit. The Ustaše ordered people to exit them. *Live* people. Nada supposed these were victims they couldn't fit in the church.

She closed her eyes and let her mind hover elsewhere as cries and wails erupted—people begging for their lives, or mourning the torturous loss of their loved ones.

Eventually the world quietened. The Ustaše murdered them all. Every last one.

The black night hovered, watching over her as she waited. Certain no more waves of death would come, Nada inched her head up to look around. The trucks remained silent and still, headlights doused. Not a soul stirred or cried, the dead now forever frozen in time.

As slowly and as quietly as she could, Nada rolled over and crawled to the corner of the pit. Muscles stiff and sore, head pounding with a vengeance, she paid them no heed as she peeked over the rim of dirt.

There had to be forty Ustaše standing around talking with each other in the forest, many of them a few steps away. One of the closest carried a glowing oil lantern at his side.

One laughed. "I have to say, you're the most innovative Ustaša I've ever come across. There's no doubt about it. Nedelko Tomič is as merciless as they come."

Nada's gaze skimmed from the lantern, along the arm holding it, and past the Ustaša's shoulder, to find a birthmark on his neck.

The Ustaša who had killed her family, her *father*, smirked. "I am. And proud of it, my friend."

Heartache shook her bones, and she crushed the button into the skin of her palm. As much as grief wanted to pull her under, as much as she wanted to seep into the dead and fade away with them, Nada had made a promise to herself. Over and over.

She would not die today. She would keep holding on.

As silent as a ghost, Nada climbed out of the pit and disappeared into the darkness, unseen.

CHAPTER 24

A HANDFUL OF THE WEAPONS THEY HAD STOLEN FROM the Ustaša safehouse sat out on the dusty dining table. Henrik stood over them, taking stock of his choices by lantern light. He picked a machine gun, two pistols, and a few daggers to arm himself with. He'd stake out Vila Rebar soon, and part of him looked forward to it. To get away from the others for a while. To get away from—

Nada came out of her and Ester's room down the hallway. She stepped into the light, saw Henrik, and turned right back around.

He wet his lips. "Nada, wait."

She took her time turning. Wearing a tight expression, she wandered over to him.

Henrik picked up a sheathed dagger from the table and held it out to her. "To take with you tomorrow night."

She shook her head. "Henrik—"

"You can't walk into the party with your Schmeisser," he said. "You'll need something with you to protect yourself."

She lifted her hands, declining the dagger. "I-I can't."

"*Take* it," he said with gentle authority. "I know it makes you nervous. But you can get past it. You need to, for the sake of your survival." It didn't escape his attention, the way she froze up or trembled whenever he reached for his dagger, let alone used it.

"How do I get past it?"

"Detach from the way you normally see it. When *you* hold it, it's not something to fear."

"Okay."

"Try to think of it as a tool. No different than a wrench or a screwdriver. It's a tool that, when used right, gives you the outcome you need. It's just mechanics, Nada."

Her brow creased and her lips parted to speak.

Henrik didn't give her a chance to protest. "If you were ever to trust someone on the art of detachment, listen to someone who's taken a lot of lives."

That sense of smallness, of unworthiness, Nada had evoked in him earlier trickled back in like acid.

"I'm surprised you think I'm capable," she said, her words quiet, "considering how weak you think I am."

Henrik frowned, searching her eyes. "What are you talking about?"

"All you've done is tell me how dangerous this rescue mission is, how I'll get myself killed."

He let out a weighty breath, slowly shaking his head. "I've never once thought you were weak, Nada. Why do you think I fought so hard to keep you from going on this rescue? It's because I *know* you're capable. Because I knew, without a doubt, you would do what needs to be done. And that's what scares—" Henrik froze, his heart stuttering. He swallowed and dropped his gaze. Gathered himself. "The Ustaše are formidable. A large number of them are just as dangerous to me as they are to you. It was never a matter of you being weak. It's because I knew you would run toward them, no matter the cost."

Her chest rose on a deep inhale. "Oh," her voice rasped. She studied his face a moment. "I can be formidable too."

A soft huff escaped him as he tilted his head. "I know." He did, infuriatingly so. Henrik looked down to focus on the blade in his hand, then held it out to her. "I also know you're capable of using this dagger when you need to."

She nodded and accepted the knife with a steady hand. "I wouldn't know what to do with it, though," Nada whispered.

If Henrik was the monster she thought he was, then at least he'd be the monster who would teach her how to stay safe and alive. He took the dagger back and placed it on the table.

Moving closer, he gave her direction, his words slow and clear and mild, so as not to overwhelm her. "If you can, the fastest way to stop someone is right here." He reached into her silky hair and pressed his fingertips to her nape. It sent his heart racing. "Don't try it if you can't get a clean shot. It's harder than you think."

Her eyes held on to his, and Henrik tried to ignore the conflicting dance between his urge to pull away and the impulse to stay.

"Here." He placed his thumb against the pulse of her throat. It thrummed under his skin. "Don't slash or cut. You want to stab, angled, toward the spine."

She swallowed as Henrik withdrew his hand.

"If he has you in a struggle or on the ground"—he demonstrated by clasping her upper arms, bringing her closer until the speed of his pulse became unbearable—"strike up into the armpit." He took her right wrist and motioned the move for her. "There's an artery there. He won't think to guard it. But if he's wearing a thick coat, something that'll hinder you, aim where the crook of his leg is, near the groin. Like this." He jabbed her fist into his palm and swiped it downward. "Push down to sever the artery there."

Henrik shifted his hold on her wrist to take her hand. "The heart is hard to get to, so aim for the lungs." He pressed her fingertips below the ridge of his ribcage. "Stab right here, angled up beneath the ribs."

Henrik's wild heart thundered, trying to escape the cage of his chest. The strong instinct to recoil tugged at him, but despite that, he ached. Ached for closeness, for connection. For Nada.

"It's just mechanics," she repeated.

He gave her a single nod and looked into those trusting eyes of hers. He loosened his hold on her. Nada's breath wavered as her hand lagged from his body, but he caught it again before she got away. His heartbeat burst into a million pieces, ricocheting through him like shrapnel.

What was he doing? He dropped his eyes to her slight hand in his, to the bracelet she wore. He took the button between his fingers and stared at it for a moment.

His brows pinched together. "Why do you wear this?"

She drew in a slow breath. "Different reasons."

"Like?"

She listed them, one by one, taking a moment between each as though they held equal weight. "It was all I had of you. It's a reminder of a promise you once made. I thought, so long as I had it, you would be okay, and you'd come home in one piece. That *I* would be okay." She paused, eyes lowering. "It brings me comfort. That day under my bed with you, holding your button in my hand, I felt safe. When I wear it, I feel like you're there with me."

We all cling to something.

Aching still, Henrik ran his thumb over the button. He frowned, remembering the distance between them. The fight they had. "I suppose it means something different to you now." Perhaps a reminder of the Ubica, no better than an Ustaša. The poor replacement for who she really wanted.

He twisted the bracelet around her wrist, unveiling the red star there. Not even the button was enough for her anymore.

While Henrik grasped tight to the notion she was pulling away—moving on, as he wanted her to—he also wrestled with the burning desire to fix it. To be someone she wanted. Because he wanted *her*.

Nada shook her head, her brown eyes full of feeling. "The day I ripped this button from your coat, you promised you'd never leave me. Then I lost my father, and you abandoned me when I needed you most. I was furious with you and more hurt than you could know. But even then, it didn't mean something different to me. And it won't now either."

Her leniency, her heartfelt grace, slapped him to his senses. "It should."

Henrik couldn't allow himself to care about her. And that meant he couldn't allow her to care for *him.* He needed to be unforgivable.

Henrik hardened himself, sliding his cold mask into place before bracing to admit his most shameful secret. "I saw them take you, Nada. You and your father."

"What?"

"I watched the Ustaše take you, and I did nothing."

The rise and fall of her chest quickened. Her eyes welled. "Don't lie to me."

The cautious look of betrayal in her eyes punched a hole through his chest, but he deserved it.

Henrik forged on. "I watched you struggle to get away. Saw the man strike you across the face. I watched them force you onto the cart and take you away. And I didn't even try to stop them. Your father died because I did nothing."

Nada stumbled back, tears spilling free down her cheeks. Her face crumpled and she spun for the hallway. She barreled past Ester, leaning against the wall there, and went to her room.

Brow creased, Ester stared at Henrik. With an arm around her middle, her free hand clasped her necklace. She must have been there a while.

Henrik averted his gaze. Closed his eyes. It was time to get out of there. Henrik turned to gather his weapons, armoring up while Ester watched. He swiped his map off the table and stormed out the door. Out into the cold, inky darkness outside.

The chilled April air contrasted with the tightening fire in his chest. He staggered around the side of the house and sank back against the wall. Now that he could drop his mask, the agony rushed in. His lungs labored, pressed with the crushing regret, with the relentless wanting. He tore off his titovka and clawed at his hair. Swallowed back the swelling in his throat. And then he launched off the wall, slamming his fist against it.

"Henrik?"

His anguished eyes snapped up. Ester stood nearby in the moonlight. "Go back inside." He turned away from her so she wouldn't see any more than she already had.

She approached him anyway, her words quiet. "Was that really necessary?"

He schooled his features as best he could, but his mask wavered.

"I see what you're trying to do," she said.

He didn't have the energy for this. "Leave it alone, Ester."

She sighed. "You forget I was your friend once too. I know you, Henrik. Yes, you've changed. But no matter how hard you insist otherwise, it doesn't mean the boy we knew is gone completely. He's just different. Transformed. Nada's changed too. So have I. There's no escaping that in times like these. Even so, the foundation of our selves is still there."

"Is there a point to this conversation?"

"I've heard things. Seen things. I know you've felt the pain of loss before."

Henrik's gaze jerked to her. How could she possibly know that?

"I know you well enough to see it's made you afraid of losing Nada."

His face pinched. He looked away.

"Pushing her away isn't the answer."

"You can't push away someone who thinks so little of you. Who thinks you're a heartless monster. No different than an Ustaša."

"You know Nada's temper better than anyone. She says things she doesn't mean in the heat of the moment."

Henrik frowned. "She meant them, alright."

Ester sighed, shaking her head. "The two of you are as stubborn as each other."

He didn't want to talk about this anymore. "Are we done here? I need to get going."

Ester stepped closer to him. Her sad eyes held his as she touched a warm hand to his face. "Don't let your fear rob you. Love is a gift, Henrik. Not a burden." She lifted onto her toes and kissed his cheek before wandering back to the front door.

Henrik tried to quiet the ache flaring inside him. Because after the things Ester said, after he hurt Nada with his secret, he didn't know what he wanted more.

To protect his heart ... or give in to it.

CHAPTER 25

THE CAR BUMPED ALONG THE DIRT ROAD LEADING TO Vila Rebar, its headlights beaming through the close-knit forest. As they passed a concrete bunker on their way in, Nada's fingers strayed to her button bracelet. She stroked its surface, adjusted the collar of her dress, and swallowed. If this plan were to fall apart, she could die before she ever came close to saving her family. And she couldn't allow that. She couldn't afford any mistakes. Nada drew a steadying breath, taking in the leather scent of the car seats.

Even though Nada faced a perilous night ahead, Henrik rarely strayed from her mind. He'd avoided her all day. Had gone as far as staying outside after he repaired the vehicle, tinkering with the car's perfectly functioning engine with those sleeves rolled up, while Nada toiled with what he had revealed to her the night before.

She thought he was lying at first. Thought he'd found a new way to be cruel. But when the truth set in, it shocked Nada more than anything. And the sudden mention of her father threw her off-center. It awakened memories she preferred to keep buried deep down.

Henrik had said he'd done nothing when he saw them get

taken. Like he expected Nada would hate him for that. But she didn't blame him at all. There were Ustaše crawling everywhere. What could Henrik have possibly done?

Nada had done nothing too. Only it was much worse. Her father died before her very eyes, and she just lay there, unable to move or scream.

Like Henrik, there was nothing she could have done. But this time there was. And she would take control. Take action. Nada refused to be a helpless victim again.

She opened the satchel in her lap, double-checking that her Partizan star remained pinned inside of it. She couldn't very well wear it on her bracelet to the party, but it comforted her to know it was with her. It kept her focused on what mattered.

Nada brushed the skirt of the deep blue floral dress Ester insisted she wear—one of a collection they'd found abandoned in a closet. Ester sat in the backseat with her, ready to blend in at the party, wearing her own findings with her hair pinned up at the sides. Vinko rode up front in the passenger seat beside Henrik, both wearing the Ustaša uniforms they'd stolen.

As Henrik steered the car around a bend, Vila Rebar came into view. Vinko let out a long, arced whistle. Nada clasped Ester's hand.

The grand house nestled into a sloping hillside, its windows alight with a warm glow—a stark contrast to the evil gathering within. Woodland hugged the mansion, leaving the front with a stretch of space—filled with vehicles—before becoming forest again. The three-story mountain lodge rose from the earth with a stone base—a series of ivy-covered arches lining the veranda all the way around—and wood log upper stories, complete with balconies and smoking chimneys. Guests milled about behind the butter-colored glass of the two bottom floors.

Henrik pulled up in front of the mansion between an array of automobiles. While no guests wandered among the vehicles, the armed guards posted at each corner of the house didn't escape Nada's notice.

Ester squeezed her hand. "We can do this, can't we?"

Nada looked at her friend—a vision in her polka-dotted red dress with bouncing blond tendrils resting over her shoulders. She had buttoned her dress up to her neck, ensuring her Star of David pendant remained hidden beneath the fabric. "We have to. So we will."

"All right, ladies," said Vinko. "No point sitting here all night. We have some fucking people to fool."

Vinko had insisted on being the one to accompany Ester and Nada to the party, stating Henrik was better suited to keep watch over their exits. Should trouble arise, Henrik had the skills to take out any guards quietly and efficiently. And so it was agreed. Henrik would remain outside while the other three infiltrated Pavelič's home.

All four of them stepped out of the car. Vinko stared hard up at the mansion while Henrik lifted the rounded hood of their vehicle, pretending to tend to some mechanical issues as planned.

Henrik bent over the hood, hands braced on either side of him, and his eyes went to Nada. Lingered on her. He'd done that a few times since she'd gotten dressed for the party. She didn't dare hope it meant something.

She moved to pass him, but he clasped her arm, fingers sliding gently over her skin, stopping her. He held her gaze with intensity. "If something doesn't feel right, if something goes wrong, you keep your head down and you walk out of there. Do you understand? Don't risk it."

Nada simply stared back at him, caught in the snare of his attention. In those blue-gray eyes that dove into hers, turning her knees to water.

His fingers pressed. "Promise me. Tell me you'll leave if something goes wrong."

Nada cleared her throat and drew the strap of her satchel higher over her shoulder. "I will."

His hand slipped away, eyes remaining glued to her, leaving Nada dazed as she staggered toward the mansion.

Ester hooked her arm through Nada's and led the way

through an ivy-covered arch. Vinko stayed close beside them. An Ustaša stood at the front entrance, welcoming them as they walked right through the doorway. Vinko's uniform worked as they'd hoped.

Laughter and chatter greeted them as the tinkling of piano and a man crooning in English played from a brass gramophone in the corner. A thin veil of tobacco smoke hung in the air, lingering within the wood paneled walls of the mansion. Women gabbled in groups—their party dresses an array of color against the muted tones of the men's uniforms—Ustaše and Nazis celebrating together. A tray of drinks passed them, but Nada couldn't even think about consuming anything. The enemy surrounded her.

She drew in a shuddering breath as they weaved through the crowd, moving deeper into hell. Shadows twisted and coiled around the guests' feet—darkness swirling in their presence as they laughed and smiled. How could they celebrate like this, as though evil and hate didn't drip from their limbs and hearts to pool on the floor?

And then there he was, visible through a gap in the crowd. Ante Pavelič. The Poglavnik. The pretty music lifting the room warped and wandered to some far-off distance.

The middle-aged man stood tall, shoulders back and chest out, as he listened to the conversation of one of his men. Dark hair brushed to one side. Neatly pressed uniform. He could have been mistaken for any normal man if it weren't for low-set, triangular eyebrows hanging over deadened eyes and the creases forming around his scornful, thin mouth. The man *was* shadow. Darkness bleeding darkness. She sensed it all around him.

An itching heat raced under Nada's skin as her eyes simmered, cold and hard. It would only take a single bullet to the head. One shot and the leader of the Ustaša regime would be gone. Farewell, Poglavnik. But though Nada fantasized about the possibility, it would be fruitless either way. Another would rise up and take his place. The regime would live on. Diseases weren't easily cured.

"Try to rein in that anger," Vinko murmured by her ear. "People will read you like a damn book."

She snatched away her gaze, eyelids fluttering as she dampened the hardness in her features. Doe-eyed and pale beside her, Ester stared at the man. At least Nada wasn't the only one affected by him. With a relaxed face, Nada let her gaze roam over the guests swarming around them. But her mind stayed glued to Pavelič. That man was the reason for everything: Nada's fear, her worry and pain. He had ripped away everyone she loved. His presence was a severe reminder of why she risked her life to be there.

Nada would hold on like hell to the rest of her family. No matter what.

Boisterous young voices cut through the din.

"And how many Serbs have *you* killed? Surely not as many as I have."

"I've lost count," said a boy. "But I must be around the six hundred mark."

"That's nothing," boasted another. "I know of a man who cut the throats of over thirteen hundred in one day at Jasenovac."

"Horseshit!"

"It's true."

Nada's stomach twisted. She fought to remain calm, to keep her pulse at a steady beat. Her gaze swung to look at them. A band of Ustaše, not much older than she, stood in the wooden archway leading to a deep red dining room. One of the young soldiers, with his hands in his pockets, watched her with interest.

Nada didn't miss a beat. She played the part of a handsome boy's fancy, giving him a coy smile and turning away before he could see her blush. But instead of blushing, she wanted to be sick.

It was then Vinko paled and pivoted to face the other way. He kept his gaze away from Nada's direction. His unsteady hand grabbed a glass of wine from a passing tray. "Pretend you don't know me or hear me."

Vinko took a sip as Nada's shoulders stiffened. She kept her eyes trained on Ester. Too nervous to be aware of the sudden tension between her friends, Ester's wide eyes flitted about her surroundings, searching for any threats as her fingers rubbed at the hidden pendant beneath the neckline of her dress.

"My brother is here," he told Nada. "He's fucking spotted me. You need to go get the map without me. Now."

Nada recalled Vinko's story. His brother had threatened to kill him. "I can't leave you alone."

"I had a feeling he would be here after we found the boy with the star cut into his forehead. Now's my chance to talk to him, but you need to go before he realizes we're together and you lose more than your map."

A young Ustaša with dark, curly hair threaded his way between the guests, curious eyes darting over Vinko's form. Over his Ustaša uniform.

Of course. Vinko could pretend he'd joined the Ustaše. It would keep him safe. But two strange girls at his side would raise questions. Nada didn't falter. She leaned into Ester's ear to whisper it was time, and they made a move toward the staircase.

A voice, similar to Vinko's, carried behind her. "Do my eyes deceive me? Have you finally come to your senses?"

Anything else said between them melted into the din as Nada and Ester neared the carpeted stairs. Henrik had said they'd find Pavelič's office upstairs on the northern side of the house. How he knew that in such detail she didn't know, but she trusted it.

Halfway up the stairs, Nada glanced back at Vinko and his brother. Both engaged in intense conversation, though Vinko's body language read far more ardent as he leaned toward Stipe, hand against his chest.

When someone on the landing above uttered the word "Jasenovac" in conversation, Nada's ears prickled. She tried to catch more fragments of it beneath the layers of noise.

"Oh, no, they eliminate most of the children ... they're only Serbs ... rid of the next generation ..."

All blood drained from Nada's body as the back of her neck prickled. She gripped the strap of her satchel until her fingers bleached white. Her breaths deepened, igniting a feverish energy that shook her bones.

"Where's Vinko?" asked Ester when they reached the landing, finally noticing he wasn't behind them. "Why isn't he with us?"

Mind swimming, Nada looked out over the railing at the crowd below. Something flashed in Stipe's hand, held low and discreet. A pistol.

Nada told Ester she would give her last breath to save her family. That she would kick and scream and claw till her fingers bled. Never had those words coursed truer through her soul. Because right now, Nada would burn down hell itself if she needed to—and dare the devil to run.

"He's staying downstairs," said Nada. "To make sure no one follows us."

If we want to find our families, we let nothing get in our way.

HENRIK'S STUDY OF THE GROUNDS LAST NIGHT HAD been thorough. He'd created a careful path to the house, out of view of the concrete bunkers littering the property and the armed soldiers within them. From the darkness, he'd watched Pavelič pacing before the glass doors of a lit room on the third floor, trimmed with a balcony. Bookshelves lined the walls inside, and Pavelič held papers in his hands. It didn't take much to deduce it was his office, and the likeliest place to find the information they needed.

The bunkers weren't the only surprising feature Henrik had found during his surveillance. He stumbled upon a tunnel opening in the thick of the woods. He'd explored and discovered a complex system of passageways sprawling beneath Vila Rebar, stretching farther into the bowels of the mountain. He didn't venture far, however. Who knew what he would find down there—or if he would ever find his way back out?

Henrik now leaned over the car engine, pretending to reach into it as his eyes skimmed the building, checking on the guards. He scoffed under his breath, noting the way his position reflected an earlier moment. One that had taken place beneath a shady tree, by an abandoned house.

The breeze had lapped against his skin, and birds had trilled as the setting sun cast dancing light over the hood of the car. Working on the vehicle all day, Henrik had maintained a safe distance from Nada while he wrestled with his feelings. He replayed the night before over and over in his mind, his frustrations ratcheting along with his tools. As hard as he tried, he couldn't stop thinking about her. About the way her pulse raced against his thumb. The shape of her mouth as she had said, *I felt safe.*

And then she stepped out of the house in that dress, her hair falling softly down her shoulders. The wind picked up, tossing strands of it across her face. Her fingers tugged them back, lingering at her temple, and those fathomless eyes lifted to his. Settled on him. The golden sunset spilled across her cheek, lighting her red-painted lips. Henrik's hands had tightened on the hood as his chest dipped. It had hurt to breathe.

Henrik now shook his head, rubbing a palm against his sternum as he refocused on the mansion. He needed to keep his wits about him. The Ustaša by the front door checked his watch and called out to the guard along the archways. The two met by the entrance, exchanged a few words, and the Ustaša went inside. Henrik continued to tinker with the engine as the guard made his way around the house to the far back corner and began speaking with his other comrade. A tiny flame flared in the darkness there, followed by the two glowing ends of cigarettes. Their voices muttered away in the stillness.

Now was his chance. Henrik retrieved their stolen sack of potatoes through the open car door and crouched behind the automobile next to him. He took a spud and wedged it as hard, and as deep, into the exhaust pipe as he could. Then, moving from vehicle to vehicle, he blocked each and every exhaust. If anyone had the notion to follow them after the theft, every vehicle parked outside the mansion would stall out. He made it to the final car across the yard, far from their own automobile, and wedged the potato into place.

Footsteps crunched against gravel nearby.

Henrik tossed the empty sack under a car and ducked low, hands pressing against the rocky ground. Held his breath, waiting.

The footsteps paused, and the scent of tobacco drifted on the air.

The guard turned on his heel. "Ništa," he announced and started back for the mansion.

Henrik's eyes closed as he exhaled. With more care, he crept between the vehicles, then back to their own. Sneaking through the open door, he pretended to step out of it, as though in the car the whole time.

But the guards paid him no attention as a canvas-covered truck traveled up the driveway, an Ustaša at the helm.

Henrik straightened, trailing the truck's movement. He and the others had the uniforms for their Jasenovac plan. But an army vehicle? That was something they lacked.

With quick and casual movements, he ducked under the hood of his automobile and disconnected the spark-plug wires.

When the truck parked, half a dozen raucous Ustaša soldiers hopped out of the back, chattering and laughing as they headed for the mansion. Henrik's eyes stayed on the driver as he climbed out and dropped the key into his jacket's hip pocket —the last soldier to make his way to the party.

Henrik called out to him. "Excuse me, comrade. May I trouble you for a moment?"

The soldier turned and took him in—no doubt seeing a clueless young man in need of help—and approached. "Car trouble?"

"Yes, I don't know why I can't get it started. Do you know anything about engines?"

"A little." The man leaned over the motor to inspect it. "Ah, here's the problem."

"Would you mind showing me how to fix it? In case it happens again."

"These here have come loose." He picked up the end of a wire.

Henrik feigned interest, inching closer as he tilted forward to get a better look. He pointed at the wires. "That's all it took to stop the motor from working?"

With the man's attention diverted, Henrik pickpocketed the key and tucked it into his own jacket.

"They're such small things," mused Henrik.

"Small but vital." The soldier reconnected the wires. "That's all there is to it."

"I appreciate your help. Enjoy your night."

"Za dom—spremni." *For homeland—ready.*

"Za dom," Henrik echoed the salute of the Ustaše.

As the Ustaša strolled away, Henrik reached back in and yanked the wires out before closing the hood. With a smirk, his gaze drifted to the military truck—his prize.

But two figures marched out of the house's entrance, and Henrik stilled as he recognized one. Jaw stiff and brows knotted, Vinko marched ahead as an Ustaša followed behind, holding a pistol to his back.

Henrik's pulse skipped and tension coiled in his shoulders. The soldier directed Vinko toward the forest behind the house, taking him deep into the night. Something was horribly, horribly wrong. Henrik's focus went to the mansion. Nada was in there surrounded by enemies. If she was captured by them ...

His heart squeezed and his hands fisted. Henrik stalked across the yard toward the mansion, attempting to slow his gait so as not to draw attention. But if anyone looked close enough, the tightness in his features and his rapid-falling breaths would give away his urgency.

His all-encompassing fear.

⁂

It didn't take long before they found Pavelič's office door near the end of the dim hallway, made darker still by the decorative wood paneling and red patterned carpet.

Nada's hand paused on the handle. Before they ventured down the hallway, she caught sight of Stipe close behind Vinko, pushing him toward the entryway. Her heart pounded for him, but she also knew Henrik would be at his post by the car. He would see Vinko and save him.

Nada hated to lie to Ester about it, but she would worry for Vinko and insist on turning back to help him. Nada couldn't allow it to stall them. The means to save her family, her defenseless little sisters, was within reach. She wouldn't let go for anything.

"Are you all right?" asked Ester, noting her hesitation.

Nada nodded, taking a quick look down the hallway. The only faces she found were stationary and framed on the wall. Together, they snuck through the door and Nada quietly closed it behind them.

Henrik's information proved accurate. They found Ante Pavelič's office, no mistake. A large desk sat in the middle of the room, adorned with a hefty typewriter, a telephone, and a brass lamp with a green glass shade. Framed paintings and rows of bookshelves lined the walls on either side, while glass doors led out to a pitch-black balcony.

Nada hurried toward the desk and searched the papers scattered on top as Ester made her way to inspect the wall of shelves.

"I saw part of your lesson last night," said Ester. "With Henrik."

The lesson that had made Nada weak in the knees. Her fingers touched the sheathed dagger strapped to her thigh under the fabric of her flowing dress. Henrik wanted her to bring it tonight, and so she did. For him. Even so, her hands remained steady, her nerve solid. She had Henrik to thank for that.

There was something about his calm, methodical instructions and commanding presence that settled her. The movements he had demonstrated with assuredness and fluidity left her awed. It reminded her of the ease with which he handled his weapons, and the trust in his own ability to wield them. The weapon didn't control Henrik, he controlled *it*.

And his faith in her, that she could take a dagger and use it without fear, made her want to rise up to meet it. There was power in that.

Nada played coy. "Did you learn something useful?"

Ester looked over her shoulder as Nada slid the drawers out, riffling through them. "Maybe. But it had nothing to do with weapons."

Nada pretended not to care, but she burned with the need to know. Ester knew she would, which was why she dangled it in front of her, waiting for Nada to take the bait.

"Okay, fine. Tell me."

Ester fidgeted with the corner of a book she'd taken from the shelf. "I think you really hurt him when you called him an Ustaša."

Nada's heart sank. She had suspected as much.

"Normally Henrik would know better, and he'd brush off something you'd say in anger. You say a lot of things. But this one hit a nerve."

Nada wilted. She opened her mouth to speak.

The door swung open. An Ustaša stepped in—the young soldier who had watched her from the archway.

CHAPTER 26

IT WAS ALL ABOUT TO SLIP THROUGH HER FINGERS. Her family. Her rescue. Her chance.

The Ustaša surveyed Nada, frozen with her hands in a drawer, and turned his focus to Ester. She stood within his reach, mouth agape, her hands paused mid-sweep behind the rows of books. His eyes narrowed, and with a dark smirk he shoved the door. It slammed and Nada flinched, launching her heart into a gallop. The Ustaša snatched Ester's arm and wrenched her away from the books, throwing her across the room as if she were light as a feather. She crashed into the desk's corner and yelped, but she pivoted, grabbed the telephone, and whirled, striking the man's skull with it.

The world around Nada spiraled slow. Sluggish. Infinite.

A conversation from days ago surfaced in her mind.

"There's no way we can go up against the Ustaše alone."

"I know," said Nada. "But if it comes to it, you should know, I'll do it anyway. I'll always choose them. I'll choose my family."

Ester met her eyes and nodded. "And as I promised, I'll be right there beside you."

Her sestra was with her. Always.

Hand to head, the Ustaša staggered, unhurried, to straighten and face Ester again.

It wasn't over. Nada could still find the map. And Ester had her own dagger beneath her dress. She would fight him off.

Snapping to action, she riffled through the bottom drawers of the desk, scattering papers and tossing books aside. She slammed them closed when they proved fruitless and turned to the bookshelves. Her fingers groped the spines in a frantic fashion, eyes darting to every nook and cranny.

Nada spared a glimpse to check on Ester. The Ustaša smacked her across the cheek. She cried out, scrambling backward until her back bumped against the wall of books. Nada gasped, her gut wrenching. He stalked across the floor, hands outstretched to grab her. Ester's fingers twitched, reaching for the hidden blade at her thigh.

Nada hurried, tackling the shelves again as her gaze fell on a quaint painting, displayed between the books, that had been knocked askew. From behind it peeked a metal door. A safe.

Nada launched at it, taking the painting off the shelf as sounds of struggle carried on behind her. The dial stared back at her. Henrik's father had a safe, and as children they used to see who could decipher the code and unlock it the fastest. She hoped it would be that easy again.

She leaned in to press her ear to the cold metal, shutting out the noise in the room, and turned the dial. *Tick, tick, tick, tick, click.* Pulse racing, Nada forced herself to draw a steadying breath. To calm down. She continued through the motions, careful and concise, until the lock unlatched.

Nada turned the knob and swung the hatch open. She tore through document after document, ignoring wads of money and velvet jewelry boxes until she spied the word *Jasenovac.* She snapped up the wadded paper and unfolded it. There it was, a map of the concentration camp. And tucked within its creases, Nada found more written documents. She didn't waste time reading them, but words like *train schedule* and *factory* jumped out at her. With quick, shaking fingers she folded the whole lot up again.

"I have it," she uttered, fumbling to cram the papers into her satchel. "Ester, I have it!"

Nothing answered but a strange quiet.

Nada spun and came face to face with the Ustaša. Her blood ran cold.

Grabbing her throat with both hands, he squeezed and squeezed. Nada fought to pry his hands away, digging her sharp nails into his strong, unrelenting arms. She tried to gasp for air, but her lungs wouldn't budge. Nada's eyes bulged, her mouth gaping open in a silent cry. Her hands slapped and scratched and pushed frantically at the man. Where was Ester?

Tiny, bright spots bloomed and glittered behind her eyes, awakening a startling, out-of-body clarity. Nada couldn't die. She needed to save her family. Save herself. The instinct to fight back ravaged through her. With a trembling hand, she hiked her skirt over her thigh and wrapped a hand over the hilt of her dagger. With blind frenzy, she jabbed the blade into his side. He grunted, but she hadn't stabbed deeply enough.

The office door flew open. Footsteps stormed across the floorboards, and Henrik appeared behind the Ustaša, eyes wild, neck corded. He grappled his arm around the soldier's head and, bracing it with his other hand, tilted and twisted. The loud pop turned Nada's knees to water as the Ustaša collapsed to the ground, and she fell forward, gasping and coughing. The dagger remained in her hand—only the tip stained red.

As Nada's lungs grated to draw air back in, she sheathed her blade and looked to the other side of the room. Ester lay sprawled and motionless on the floor. Ice trickled down Nada's body, and she crawled over, but Henrik beat her there, face drawn.

He checked Ester's pulse and a breath loosed from him. He tapped at her face. "Ester, wake up. Ester."

She stirred, wincing before turning her head to peer up at Nada.

Tears welled in Nada's eyes as she slumped forward, pressing a hand to her forehead. She almost lost her sestra. How stupid she was to make such a feeble-minded choice in the heat of the moment. She should have helped her when the Ustaša came in.

Henrik darted back to the door, checked the hallway, and closed it, locking it shut.

"Are you okay?" Nada fretted, brushing Ester's hair from her face. "I'm sorry, Ester. I'm so sorry."

Ester reached up to touch the back of her head and grimaced. "I'm all right," she breathed.

Nada tilted her gaze up to Henrik, who stood utterly still as he stared at her, his eyes glazed over. The muscles in his jaw twitched.

"I have the map," she said. "We need to go."

It nudged him to life. "Not before we hide him and clean this mess first." Henrik made his way to a door by the bookshelves and found a closet hidden behind it.

Nada frowned. "We should go now, before anyone finds us."

"If we leave and someone finds this mess a moment later, every man in this house will hunt us down like dogs."

He was right. If everything seemed in order, it would at least buy them enough time to escape back to their abandoned house.

Henrik grabbed the soldier by the arms and dragged his body across the floor. Nada helped Ester to sit up. She stood on shaky legs, her jittery fingers brushing down the folds of her dress. As Henrik pulled the body into the closet, Nada hastened over to grab the Ustaša's legs and helped to stuff him inside. She glared at the Ustaša folded in the closet. He could have killed Ester. Could have killed *her*. The longer she looked at him, the more her gut simmered. The man had his hands around her throat. Had control over her. Made her feel powerless.

Every muscle in her body burned. Toughened. Her fists curled until her nails dug into her palms. Nada swung her leg back and kicked him in the side. Pain shot through her toes, but she gritted her teeth and booted him harder. Grasping the doorframe, she kicked him again, and again, and again, her breaths frantic and loud in the silent room. For every nightmare she endured, every strike she suffered, every drop of blood spilled, for every hurt and loss and gasp of heartache that wrenched from her lungs, she beat him. She beat him with all the might she possessed.

Henrik grasped her arm. "Enough."

She stopped and looked at him from beneath the disarray of her hair, panting in rapid, feverish bursts.

He held her gaze firm. Steady. "He can't be killed twice, Nada."

Her recent perception that his blue-gray eyes were often cold and emotionless dissipated. Because right then, she understood him. A ferocious fire consumed this new Henrik, the same fire burning through Nada that very moment.

But while Henrik kept it contained beneath intensity and control, Nada couldn't wait to unleash it.

If Nada hadn't lashed out at the dead Ustaša like she had, Henrik might have. Killing him hadn't been enough, though Henrik *did* find cold satisfaction in the snap of his neck. He latched onto the solace of that as the three of them hurried to tidy the room and leave it as they found it. As soon as they were done, Henrik informed the girls that he'd witnessed Vinko being taken away at gunpoint.

"As soon as I saw him, I knew something was wrong and came straight here," he told them.

Ester shuddered, hand flying to her chest. Nada sank into the office chair, staring at the wall of books, and remained silent.

Henrik gave the room one last glance. "Time to go. I don't think we should leave the way we came. I know of a hidden exit." He made his way across the room. "I'll lead you out of here."

When Henrik had explored the tunnels beneath the mansion, one in particular led him to the kitchen—dark and vacant at such a late hour. That would be their escape now. Henrik didn't know what had happened for Vinko to get caught, but he wouldn't risk traipsing the girls out through the front door.

"Are you sure we shouldn't exit through the party instead, and act as if we've nothing to hide?" Nada's voice rasped after having her throat crushed.

Henrik turned away to hide his faint wince, doing his best to appear unaffected by it. "For all I know, Vinko's captor has posted more guards at the door, or sent men to look for us in the crowd. Our best bet is to get out as fast as possible, from a place they won't be patrolling."

"Which is?" asked Ester.

"The kitchen."

"You don't think the three of us sneaking into a kitchen will look suspicious?"

"There'll be fewer eyes on us that way," said Henrik. "And less dangerous ones. It's likely we'll only come across the staff, and they won't think much of our presence."

Nada twisted her bracelet around and around her wrist, her brows drawn together. "We can't leave Vinko behind."

He shook his head, lifting a hand to keep her from barging forward with any risky ideas. "I'm getting you two to safety first. If he's not at our meeting point, I'll double back for him."

Henrik cracked the door open and peered through the gap. No one walked the hallway. He gestured for the girls to come and stepped out of the office. They strolled toward the stairs, Nada quickening to his side as they descended the two flights. She hooked her arm through his, for appearances' sake, he assumed, and chattered about inane subjects like the weather as they passed the guests milling about.

Henrik glanced over his shoulder as they reached the bottom floor. No one followed.

Passing around the edge of the mingling guests and gaiety, Henrik led them into a hallway where a door flung open as a waiter burst through it carrying a tray. Henrik marked his movements from the corner of his eye. The man turned his attention to their group, eyes flitting over them as they walked away from the festivities, but in the end, he melded into the party to carry out his job. Henrik released a tense exhale.

Once through the door, the kitchen staff bustled around them, too busy to pay any notice to the three strangers. Pots and pans clanged, cooks barked orders to waiters, and the scent of roast chicken and vegetables taunted him as they rushed toward the back. There, beside a well-stocked pantry, Henrik opened a door. The moment he ushered the girls down the cement stairwell, a burly, middle-aged woman cleared her throat. The kitchen-hand eyed them, her gaze darting from him to the girls and back. Henrik plastered on a roguish smile for the woman. He winked and brought his finger to his lips, making her see nothing more than a scoundrel Ustaša with dishonorable intentions sneaking two beautiful girls out. Fists on her hips, the woman shook her head at him, and Henrik closed the door behind them.

The brick blocks and cement of the arched tunnel stretched along to their left and right. A thin gutter cut straight through the middle of the tunnel floor, complete with patches of stagnant water, making the air smell stale and dirt-like. Though dim inside—the lightbulbs along the low ceiling few and far between—enough light glowed for them to see their way. Which also meant they were visible, and therefore vulnerable in such a confined space.

Henrik remained alert, eyes sweeping forward and behind as they crept in silence through the passage. He led them down to the left, then the right, through a series of orderly, straight corridors. Moving from shadows to light to shadows again.

He glanced back to check on the girls. Nada watched the ground as she walked, her hand lightly bracing her neck. Henrik turned back around, letting his face darken at the vacant tunnel ahead. The Ustaša had been merciless. The man's fingers had pressed so tightly into her throat that her skin around them had turned white. That split second, when Henrik walked in and found her like that, a raging heat he'd never known before burst inside him, alive and writhing.

It simmered down after he killed the man. But when his eyes had fallen on Nada, weakened and gasping on the floor beside Ester, it altered. The heat gave way to a slow, cold prickle, lifting the hair on his arms, crawling through his seams. He'd failed her again.

Men's voices swelled and bounced through the tunnel.

Pulse racing, Henrik gestured for the girls to hurry ahead. They turned a corner and he guided them into an indented space, exactly where he remembered it would be, used as a storeroom of sorts. A few stacked boxes sat by the entrance, but toward the back stood a tall wooden shelf housing crates upon crates of rakija and vino.

They slipped behind the shelf and pressed against the cool stone wall, cloaked in the shadows of hundreds of bulbous bottles.

The voices grew louder. Henrik's pulse thundered harder.

The nearing footfalls scuffed against cement, and Nada flinched beside Henrik. The same way she'd flinched in a certain house in the woods, sandwiched between a wall and some furniture, much like this. A place where the sound of footsteps made Nada grow pale. Where she had grabbed at his shirt and started to panic.

Henrik grasped her hand and tried to steady her with his eyes. Though, after the last time, he doubted she trusted him to keep her grounded anymore. He'd told her he was playing a part. Giving her a fantasy so her hysterics wouldn't get them caught. No wonder Nada thought so little of him.

Henrik's eyes lowered to the redness ringing her neck. A heavy pressure sank onto his chest, making it hurt to breathe. A wave of protectiveness surged through him. Never again. He'd never fail her again.

Nada's gaze softened, recognizing the traitorous emotion twined in Henrik's. "I'm okay," she mouthed, assuring him.

He forced himself to turn and stare out at the tunnel between the rows of bottles.

Nada's thumb lightly brushed over the back of his hand. His lungs ached in response.

Scraping footfalls came to a stop as two Ustaše entered the storage room. Henrik stiffened, his heart pounding in his temples.

"What do you think? Two bottles enough?" one asked.

"Take a third and keep it for ourselves for later. He won't miss it."

They chuckled and helped themselves to a crate on the middle shelf. Ester's eyes widened as she and Nada froze against the wall. A small patch of light filtered through the now-empty space to light the stone between the girls. Henrik readied himself, muscles tensing, prepared to attack if it came to it.

Then the Ustaše's shuffling footsteps carried them out and back down the tunnel.

None of them dared to breathe as they waited for complete silence, for safety. While they remained tucked in the shadows, Henrik closed his eyes and let out a wavering breath as he squeezed Nada's hand, still delicate and warm in his.

THE FAINTEST OF STARLIGHT ILLUMINATED THE opening of the tunnel ahead. Fresh air whispered its way inside, rippling against Nada's face and dress, mingling with the stale scent of the stone walls. With the forest in sight, she walked faster. Vinko was out there somewhere, in danger. Nada knew Henrik and Ester were unaware the Ustaša with him was his brother. And only Nada knew Stipe had threatened to kill him once.

Yet she couldn't bring herself to tell them.

Her stomach knotted. She hoped Vinko had escaped his brother somehow. Her desperation to find her family meant she had made too many poor choices tonight. The only thing that had gone right were the maps she carried in her satchel.

Nada rushed forward near the end of the tunnel. Henrik grasped her shoulder to stop her before she could go barreling out into the open. He held up a hand in signal to her and Ester. They waited for him as he crept to the opening.

Henrik observed the woods for a minute, listening for any sound, watching for any movement. They encountered nothing but the crisp, green scent of nature. He gave them a nod, and they immersed themselves into freedom again.

It didn't take long to descend the sloping hillside, and Nada waded through grappling twigs and long grass until she stepped out onto the dirt road—their meeting point.

She spun on the spot, peering into the dark distance, searching every shadow. Nothing but silence.

She braced a clammy hand against her creased forehead. "We have to go find him."

"I'll go right now," said Henrik. "You two start walking down the road, but if you so much as hear a rustle in the grass, hide. Vinko and I will catch up. I stole the keys to an army vehicle, so keep an eye out for it."

Nada moved toward him, shaking her head. "I'm coming with you."

He swung away, wincing, and wiped a hand down his face. Then he stepped close to her, clasping her arms as his chest rose and fell faster. He leveled his intense eyes with hers. "*No*, you're *not*. You're staying with Ester. There are armed soldiers in bunkers all over—"

The clap of a single bullet fired, echoing through the forest.

Henrik paled, turning in the direction of the mansion. Ester covered her mouth, eyes glistening.

Nada's heart stopped. She staggered backward. "No." A rush of breath escaped her as a sharp pain lanced through her heart. Her eyes, fixed wide, locked onto the dark divide of forest between her and Vinko. The ground swayed beneath her, causing her knees to rattle. A sob, waiting to burst, expanded hot in her chest. Tears flooded in. "No, no, no, no, no, no." She erupted, chugging as she charged blindly for the woods.

Strong arms caught her and wrapped firmly around her middle.

She struggled against Henrik's hold and cried though her teeth. "*No!* Let me *go!*"

"It's too late, Nada," Henrik murmured, voice cracking. "We're too late."

"*Please.*" Her cries tilted into wails.

"Sssh. I'm sorry. There's nothing we can do. I'm so sorry."

Nada sagged against his chest as she fell apart, unable to hold herself upright any longer.

"You need to get going." Strain colored his voice in her ear. "I have to go back for the truck before there are Ustaše crawling all over the place."

How many more loved ones could she possibly lose? Nada's heart had already hollowed out until there was nothing left but a pulsating husk—frail but enduring. What would happen if its thin walls caved in? Would it cease beating? Or would it continue to stubbornly persevere, no matter how crumpled or ruptured or mangled it became?

CHAPTER 27

Before

THE ACHE DIDN'T FADE. DIDN'T LEAVE HIM AS HENRIK looked at the shovel in his trembling hands, his chest heaving. The metal had dents in it now, and violent scratch marks, but it was still intact. Solid. It was still useful.

Henrik's mind sharpened. He didn't have his father's rifle, but he had the shovel. And it had been enough to chip away at the brick of his house.

Would Henrik really give up because his father was a coward? Because he wouldn't help his son? He clenched the handle tight. No, he wouldn't.

He didn't waste a second. He didn't give it another thought. He ran.

Take them to the town hall.

That's what the pillaging Ustaša had said. Henrik knew where they would be and so Henrik sprinted hard, feet pounding against the road toward the next village. As long as he kept fighting, there would be hope. And he didn't care if he died trying, he would get to Nada and save her.

Henrik reached the street that led to the town hall when the chuffing of a train drew his eyes toward the station. Cattle car after cattle car rattled over the tracks there as they snaked away into the distance, Ustaše buzzing at the station from where it had departed.

He stumbled to a stop. His shoulders slumped. *No. Please, no.*

Henrik knew, deep in his gut, the Serbs they had corralled were on that train. He lifted his chin, allowed himself to gulp a few breaths, and then Henrik slunk away into the village, taking a roundabout way into the woods where he could follow the tracks, out of sight of the Ustaše.

Henrik jogged for hours along the train tracks, slowing to catch his breath at times before speeding up again, never once letting go of his shovel. Night descended and crickets chirped. His feet and his back ached. Exhaustion screamed through his body. Still, he ran.

Soon, a new village unfolded before him. A new station. The train he followed sat silent in the darkness, cattle car doors wide open and empty. But the nearby rumbling of vehicles pulled him forward. Ustaše milled about ahead, down by a cream-colored church. Multiple truck headlights beamed, throwing light onto its walls and casting tall silhouettes of the figures sweeping around them.

I'm coming, Nada.

Henrik kept to the shadows as he crept closer, ducking behind vacant buildings. He darted across the street to the foot of the church grounds. He slipped into a small grove of trees there and hid behind the bushes to peer beyond.

And he jolted as a shock punched through him.

Bodies upon bodies were piled high in the trucks. All of them drenched in violent red. With too many of them to fit, two Ustaše dragged the dead from one of the vehicles. They grabbed the ankles of a body and slid it off the pile. A girl thudded to the ground, covered in blood from head to toe.

Nada.

Henrik stopped breathing. All feeling, all warmth, drained from his body. His ears rang and reality warped.

The Ustaše lifted her flaccid body and tossed her onto another truck, out of his view.

Henrik crumbled and fell to his hands and knees. With shaking palms against cold grass, brutal gasps sawed in and out of his throat. His face contorted with the crushing pain in his chest, and then he heaved. Retched and retched into the bushes until there was nothing left inside, and still his body tried to expel more. The groan of the trucks accelerating drowned out the helpless sounds of him breaking.

He was too late. He was too late. He was too late.

Henrik dug his fingers into the soil as he shattered. A vital part of himself had been taken, ripped from his bleeding chest. It destroyed him. He'd failed her. She was gone.

Somehow, in a haunted daze, Henrik picked up the pieces of his remains and staggered away from the church. Went back to the train tracks, welcoming the darkness. The silence. Body wracking with sobs, he followed them home. One hand gripping at his aching heart, the other holding fast to the shovel.

HENRIK COLLAPSED ONTO THE DARK STOOP OF HIS house—drained enough for his body to stop moving, but not enough to end the heartache. He sat there, unable to go inside, enduring waves of grief that threatened to take him under. Was it possible to drown without water? He wanted to. Only emptiness stretched out before him now. Life would never be whole again. And it hit him, all over again, that Nada was gone. A vicious cycle, rousing another painful throe, another teary grimace.

He didn't know how long he sat there, steeping in his suffering, when the shuffle of footsteps had him glancing up. A teetering figure, framed in moonlight, made its way along the street. Nearing his house.

A strange tingling crawled over Henrik's skin. He stood. Stepped closer.

A face, bruised and beaten, lifted to look at him.

Nada?

His heart flew into his throat, and he stumbled toward her. His face twisted. Fresh tears welled in his eyes. He couldn't believe it. It was her. But how?

His arms reached out, needing to feel she was real, and the moment he touched her face, Nada's legs gave out and he caught her to him. He scooped an arm under her legs and picked her up.

"Nada," he breathed, brows furrowed and eyes glistening. With a thick swallow he took in the sight of her dark hair hanging ratty and limp down her shoulders. The rust-scented blood that saturated every inch of her. She clutched at his collar, gazing up at him—her wildness and her fire now bleak and depleted. "I've got you. I'll take you home."

He carried her down the street in the deep silence of night. Nothing existed but the two of them—her warm breath against his neck, his footfalls against the pavement. He had her. Alive and in his arms. But how long would that last? As long as the Ustaše continued to ravage and murder, the world wouldn't be safe for her.

The immense pain of losing Nada still lingered, and Henrik never wanted to experience that again. He'd sooner die. He'd sooner bleed. He'd sooner fight.

Maybe that was all the hope he had left. To fight for a world —a life—she deserved.

Henrik tightened his hold on Nada and pressed her closer to him. Nothing mattered more. He would fight for an end to the madness. And he'd do whatever it took, for as long as it took.

Like the shovel he'd smashed against his house, Henrik would chip away at the enemy.

CHAPTER 28

Henrik parked the truck beneath a shadowed cove of trees by the abandoned house, keeping the vehicle hidden from view. When he turned off the engine, a silence as thick as fog rushed in to swallow them. Starlit leaves rustled outside the window as a steady breeze lapped at the glass, and the engine ticked away as it cooled from their getaway.

Nada peered sideways at Henrik. His hands wrung the steering wheel, and his throat bobbed up and down. He lurched at the door to fling it open and stumbled out. It slammed closed and Nada flinched, causing her eyes to prickle.

She climbed out of the passenger side and joined Henrik and Ester in standing around like statues, the long grass wavering about their ankles in the wind. Nada couldn't believe Vinko was gone. Her heart ached from the loss, heavy and insistent. She hadn't known him long, but she had come to love him dearly.

Henrik's shoulder blades slumped back against the house and his knees gave out, dragging his body against the brick until he sat. He wiped a hand over his face. "I wish I knew how he got caught. What went wrong."

Nada looked at Ester. Eyes downcast. Arms wrapped around herself. She didn't know either. Only Nada did.

She swallowed back the tightness in her throat. "His brother Stipe was there. He saw Vinko. He was the one who took him away at gunpoint."

Ester glanced up at her, her lips parting.

Henrik's brow knotted. "You saw this happen?"

"When Vinko realized he caught the attention of his brother, he told me to go find the map. And I listened."

Ester's arms fell to her sides. "You knew he was in trouble?"

"I thought he was safe. He was dressed as an Ustaša. I thought he would convince his brother he was one of them now."

"But you never said a word of this to me." Ester's voice was small, but her eyes were large, burning a hole through Nada. "When we made it upstairs, I asked you where Vinko was. You told me he was staying downstairs to make sure no one followed us."

"I was afraid you wouldn't go through with it. That you'd give up everything if you knew."

Her arm slid around her middle as she looked away, her free hand splaying at her collarbone. "So you lied to me?"

Henrik's eyes hardened. "You lied to Ester and fed Vinko to the wolves."

Nada grimaced. "I was doing as he asked."

"We could have helped him," said Ester.

"Did you..." Henrik glanced away. Clenched and unclenched his fist. "Did you let him go as some sort of sacrifice to distract the enemy?"

Her shoulders dropped as she took a step back. Did he really think her capable of something like that? "Of course not. It wasn't like that. And we needed those papers."

"The papers." Ester's brows drew together, her gaze falling away in thought. "When I woke up in the office you had the map already. You kept saying sorry. Why were you apologizing, Nada?"

A soundless sob wrenched from her chest, but she squeezed her eyes shut and fought it back with a thick swallow. "It's not how it sounds. When the Ustaša came in we were about to lose our chance to get the map. I thought you had a handle on it, so I hurried to find the papers. I thought you would be okay. You had a dagger with you."

Henrik stood. "She *wasn't* okay. She was knocked out cold when I arrived."

Ester lowered her chin, shrinking.

Nada would never forgive herself for it—that one fleeting moment of human error in the chaos. She settled her watery gaze on her best friend. "Ester, you know I'd never let anything happen to you."

"You *did* let something happen to her."

Nada's cheeks burned. She angled away from them, arms curling up to wrap around herself.

Henrik's hands fisted as his body turned rigid. "What happened to walking out of there if something wasn't right?"

She looked back at Henrik and lifted her chin through blurry eyes. "Ester and I have been in this together from the beginning. She knows we can't let anything get in our way. We were *both* fighting for our families in that office. And if it were me who was attacked first, I'd want Ester to carry out the plan no matter what. That map is important. It was the whole reason we came here. Even Vinko knew that."

Henrik ripped off his Ustaša hat and threw it to the ground, eyes flaring. "And now he's dead. Ester was unconscious. *You* got hurt. You were so caught up in your desperation, all you cared about was your stupid map! Do you have any idea how much worse it could have gotten back there?"

Nada's chest tore open at his words. At his anger.

"You could have died!" A fleeting ember of stricken emotion pulsed through his outrage. "Everything would have been for nothing."

Her brow pinched. "What?"

He squeezed his eyes shut, turned his face away, and swallowed hard. "You shouldn't have left Vinko like that. You should have made the hard choice right then and there to forget about the map and keep you and everyone else safe. You should have aborted the whole plan. Like you promised me you would."

She shook her head, biting down on her lips. "You saw the Ustaša take Vinko away. Why didn't *you* go after him?"

"Because I chose *you*, Nada!" Henrik puffed and clawed his fingers through his hair, leaving it in a tousled mess. "I ran to save you instead."

She scrubbed her face, rough and fast. "How many times do I need to tell you, I don't need you to save me? I can save myself. I've done it enough times since you abandoned me to prove that."

Henrik looked at her as though she had stabbed him in the chest.

Nada turned to Ester, pleading. "You understand, don't you? We agreed. We have to get our families back."

She glanced up, eyes glistening. "I didn't have a handle on it, Nada. Far from it."

Her heart sank as Ester let herself into the house and quietly closed the door. The color drained from her face. What had she done? How had she messed up so horribly? Nada stared at the grass around her feet for an eternity. It rippled and waved at the mercy of the whirlwind around it. She needed her sestra by her side. Always. But Ester had walked away from her, hurt, and without a hint of forgiveness. Did she hate her? Nada couldn't stand it. Her breaths tightened as her body grew too hot. She wavered on her feet.

"You could have died tonight," said Henrik, his voice low and rough.

"But I didn't."

"You're being reckless because you're too desperate. This is all getting too dangerous."

She folded her arms around herself. "We knew it wouldn't be easy."

"Wouldn't be easy? Nada, tonight was *nothing* compared to what we'll face in Jasenovac. I know you're smart enough to already realize that. Which only makes it clear to me *you're* willing to take a huge risk like that, but I'm not."

"What are you saying?"

"I'm saying forget Jasenovac. I'm done. It's over."

She frowned. "No. It's not."

"Do you want to die like Vinko?"

Nada winced, averting her gaze.

"Because you won't be as lucky as him. You won't get the mercy of a single bullet. I've heard stories about that place. Of what they do to people there. To girls like you. Is that what you want? To run right into their trap and be mutilated, violated, and God knows what else?"

She fought back the tears threatening to rise. "We can find a way."

"I know this is hard, Nada. I know it's awful to give up on your family like this, but the odds aren't in our favor. We're not going. We can't. It's time for you to make peace with that. I never should have entertained this in the first place. And I wouldn't be surprised if Ester wants to back out too."

Nada shook her head. "We promised each other."

"Ester was overpowered at a *party!* You think she can handle Jasenovac? She can't even fire her weapon for fear of hurting someone. You need to let it go."

Nada looked at Henrik, her heart wrenching. "I've lost my father. I've lost Vinko. Ester is upset with me. For all I know I've lost her too. I've even lost you. And now you're telling me I'm going to lose my mother too? Ana? Maša?" Strands of Nada's hair danced across her face. Her skirt licked around her knees. Henrik remained silent. "Don't you *care?*"

Henrik held her gaze, then spoke in a flat tone. "No. *Ustaše* don't care about anyone."

CHAPTER 29

NADA CREAKED THE BEDROOM DOOR OPEN AND PEERED inside. Curled up on her side on the bed, Ester wept, her tears reflecting Nada's.

"I'm sorry, Ester," she whispered, her words catching in her throat. "I'm so, so sorry."

"I'm not going anywhere, Nada." Ester patted the vacant half of the bed, beckoning Nada to join her.

She closed the door and climbed into the space in front of her, the springs of the mattress squeaking from the movement.

"I won't leave you." Her oldest friend locked her fingers through Nada's, trying to still the tremors in them. Ester sniffed, forcing a smile through her tears.

"How can you stay by me when I've hurt you this much? I've been unforgiveable."

"I'm not upset because of *you*, Nada. I'm upset because of me."

"What do you mean? I left you to fend for yourself."

"I would have done the same," Ester said, shaking her head. "I'm glad you carried out the plan. That you found the map. You were right when you said we can't let anything get in our way."

Nada's brow creased. "So what is it?"

"That's just it. We can't let anything get in our way." She slowly shrugged as fresh tears spilled. "What if *I* get in our way? I'm not like you. Like Henrik. I failed to protect myself tonight. Even you know I'm not capable of these things. It's why you lied to me about Vinko. Because you were worried I'd become afraid and wouldn't go through with our mission."

"No, that's not why—"

"This whole plan, what we're doing, it's so much bigger than me. It terrifies me, Nada."

Nada clutched her hand back, her wooden button brushing against Ester's wrist. "We're all scared."

"No, not like this." Her chin wobbled. "I'm not so sure you should let me be a part of it. I'll only be a liability. I'll fail you."

"That's not true."

"I panicked in that office. I reached for the dagger but the thought of taking someone's life ... I couldn't go through with it. I hesitated. I really did try to fight back with all my might. But how can I maintain my compassion, my humanity, if I choose to kill someone? I'm afraid I'll lose a part of myself I won't get back."

Ester—the epitome of compassion—wouldn't be herself without it. Nada's brow wrinkled, her eyes brimming with sadness. "Ester—"

"And if I can't surrender that, then how can I succeed with this rescue?"

If there would be a rescue at all after tonight. Henrik had declared it over, not that Nada had agreed.

Ester inched forward on her pillow. "Because if it comes to it, I don't know if I have what it takes to save my family. To help you save yours."

It hit Nada like a ton of bricks. The sheer enormity of what she expected from them. How could she drag these people—her dearest and oldest friends—into a fight *she* had decided to chase? A fight that would put them at risk and in a position for Nada to lose them too. After Ester shared her side of it, Nada couldn't blame her for her trepidation.

Her sestra had come as far as she possibly could with Nada. Had pushed beyond her boundaries and remained at Nada's side through all of it, as promised. But it was time Nada remained by hers.

"There's not going to be a rescue, Ester." Her heart tore in two as she said it, bringing on the sting of tears. "This is as far as we go."

Ester's voice choked with emotion. "No."

"Henrik won't help anyway—"

"*No.* You're wrong." Ester wrapped her free hand over their adjoined ones. "The rescue is going ahead, and it's going to succeed."

Nada's chin quivered.

"Listen to me, Nada. Do you know how I know we'll succeed?" Ester held her eyes with sincerity. "Because of *you*."

Her words stunned Nada into silence.

"That fiery streak in you lends to fierce determination, to intense focus on what's important. I could barely fight back tonight. But you? You never give *up* fighting. Not for our whole journey here, for *both* of our families. You're relentless and I admire you for that—for the part of me that's lacking. You're capable of so much more than me, sestra. How can I let you give up, when *you'll* be the one to triumph in rescuing my parents?"

Nada closed her eyes, pressing tears free.

"Nothing gets in our way, remember? Not even your doubts. I won't let them."

They stared at each other across the pillow, a breath of hope apart.

"Do you want to know why I refuse to take off my necklace?" Ester asked. "Because it's a reminder that King David was successful in defeating armies much greater than his own."

With a small shake of her head, Nada splayed her hand against her chest. "Have I ever told you you have a way with words?"

A faint smile crept over her sestra's features.

"And what of *your* doubts, Ester? You *are* capable. Of so much. There's more to this rescue than needing the ability to fight and kill. You're important to our success in different ways. If one of us gets hurt, your medical knowledge will be a huge advantage. And you have a level head on your shoulders. You're the calm. I'm the storm."

Ester's smile grew.

"You're always the voice of reason," Nada continued. "The compass that keeps us on course, aimed toward what's important. You keep us from making poor choices."

"Stupid choices," she clarified with raised brows, grinning wide. "*Pigheaded* choices."

Nada chuckled. "See? I admire *you* for the part of me that's lacking."

Ester laughed and wiped the tracks of tears from her face. She nodded and settled into her pillow. "What about Henrik?"

"What about him?"

"I can help you convince him to follow through if you want. But honestly, I think you should be the one to do it. You need to talk with him."

Nada's gaze lowered. "I tried. He said he doesn't care about me."

Ester sighed. "He pushes everyone away because he cares *too* much. But he'll open his heart for you. You just need to try."

An ache stirred in Nada at the thought. "How can you be so sure?"

Ester smiled. "I've been a side character to the Henrik and Nada story for a long time."

Nada's face dropped. Had she really made her feel that way?

"I don't mind," she said with a laugh. "In fact, it's been a beautiful show. The two of you were always a force nothing could contend with. I've always felt lucky to be a part of it."

Nada half-laughed, thinking of all the fights they'd had. "I'm sure you haven't felt so lucky recently."

"Well, yes, I *have* always been partial to a happy ending. And I've yet to see one."

"I wouldn't hold your breath."

"Oh, please." She grinned. "This is the first time you haven't denied your feelings for him. It's coming."

A fluttering spiraled in Nada's chest. "I miss him."

"He's right here, Nada."

"He might as well be oceans away."

"Only if you let him be."

Nada rolled her eyes, smiling. "And you say *I'm* relentless."

Ester chuckled, rolling onto her back. It made the mattress bounce.

Nada shifted to get comfortable. Her mood sobered as she picked at a loose thread on the blanket beneath her. "I think you're right. I hurt him when I called him an Ustaša. I *wanted* to hurt him because he hurt me."

Ester turned her head on the pillow, meeting Nada's gaze with softness, nodding.

"I've been awful to him. I fought so hard to make him who I wanted, I never took the time to really see who he *is*."

"So take the time."

Since the moment Nada had stumbled upon him outside the Partizan camp, Henrik had been cruel and distant. Had battered her heart more times than she could count. But when she peered beneath the surface, truly glimpsed at things closer, she found … *Henrik.*

He had protected her, saved her multiple times. He came with her on this rescue. Shared a blanket with her and eased her bruising with his cold hand. He trusted her judgement and her plans of escape. After she panicked that day behind the stairs, he never once looked at her like she was broken or ridiculed her for being weak.

But Henrik was also different. Grown up. He had shouldered the burden of burying the Partizan boy himself. The other Partizani respected him, and Jakov clearly counted on him.

He gave Nada the knowledge to defend herself and believed in her ability to do so. He was strong and confident and fierce.

He was achingly beautiful.

Her heart stirred and her breaths deepened. Nada couldn't let it go a second longer. She needed Henrik to know she accepted him and valued him as he was.

CHAPTER 30

HENRIK SAT ON THE EDGE OF HIS BED IN THE DARK, rubbing at the burn mark on his forearm. He watched the silhouettes of trees dancing and undulating against the midnight sky through the window in front of him. He didn't want to think about Vinko, but he couldn't ignore the unnerving sorrow hammering at his chest. Henrik wasn't supposed to care about it. To feel *anything*. Henrik had been so careful. He formed no friendship with Vinko. No laughter was shared. He only spoke to him when he had to. Henrik did everything he could to avoid a connection with him. So why didn't it work? Why did it hurt?

Henrik swallowed and yanked his thoughts away from Vinko, only to settle them on Nada. She had promised him. Reassured him if something went wrong at that party, she would walk out of there. And then she hadn't. She'd barreled through the way only Nada would. The way he feared she might.

He slumped forward, raking his fingers through his hair as he rested his head in his hands. She had come so close to getting herself killed tonight. Henrik almost lost her. If he hadn't gotten to that office on time, if he'd walked in a minute later... His breath quaked as it left him. He had no choice but to put a stop to the madness. To make her forget about Jasenovac.

A quiet knock rapped at his door. He glanced over his shoulder to find Nada opening it—a murky figure in the shadows, pausing at the threshold. "Can I talk to you?"

He sighed and turned back around. "I'm not going to change my mind."

"I'm not here for that."

Was something wrong? He looked to the side. "Is Ester okay?"

"She's fine. I practically interrogated her on how she was feeling. She swears she's okay. Just a bump on the head."

He nodded, staring out the window as she closed the door. Her footsteps hushed against the carpet as she drew closer.

"I wanted to say I'm sorry about Vinko," she murmured behind him. "For a moment there I forgot you've lost him too. And I ... I didn't want you to be alone."

"No need." He stood, his gut crawling with discomfort. "Vinko wasn't my friend. I barely knew him." Henrik rounded the bed to head for the door.

"Where are you going?"

"To do a perimeter check."

She grabbed his arm as he passed, wrinkling her brow. "*Stay.* Fight with me if you have to."

"You think I *want* to fight with you?"

"Maybe *I* want you to. I'm partly to blame for Vinko. Stay and yell at me."

He narrowed his eyes. "First you say you don't want me to be alone, and now you say you want me to fight with you?"

"It's better than nothing. If the only time I can talk to you is if we argue, then I'll take it."

Henrik huffed. "What do you want to talk about, Nada? How tonight was such a failure? You want me to console you over the loss of your new boyfriend?"

Her jaw dropped. "My what?"

"Talk to Ester about it. That's what girlfriends are for."

She closed her eyes as she shook her head, then pressed her face into her hands for a moment. "I can't even tell you how wrong you are. Trust me when I say I'm not Vinko's type. *Wasn't* his type."

"I suppose all that flirting was my imagination then?"

"*Yes.*"

He scoffed and wandered back to the window, keeping his back to her. "I don't want you here, Nada. Go back to your room."

"Why do you do this?" Her words cracked. "Why are you so cruel to me? Do you really not care about me anymore? Are we not even friends?"

He let out a dark half-laugh. "You don't care about me either. Let's not pretend otherwise."

Who would *want to find an ubica? A cruel, heartless monster. Who would* want *that?*

"Are you sure about that?" Her voice came from closer behind him. "Because the last time I checked I prayed for you every day. After you left, I couldn't sleep for weeks because I worried for you. Anything could have happened, and I wouldn't have known. I wondered, daily, if I would ever see you again. Does that sound like I didn't care?"

Her words pulled at his chest, the strain building until he trembled and fisted his hands against it. She needed to stop talking like this. It only made him *feel,* and he needed distance now more than ever.

She tugged at his arm, forcing him to face her. Her eyes, dark and shining, darted between his. "Or what about the fact that it *hurt* me?"

The ache in him intensified. He broke away from her gaze, but her grip on his arm pinned him in place.

"You left me when I needed you most."

Like a caged animal, breathing hard and pacing, Henrik wanted to claw at the bars and escape her words. "Get out of—"

"You were always an anchor for me," she forged on, inching closer. "And you left me untethered. I felt your absence as though you *died*. You have no idea what that feels like. That kind of loss."

He wrenched from her hold, grimacing as his pulse raced. He glared at her. "I don't know what that feels like? For an entire night I believed you were dead. So don't tell me I don't know about loss."

Stunned, her eyes searched his face.

"I went back for you. Followed the damn train they took you away in. I ran for hours to get to that church, only to see you dead in a pile of bodies." His eyes turned glassy as his chest hitched up and down. "You think I don't care about you? I became *who I am* for you, Nada. This thing you hate! The Ubica. The monster. I wanted to make a world where you would be safe. You were the whole reason I became a Partizan."

Her eyes welled. She reached out for him. "Henrik—"

"Don't." He pulled away.

"If you cared about me that much, then why are you cruel to me?"

When he didn't answer, she approached him. He turned his face away, and she clasped his shirt to keep him there.

"Why do you hate me now?"

"Nada, please."

"*Tell* me."

His breaths heaved, bordering on agony. "Because I never want to go through that again. If you mean nothing to me, it won't hurt to lose you."

Her hands dropped from his shirt. She backed up a step, brows knitting together. "So you were doing it to push me away? You were hurting me so I'd never hurt *you*?"

He couldn't look her in the eyes.

"I didn't mean it when I called you an Ustaša. I never truly thought of you as a monster for a second. But now I'm not so sure."

His chest coiled tight. When she moved away, he let her.

Heading for the door, she paused by the dresser. Nada stared at his titovka, resting there. She reached out to touch the star, then glanced back at him. "Tell me one thing, Henrik. If I *had* died tonight, would you have been fine?"

He clenched his jaw against the truth pounding through him with each painful beat but didn't answer. Nada took it as one, though, and her lips parted on an inhale. Her eyes flooded, glistening in the dull starlight.

He paled, lowering his head. The hurt in her expression drained all the fight out of him.

"No, I wouldn't be," he murmured. Lifted his gaze to her. "I'd be the furthest thing from it."

Losing Nada would shatter him. Of course it would. Pushing her away, keeping her at arm's length didn't work, like it hadn't worked with Vinko. So what was the point anymore? All that cruelty and harshness now seemed senseless.

Her voice wavered as she spoke. "Then your plan was a waste of time. And at my expense. Well done, Henrik. You've lost me anyway."

His stomach plummeted as she turned for the door.

"Wait." He surged after her, catching her hand before she could leave.

Even if losing Nada was inevitable, he'd rather keep her close, to soak up every glorious minute with her. Hadn't it always been what he wanted? What he *still* wanted?

Nada was a gift, not a burden.

His heart thrashed and his hand shook around hers. "Stay. Fight with me." His eyes blurred with moisture. "I deserve for you to rip my heart out."

Her eyes fell to the ground, as if attempting to resist his persuasion.

"I'm sorry, Nada." He stepped close. He brushed his finger under her chin. Asking. Begging. "Don't go. Hurt me like I hurt you."

She finally looked up at him. "Why?"

"Because as long as you stay here to fight with me, I'll still have you." With nerves firing, he traced his fingers along her jaw to settle lightly against her cheek. "Because you have *me.* All of me. You always did. Always will."

Her eyes locked onto his, tempered with tenderness. Henrik

gathered his courage. He cradled her face and delved his fingers into her hair. His entire body thrummed electric when she didn't pull away. Henrik had wanted to belong to her for as long as he could remember. But never had that yearning moved so deeply—so intensely—like a grinding shift beneath the surface of the Earth. Monumental. Pulsing. Powerful.

"If you don't kiss me now, Henrik, so help me I'll—"

He dipped his head and grappled her lips with slow, restrained fire. His brow furrowed from the radiant, warm ache overwhelming his heart. A pain that hurt so good he wanted more of it. Henrik snaked his arm around the curve of her waist and drew her against him. He became a bundle of senses in the dark of the room. Only her body, and the way she melded into the shape of him, existed. The fabric of that damned dress, so soft against his palms. Her gentle hands roaming his chest before grasping his shoulders.

Everything in Henrik burned for her. He couldn't believe she wanted him like this. Until now, every thought of Nada had been wishful. Dreamlike. Yet here she stood in his arms, clinging to him like he was air and she was drowning.

And he let her. Henrik could never push her away again, even if he wanted to. Not after this.

KNEES WEAK AND HEART THUMPING, NADA FELT A sunburst spiral through her entire body. Henrik's hand nestled in her hair, and his arm was firmly locked around her, pressing her to him as if he hungered for it. Chasing after the headiness his touch gave her, Nada continued to reach blindly. She grasped the shirt at Henrik's waist, keeping him there. Trapping him so he wouldn't go. So he couldn't escape if he wanted to.

All that time she had spent denying her feelings for him, brushing off Ester's teasing comments, had been because she thought Henrik didn't care for her. Because her childish humiliation prompted her to hide it. She had no idea of the sacrifice Henrik had made for her. And she'd unknowingly thrown it back in his face during a stupid argument. Had crushed his selflessness under the heel of her boot as if it was of no consequence. And it killed her.

Henrik let the kiss go and inched away, still close enough for Nada to feel his warmth. He remained silent, his chest moving in time with hers, arm sliding back to rest his hand on her hip. A hurricane of emotions swirled behind those blue-gray eyes. She wanted to reach in and snatch one from the gale, to see what he felt so deeply.

"Don't you dare push me away," she warned.

His face tilted. Lips—light as a whisper—brushed hers, then pulled back. His shaking breath skated through her parted mouth and teased her tongue. Her grip tightened and her brows knotted, straining with the need for more. With both hands, she reached for his jaw and lifted to her toes to claim his mouth again, eyes falling closed. His kiss deepened and fire raced through her bones at his responding intensity.

Henrik's hands slid around her waist, and the fabric of her dress was so thin she could feel the heat of their trail. His arm hooked around her back. A hand skimmed down to grasp her thigh, and he lifted her, cradling her tightly against him. Her sharp breath rushed into his mouth, and he placed her on the dresser.

Nada broke away, breathless, stripped of all hesitation in the dark. Her hands found their way to his top shirt button, where she proceeded to undo them, one by one. Henrik's kisses drifted light against her temple, her jaw, her neck, showing no objection to her advances. She tipped her head back, inviting more. His mouth and breath made her shiver. Made her toes curl. When she untucked the shirt from his slacks, Nada's palms braced the hot skin of his heaving chest, then slid them lower, unable to get enough of him.

Henrik found her lips again, and gliding a hand over her knee, he slipped beneath her skirt, along her thigh. He met the sheathed dagger she still wore. Pulling away to look down, he pushed the fabric up high enough to make her heartbeat skitter.

He ran his fingers over her leg, over the weapon, as if marveling at it. "You took it with you."

"You wanted me to."

He brought his gaze to hers. "But you didn't kill him." It wasn't an accusation but an observation.

"I tried to. It was harder than I thought. I didn't put enough strength into it. But I will next time."

Was it surprise and admiration that flickered in his eyes?

"I'm done being afraid, Henrik."

He softened. Drew a slow breath. "Me too."

He unbuckled the weapon for her and let it fall to the floor. He reached around to scoop her closer to him, prompting her knees to latch around his hips. She took in the sight of his solid body as he fumbled with the buttons running down the front of her dress.

Nada's lips twitched. She couldn't help herself. She raised a brow. "It's just mechanics, Henrik."

With a quiet, simpering laugh he dropped his forehead against her shoulder. His hands moved away to grip the dresser.

It made her smile. "My Ubica can disarm a man in two seconds, but give him a button..."

He drew back, looking at her with a crease in his brow, his breaths shallow. "*Your* Ubica?"

Her heart twinged. Nada hated that she had hurt him the way she had. That she ever tried to make him feel ashamed for it. She slipped her palm against his face. "You became an ubica for *me*, didn't you?"

He nodded, slow.

"Then you're mine."

His throat slid up and down in a swallow as the words hung between them. As his eyes shone and his furrow deepened.

Nada sank forward and kissed him to burn away any shame or hurt that might have remained inside him as she finished unbuttoning her dress. Henrik slipped it down to her elbows so he could touch his lips to her shoulder and lingered there—as if he needed a moment to collect himself. His warm breaths washed against bare skin as she reached up to cup his nape, fingertips curling into his hair. If Henrik belonged to her, she wanted to belong to him too.

Her heartbeat quickened. "Take me to the bed," she whispered.

He stilled, but Nada wouldn't have it. She took his face in her hands, meeting his mouth in a way that defied contestation. Henrik picked her up. Moved blindly as he turned. Laid Nada down on the bed and positioned himself above her. With one arm braced by her head, his other hand glided up the side of her body, drawing goosebumps in its wake. He paused when he touched the cotton seam of her brassiere and broke their kiss to keep himself from going further.

Nada skimmed a hand over his chest, past the heart thrashing beneath his ribs, her fingers trailing up his neck until coming to rest against his cheek. Henrik leaned into her palm. She wanted more of this. More of him.

"Please don't stop. Don't pull away."

His throat moved up and down against the edge of her hand. Nada leaned up to brush his lips with hers, gentle and purposeful and sweet, asking and tempting him to stay with her. A rush of breath left him, along with his resolve, tension slipping from his body as he allowed himself to let go.

They moved together, exploring beneath a blanket of heady darkness, coming to know the feel of each other—all senses crackling where sight was lacking. Losing time and all thoughts of past and future. So much spoken—not with words, but tenderness and want.

CHAPTER 31

In the gray light of early morning, Henrik stroked Nada's temple, brushing her hair back from her face. She hadn't taken her eyes off him for some time as she lay beside him —both resting in silence, needing no words. Content to just be together. Like their night at the river's edge.

"Henrik?" she whispered.

"Hm?"

"Tell me about Katarina."

His brow pinched. "*Partizanka* Katarina? Why?"

"Vinko told me about her."

"Okay?"

"Matej once told him how you tried to save her, but you were too late." Nada lowered her gaze and picked at the blanket between them. "I know she died. I heard you and Jakov talking about it."

He searched her face. What was she talking about?

"It's okay. You can tell me about her."

He shook his head. "I don't—" And then it clicked. He closed his eyes, a small grin surfacing. He couldn't help it. "Nada, those were two separate instances. You've assumed they go together, but they don't. I never tried to save Katarina."

Her focus jumped back to him. She blinked.

"Yes, Katarina died. About a year ago. But I was talking about *you* when I told Matej that story, right after I joined the Partizani." Back when he hadn't started pushing people away yet. Before he started to fear connection with those around him.

"Me?"

"I was talking about when I went after you, after you were taken. When I got there, I thought I was too late." A heaviness sank over his heart. Henrik took a deep, pained breath and closed his eyes. "I should have been there by your side. When I saw them take you, I should have let them take me too."

"No." Nada inched closer, bringing her hand to his face. "Don't talk like that."

"I should never have left you. I'll never forgive myself for that."

"Stop it," she whispered, shaking her head. She pressed a light kiss to his lips. "If you were there, you could have died too."

"I would have preferred it. Because Nada, when I saw them pull you from that truck full of bodies ..." He swallowed back the swelling in his throat. "You were completely covered in blood. You weren't moving. I thought you were dead and it broke me." His voice cracked. "Utterly and completely broke me."

Her eyes glistened in the dimness. "I was pretending. To survive."

Henrik nodded. "You were always smart like that." He clasped her hand where it rested against his cheek. "You even had *me* fooled." The one person he knew better than his own heart.

"You didn't look close enough," she said.

An ache took hold in his chest.

"If you had, you would have seen my fist was clenched."

He questioned her with his eyes.

Nada withdrew her hand and toyed with her bracelet. "I was holding your button. You were with me the whole time, you just didn't know it."

Henrik winced and rolled onto his back, covering his eyes as his heart broke in two. In the darkest moment of her life, she had held on to him. The weight of that brought a sting to his eyes.

"Be careful, Nada," he whispered, the sound thick. "You might break me all over again."

She reached for his arm, tugging him so he would roll back to face her. He met her teary eyes with his own. "Tata always said with destruction comes renewal. There's nothing wrong with breaking, Henrik."

How he marveled at this creature before him. He could never gather the right words to convey how much he admired her. How she inspired him. He could only settle for stroking her cheek and running his thumb over her lips.

When he drew back, Nada grew still. Her gaze shifted from his, landing on the blanket covering his waist. "So, you and Katarina..."

He breathed a short laugh despite the moisture in his eyes. "Were never anything. I only trained her for a while. Nothing more."

She looked at him again. At the grin he couldn't hide. He enjoyed it far too much.

Her own cringing smile bloomed, and she rolled her eyes, knowing full well he was eating up her apparent jealousy.

"Don't fret," he teased. "You won me in the end."

She chuckled and pushed his chest.

"I'm all yours now," he said, and he meant it. "I'll never leave your side again." He'd never *fail* her again.

Nada's smile dimmed. Her gaze lowered. Had he said something wrong?

His stomach hollowed. "What is it?"

"Henrik." She took a moment, then continued. "I've decided I'm going to Jasenovac tonight."

He launched up onto his elbow, looking down at her, frowning. "What are you talking about?"

"You're right. It's too dangerous. I never should have put that on you and Ester. On Vinko. So I'm going by myself."

A tingle crawled over him. "*No.* You're not."

"It'll be easier with only one person. Harder for them to notice me."

His pulse picked up. Henrik needed to make her see reason. "I heard what that German soldier told you. The place is a fortress."

"He said no one escapes Jasenovac. He didn't say no one can get in."

"Nada, what kind of logic is that?"

"I can't live without trying," she said, eyes growing glassy. "I did nothing to save Tata. I watched him die right in front of me, and all I could do was play dead. I was trapped in my frozen body, screaming on the inside." She swallowed hard. "If I don't try to save them, I'll live the rest of my life feeling that way. And I can't do it, Henrik."

"Please don't do this." He hung his head as he let out a shuddering exhale. His focus darted over the bed as his breaths fell faster. Shaking his head, he bent down to cradle her cheek and grasp her lips in a gentle pull that pleaded with her. "You can't," he whispered against her mouth, eyes clenched shut. He kissed her again and again, begging her, each kiss laced with urgency, until he pressed his forehead to hers. His heart strained beneath his ribs. "I want to spend endless days with you, hearing you talk while watching the stars. Racing you for fun. Making each other laugh like we always did. I want sunny days by the river with your lips on mine and lazy afternoons listening to music. I want to argue and get mad at you, only to kiss you and forget it all in an instant. I want to hold you until you fall asleep and still wake up beside you when we're weathered from age. Don't take that away from me, Nada."

Her chest dipped beneath him as all breath left her. "I'm not planning to."

"It doesn't mean it won't happen."

She tilted to kiss him. A soft grapple. And then Henrik drew back to look at her.

Nada's watery gaze, the sincerity in it, held him there. "If it does, if I don't make it out alive, you'll go on."

His heartbeat slowed. Throbbed in his chest. He sank onto his side, staring at her with wide eyes and a furrowed brow.

"Listen to me," she said, taking his hand. Her lips trembled. "I'm not saying you wouldn't grieve. You would. Hard. But it's human nature to go on, to keep moving. People can endure anything, Henrik. I'm testament to that. Sometimes I think it's a miracle I can remain standing. Sometimes I feel so broken, so beyond repair. But I'm still here. I'm still breathing. And you will too."

He darkened. "I don't like hearing you talk like that."

"But it's true. I know how resilient you are. The things you gave up, the things you've done for me. You'll never know how much—I'll never—" She huffed and planted her face in the pillow.

Henrik slipped his arm around her. Tugged her closer. Kissed her shoulder.

Nada emerged from hiding and tried again. "I see you. As you are now. And I'm far from disappointed. I'm sorry I ever said those awful things to you."

Glowing warmth blossomed in his chest. "Nada apologizing," he mused, his faint grin chased by intense heartache. "Now I'm *really* worried you won't make it out alive."

Nada shifted to push him back on the bed, leaning over him, the weight of her on his chest a comfort. Henrik brushed the bare skin of her back, so warm and soft. He didn't want to lose her. Lose *this*.

"Then come with me," she murmured. "Not as my protector, but as my partner. There's no chance we won't succeed if I have my Ubica with me. We were always a good team. Imagine what we'd be like *now*. Besides, there's no Nada without Henrik."

He sighed, torn between giving her what she wanted and keeping her safe. He knew which way he leaned. "It would take an army to go in there and save them. We're three people. Against who knows how many Ustaše."

Her focus drifted, eyes searching in that way he'd seen a hundred times. "I know what we're going to do."

He sighed. "Of course you do." His face softened as he shook his head. "My wily Partizanka. If anyone can plan something like this, it's you."

Her lips curled. "Does this mean you're coming with me?"

A crease formed in his brow as he studied her. When Henrik first decided to join her on this journey, it was a decision born from fear. He came solely to keep her safe and alive. But now he could see his actions often stifled her. If he wanted Nada to succeed, he needed to step back and give her room. As she said, she needed a partner, not a protector.

If Henrik decided to join her now, it would be because he wanted to be by her side in everything. He wanted to be what *she* needed. To have her back while she led the charge. To bolster her while she fought for her family unhindered. Wasn't that always Nada's way?

"Do you think we'll ever be forced to fight in the war?" Nada asked.

Henrik's expression grew serious. "I don't know."

"If we did, I'd want to fight beside you."

Henrik nodded. "I promise I'd keep you safe."

"That's not why I'd want you there. If anything, I'd keep you *safe."*

Even when Henrik failed to convince his father to help him, when he failed to save Nada from the Ustaše and the church massacre, she had saved herself.

Henrik had been so bitter about his father since that day. Unable to forget the words he had said. *These things happen all around us. We can't save everyone.* Henrik didn't want to make the same choices as his father. He didn't want to believe saving everyone meant falling into an early grave. At what point did it stop being about the bigger picture, about the hundreds of helpless victims being slaughtered every day? Enough was enough.

"If we're going to do this," said Henrik. "I want to save them all. Not just your mother and the girls. Not just Ester's parents. But everyone."

"Then we'll save everyone." Her eyes glittered and the tilt of her mouth hinted at mischief. "On one condition. Once we're done with Jasenovac, you follow through with all those moments you want to have with me."

Henrik drank her in, hovering above him with her mess of hair tickling his skin. A sense of warmth and calm settled over him. "I'll conquer the impossible to have that with you. I mean it. I will wear myself down to the bones if it means having a life with you."

Her grin eased as she held still. "Promise me."

He gave her a soft smile and brushed his knuckles against her cheek. "I promise."

Nada tipped forward and caught Henrik's lips with hers. Nada's hand pressed over his heart, her makeshift button bracelet dangling against him. He melted into her, enfolding her with his arms, bringing her closer.

It seemed Henrik would still follow Nada anywhere, like he did when they were kids. Maybe he wasn't so different after all.

CHAPTER 32

WANING GOLDEN SUNLIGHT FILTERED THROUGH THE trees, providing Henrik, Nada, and Ester cover as they gazed out at the railway tracks nearby. The vehicle Henrik had stolen sat hidden, farther back in the forest. It had been a smart move to take it. If anyone saw them traveling in the direction of the death camp, no questions would be raised at the sight of an Ustaša's truck.

Dressed as Ustaša soldiers, the three of them carried daggers tucked into their waist belts, along with a machine gun across their backs. Like Ester, Nada had gathered her hair, pinned it beneath her cap, and wrapped and flattened her chest with bandages in hopes she would be perceived as a man once they set foot in Jasenovac. Nada detested putting on the Ustaša uniform, and so, for comfort, for hope, she stowed her red star pin in her breast pocket.

Her cells raced, electric, as they waited and watched. Nada closed her eyes and breathed deep to try to calm herself.

"What do you think he would say?" asked Ester. "If Vinko was with us right now?"

Moisture sprung to her eyes. Nada wasn't sure what he'd say, but it didn't matter, because her lips twitched at the thought anyway. "Probably something with a mouthful of curse words."

Henrik chuckled, and Nada turned to smile at him. He was different again. More at ease. A little lighter, despite the peril they faced.

Like she had done a hundred times in the past, Nada checked to see that Ester's Star of David pendant remained hidden. But no chain glinted against her neck. "Ester, where's your necklace?"

Ester's hand flew to her throat, finding nothing but bare skin. Her brow creased. "I don't know. I didn't take it off." Her face fell as her hand dropped. "I must have lost it."

"Here." Nada dipped into her pocket for her red star pin and slipped it into Ester's. "It'll be your replacement until we find it."

Her sestra grinned and pecked her cheek in thanks.

The far-off huffing of a train interrupted them. The three of them spun in its direction. There it was, right on schedule—the last prisoner train for the day, bound for Jasenovac.

"This is it." Nada's heart skipped a beat and her wide eyes turned to Henrik. "No turning back."

His steady gaze held hers, calm and immovable. "No going back."

She took Henrik's hand, took Ester's, threading her fingers through theirs as the train drew near. "For Vinko?"

"For Vinko," they echoed.

With a final squeeze, she let them go.

Closer and closer the train came toward them, slowing as it neared Jasenovac in the distance, but still traveling faster than Nada would have liked. Her fingers tingled and she shifted from one foot to another, readying herself.

As the head of the locomotive barreled by the trees, rattling over the tracks, Henrik, Nada, and Ester burst from their cover. They sprinted alongside the train, as near as they dared and as swiftly as they were able. Nada's legs and arms pumped, charged with the rush of adrenaline. Her lungs burned, filling with the acrid scent of coal and steam, and her weapon clapped against her back.

Henrik kept pace beside her. Either he had become faster over the years or Nada was out of practice. Ester, as always, lagged behind.

The tail-end cattle car crept up next to them, and Henrik leapt, gripping the iron railing at the back of the carriage, and hauled himself up onto the small landing.

Nada reached for the railing, but her fingers fell short, and a jolt went through her chest. Henrik's hand snapped over her wrist and he pulled, lifting her off the ground, and she grabbed the railing with her free hand, swinging up beside Henrik.

Panting, Nada turned to face the tracks below—a rushing, metal stream beneath them—as wind buffeted her. Ester sprinted after them, her arms reaching out. Grasping the railing, Nada and Henrik leaned out over the edge to snatch her hands and yanked her up and onto the landing with them.

Nada turned to them both, catching her breath.

"That was the easy part," said Henrik, sunset painting his face with amber light.

He gave her a small smile and clasped her hand. Gave it a squeeze. He didn't let go, and Nada didn't pull away. Night was closing in and soon, under cover of darkness, they would face the devil in his domain. And if fate decided these moments would be her last, Nada was glad they would be by Henrik's side.

With acceptance, she turned her eyes forward. Toward Jasenovac. Toward her family.

AN EMBANKMENT CIRCLED THE CAMP LIKE A GIANT coiled snake sleeping beneath a layer of soil. As the steam train neared, the main gate opened its jaws and allowed the train to chug through, slow and steady, into the belly of the beast. To Nada's right, a falling sunset glinted fiery and golden on the surface of the Sava River, which ran parallel to Jasenovac's southern border. As the last cattle car made its way inside, crawling through the barbed-wire fencing that corralled the entire camp, Nada let out a shaky breath.

They did it. They were inside the camp. Nada straightened her back but kept her chin low while her heart thundered within her chest. Then she froze, a heavy weight sinking in her gut. Rotting weeks-old corpses littered the grounds, left out in the sun and treated like flies, swatted away and ignored. The putrid scent of death lingered in the air—a reminder that any moment could be their last.

The train wormed to the left and deeper into the camp, away from the dead. As their carriage turned, Nada looked up from under her lashes and scanned her surroundings. The entire world muted to a dull gray inside those walls. Buildings clustered here and there, a large pond visible between them. As the train eased toward the yawning, dark mouth of a tunnel, the camp's brickworks came into view. Emaciated men, shirtless in the cold, finished up their day's work in the distant brick pit, carrying round baskets and huddling in groups. Some of them wheeled metallic bins along tracks to one of the many brickworks' constructions.

Beyond all of them sat the prison camps—one elongated roofline after another.

Their cattle car coasted into the awaiting tunnel, dousing them in darkness as the train hissed to a stop, jostling them. Ustaše spilled out of the shadows on one side of the tunnel, ordering the prisoners out of their carriages. Biting at her lips, Nada looked to Henrik, and his solid gaze buoyed her. She squared her shoulders and readjusted the strap of her Schmeisser, moving it against her back. Reminding her she wasn't defenseless. *No turning back.*

Henrik led the girls off the cattle car landing and onto the tracks. Nada's pulse pounded in her temples as they strode with wide steps, chins high and chests out, to the opposite side of the tunnel and into the patches of dimness there. She hoped the darkness would be enough to hide them from plain sight as she,

Henrik, and Ester observed the new prisoners being gathered and directed outside into the open.

Around fifty in number, the train prisoners waited in silence, faces drawn and shedding tears for what might come next. A shackled inmate jangled as he approached an Ustaša soldier and held open a hefty sack for him. From its contents, the soldier passed weapons around to some of his comrades. Daggers and knives and axes.

One of the Ustaše stepped forward—broad shoulders pulled back, chin set with an air of importance. The other soldiers nodded with respect as he passed to approach the inmate. The Ustaša dug into the sack with a smirk and withdrew his weapon of choice—a srbosjek. *Serb cutter.*

The ground beneath Nada shifted. She had seen the weapon before, designed to make slaughter quicker. Easier. More efficient. Her stomach roiled as he threaded his thumb through the leather cuff and strapped it to his palm. The blade protruded from the outside of his hand like a fin.

The Ustaša called on random prisoners, one by one, both men and women, and his weaponless comrades swooped in to beat them. Eyes wild and chests heaving, they pummeled and kicked and struck the prisoners until they collapsed and begged for mercy, shielding themselves with trembling hands.

Nada cringed and kept her gaze on Henrik, her hand gripping his arm tight. A cold sweat turned her skin clammy as that old demon yawned, tremulous, inside her. Waking. Henrik's jaw remained clinched as his eyes dropped to the ground. Ester turned away, covering her mouth.

A strange stillness settled, thickening the air and raising the hair on Nada's arms—like her body sensed and recognized the creeping whispers of evil, slithering through the camp and curling toward the group of prisoners. Nada looked over, unable to stop herself.

Darkness whorled among the soldiers, writhing up the length of their bodies and along their blades. Without warning, the soldiers wreaked havoc, slitting throats and slaughtering the beaten prisoners with barbaric abandon. Nada gasped and buried her face into Henrik's shoulder.

"Don't look, Nada," he rasped.

But it was too late. She had seen the horror already. A sight all too familiar.

The brutal sounds of death continued amid a cacophony of cries and pleas and tears. Once the soldiers slew the crumpled and beaten, they moved on to those still standing.

When all fell quiet, a leaden pall burdened the atmosphere. Nada couldn't help herself. She peeked out into the open.

More than half of the gathered prisoners lay in the dirt, all killed in a handful of minutes. The remaining survivors stood transfixed and shuddering, covered in the victims' blood. A boy, not much younger than Nada, panted and trembled and stared at the corpses, open-mouthed, his face and body painted with sprays of red.

Bile threatened to rise in Nada's throat. She knew that boy. He was *her*.

The clanging of blades being tossed back into the sack woke Nada from her numbed stupor. She began to shudder all over.

"Take them to the iron factory to be sharpened," the Ustaša ordered the shackled inmate. "We'll need them for tomorrow's slaughter."

As the inmate trudged away, another soldier approached the scene, leading a horse with a pristine and shiny chestnut coat. He mounted the animal and, with nostrils flared and lips pulled back, he urged the mare forward to trample the battered, lifeless bodies.

"Step on them!" he shouted, spittle flying from his mouth. "Step on them and their Serbian, Jewish, and Communist mothers!"

Nada ignored the burn of tears in her eyes. Didn't blink them away. Didn't try to stop her body from racking with fear. She wouldn't close her eyes to the truth of what happened around her. This was the world they lived in. The hand the devil dealt them. This was the reality of her situation.

And for the first time since Nada began this journey, after all she did to claw her way into this hell, she grew petrified she might have no family alive to rescue at all.

THE BRICK KILN SAT ALONGSIDE THE TUNNEL, WHICH meant their next destination was a short distance away. But still, Nada's nerves rattled, and her stomach turned as they crossed the open space toward it.

"Get on your knees! Quickly!"

Nada whirled toward the voice, expecting a threat, heart pounding out of her chest.

A guard stood over a wilted and feeble inmate who stumbled to the ground, losing his balance. Fellow prisoners looked on, keeping their chins tucked and their hands still, faces slack and carefully impassive.

"Not like that! I said quickly!" The guard raised his pistol and shot the man through the chest.

The inmate tipped sideways to the dirt. He gasped for air, reaching a weak hand out for someone to help him. Seeing him alive still, the guard grunted, sneered, and crouched beside him. In a swift, practiced move, he slit the man's throat.

The guard bent down, his hand scooping up the life pouring out of him. And he drank.

The guard stood—hot scarlet covering his mouth and chin—and turned to the prisoners scattered around him, pale and shaking. "You see, this will happen to everyone who tries something like that!"

Bile burned in Nada's throat. She tried to swallow it down as Henrik quickened his pace, prompting the girls to do the same. Nada needed to get away from there. Her lungs tightened as the inevitable rise of panic bubbled up inside her. At least the Ustaše were too distracted, relishing in their torture of the inmates, to see them as they slipped through the kiln door and closed it behind them.

The scent of soot and woodsmoke hit them. As the workday had come to an end, not a soul moved in the dark and narrow building. Brick walls led up into a low but peaked ceiling lined with ashen residue. The still dying embers—hidden behind a row of closed hatches along one wall—wrapped them in thick warmth, and goosebumps prickled over Nada's skin, a strange sensation in the sudden heat. Stacks and stacks of chopped wood, as tall as Henrik, spanned the room in sections, awaiting another day of firing clay into bricks.

Henrik tilted his head toward the front corner of the room. "We'll hide near the exit. If someone comes in, we don't want to get cornered in the back."

Nada tried to draw a deep breath, closing her eyes a moment to quiet her nerves. *We're safe now. We're out of sight.* And they would stay there until nightfall, until they could slip out again under the cover of darkness. She wiped her shaky hands against her slacks.

Henrik and Ester rounded a pile of lumber and stepped under deep shadow, but Nada staggered behind them. That boy, covered in blood, looking down at his loved ones, haunted her. The image wouldn't let her go, digging its claws into her thoughts. Her chin shivered as if she stood in a snowstorm, but the room weighed heavy with heat.

A crease formed between Henrik's brows when he noticed. He rushed over to her. With gentleness, he cradled her face. "Hey," he whispered. "You're safe right now. I won't let anything happen to you."

"I'm okay," she nodded, though her entire frame quivered where she stood. She forced herself to draw deep, even breaths in an attempt to calm herself. Her hands continued to shake at her sides regardless. "It's just my body. It reacts sometimes, whether I want it to or not."

Her teeth chattered and she dropped her chin, cheeks warming as her eyes blurred with tears. She hated it. Hated the way it took over despite knowing, logically, in that moment she was safe. Hated the disconnect between mind and body.

"Look at me, Nada."

She did as he asked and blinked away tears until his handsome face came into view.

"It's all right. You don't need to be ashamed of it."

"I don't want you to lose faith in me because of it. I can do this. I swear."

"I could *never* lose faith in you," he said, full of sincerity. His thumb brushed against her cheekbone as his ardent gaze locked on hers. "I know my Nada. You're so strong. Even stronger than the Nada I knew before. And it's you who taught me it's human nature to keep moving. You've been a shining example of it from the moment you set foot in my camp. You always persevere, no matter what obstacle gets thrown your way."

Nada's lips inched into a faint smile through the welling of fresh tears. Her trembles eased a little.

He gave her an incredulous grin, shaking his head. "I already know you can do this. It's why we're here."

"Our faith in you is the *only* reason we're here," Ester told her in earnest.

Nada inhaled deep again, nodding, flooded with gratitude for these two whom she loved so dearly. She offered them a weak smile. She could do this. She would summon all the strength and fortitude she possessed tonight, and she would charge ahead through whatever came, fortified by their belief in her.

She moved to join them in sitting against the brick walls in the corner, the mountain of chopped wood shielding them from the door's view. Henrik reached his arm around her, tucking her close to his side, and pressed a kiss to her head. She let the comfort of it spiral through her. Nada's gaze darted toward Ester, who sat watching them, a pleased, knowing grin on her face. She had pushed for this, and now she was witnessing her happy ending. But her smile didn't last long as her focus drifted to the darkness in the room.

"Are you doing all right, Ester?" Henrik asked.

"As much as one can expect, considering what we've walked into." Her brow pinched. "I'm scared, though."

"That's understandable."

"Not only because of what's out there." She wrapped her arms around herself. "You and Nada are both so strong. So capable. But me?"

"You've made it this far," Nada reminded her. "Don't sell yourself short."

"I made it here because you two did the heavy lifting."

"Ester—"

"I'm not feeling sorry for myself when I say that. I'm *worried*. I couldn't fight, couldn't use my weapon during the ambush. I didn't try to kill the Ustaša when he attacked me. How can *I* save my parents from a place like this?"

"You're not alone," said Henrik. "We're doing this together."

"I know that. But you can't always be there to pick up my slack. You don't know what we might face tonight. I might not have any other option. Either I do what's necessary to save my parents and lose a part of myself, or I don't, and carry the guilt of that choice. I feel like my fears are pulling me in two different directions. How do I know which is the right choice to make?"

"You choose your family," said Nada. "You choose yourself. God will forgive you."

"The Ustaše don't concern themselves with guilt," said Henrik, his voice low and steady. "They won't hesitate to take your parents' lives, or yours. So don't give a single thought to theirs."

Booming voices outside the kiln silenced them. Nada held her breath as Henrik stiffened, slanting his head to listen in.

"Speaking of games," said a man. "Blago and I came from our favorite one yet."

"The way the mothers wept," said another with a chuckle.

"What kind of game?" asked a third.

"We throw infants into the air, and the first of us to impale them on our dagger wins."

"I won twice."

"I'll beat you next time, Blago. You can be sure of that. I need to win back my cigarettes."

They laughed, chatting away as they moved on past the kiln.

Nada blanched as her pulse throbbed in her ears. As her breathing shifted into a furious rhythm.

Ester clamped a hand over her mouth as tears spilled down her ashen face.

Henrik squeezed his eyes shut and turned his face toward the darkness. His hand tightened into a fist.

Nada leaned over and took hold of her sestra's hand, fire burning in her heart. "You worry you'll be less of a person, that it's shameful for making such a choice, but Ester, there's humanity and compassion in standing up and fighting back."

CHAPTER 33

THE SCENT OF BLOOD AND VOMIT TINGED THE NIGHT air—a stark contrast to the smoky warmth of the kiln. Mournful sobbing hovered, close enough to touch. Without electricity, the camp was swallowed by darkness, and Nada stuck closely to Henrik and Ester as the trio crept along the railway tracks. Though no Ustaše were to be found, the surviving new prisoners remained. Some tried to curl up on the ground and sleep, while others cried—many of them clinging to the dead.

"They didn't take the bodies away?" whispered Nada.

They didn't house the new inmates either. They were left to scatter and find rest where they could.

A man paced by the track, pulling on his graying hair while he muttered and wept. A spattering of blood covered his threadbare shirt.

Henrik brushed Nada's elbow in a prompt to keep her walking. "We should go. The sooner we get these people out the better."

They turned, but Henrik suddenly lurched, thrown to the ground. His knee cracked into the metal of the railway track. Henrik moaned from the agony, gritting his teeth to try to keep quiet. The pacing man's arm latched around Henrik's neck, squeezing tight.

Nada swung up her Schmeisser and aimed at the man's forehead, her heart racing. "Get back."

He released Henrik, straightening to face Nada, his eyes feverish.

"Get back!"

"I don't care." The man panted, patting his chest. "Kill me. Get it over with. Please."

Nada's steady weapon dipped as her mouth opened, but she corrected it again.

Henrik struggled to his feet, grimacing from the move. "You don't want to die yet, my friend." He held his palms out to calm the man. "There's going to be an escape tonight. Be ready for it."

His eyes darted between them as his lip curled. "What lies. You filth. You murderers."

"We're not Ustaše," Nada mumbled so no one else would hear.

The man studied her, and his expression faltered as he finally realized she wasn't a man. "What kind of game is this?"

"No game at all," said Henrik. "If we were truly Ustaše, don't you think you would have been killed the moment you kicked me?"

The man had no response for that.

"If you tell the others, make sure they stay calm and don't raise alarm," said Nada. "Stay here. You'll know when it's time."

Eyes wide, the man stared as Henrik, Nada, and Ester moved on toward their next destination.

As Henrik walked on his injured knee, he tried to straighten his back and carry the arrogant air of the Ustaše. If they played the part and looked like they belonged, no one would question them. But trying to hide his limp proved difficult.

"Are you all right?" Nada reached out to help him walk.

He gave a small shake of his head toward her offered hand. "Ustaše don't seem like the caring type. I don't want to draw attention by doing something out of the norm. I'll be okay."

They traveled the road running parallel to the railway track, past the administration office, and tucked themselves between the last two buildings along that stretch. Not too far away stood the southern gate. Beyond it snaked the Sava River, and floating at its bank would be the raft-like ferry that transported inmates across the water to dig their own mass graves.

Nada glanced to her left. Across the road and tracks, down by the gate, stood the guard house. A flutter of nerves went through her. It wasn't time for that yet. It was time to focus on the task at hand.

Nada and Ester followed as Henrik melded farther into the darkness between the offices, crossing to the other side so they could study the area ahead. A long run of barbed-wire fencing separated them from a smattering of warehouses and a wood-paneled watchtower by the outer fence. High on its second level, an Ustaša kept watch from a thin, rectangular window.

Nada towed Henrik back into the shadows with her. "You need to let me do this."

He looked at her, brow creasing.

"You can barely walk, Henrik. I'm the fastest between us."

"You always were boastful."

"I mean it. I'm our best chance of this going smoothly. We can't take any risks. And I won't ask Ester to do it."

Henrik studied her a moment with a softness in his eyes.

"I can do it, Henrik."

"I know you can," he said, his tone full of assuredness. "Go, Partizanka. We'll be waiting here for you."

Her chest swelled as she gazed at him, at the belief he had in her. Like the night he had taught her to use the dagger. There was power in his faith in her, and Nada would soak up every drop of it.

Henrik withdrew the wire cutter he kept in his pocket and handed it to her. With a grasp of his collar and a quick kiss, she left his side and crept over to the fence, cloaked in the thickest of shadows from the warehouse. One by one she cut the strings of wire, glancing often at the guard in the tiny watchtower window.

Nada snipped through the final strand. It twanged and coiled, causing the wire to ripple along the entire fence line.

The guard's head snapped to the ground below him. The barrel of his weapon followed.

Nada's heart clobbered beneath her ribs as she ducked and bolted through the break in the fence. The guard's machine gun trailed along the barbed wire to the point of Nada's entry and stopped. Under the cover of shadows again, Nada slowed, quietening her steps as she neared the windowless side of the watchtower. With the guard around the corner from her, Nada pressed her back to the tower, making herself as flat and invisible as possible.

She looked across the way. Ester stood alone, sandwiched in darkness between the two offices. Her chest heaved in time with Nada's. Hands flat against the rough wood planks, Nada thrummed with adrenaline. But she remained silent and fought the urge to lean to the side and peer up to the top of the watchtower. Instead, she locked eyes with Ester and jerked her chin in the direction of the guard.

Ester gave her a terse shake of her head, holding up a hand.

Nada couldn't mess this up. Far too much was at stake. And on top of it, Nada wanted to prove she could do this on her own, to show Henrik his belief in her wasn't misplaced.

Movement caught her eye beyond the offices, along the road. Out from behind the buildings appeared Henrik, staggering in clear view of the watchtower. Shoulders hunched, he dragged his feet as his body listed to the side. He began to sing *Ja Sam Sirota* to himself, his words drawling, and she swore his eyes darted toward her for a split second. He knew she needed him to create a distraction. Favoring his good leg, Henrik began to stumble his way through a dance with an invisible partner and Nada had to fight not to laugh.

Ester, watching the Ustaša guard above her, waved her on and mouthed, "*Go.*"

Nada rounded the back of the watchtower and its doorless entry.

"What are you doing?" the guard above called out to Henrik.

Nada unhooked the Schmeisser from her shoulder and slipped into the dark opening of the tower. Dusty wooden planks made up a floor in the gloom, and a ladder stood to one side of the small space, leading up to the square loft where the guard kept watch. Tension tingled along her skin as she inched toward it.

"Hey!" he shouted when Henrik didn't stop singing. "Are you deaf?"

Nada climbed the ladder, her feet falling as quiet as humanly possible while the guard continued to question Henrik.

"Why are you having such a good time? Are you drunk?"

Henrik sung out his reply. "I aaaammm."

The guard muttered a curse word. "Why don't you bring me whatever you've been drinking? Then we can both have a good time."

As he spoke, Nada stepped onto the landing and aimed her gun at his silhouetted back. Her pulse hammered through her body, yet her hands steadied to a frightening calm. This was the moment. Nada would finally unleash the fire that had consumed her since Vila Rebar.

"Put down your weapon and turn around. Slowly."

The Ustaša guard glanced over his shoulder and did a double take. He laughed at the sight of her. His eyes slithered up and down Nada's body, so idle she could feel it. Standing this close, not even the uniform and her bound breasts could disguise her gender. The man turned to face her, a sly grin in place. He feigned compliance, raising his hands, though he still held his weapon in one of them, and ogled her.

"An Ustaša angel," he mused with mock reverence. "Well, well. Aren't my comrades full of fun surprises. Where in heaven did the boys find *you?*"

Stupid, stupid man. He thought his Ustaše friends had sent her to him as some form of entertainment.

Nada smirked. "In Tito's army." She stepped forward, raising the barrel to his face.

His lascivious grin fell away and his skin paled.

"Put. It. Down." Her steeled gaze didn't falter. While she couldn't afford to fire her weapon and alert the Ustaše of their presence, *he* didn't know that.

Taking his time, the Ustaša lowered his gun and placed it on the floor. Darkened eyes lifted to hers. "Partizanka." The word rolled in his mouth like bile.

As he straightened, his hand shot out and knocked the barrel of her gun away, wrenching it out of her loose grasp, before snatching her throat. The wall smacked into her back as he pinned her against it. Her chest hitched up and down as she glared at him. Shadows simmered in his eyes and he salivated black smoke—a demon, through and through.

"Partizanka *whore*." He tossed her gun aside to thump on the floorboards. "Pretending to fight like a man. I'll show you the only thing you're good for."

He moved to unbuckle his belt. Nada moved to grasp her dagger.

"This here—*women*—is why the Partizani will lose this war."

"You're wrong," she snarled. "It's why we'll win." With a swift and powerful thrust upward, she stabbed him beneath his ribs and into his lungs. "You're all too busy with your hands down your pants."

The Ustaša choked before his wide eyes deadened. He collapsed in a heap, vibrating the floor.

Nada stared, breathless, at his motionless body. At the bloody hilt protruding from his torso, scarlet spreading like a cloud around it. She waited for the nausea and the tremors to wash over her, for the remorse and the disgust to rush in. But it didn't come. Nothing rustled inside her but a fierce sense of accomplishment.

Nada wrenched her dagger out of his corpse and wiped it

clean on his coat. She placed it into her waist belt, and then Nada stepped around him to pick up her Schmeisser before climbing back down the ladder.

When she turned to face the opening, Henrik waited for her outside in the starlight. At the sight of her, his tense shoulders relaxed. Deep, wintry eyes flitted over her, checking for signs of harm. Then, without a word, he reached out his hand for her.

WITH THE AREA IN SIGHT OF THE WATCHTOWER NOW free to roam, they kept a watchful eye on the guardhouse as they slunk their way across the road and beyond the railway tracks to the clusters of buildings. After a few turns through dirt walkways, they found a space between some buildings deep in shadow.

Nada slid her Schmeisser off and gave it to Henrik.

He frowned. "Maybe you should take it with you."

"It'll get in the way."

"Are you sure about this, Nada?"

Her heart raced but there was no way she'd back out now, after they'd come so far. "I'm positive. This was tailor-made for me. You know that."

He pressed his lips together. Nodded fast. He leaned her Schmeisser against the wall and took her face to kiss her, the warmth of it tangling through her ribs. "Be careful."

"I promise." She gave him and Ester an encouraging grin. "I'll be right back."

"We'll be waiting," said Ester, eyes tight as her hand braced against her collar.

Nada slipped around the corner and crept along the darkness spilling from the buildings. She made her way to the guardhouse. The windows were lit by the soft glow of lantern light. As far as she could tell, only two Ustaše were inside. Perfect. It would make this a little easier.

As the men sat at a table together, playing cards near the

front of the building, Nada circled around to the back. She prayed it wouldn't be locked and glanced around to make sure no one was nearby. With the slowest and lightest touch, Nada gripped the doorknob and turned it. It moved, shifting with the twist of her wrist in silence. Once it stopped, her pulse launched into a thumping rhythm. Continuing her slow movements, she pressed a palm to the door and pushed. Her tight brow relaxed when the door didn't make a sound. She crouched as she stepped inside, keeping an eye on the preoccupied Ustaše, and closed the door again in the same way.

Nada ducked behind a short wooden bookcase dividing the room, pausing to calm herself and catch her breath. The men murmured about the game, one of them accusing the other of cheating. The other gave a hard laugh. Nada tipped to the side to peer along the southern wall of the guardhouse. Gun racks lined the wall near the men, followed by a simple bench and then a small fire stove. A few steps out of reach, rows upon rows of keys hung from the pegs on a board, all of them labeled for convenience.

She tucked back behind the bookcase to gather herself. She wet her lips. As long as the men stayed focused on their game, Nada wouldn't be noticed. Heart in her throat, she inched past the edge of the bookcase. The Ustaše chuckled about something, doubling over with laughter at the table, and Nada took her chance, slipping out from behind it.

Her elbow caught a stack of papers, sending them fluttering to the floor.

CHAPTER 34

NADA'S HEART STOPPED BEATING. THE USTAŠE looked at her. There was nothing left to do. Her eyes snapped to the keys labeled *Prisoner Barracks*. She dove for them, snatching them from the peg. Nada turned to bolt for the door, but she wasn't fast enough. Meaty hands grabbed at her, pulling her back from her escape.

She fought against the Ustaša holding her, trying to wrench from his grip, but his fingers pressed deeply into her arms. Growling through clenched teeth, the keys digging into her palm, she kicked back at him. She struck his shin, but the man didn't so much as flinch.

"Get the chair, Blago."

He dragged Nada backward and shoved her into the seat, warm from their card game. It made her skin crawl as the man clasped his hand around her throat to keep her there.

The second Ustaša, Blago, appeared before her, pointing a pistol in her face. "What have we here? A girl?"

Nada glared up at him. He was young. No older than twenty-one. Dark hair and dark eyes framed the hateful gleam in his smirk. It was his voice she'd heard outside the kiln. Putting a face to it only painted a more vibrant and sinister picture of him.

Nada hoped with all her might that the Ustaše would take pause at the sight of her. That their immediate reaction in this situation would be curiosity, and not the urge to kill her where she sat.

The first Ustaša—older and graying at his temples—pried her hand open and tore the keys from her grip. He looked at them, then threw them onto the table behind her. "What are you doing here?"

"Visiting my brother," she said. "He's in one of the watchtowers."

The man let out a hard laugh. He ripped her dagger from her belt and, with a glance at it, tossed it onto the table too. Only then did he release Nada's neck. "That's the best you can do?"

Nada's eyes went to the gun aimed at her. "He asked me to get the keys for him."

"I've never seen such pathetic lies, Patrik," said Blago.

Patrik smirked. "And visiting your brother required you to dress in a man's uniform?"

Nada clenched her jaw. "It's a long story."

"I'm sure it is," he mocked. "If you don't tell us why you're really here, I'll have Blago question you. He has a knack for making prisoners talk."

"I'm not a prisoner," she argued.

"Yet."

Her heartbeat jolted.

Patrik squatted in front of her and cocked his head as he searched her eyes. "You're dressed as an Ustaša, you tried to steal the keys to the prisoner barracks, your dagger has blood on it, and you reek like a filthy Serb."

Nada's instincts screamed at her to fight, to run, but she forced herself to stay calm. To keep the upper hand. She held her gaze steady. "Actually, I think that's the uniform. The Ustaša I took it from pissed his pants."

"Aren't you a wild one?" he said, straightening to his feet. "But the thing about wild animals is they tend to travel in packs."

"The only animals I've met are Ustaše."

He struck her across the face. She gasped as her head snapped back. The sharp burn of his lingering handprint only made her seethe. Only motivated her.

"How many more of you are there?" he asked.

She returned her gaze to him, unafraid. "I came alone."

He withdrew his dagger from his belt. "I'll ask you again. How many?"

Hair lifted along Nada's skin at the sight of his blade. "I told you. I came alone."

"More lies." His hand tightened on the hilt. "I'm running out of patience."

Her eyes froze on the glint of the metal, and her breaths fell faster. Shakier. "Why don't you sound the alarm if you're so worried?"

He lifted his brows. "And warn your friends we're coming? I don't think so." Patrik pointed the dagger at her and Nada flinched—the slightest move—but he noticed. "No. You're going to tell us what we need to know."

"I'm here alone."

Patrik stepped forward and held the knife against her throat. She squeezed her eyes shut at the press of the thin, cold blade against her supple skin. Her insides turned to lead.

"Please don't," she whispered, heartbeat pounding in her temples. Her chin quivered. "Don't hurt me."

Patrik grinned at the change in her. "Interesting how a pistol didn't scare you, but a blade did. You must have come face to face with a dagger before."

Tears escaped, spilling down her cheeks. Nada's hands, her body, trembled. She couldn't stop it if she tried.

"Do you know how easy it is to slit a throat?" he asked.

"Please," she begged. "Get it away from me."

"If the weapon is sharp enough, all you need is a little momentum, the lightest pressure, and it does the work for you."

A sob erupted from her chest. "Stop. Stop talking about it."

"Tell me how many of you there are, and I'll stop."

Nada gave him nothing, fighting back her tears.

"Let's try another approach. You have three seconds to tell me before I slit your throat right here, right now. And I'll go find them anyway."

He pressed the blade harder. It stung, cutting into her skin. She moaned and gripped the seat of her chair.

"One."

Nada panted. "Please."

He pushed a heavy hand over her head, tilting it back, exposing her throat further. "Two."

"Please, shoot me instead."

"Thr—"

"Okay! Okay!" Nada shuddered. "There's two more of us. Only two, I swear." She didn't hide the shame from her expression.

"Where are they?" he asked.

"I-I can't think." If Nada told them outright, they would kill her right now. She needed to string it out, to try to survive a little longer.

"You can't think?"

"They're over in the, in the building, with the—" Another sob wrenched free from her. "They all look the same. I can … I can show you."

His tone mocked her as he repeated her words. "You can't tell me, but you can show me."

"The knife. I can't think straight." Her ragged breaths peaked with panic. "I'll take you to them. I swear. But I'll only show you if you promise to let me go. If you promise not to kill me."

Patrik grinned, exchanging a look with Blago. He pulled his dagger away and watched her as she folded over, gasping.

"Let you go?" he asked and clicked his tongue. "Now, why would I do that?"

Nada brought her hands in front of her, shaking beyond control. "What harm am *I* going to do? *Look* at me. I couldn't even sneak in here to get those keys."

"What were you planning to do with the keys anyhow?"

She kept quiet. The faces of her mother, her sisters, came flooding in. She was doing all this for them. *If we want to find our families, we let nothing get in our way.*

Patrik moved to raise his dagger again.

"I have family here," she blurted, wilting. "We were trying to rescue them."

The men laughed at her, the sound so jovial.

"Please," she whispered, hanging her head. "I'll take you to them if you let me go. I just want to be with my family, even if it means being trapped here with them."

"Fine, then," said Patrik. "We'll let you live and throw you to the Ustaše instead. By the time the men are done using you as a plaything, you'll be begging us to kill you anyway. That's assuming you survive the mutilations first."

She winced, wrapping her arms around her middle.

Patrik grabbed her arm tightly and dragged her from her chair. "You'll show us the way, and you'll do it without making a sound. Don't even think about alerting your friends or we'll cut your throat before filling you with bullets."

Her legs were water beneath her as they forced her out the door. She stumbled along the dirt path toward the buildings. Patrik kept a firm grip on her as she took them back the way she came. Heart racing, Nada hesitated, pausing before she reached the buildings where Henrik and Ester were waiting for her return. Blago readied his pistol, keeping it aimed at the ground, his arms taut. Patrik nudged her forward, raising his dagger to hover it by her throat, reminding her of the deal she made.

Nada and the Ustaše turned the corner and were met with two Schmeisser barrels, already pointing right at them.

"Drop your weapons," said Henrik. "Before I shoot your hands clean off."

Ester stood at his side, keeping her own aim steady and true.

Blago whipped up his gun, directing it at Henrik regardless.

"I wouldn't do that. We have you surrounded." Blago faltered for a moment, looking to Patrik, but Henrik continued.

"We chose our position wisely. There's over a dozen weapons pointed at you right now and we're all well out of view of your watchtowers. Now, drop your weapons and let her go."

Blago swore and tossed his pistol to the ground.

Patrik sneered. "Pick up your gun, Blago. They won't shoot."

"Why not?" he asked.

"Because if they fire on us, our people will hear it and come running. They'll be overtaken in minutes."

"I doubt that," said Henrik. "I've seen how commonplace it is for you to kill a prisoner at whim here. I doubt anyone will even flinch at the sound. And I'm willing to bet you won't risk your life to find out."

"Let her go, Patrik," said Blago. "They'll never make it out of here alive anyway."

Pinching his lips, Patrik dropped his dagger and released Nada with a shove. She walked away, body loosening, and swooped up her Schmeisser from where Henrik had left it. She turned and aimed at the men with a smirk.

Henrik kept his sight trained, but he grinned. "Nicely done, Partizanka."

"I told you this was tailor-made for me." It had been their plan for Nada to get caught. For her to be questioned and give up her friends in desperation, all so she could lure the men away. Patrik was right when he said Henrik wouldn't shoot. They needed to disarm the Ustaše quietly and avoid notice. Which meant bluffing there were more Partizani around to keep them compliant. And they couldn't very well threaten that the Ustaše were completely surrounded while still in the guardhouse. It needed to happen out in the open. "It was my idea, after all."

"Did they hurt you, Nada?" asked Ester.

Nada couldn't help the bubble of a laugh. "Not as much as I hurt them."

Patrik narrowed his eyes at them, slowly catching on.

"It must sting to be outsmarted," said Henrik, slinging his Schmeisser across his back.

"Yes," said Ester. "Our Partizanka wields her cleverness like a weapon."

Nada couldn't help her smile at Ester's choice of word. "What was it you said?" she asked Patrik, tilting her head. "If the weapon is sharp enough, all you need is a little momentum, the lightest pressure, and it does the work for you."

Patrik's eyes burned. He turned them to the buildings around him, looking at each corner, every shadow, up at the eaves. "There are no men here," he realized. "It's only you three."

"What can I say?" said Henrik. "Bluffing worked for us once before. We thought we'd try it again."

The men lunged, but Henrik expected it. He went for Blago first, before the man could dive for his pistol on the ground, giving Patrik the opportunity to snatch up his dagger. It didn't matter, though. As Blago reached for his gun, Henrik knocked his arm upward with a kick, and snapped his finger before striking a blow to Blago's face that sent him reeling, then whirled to attack Patrik in the same breath. With a fast, precise move, Henrik wrested the blade from Patrik with ease and turned it on him. In a matter of moments, he'd used their own dagger on them, leaving the Ustaše crumpled in the dirt. All of it done quietly and without drawing attention.

Nada's mouth slackened as she sucked in a breath. She could only stare at him as her body warmed. Flushed. She'd never seen anything like it. Anything so impressive, so fluid. Powerful. This. *This* was why they called him Ubica. She swallowed, her mouth cotton dry.

Her Ubica.

As Henrik moved to drag the Ustašes' bodies, she collected herself enough to hasten to his side. She helped him and Ester take the bodies around a corner and leave them in the darkness, out of immediate sight.

"All right, let's go get the keys," said Nada.

"Wait, Nada, you're bleeding." Henrik stepped to her side, brushing his fingers along her throat with the lightest touch, inspecting the thin cut Patrik's blade had made.

"I'm fine, it's barely a scratch."

He looked at her, brow furrowed while clenched muscles feathered along his jaw.

She didn't want to think about it. As much as it had been an act, feigning being caught, pretending to yield just to ambush the Ustaše, her fear and panic had been real. She had embraced it in the moment. Worked it to her advantage. But she didn't want to dwell on the thought of the knife at her throat when time was ticking away. "We need to keep going."

She led the way toward the guardhouse—empty now that the men had been taken care of. Nada swiped the prisoner barracks keys from the table, along with her dagger, as Henrik collected other keys he thought they might need. As they were about to leave, Nada's gaze snagged on a chalkboard. She stopped short, staring at the sign-in list of names. She paled as a cold sweat prickled over her body. There, written in white chalk, was the name *Nedelko Tomič*.

CHAPTER 35

Nada froze, her face drained of all color as her breaths fell faster. Henrik followed her line of sight to the name that sparked recognition. *Nedelko Tomič*. The name Nada screamed out every night in her sleep. He was here. Henrik didn't know who he was or what he had done to haunt her nightmares, but he could guess.

"Nada?"

She woke from her daze and drew a shaky breath. Without a glance his way, she rushed out the door. Henrik's brow creased and he wiped a hand across his mouth. Knowing Nada, she wouldn't say a word about it, and now wasn't the time to ask.

Staying focused on the task at hand, Henrik and the girls made their way to the southern gate, and with the keys they collected, he unlocked it and ushered the girls through. Once he followed, Henrik kept it ajar, enough to not be noticed from afar. But if anyone went by on a perimeter check, they would see clear as day it was a point of escape.

Despite the slight hitch in his gait, the ache in his knee present but easing, Henrik led Nada and Ester along the outer fence toward the eastern side of the death camp. Another watchtower loomed ahead, but no face appeared in the window.

They slowed as a unit to stare up at it from a safe distance.

"Is anyone in there?" asked Ester.

"They'll be in there," Henrik assured her. "Give me five minutes."

He broke away from the girls to approach the watchtower. Too exposed for his liking, without the cover of any buildings, his eyes flitted in every direction around him.

Nada hurried after him. "Henrik, your knee."

He stopped to wait for her. "I took out those two guards with no problem."

"But can you climb a ladder? Quietly?"

Though Nada showed no outward signs of it, she had to be shaken up after the cut to her throat and discovering Nedelko Tomič was at Jasenovac. Who wouldn't be? But distractions like that led to mistakes. Nada was capable, no doubt about it, but Henrik would take this one for her. He'd always have her back.

He brushed his hand down her arm and gave a gentle squeeze. "It's not hurting anymore, and I can use it just fine. Wait here with Ester."

She nodded and doubled back.

As Henrik neared the watchtower, the viewing window remained vacant. He frowned, looking the structure over for any sign of movement. It didn't seem right that a watchtower would be without a guard. Henrik would have to proceed with caution. With light steps he slipped through the doorway of the tower and paused to listen, searching the darkness as he waited for his eyes to adjust. He tightened his fists, then loosened them. Only silence and empty space greeted him. Henrik crept up the ladder, clenching his jaw at the throb in his knee, and climbed onto the landing.

Someone barreled into him, throwing Henrik off balance. They'd been lying in wait for him. Henrik corrected fast, cracking the guard's face with his elbow. In a series of quick and powerful moves, Henrik disarmed him and pinned his front against the wall, hands twisted in awkward angles behind his back. The guard struggled against his hold, but Henrik, barely out of breath, was strong and had his arms in a lock.

The Ustaša must have seen Henrik and the girls coming and found them suspicious. Despite his best efforts to attack Henrik, the guard would die now. Henrik kept the guard immobilized with one hand as he flipped the dagger in his other, but then hesitated. This man was the last guard they would come close to tonight. The last Ustaša he could pry information from.

Henrik planted his feet. Leaned toward the man's ear and ground out his words. "What do you know about Nedelko Tomič?"

The guard said nothing.

Henrik turned him as he shoved him into the corner, knife held to his throat. "Do you know him?"

The Ustaša only smirked.

Henrik narrowed his eyes and tilted his dagger so the point of it pressed into the guard's skin. His pulse rose to an insistent beat. "Where do I find Nedelko?"

The man breathed heavy through his nose and stared Henrik down with a death glare, but he kept his mouth shut.

"Last chance."

The Ustaša drew his head back and spat at him. Henrik flinched as saliva splattered onto his face, and his eyes darkened as he lifted his chin. As his muscles tensed. The guard was a waste of time. Henrik thrusted the blade into his neck. The Ustaša's knees gave out under him, and he slumped to the floor.

Henrik wiped his sleeve over his face as a heaviness fell over him. He wanted to learn of Nedelko's whereabouts. Perhaps Nada could find some justice if he did. But Henrik had dealt with enough Ustaše at the end of his blade to know the guard wouldn't talk. And they didn't have all night for Henrik to tear it out of him.

Henrik wasted no time hurrying back down the ladder. He stalked back through the darkness to where the girls waited. "Let's go. It's done."

Together, they passed the watchtower that Henrik had come

from and rounded the corner of a building sitting behind it. Nada tossed Henrik a ring of keys, and he snatched it out of the air. Once he found the right key and unlocked the door, he pushed it open.

They took a collective breath. A well-stocked assortment of rifles and machine guns lined the windowless walls of the armory, while various hand weapons and pistols loaded the benches around the room.

Everyone set to work, taking the folded hessian sacks from Ester's satchel to fill with every weapon they could get their hands on. But Henrik could only think of Nedelko. Of the way Nada stilled at the sight of his name. Of the way she whimpered in her sleep in the bed beside him. An edgy, restless sensation coursed through him.

If Henrik crossed paths with the man at Jasenovac, he would kill him for her.

THE BARRACKS OF THE PRISON CAMP CRAWLED WITH eerie silence. The moon, waning with a sliver of shadow in the sky, offered little light to see by. For this, Nada was glad. If she couldn't see the guards in their watchtowers, surrounding the barracks on two sides, it was unlikely the guards could see them in return. And if they did, the uniforms they wore alone would ease the guards' concern.

Nada tried to squash down all thoughts of Nedelko. But even if her mind ignored his presence at the camp, her body didn't. Every cell quaked, radiating unease. The ground rumbled unsteadily beneath her. She prayed she wouldn't catch sight of him. An electric jolt went through her chest. Nada looked over her shoulder and scanned the camp as her hands grew clammy. With nerves raw and muscles tensed, she turned back to the barracks. What if Nedelko had taken more from her than just her father? Were her mother and sisters even alive? Nada chewed the inside of her lip. She'd lost so much already. Why would tonight be any different?

She glanced over the three rows of buildings while they made their way to the northernmost ones first. If they were alive, her family could be in any of them. They found the entrance for the long and narrow structure, made of nothing more than corrugated metal and wooden planks.

Henrik adjusted his grip on his weighted sack of weapons and checked the area around him. "Okay. Hand me your guns."

Nada passed Henrik the heavy sack she carried and withdrew the set of keys marked *Prisoner Barracks* from her pocket. It took a few tries with different keys before the lock unlatched and Nada could swing the door open. With a final glance around the camp, Henrik and Ester followed her into the darkness and pulled the door closed.

The stench of excrement hit her first, tangled with something sour like bile. Rats scuttled and squeaked. It took a moment for her eyes to adjust to the darkness. Small windows ran the length of the building, providing enough illumination for her to make out the inmates huddled together on the concrete ground. Their startled and wide-eyed faces stared in her direction, disembodied by the paper-thin blankets they wrapped around themselves. Someone deeper into the barrack sputtered in a fit of coughs.

A solid force shoved into Nada's side, knocking her to the ground. She landed with such a blow it winded her. Nada gasped, fighting for air as a man's face sneered above her, his weight pressing her to the floor, pinning her there.

"Stop!" Henrik dropped the sacks of weapons and hooked an arm around the figure's neck, trying to pull him back. "We're not Ustaše! We're not Ustaše!"

But two other men jumped in, latching their arms around Henrik, and pried him from their fellow inmate.

Free once more, Nada's attacker raised a brick, ready to strike her with it. Nada braced herself as he seized her by the collar of her jacket, lifting her shoulders off the floor. Her cap slipped off.

"Don't hurt her!" Henrik strained to break from the arms holding him.

Nada's attacker paused. His brows inched together. "Her?"

It was then he had his first good, hard look at her. Long brunette strands fell loose from her pinned-up hair—as good a sign as any proving Henrik's words were true. As she panted, regaining the ability to breathe, the man stared into her wide eyes and lowered the brick.

"Who are you?"

Nada's voice rasped. "Look inside my cap." When the man frowned, she said it again. "Turn it inside out."

He let her go to reach for it and did as she asked. The man paused at the sight of the red, five-pointed star Ester stitched inside the brim.

A bright fire lit in his eyes. "Partizani." He turned to grin at the inmates.

Henrik's captors released him, and Henrik removed his cap, flipping it inside out to show everyone. "Partizani," he echoed.

A prisoner let Ester go from where he'd shoved her against the wall.

Henrik strode to Nada's side and, as her attacker moved away, he helped her back to her feet. His hand came to her cheek. "Are you hurt?"

Nada's adrenaline continued to thrum. "I'm okay."

The attacker returned her cap to her. "Has liberation finally come? Is Tito sending his army to drive out the enemy?"

Inmates began to stand, eager for the answer.

"I can assure you, Tito's men are closing in, though the Ustaše are retaliating with force," Henrik told them. "But tonight, the only liberation you'll find is with us. We came to set you free."

"We've brought weapons for you." Nada pointed to the sacks. "But we need your help handing them out to all the prisoners."

The man who attacked Nada smiled. "We've been planning a revolt. For the past week we've been collecting bricks and tools, anything we can find around camp to use as weapons. But this? This is much better." He took the sack and looked inside it. He noted there were only three sacks. "This won't be enough. There are six hundred souls dwelling in this camp."

"There's more in the armory," said Henrik. "But not enough for six hundred by a long shot. If you're willing to collect them, the door is unlocked."

"If I go to the armory I'll be shot on sight."

Nada shook her head. "We've taken out the guards posted along the southern fence by the river. If you're careful, the southern side of camp is clear. And that's the direction everyone should stick to when they escape, in small groups, as quietly as possible. The weapons should be a last resort."

Tense whispers gathered in the quiet.

"Where are we escaping to?"

"The prisoner train." Ester stepped forward, eyes groping the crowd. "Tata, are you here?" she called. "Does anyone know if Ivan Novak is—"

A man rose from farther back, hobbling his way to the front of the building, catching Ester's eye. Black and blue bruises marred his face, one eye swollen shut, and he walked with a tender limp.

His lips trembled as he parted them to speak. "Estera?"

That voice crashed into Nada. She hadn't recognized him.

"Tata!" The word wrenched from Ester's lips in a sob. She rushed at him and threw her arms about his middle, crying into his shoulder.

Ivan wrapped her close, stroking her hair as they wept. "Estera," he whispered. "Don't cry, Estera."

Their reunion made Nada's chest squeeze. While glad Ester found her father, the loss inside her stirred.

"What are you doing here?" he asked.

"I came to rescue you. We're getting you out of here."

Ivan's sigh shuddered. "You should have stayed home. Where it was safe."

Ester looked at him, at his bruises, and her brow furrowed. "What did they do to you?"

"I'm all right, Ester."

"You're not all right. You could barely walk over here."

Ester pulled back and inspected him with a sharper eye. Ragged clothing and hand-fashioned sandals replaced her father's usual neat and proper attire. "We need you to drive the prisoner train, but—" Ester spun to look at Nada, face pale and wincing. "He can't shovel coal. Not in his condition."

"I can manage," said Ivan catching on to their idea. "I'll take men with me to help."

Nada's attacker turned to Ivan. "How long until the train can be ready?"

"The boiler should still be hot from its last arrival. If I can get it fired up again right now, it would take maybe thirty minutes if we're lucky. An hour at most."

"I'll spread word through the barracks that it's time for us to escape," said the man. "And then I'll go gather more weapons to hand out to the inmates."

Nada handed her attacker the keys to the barracks. He called for his friend nearby to go with him, and the two of them crept out of the building.

"Where's Mama?" asked Ester.

"They forced her to work in the hospital. I haven't seen her since the day they took her there."

"Do you know if she's all right?"

"I think so. I've heard people with occupations such as hers are safest here. They're useful."

Nada scanned the crowd of inmates behind him. "Have you seen my mother? My sisters?"

His expression dulled. "I think your mother might be with my wife. I can't be certain, but I heard my wife convinced the Ustaše to bring another nurse with her."

"My mother's not a nurse," said Nada. "You think she lied to save her?"

"If I know my wife, yes, I do."

"What about my sisters? Where are they?"

Ivan's eyes watered, still visible in the dimness. "The little ones ..."

Nada's heart throbbed in her chest. Her fingers turned to ice. "What happened to them?"

He buried his face in his shaking hand.

"Tell me."

"The moment we arrived, the Ustaše ..." His murmured words rattled. "I watched them gather all the children off the train. Maybe a hundred of them. They took them to the tailor shop. The building was so full of children already, they could no longer fit them through the door. So they began throwing the children through the windows, on top of the others." He paused to let out a weak breath and wiped his trembling fingers over his eyes. "There must have been five hundred children in there. The Ustaše forced some prisoners to seal the doors and windows with tape. Then they threw cyanide inside."

The air in the room deadened. Breath expelled from Nada's lungs and didn't return. Her chest went through the motions. In. Out. In. Out. In. Out. But still her head spun, and her ribs ached with the desperate need for air.

They're gone.

Nada pushed past Henrik and shoved her way out the door and into the cold night. The ground tipped under her feet. The barracks around her swayed. Nada stumbled to lean her back against the building. In. Out. In. Out. In. Out.

Her gasps peaked, falling into a rhythm of hoarse sobs. A moan wrenched out of her.

And then Henrik was there, all warm hands and watery eyes. He cradled her face. "Come inside. It's not safe out here for this."

"I was too late. I failed them."

"You did what you could."

"They're gone. My little sestre." Her chest chugged as hot tears tracked down her cheeks. "They were *babies*, Henrik."

His face twisted, and a wretched breath heaved from his

lungs. Henrik touched his forehead to hers. "It was better for them, Nada," his voice broke. "It was better they were taken right away than to suffer cruelty. They knew none of this hell." Henrik's fingers slid behind her neck with gentle purpose. "They were spared from this place. Hold on to that, Nada."

With the cap still in her hand, Nada brushed her thumb over the soft ridges of the star-shaped stitching inside it. And then she clutched it tightly in her palm, knuckles turning white as a wave of heartache tore through her again.

"Hold on to it."

Hold on to it.

A HEAVINESS CLUNG TO HENRIK AS HE MANAGED TO escort Nada back into the barracks, where it would be safe for her to fall apart. Ester wrapped her up in a hug and whispered words of comfort in her ear before she met Henrik's eyes and tipped her head in the direction of the door. Ivan had already gathered two of the inmates to help him with the train. They stood waiting. They all needed to go, to keep moving.

With a swallow, Henrik nodded and darted toward the sack of weapons. He gave Ivan and the men a pistol each. "Go. Hurry and be careful. Stick to the shadows and try to blend in with the new prisoners."

"I'm going with him." Ester appeared at his side. "We need that train, and I can show them the safest way there."

"All right," said Henrik. "Be safe. Nada and I will bring your mother. I just want to give her some time."

"Of course." She pressed a quick kiss to his cheek. "You two be careful too." With a watery glance at Nada sitting huddled in the shadows, Ester slipped out the door with her father and the inmates.

Henrik sank beside Nada on the cold, hard floor. She leaned against the wall, arms wrapped around her knees as she stared in numb silence, tears falling of their own accord. Henrik's brows drew together. Nada was always more likely to rage than slip into blank hopelessness.

"I've never known a heart could feel so heavy," she whispered.

"I'm so sorry, Nada."

Henrik didn't know what else he could possibly say, so he took her hand and sat with her. Grieved with her.

Eventually, the inmate who volunteered to spread word through the barracks stepped back inside. "They're all ready and I gave them the weapons you brought. Did the others go to fire up the train?"

Henrik nodded. "About twenty minutes ago."

"Good. I'm heading to the armory now to get—"

The wail of a siren pierced the quiet, rising in an intensifying arc. Nada's wide, reddened eyes went to Henrik. A quake went through him. The Ustaše knew they were there.

CHAPTER 36

Either the Ustaše had stumbled upon their dead guards or they had found the gate Henrik had left open. If everything went according to plan, the Ustaše would swarm the gate, thinking prisoners had escaped through it. Maybe even search along the river for them. The Ustaše would be looking in the wrong direction as Ester and her father readied the train. As hundreds of prisoners followed them.

Still, Nada and Henrik leapt to their feet. The siren wasn't part of their plan. An empty pit formed in Henrik's stomach as they barreled out the door for the hospital.

A whirlwind of chaos surrounded them. Inmates fled from the barracks in a rushing tide, bumping into Henrik and Nada in their haste to escape. They panicked at the blaring siren, afraid their window for escape was closing. When gunfire erupted from the southern side of the camp, Henrik grabbed Nada's hand, shoving his way through the gaps between the prisoners. They ducked into the next long aisle between barracks across the way. Few inmates ran through there, and the buildings shielded them from the northern watchtowers.

At the other end, Henrik paused to take stock of the situation, their new position allowing them to get a good view of the Ustaše shooting toward the barracks. Some prisoners fired back while others fell to their deaths amidst cries and shrieks of pain and fury. More than half of them turned to run the other way. That was when the guards in the northern watchtowers opened fire. With the prisoners being attacked on both sides, and with the barracks and fences behind them, there was only one direction left to run—across the wide-open expanse.

Their plan was going to hell, but Henrik wouldn't go down without a fight, doing whatever he could to get Nada safely out of there. And he wouldn't leave this camp without finding Nada's and Ester's mothers first.

The hospital looked like the barracks—long-stretched structures made from wood and corrugated metal. With bedlam erupting in the camp, Henrik was glad the hospital buildings were close.

He turned to Nada. She stood solid, pressed against the wall beside him, jaw set, with fire in her eyes.

"We'll go to the first building." She gestured to the one across from them. The one facing out toward the battle. "If they're not there, we'll go to the next."

Even in her grief, she wasn't giving up. It made his heart warm. Henrik admired her for it. No matter how many hits Nada took, she kept going. Relentlessly.

In response to Nada's instruction, Henrik readied his Schmeisser, and she followed suit. With their weapons at the ready, they charged across the aisle and swept through the door of the hospital, closing it behind them.

Henrik rested his finger by the trigger as he made a quick scan through the darkness, heart racing as he searched for threats. He only found dim stillness, made eerie by the muffled sounds of gunfire. The dark entryway, laid out like a hallway, partitioned the main body of the hospital with two open doors either side of Henrik and Nada. Stepping through the opening on the right, a wall to their left bisected the building down the middle. Rows of rickety cots lined the length of the wall and beneath the windows across from it, ending with yet another hallway and a back exit. With nothing but thin mattresses and a tin cup floating in a metal bucket of water, the place hardly resembled a hospital.

Crouched behind a tiny bed, two figures hid themselves from the battle outside. They shrank lower as Nada and Henrik moved closer.

"Mama!" Nada leapt into a run.

Teodora, gaping at her daughter, rose from her place behind the bed. She stumbled out into the room and met Nada in a crushing embrace and a flood of tears. Ester's mother Maria stood, watching wide-eyed, as Nada filled her mother in on the reason for her unexpected appearance. On their plans of rescue.

Without a word, Maria rushed off into the entrance hallway, and Teodora's eyes went to Henrik.

She came over to him, wearing a tearful smile, and took his face in her hands. "Henrik. I'm so happy to see you're all right." She pulled him into a tight hug, the kind his own mother would give. It warmed him through. "I've had you in my prayers."

"Thank you, Teodora."

She pulled away, grasping his shoulders to get a good look at him. "What a fine young man you've turned into."

He gave her a smile and jerked his chin toward the room. "There are no patients?"

She shook her head, mouth pinched. "The sick inmates are only sent here to die or be executed. The only real care we give is to the Ustaše."

Nada gasped sharply behind him and Henrik spun, his frame rigid and ready.

Maria ushered Ana and Maša into the room. Nada burst into tears as she crouched and the girls ran into her open arms.

Henrik's mouth fell open as the heaviness in him lifted. "How? Ivan told us they—"

Maria grabbed his arm. "You've seen Ivan?"

"Yes. He's with Ester, getting the train ready to leave." Henrik turned back to Teodora. "He said the girls were gone."

"We were separated from him. He must have assumed. But

Maria helped me hide them when the other children were taken," said Teodora. "We've been keeping them hidden in the supply closet ever since."

Nada clung to her little sisters and a slow smile crept over his face. They were alive. Which meant Nada would be all right. Henrik left them to their moment and approached the line of windows facing the rest of the camp. The handful of Ustaše at the southern side were closing in, pushing back the straggling inmates who continued to fight. Henrik caught movement to the left of the building. His body tensed, heart kicking into a fast beat.

"Ustaše are coming straight for us," he announced. "Nada, hide them somewhere and stay quiet. I'll take care of it."

Adjusting his hold on the Schmeisser, Henrik followed them into the entry corridor and kept an eye on them as Nada and the others hurried into the supply closet at the end of the hallway. The second they all tucked in there, the door across the building opened.

Six Ustaše bustled inside.

Painting on his best, arrogant Ustaša attitude, Henrik stepped into the infirmary to bark at them. "What are you doing here? You should be out there shooting them all."

"They're fighting back," one replied. "Somehow those fucking Serbs got their hands on our weapons."

"We thought we could use this place to keep cover while we take aim," said another. "We've lost a few of our men already."

The first Ustaša turned to one of his friends—a man Henrik marked as a threat for his tall, broad build. "Franjo, help me search the building."

Henrik's pulse staggered but he kept his face straight. "No need. I've already done that."

"Better to double check. These animals are tricky."

His friends seemed to agree. Four of them broke away and moved back into the corridor they had entered through.

Henrik's nerves hummed. He shot a quick glance into the dark hallway behind him, the grip on his Schmeisser growing slick. Nada and her family hid undefended in that closet. The Ustaše would find them in a matter of minutes. The quiet exhale escaping him shook. It was up to Henrik to protect them. They had come so far, and gotten so close to the finish line, he couldn't let them falter now.

The muscles in Henrik's jaw feathered as he steeled himself. He refocused the tension wound tight in his body, tuning it to a dangerous but static calm.

The remaining two Ustaše strode into the room and, using the butts of their weapons, smashed the glass of the windows—pieces tinkling to the cement floor as the volume of outside ammunition heightened. They kneeled and propped their machine guns on the sills.

Henrik knew what needed to be done now. He didn't hesitate.

He slung his Schmeisser behind him and withdrew the knife from his waist. As the Ustaše squeezed their triggers, sending bullets flying and their guns vibrating against their shoulders, Henrik crept with sure and deliberate steps to the closest soldier. In a swift and practiced move Henrik slipped behind him and slit his throat. When the man's body slumped and his weapon silenced, his friend glanced over.

His brows twitched for a fraction of a second. And then he yelled, "Traitor! He's a—"

The Ustaša didn't get the chance to finish. With his free hand, Henrik whipped up his pistol and fired. The Ustaša dropped to the floor, his gun following in a clatter.

A shadow caught Henrik's eye and he looked up. The big Ustaša stood by the back entrance, his body filling the doorway. He saw what Henrik had done.

"He's Partizani!" the big Ustaša shouted into the hospital, his voice booming.

It was then a scuffle sounded from the front entrance. Nada's unmistakable growling cry had Henrik whirling toward her. A mustached Ustaša gripped her arms, dragging her backward into view through the doorway. She fought against his hold, gritting her teeth, as another advanced toward her. She kicked at him, booting his gut. He retaliated by striking her across the face and withdrawing his dagger.

Henrik's heart stopped as a tremor took hold in his chest. The world slowed. All he could see was the way Nada and her father had fought as the Ustaše forced them into the horse-drawn cart. The way Henrik had watched, helpless to do anything. It was going to happen again. Only this time, death would not be a deception.

Nada's desperate eyes shifted to Henrik through the door. The second Ustaša noticed, following her line of sight, and spotted Henrik, frozen in place.

The Ustaša sneered and pressed his blade against the pulse of her neck. "Surrender now or I cut her throat."

Lies. He would kill her anyway.

A flashfire seared through him, making his fingers throb and his ears pound, waking Henrik out of his crippling fear. He clenched his fists. His muscles strained against his skin. No. It would *not* happen again. He wouldn't let it. Because he wasn't the same Henrik anymore. He wasn't helpless. He wasn't a coward. He was Nada's Ubica—a merciless weapon forged from his determination to keep her safe. Nothing could defeat that.

He had resisted the title of "monster." Now he would embrace it. Become it.

Henrik let the rage take over.

He dropped the bloodied knife and snapped up his pistol with both hands. Squeezed the trigger. The shot reverberated in his ears as the bullet struck the man dead between the eyes. He flung backward and hit the ground.

"Henrik, behind you!"

Nada's shout stoked his instinct. He began to turn, but the big Ustaša's meaty fist came down hard over his hand, causing the pistol to fall from his grip.

Henrik reacted fast. He hooked his leg behind the Ustaša's while snatching the man's wrist and shoulder, shoving the Ustaša's body forward as Henrik swept his leg out from under him. The man thumped hard to the ground. A quick and thorough glance told Henrik the Ustaša was unarmed. Good. Henrik stomped on his lower ribs, and they gave under his boot with a crack.

The man lurched with pain, grunting, then rolled away and scrambled onto his knees, lunging to grab Henrik's calf. He didn't fight it. Henrik followed the motion and gripped the man's hair, thrusting his knee upward and smashing it into the Ustaša's face. Blood gushed from the man's nose, and he pressed his hands to his face.

With the Ustaša distracted, Henrik stalked to the other side of the room in search of his dropped pistol. He crouched between two beds, checking underneath them. The big Ustaša leaned over his dead comrade and grabbed the dagger from his waist. He barged toward Henrik, poised to run the knife through him with the weight of his large body behind it.

At the last moment, Henrik tossed the cot up on its side to shield himself, clamping his jaw. The dagger stabbed through the flimsy mattress and caught between the spring coils of the bed. Face to face, Henrik thrust the heel of his palm up at the Ustaša's already broken nose. The man clutched at his face with a moan.

Cheeks mottled and baring his teeth, the Ustaša rounded the bed to Henrik's side. Henrik stood and unhooked his Schmeisser, nose flaring. He brought down the butt of his gun hard, slamming it against the Ustaša's clavicle. It snapped and his arm fell limp. As the Ustaša screamed, Henrik grasped each end of his Schmeisser and swung it to strike his opponent's temple. The force and disorientation of the blow made the man tip backward. Following the momentum, Henrik pushed his weapon against the soldier's throat and hooked his ankle in another sweep to loosen his footing. The Ustaša dropped onto the upended cot, landing with a crunching whiplash.

Henrik's focus darted to the water bucket nearby. With heat burning through his veins, he dropped his Schmeisser to latch a firm grip on the Ustaša's neck. Henrik dragged the bucket over and plunged the man's head into the water. The big Ustaša's survival mode kicked in and he grappled to push Henrik away with his only functioning arm, entirely at the mercy of Henrik at such an angle.

As he drowned the man, Henrik's focus flitted to Nada. The Ustaša with the mustache now had her on the ground beneath him. Nada fought him, savage in her attacks. The Ustaša grabbed her head and smacked it against the floor. Her whole body slackened, her eyes falling sideways in a daze. Then her attacker pressed a pistol to her head.

All breath left Henrik's cold, cold body. Outside the battle waged on. The siren, the bullets, the screaming, the panic—it all washed away in a muted haze.

NO.

Henrik wrenched the bucket away from the dead Ustaša's head, tipping the water across the floor. He hurled the metal bucket right at Nada's attacker. It cracked against the side of his head. The man cried out and jerked his face toward him, claiming his attention as Henrik intended. The Ustaša launched to his feet, knowing he'd be too vulnerable on the ground. And then he stormed for Henrik with his gun aimed.

At the same time, footsteps hastened behind Henrik, alerting him of a rear attack. Henrik's next moves played out quickly and with precision. Henrik snatched the Ustaša's hand holding the pistol, pulling the man toward him. He pressed the barrel to the fleshy side of his own waist as he pivoted ninety degrees and squeezed the trigger over the man's finger. Jolting pain lanced through Henrik's side as the bullet went through him and struck the man behind him in the groin. He collapsed to the ground, screaming.

While Nada's attacker's eyes bulged, Henrik disarmed him, then fired the weapon at his face, but it clicked empty.

Changing tactics, Henrik clobbered the man's ear with it in one solid hit. Off balance from the strike to his eardrum, Nada's attacker staggered sideways. Henrik dove for the dagger he had dropped earlier, then spun to circle the Ustaša he had shot. With the man groaning on hands and knees, Henrik reached around his head to pull at his nostrils, forcing the man's head back, exposing his throat.

As soon as he sliced the Ustaša's neck, Nada's attacker regrouped and barreled into him. He knocked Henrik to the ground, and they landed in the shattered window glass. Henrik swiped for broken shards and threw a fistful at the Ustaša's eyes, then yanked another dagger from a body. Nada's attacker recovered from the glass and aimed his fist, but Henrik was ready. He cross-slashed the two blades against the Ustaša's throat. Hot liquid spilled over Henrik, and he shoved the slumping soldier's body aside and got to his feet.

Chest heaving, Henrik's focus darted around him, checking all corners for another threat. But there was only Nada sitting in the doorway, pale and shaking, with her glassy eyes frozen on him.

So much like the way she had looked at him in terror after he had slit the German soldier's throat. She was afraid of him then. He could only imagine the fear she had now. Agony pierced his heart as he stood, immobilized.

He slowly slipped his bloodied dagger into his belt. Calmly lifted his hands, palms out. "Nada," he rasped.

"You're hurt," she said, her lip quivering. "You're bleeding everywhere, Henrik."

A rush of air left him. She wasn't afraid of him. She was afraid *for* him.

Henrik swept in to gather her up and draw her away from the havoc waging outside the windows, moving them to the hallway. Breathless and with a furrowed brow, his hands skimmed over her hair, her face, her neck, checking her for signs of blood or injury as she trembled within them. He finally settled on cradling her face as he let his eyes roam hers.

The moment he saw that pistol aimed at her head, his soul had heaved inside him. Begged to leave his body. He thought he was about to lose her despite all he'd done to fight it. And in that hovering, endless heartache, he realized how violently—how absolutely—he loved her. Of course, he'd always known it, but it wasn't childhood adoration anymore. Not just a lifelong knowing they were two halves of a whole. It was more than the years of infatuation and secret yearning. It was immovable and resolute.

"Let me get Maria to look at you," she said. "She can—"

"I'm all right," he assured her. "It's not all my blood."

"I know. I saw. Your side, Henrik."

"I promise I don't even feel it." He would. Later, once the adrenaline wore off. But for now, he only wanted to be still and sit in the moment. Nada was okay. It was all he cared about.

Nada dove into Henrik's arms and he wrapped her against him. Tendrils of her hair had loosened from their pins, tangling between his fingers as he held her against his shoulder. Henrik's chest swelled. He had her. Alive and whole and with a future full of promise. As her heart thundered in time with his, Henrik wanted to live for nothing more than this.

"Is it safe?" Teodora hissed. She had cracked the storage room door open, peering out.

Still clinging to Henrik, Nada turned to look at her. "Yes, it's clear."

The second her little sisters and Maria appeared behind Teodora, Henrik stepped away to close the door to the infirmary, closing off the vicious scene he had created.

The girls ran over to them, and Nada picked up Maša. "Maria, Henrik needs your help. It's his waist."

He shook his head. "I'm all right. Really." It wasn't the first time this had happened to him.

Maria took in the blood seeping from his side before her eyes flashed sternly. "Let me see."

Despite his protests, she yanked his jacket and shirt up to inspect his wound, like he was still a child.

"The bullet went straight through," he said. "I'll be fine."

She nodded. "You will. But I'll bandage it now and we can tend to it later."

Maria bustled about, collecting her supplies. Henrik sighed. It was easier to back down and let her take the time to patch him up. Maria may have been a nurse with a gentle bedside manner, but she was brusque and commanding when she wanted to be. She proceeded to wrap a bandage around his middle.

"We need to make our way to the train," said Nada once Henrik was taken care of. "Ivan should have it ready by now."

Henrik finished buttoning his jacket. "Let me check on things first."

He cracked open the door to the infirmary, careful to keep the girls from seeing inside, and slipped through. He took a moment to search for his pistol and Schmeisser, boots crunching over bits of glass as he reclaimed them. Through the broken windows, the Ustaše were still firing toward the barracks, far too close to the southern end of the hospital. His nerves jangled.

Henrik stepped back into the hallway. "We can't go," he said. "Those Ustaše haven't left. We'll be caught in the crossfire."

"If we wait too long, we could be in a worse situation," said Nada. "Or the train will leave without us because we're presumed dead. We're running out of time."

Teodora looked at her three daughters. Maša in Nada's arms and Ana latched onto her big sister's side.

"Give me your pistol, Nada." Teodora didn't wait for her daughter to hand it over. She took it from her hip. "I'll draw the Ustaše away while you take the girls and escape."

CHAPTER 37

Coldness rattled in Nada's chest. "No, Mama."

"Take the girls. Now. Get them to safety," she said. "You too, Maria."

"I'm not leaving you here."

"I'll get their attention," her mother continued, ignoring her. "You all go around the back of the building. When you see the Ustaše come into the hospital, you run."

Nada shifted from one foot to the other, her fingers restless and twitching where they rested on Maša's side. "*No!* I came here to save you. You're coming with us."

Teodora turned to the young man beside her. Met his gaze with unwavering steadiness. "Henrik, take them. You know we have no choice."

He looked at Nada, face drawn, and crouched to face Ana. "Do you remember when I used to give you piggyback rides?"

The girl nodded, her eyes large.

Henrik slid his Schmeisser around to hang across his chest and tapped the back of his shoulder. "Hold tight onto my shoulders, not my neck."

"I remember," she said, circling him to climb onto his back.

Henrik straightened, Ana perched behind him, as Nada

watched on, helpless, with Maša's small hands fisting the collar of her coat. The air around her grew thin.

Maria shook her head, wringing her hands. "This isn't right. You should be going with your daughters. I should be the one to stay."

"If they get hurt while trying to flee, they will need a nurse," said Teodora.

Nada's chest hitched up and down as an ache writhed around her throat. She couldn't lose her mother. How could she live without her? Without *both* her parents? "Mama, please. I promised Filip I'd bring you home. We can find another way."

Teodora stepped close to kiss Maša on the head and Nada on the cheek. "You go and you don't look back." Then she turned to Henrik, her eyes glistening. "Take care of them."

Henrik returned her gravity. "Always."

Teodora took Ana's hand and clasped it in hers to kiss it.

"Mama, stop this," Nada begged, her voice breaking, but her mother pushed her toward the door. "Don't do this."

Henrik cracked the door open to the outside, checking it was safe. He slipped out, followed by Maria.

"Be careful, and be smart," said Teodora, her forced but faint smile trembling. "I love you all."

With a final shove, she pushed Nada outside and bolted the door closed.

Nada gasped, her vision blurring. Back in the thick of pounding gunfire, facing the loss of her mother, she reeled. Henrik grabbed her arm and pulled her around the corner, to the walkway between the two hospital buildings. They inched along it until they reached the end. Henrik peeked around the wall.

A series of gunshots fired inside the hospital. Teodora's voice rang out inside, her words indistinguishable in the chaos. But the intention, the feeling, behind it was clear. It screamed *come and get me.*

Nada shut her eyes, biting down on her lips. Her heart broke in two.

Henrik snapped back behind the wall with a pained expression. "They're coming."

Nada gulped for air, fighting back the urge to cry. She needed to save her sisters now. Needed to focus and make it out of there alive.

Henrik checked again and gave them a nod. The Ustaše were inside. Together, they jogged away from the building, Maša bouncing on Nada's hip. Multiple gunshots thundered in the hospital behind them. Nada gritted her teeth as tears spilled over. But she kept going.

They headed for the south side of camp while giving a wide berth to the fleeing prisoners. They dropped like flies, and Nada's gaze darted to them often, hoping her mother was among those trying to escape. But she recognized none of them. When Nada turned back around, at least twenty Ustaše traveled along the southern fence. Nada froze. Their route was blocked.

"What do we do?" asked Maria. "Once they see us, we'll be cornered."

Nada's gaze grappled across the camp, searching for a way out. Inmates continued to flee, crossing the stretch of dirt between the brick pit and the pond, but many of them fell as they ran, tumbling over, one after another. The watchtower's gunfire could reach them there. Which left only one option.

"The pond," said Nada. "We have to get under water before those Ustaše see us. And we'll need to make our way across it to the buildings on the other side."

Ice cold water swallowed her legs when Nada and the others waded into it. She gasped at the temperature but forged on in her hurry to hide. She sank Maša and herself into the water, up to their necks. Henrik and Maria did the same. The Ustaše drew closer and closer.

Nada turned to her sisters. "Do you remember when I took you both swimming in the summer and I taught you how to hold your breath under water?" They nodded in reply. "We're going to do that now. When we go under, I want you to count to five in your head. That's when we'll come up again for air. When we do, take a deep breath for me. Then we'll go under and you'll count to five again. We're going to do this over and over. Do you understand?"

"I'm scared, Nada," Ana whimpered, her small hands gripping Henrik's shoulders.

"I know you are. I am too. But I promise we'll be okay. We won't let anything happen to you." Nada looked at Maša and her pale little face. "Can you still count to five?"

"Jedan, dva, tri, četiri, pet," she recited, her voice strained.

"Good girl. All right, everyone. On the count of three, take a breath."

The Ustaše's faces were clearly in sight now. Nada trembled, and not just from the cold of the water.

She whispered, counting them down. They drew a collective breath, and under they all went. The frigid liquid blocked her ears in an echoing whoosh, dulling the sounds of gunfire. Nada grappled her footsteps against the muddy bottom, pushing her and Maša through the water, until they came up gasping. Maša's little face and hair dripped with dirty water as her mouth opened like a gaping fish. Again and again they moved through the motions, counting to five, surfacing, dipping under again. Until the pond became too shallow to continue.

They kept low in the water, surveying their surroundings. A long building rose from the ground before them. To the right, the luckiest of the prisoners ran through to the brickworks' structures, disappearing into the darkness between them. The more inmates that made it through toward the train, the more it would increase the risk of drawing Ustaše attention their way. They needed to cross the grounds unnoticed. Nada's focus went to the small excavation pit nearby and the metal bins sitting on the thin tracks, trailing away into the brickworks. "Follow me."

Glancing to make sure no Ustaše were near and watching, they climbed out of the water. With rivulets streaming from their heavy, wet clothes, they hurried over to the metal bins.

Nada sat Maša inside one of them. "Duck as low as you can," she told her, and then turned to Maria. "I need you to push Ana in one of them. Henrik, aim your Schmeisser at her back so it looks like you've caught an escaped prisoner."

Even though they dripped with water, Nada hoped from afar no one would notice. She pushed the bin forward on the tracks. It squealed along the metal, but the gunfire hammering through the camp drowned it out. She quickened her pace, eyes darting all around in search of Ustaše. They wound their way between the brickworks' buildings: Nada leading, Maria behind her pushing Ana along, Henrik following in the back as they fell under shadow.

"I'm cold," Maša cried. Her skinny little arms wrapped her shivering body.

"I'm going to take you someplace warm," said Nada. "We're almost there."

The tracks stopped behind the brickworks' structures, near the end of the train tunnel. Nada peered around a building to check the watchtower in sight. The guard fired his weapon at the prisoners crossing the expanse, his attention diverted. Confident they could slip by him, Nada picked Maša up and set her on the ground. Henrik followed her lead, taking Ana out of the metal bin, and together they circled around the back of the train tunnel, keeping the girls between them and the wall. As they approached the kiln beside it, a figure stalked out from the buildings beyond, pistol in hand as his focus swept over the fence line.

Nada's heart burst into a frantic rhythm. When the Ustaša's eyes landed on them, he started. He looked from Nada and Henrik to the girls they had shielded against the wall, then at the prisoner walking with them. Henrik reached for his pistol, but the Ustaša whipped up his weapon first as Nada stepped in front of the girls.

A crack rang out as a force clapped against Nada, throwing her back. She smacked against the ground.

A series of shots followed, lost in the thunder of a thousand bullets.

Nada lay breathless and stunned, staring up at the stars.

They whirled overhead as a stinging pressure erupted in her left arm.

"Nada!" Henrik's voice cracked as he dropped to his knees, tossing his pistol aside. Gasping, his hands flit over her, searching. "Nada, where are you hit?" Then he clasped her shoulder, wild eyes resting on her sleeve. "It's her arm. Maria!"

"I'm here."

Maria appeared above her, mouth open with a hand to her chest, and Ana and Maša approached, faces ashen and crumpling. Maša's chin quivered as she began to cry.

Nada found her voice. "I'm okay," she told her sisters. "Don't cry. I'm all right." Breaths falling fast, she sat up with the help of Henrik's palm between her shoulder blades. She gave them a weak smile, her body shaking. "See? Don't cry, Maša."

"We're too exposed out here," said Henrik, his gaze darting all around them.

"We need to get to the kiln. Get the girls warm."

Maria nodded. "I'll tend to your arm there. Ana, you stay close to me." She picked Maša up, carrying her on her hip.

Henrik shifted to his feet and slipped his arms under Nada's knees, behind her back, lifting her from the ground.

"I can walk," said Nada, hooking her good arm around his shoulders.

"I don't care." Jaw tight, the muscles in his neck bulged as he carried her. While his body read rigid and strained, his breathing tight and rapid, his glossy eyes screamed with agony.

Maria led the way, Ana glued to her side, as they rounded the back of the kiln. As they passed the Ustaša who shot her, now motionless in the dirt.

From there, they had a straight view down the road to the southern gate. Ustaše swarmed in front of the now-locked gate, keeping their attention off the kiln and the nearby train tunnel. Maria and the girls turned the corner, Henrik right behind, and they slid through the door to the kiln undetected.

Warmth and dimness swallowed them as they entered, offering a reprieve after the cold of the pond.

Henrik stormed toward the wall. To the space where they had waited for nightfall when they first arrived at this godforsaken camp. The lantern they found and lit to push back the darkness still glowed in the corner. Maria ushered the girls to sit by the hatches to warm up—and to keep them from seeing what damage might be done to Nada's arm.

Henrik set her on the floor. As she leaned back against the wall, he unfastened the belt around her waist and unbuttoned her jacket, his hands shaking.

"You really are terrible with buttons," she breathed, her mouth curling up.

"Don't even joke." His eyes glistened as his jaw feathered. He helped her out of the coat.

Maria rushed over and sank by her side, taking over. Her hands moved swiftly to unbutton Nada's shirt and carefully pull off her sleeve. Nada couldn't look. Didn't want to see.

Maria exhaled. "You were lucky. The bullet skimmed you."

Henrik's eyes closed and his face twisted as he lowered his chin.

Nada slid her hand against his cheek. "Hey, pull yourself together," she whispered with a gentle smile. "I need my Ubica."

He opened his watery eyes again. Held her hand in place, nodding. Then he turned to kiss her palm.

Maria fished into the pockets she had stuffed with bandages before they left the hospital. "They're wet, but they'll have to do." She began to wrap her arm and Nada lifted it to give Maria room.

Henrik's expression remained pained as he took her trembling hand from his face, clasping it between his.

"I'm okay. Really," she told him. "It barely hurts and I can move it fine."

He smiled but it didn't reach his eyes. "That'll change tomorrow. You'll feel it then, and your arm will be too stiff to move."

Henrik would know. The number of scars adorning his body told a more visceral story now. Nada's wound was only a taste of what he'd endured these last two years. It made her heart ache.

Once Maria finished bandaging her arm and Nada had dressed herself, Maria and Henrik helped her to her feet. Her legs wobbled beneath her, but they held.

"We should check that Ester and Ivan made it to the train," said Nada. "Maria, can you stay with the girls?"

"Of course."

"We'll come get you all when it's safe," said Nada.

She went to her little sisters, their knees curled up to their chins where they sat, and crouched. She took each of their arms. "I'll be right back, okay?" They only blinked as Nada pressed a kiss to each of their foreheads and slipped back outside with Henrik.

Though Nada's bullet wound wasn't as bad as it could have been, Henrik's lungs remained tight. He held fast to the knowledge she was all right and would recover. Tried to use it to ease the knot lodged in his gut. But he hated that Nada had been hurt. Approaching the opening of the train tunnel, Henrik's skin prickled all over as his steps slowed, dousing his anguish over Nada's injury. The newly arrived prisoners who had survived, lingering among the dead by the railway tracks, were nowhere to be found.

"Where are they all?" asked Nada.

Henrik stared at the area ahead. "I don't know."

The uncertainty put him on edge. Made his pulse quicken. Had the Ustaše come to corral them? What did that mean for Ester and Ivan and the men who were supposed to be preparing the train?

Pulling his Schmeisser in front of him, Henrik pointed the barrel at the ground while leaving his finger loose on the trigger and crept to the mouth of the building. Pressing his shoulder to the brick, he peered around the corner into the tunnel's opening. A minute passed before he stepped into it and out of view.

Nada followed a beat later. Nothing met them there but darkness and an idle but steaming locomotive, wisps of fog curling upward from its chimney as the engine ticked and hissed.

Henrik hunched and inched his way into the tunnel, being sure to keep his footsteps quiet. With his eyes skimming in every direction, searching for any threats, he sidled up to the train's cab.

A shovel swiped out of the cab to strike at him, and Henrik ducked in time. He twisted, swinging his gun's barrel up to aim at a man's face.

With a start, Henrik swore and lifted his finger from the trigger, lowering his Schmeisser. Ivan and his fellow inmates gaped back at him.

Ivan let out a sharp exhale. "I saw an Ustaša snooping around. I didn't realize it was you."

The two men, crouching in the cab, straightened and took the shovel back to continue loading coal into the firebox.

"Where are the prisoners that were outside?" asked Henrik.

Ivan jerked his chin toward the cattle car beside them. "They're with Ester."

Henrik and Nada went over and peeked through the half-open door. There they were, bunched against the walls of the wagon, blinking and staring out at them like mice cornered by a cat.

Ester, sitting with them in the dark, launched to her feet. "You made it. Did you find them?"

Nada nodded. "Your mother's waiting in the kiln with Ana and Maša."

Her eyes widened. "They're alive?"

"Yes. Your father didn't know, but they were hidden from the Ustaše."

"What about Teodora?"

Nada's eyes fell. She swallowed hard. Henrik gave Ester a

quick shake of his head. Her face crumpled and she climbed down from the cattle car to sweep Nada into a hug.

Ivan leaned out of the cab. "We're working as quickly and quietly as we can, but she's heating up well. We've had a few prisoners come through, but where are the rest of them?"

Nada turned to them. "They're coming. But they're under heavy attack over by the barracks. We need to wait."

"I worry about waiting too long," said Ivan with a frown, ducking back into the cab.

The rumbling engine of a vehicle revved and groaned. Henrik spun in the direction of the road outside the tunnel. A canvas-covered truck sped and swerved around the bend behind the offices as the driver hung his head out the window and shouted out warnings to the Ustaše in the camp.

"Breach! Breach! Arm yourselves!"

Henrik grabbed Nada's hand and drew her behind the lip of the tunnel with him. Pulse racing, he stared outside.

The truck skidded and swerved to a stop, its headlights beaming bright pillars through the billowing dust to shine on the administration office. The scent of burning rubber hovered in the air. More soldiers bled from every building, every corner, swarming and calling out to each other with chaotic urgency.

The passenger door of the truck opened, and a soldier stepped out.

Henrik stiffened. "It's him. The Ustaša that took Vinko into the woods."

"His brother?"

His eyes tightened as he clenched and flexed his hand. "He'll die before the night's end. I'll see to it myself."

"What breach are you talking about?" an Ustaša called out to Stipe.

"I've come from the Poglavnik's house. We found one of his men dead in his office, and a Jew's necklace. Someone stole all his Jasenovac documents. We believe someone's trying to free the prisoners."

As the commotion waged on, a figure slipped out of the

back of the truck, unnoticed. He brushed the arm of his Ustaša uniform as he took in his surroundings, keeping his head low.

Henrik stopped breathing. And then fought the urge to laugh out loud.

There was no mistaking his—as *he* once called it—winsome profile. Certainly not that lean build or the dark, messy curls sticking out from under his cap.

"Nada, look."

Henrik smiled as Vinko darted into the darkness between the buildings and disappeared.

That was when the inmates began flooding toward the tunnel.

CHAPTER 38

AMIDST THE POPPING AND CRACKING OF DEADLY FIRE, men and women ran for their lives. Passing the massive brick pit, they headed straight toward Henrik and Nada, for the cover the brick factory and buildings would afford them. One after another they toppled to the ground. But still the others kept coming.

"I'll go find Vinko," said Henrik. "Take Ester and get your sisters and Maria to the train. We're about to draw a lot of attention this way."

As soon as Henrik readied his Schmeisser and hastened toward the buildings, Nada gathered Ester to her side. Together, they swept toward the kiln. The moment they entered, Ester crushed her mother in a fierce hug, then Ester and Nada picked up her sisters and prepared themselves to run.

By the time they set foot outside again, inmates were bolting into the train tunnel, circling to get in at its entrance. Heart racing, Nada and Ester jostled between the prisoners, fighting to get into the tunnel as the Ustaše congregating by the gate began to open fire on them. Ester and Nada finally broke through into the shadows, charging toward the far end of the tunnel. They put the girls into the first cattle car, right behind the locomotive.

"Hide in the back corner," Nada told them. "Stay low on the floor."

"Mama!"

Ester's cry had Nada whirling. Maria, caught farther behind in the melee, fell in the rush of bodies outside the tunnel entrance and became trampled by the stampede of prisoners.

"No!" Ester shoved her way through the crowd toward her.

"Ester, no!" shouted Nada. "You'll be crushed!"

But Ester paid her no heed. "Mama!" She barged through the inmates. "Mama, I'm coming!"

Tousled in the hysteria, Ester fought against a strong current powered by fear as the more-exposed prisoners began dropping, one after another, under gunfire. Ester dove to her mother and helped her to her feet, then turned them both into the tide heading for the train tunnel.

An Ustaša with stiff posture stalked toward Ester, shoving inmates out of his way as he focused on her.

"Ester!" Nada pushed her way through the panicked inmates as the barrage of shots crept closer. "Ester, run!"

The Ustaša swooped in. A blade flashed in his hand. He stabbed Ester in the stomach.

Her sestra fell and Nada's heart seized. *No, no, no.* She hastened, cutting her way through the prisoners with clenched teeth. Maria cried out and dropped to Ester's side as Nada reached them. But the Ustaša stepped in front of her, blocking her path.

Nada looked up at the man and froze. Her eyes locked onto the birthmark against his neck. Nada stood face to face with Nedelko Tomič.

CHAPTER 39

Henrik heard Vinko's voice before he saw him. He talked with someone in the shadows, prompting Henrik to proceed with caution. He tilted around the corner of a building to peer into the alleyway. With Vinko's back to Henrik, he blocked the view of the Ustaša before him.

"I knew you were part of this," the Ustaša spat, his tone spewing venom. "You were lucky to get away last night, but you won't get away from me this time."

Vinko's voice wavered. "Stipe, don't do this. Please."

"You're better off dead."

Stipe. Vinko's brother had him cornered. Henrik's fingers tightened against his Schmeisser as his lips pressed together. He could taste the violence hanging in the air. Certain the Ustaša was about to kill Vinko, Henrik needed to put a stop to it. But he couldn't get a clear shot at Stipe from where he stood.

"How can you think what you're doing is right?" Vinko asked him. "Look at you, Stipe. Are you really willing to kill your brother for this cause? Think about it. Think of the influence they have over you, to the point you would hold a gun to your own fucking family."

Henrik tipped back around the corner and slung his

Schmeisser over his shoulder. He hopped onto the barrels lined against the wall there and, gripping the gutter, swung himself up onto the roof. Keeping low, he inched across it, over to the far edge, and looked down.

The resemblance in their features, the same shape in their eyes and curl in their hair, confirmed he was Vinko's brother. And he pointed a machine gun at his chest.

"I *know* what I'm doing is right," argued Stipe. "Croatia is our home. *Ours.* And yet Serbia was the one with the power. I fight for freedom from our oppressors. There's nothing more noble than that. Only the destruction of Jugoslavija can liberate Croatia."

"The destruction of innocents, you mean. You think you can murder children for the sake of liberation? The elderly? You think that is fucking noble?"

"God is behind our cause. It's no longer a sin to kill a child."

Henrik darkened and reached back for his Schmeisser, then hesitated. He had a clean shot from his position on the roof. It would have been so easy to add another Ustaša to his ever-growing number of kills. But Stipe wasn't just any other Ustaša. Not to Vinko. He heaved a sigh and wiped a hand over his face. For *Vinko's* sake, Henrik left his weapon hanging across his back.

He crept to the end of the building, right around the corner from Vinko and his brother. Henrik descended the roof much the same way he climbed onto it and dropped with a soft landing.

"You're lost," Vinko murmured. "I thought there was still hope. But I see it now. You're lost. There's no saving you."

"I'm not the one who needed saving."

Henrik rounded the corner the moment Stipe lifted his weapon and centered his aim at Vinko.

Henrik didn't give him the chance to fire. "What do you think you're doing?" Henrik barked. "The prisoners are trying to escape and you two are here taking a break? This is no time to catch up on chit-chat."

Vinko's jaw dropped, not even trying to hide his surprise.

But Stipe turned to Henrik, distracted from his aim, and Henrik took his chance. In a few swift moves he stole the weapon from Stipe, struck his temple, then smacked the back of Stipe's head with the butt of his gun. Stipe hit the ground, knocked unconscious.

Vinko stared at Henrik, his eyes large.

He handed Vinko his brother's machine gun. "He'll be all right. But it won't be long before he wakes up. We should go."

"I thought you would kill him."

The surge of old habits made Henrik reluctant to say his next words, but he didn't want to be that way anymore. He rubbed the back of his neck. "I wouldn't do that to you. To my friend."

Vinko's eyes shone as a faint, lazy grin alighted on his face. "Friend, huh?"

Henrik looked away, shaking his head while his lips twitched. "Not if you make it difficult."

He chuckled. "Nada's made you soft."

Warmth wrapped its way around Henrik at the mention of her name. No, she'd just made him see what he needed.

Vinko's gaze went to his motionless brother. He winced as his chin tilted down, as his shoulders lowered. He crouched to unfasten Stipe's magazine pouch, keeping it for himself. Vinko then turned around, his eyes still glassy as he nodded. "Time to walk away."

With that he moved forward, and Henrik joined him.

Vinko cleared his throat, blinking as he looped the magazine pouch across his chest. "I'm glad I found you here. I was beginning to worry I'd lost you all for good."

"Vinko, we thought you were *dead*. How are you here right now?"

"Stipe tried to shoot me when we were at Vila Rebar, but his gun misfired. It only clicked. The second he tried to fix it by slamming the magazine into his palm, I saw my opening and lunged at him. I grabbed for the gun and it went off, but I managed to wrestle it from him and crack him over the head with it. I knocked him out. That's when I fucking ran to hide in the tunnels you told me about."

Henrik lifted his brows.

"Don't be too impressed. While I was up all night waiting for it to be safe to sneak out, I fell asleep. I woke this afternoon and snuck into the kitchen to get some food. I overheard that they'd found a dead Ustaša and some missing papers. That was all I needed to know the plan was going ahead. But the Ustaše at the house figured out what you might be up to, and Stipe volunteered to drive to Jasenovac to alert everyone. That's when I took the opportunity to sneak into the back of his damn truck."

Henrik shook his head. He'd underestimated Vinko. He might have had terrible aim, but he was quick on his feet.

Vinko looked at him sideways, his brows quirking. "Hey, Ubica?"

"Yeah?"

"Why are you wet?"

Persistent, peppering gunfire erupted from the direction of their planned escape, and Henrik spun toward it, heart racing.

Vinko's eyes widened. "Where's Miš and Ester?"

Henrik nudged Vinko forward as he stormed ahead. "On the train. Hurry. Get to the front cattle car. They could leave any minute."

They ran, leaving the cluster of buildings and finding themselves thrust into a throng of inmates fighting to get into the train tunnel. Those who gathered on the outside of the crowd were gunned down with abandon.

Henrik's eyes turned toward the train and his heart stopped. Nada stood facing an Ustaša outside the tunnel, pale and still as a statue.

"Nada!" Henrik threw himself into the river of bodies, his eyes anchored to her. "Nada!" But he was too far away to reach her in time.

The Ustaša grabbed her. He ripped her cap off to take a

fistful of her hair. He wrenched her head back as he snarled words into her trembling face.

Muscles straining, Henrik bulldozed against the crowd.

NADA'S SCALP SCREAMED WITH PAIN AS NEDELKO'S fingers fisted her hair, but all Nada could notice were the black pits of his eyes. He snarled in her face, uttering words she couldn't grasp over the quaking in her bones. The scent of blood mingled with the cool air brushing against her exposed throat, and she stared at the birthmark on his neck as that all too familiar tremor woke in her veins again. The world ceased to exist. All sound deadened.

Silence was an ocean—vast and depthless. And Nada, lost and adrift in its murky waters, stood frozen in Nedelko's grasp. How was this happening again? Why was she here with those bodies heaped at her feet, with the man whose presence suffocated her? The cracking of gunfire in the distance, the contrast of it, muddled her.

"Nada!"

Henrik's voice slammed her back into the present, into her shuddering body. Instinct took over. Her hand shifted to her belt.

If he has you in a struggle or on the ground—

Nada gripped Nedelko's bicep and thrust her dagger up into his armpit. Then she beheld the fear in his black eyes as she tore it back out.

THE USTAŠA COLLAPSED IN A VIOLENT WASH OF BLOOD as Henrik reached Nada's side. Immense pride lifted his chest. She did it. She took what he'd taught her and used it to save herself. He wanted to pick her up, squeeze her tight, and then sweep her out of there. But then his eyes fell on Ester, on her mother pressing frantic hands against a scarlet bloom at her middle. His stomach lurched.

The Ustaše's gunfire continued mowing down the inmates around them.

"Get to the train, Nada!" Henrik stepped in to scoop Ester up into his arms. Her head lolled but she was still breathing, her dazed eyes glued to him. "Stay with me, Ester. Stay with me."

He carried her through the chaos, ducking from the resounding shots as Maria followed behind, wheezing from breathlessness.

Ester mumbled by his ear. "I was never able to ... keep up with the two of you."

"Hold on a little longer. We're almost there."

Nada kept to his side, unwilling to leave them. "What about Vinko?"

With a quick glance Henrik found Vinko pushing into the dark train tunnel ahead of them. "He's right here. He's coming."

The train hissed with a surge of steam as its brakes released and the locomotive rolled backward without them on board.

"Hurry!" Henrik tightened his grip on Ester.

As soon as the Ustaše realized the train was pulling out of the tunnel, even more gunfire rained down on them. Nada ducked her head as she cut through the thinning crowd beside them. Henrik's pulse beat loud through his entire body. They were so close.

Rapid bullets thudded from the train's front carriage. Vinko peered out of the slow-moving cattle car's opening, firing back with his brother's machine gun.

They reached the front car and Nada clambered into the carriage behind Vinko and his aim. She helped as Henrik set Ester inside, dragging her away so Henrik could throw himself onto the wooden floor. He grabbed Maria's hand, pulling her into the carriage after him.

Maria crawled over to Ester as bullets struck the walls around them, piercing holes in the panels. Henrik threw his body over Nada to shield her, adrenaline coursing through him like wildfire.

As she pressed herself to the floor of the wagon beneath him, her eyes turned to the other side of the carriage. There, her little sisters huddled together.

With the train reversing into the bend that would carry them out of the camp, they were about to be on display to the Ustaše, exposed to their volley of bullets.

Launching to his feet with his Schmeisser, Henrik met Vinko's side at the wagon's opening. Nada swept in to pull on the cattle car door, tightening the gap they fired from, shielding them. As Henrik's gun shuddered in his hands, Vinko tucked back against the wall to switch out the magazine in his weapon.

Nada didn't miss a beat, stepping in to shoot with Henrik. Guards convulsed and flung back into the dirt. As Vinko swung back into action, their carriage curved, and together they met the bulk of the attack head on. White-hot pain lanced through Henrik's calf, but he gritted his teeth and kept his aim steady.

Ustaše chased the train as it wound around the bend, shooting at them in vain when the carriage angled away from their line of sight. Gaining momentum, the train steamrolled for the exit. It barely jostled as it shattered through the locked main gate. As it threaded out through the fence and out of reach, the Ustaše's gunfire tapered off.

But they weren't home free yet. The tracks were only long enough for the train to reverse out before they'd have to roll forward into a curve, passing the camp again before finally carrying them to freedom.

"Hold your position!" Henrik shouted over the sluggish chuffing of the locomotive. "When the train starts to move forward, we'll be passing the main gate!"

The engine hissed as they came to a clunking stop, and then they crept along the tracks. The cattle cars slithered and swung out in an arc to the left. Henrik, Nada, and Vinko blasted their gunfire as the gate came into view. As expected, the Ustaše shot back at them, but with such distance from the camp, their ammunition failed to strike.

Gathering speed, the train pushed on, passing the embankment of the death camp. The gunfire stopped. Vinko lowered his weapon and Henrik slumped against the door, catching his breath as his leg continued to burn.

Nada stared blindly at the rushing, starlit scenery. "We did it."

Wind lapped through the doors to ruffle Henrik's hair, bringing with it scents of coal and iron. The train chuffed on, faster and faster, farther and farther away from Jasenovac.

Henrik removed his Ustaša cap, and with one last look at the metal U pinned at the front, he tossed it out into the night.

Nada crashed into him. He tucked her head beneath his chin, held her close, and closed his eyes. With her safe and whole in his arms, Henrik's body loosened. His heartbeat eased. They'd made it out. *She'd* made it out.

Vinko closed the cattle car door, dimming the already low light inside, and around them inmates wept tears of joy and loss. They were free.

Then Nada's body melted against his, and Henrik held her as sobs overtook her—free, but not from grief.

CHAPTER 40

HENRIK'S ARMS TIGHTENED AROUND HER, ENFOLDING Nada as she jerked with quiet, frail sobbing. Nada's fingers clawed at his damp coat, clutching onto Henrik's strength. Holding on to him to keep her steady from the storm wreaking havoc in her mind and body. She was gone. Her mother was gone. Nada's heart broke in two—one half bleeding for her mother, the other for her failure to save her.

Henrik pressed a kiss to her hair and rested his cheek on her head, letting her fall apart in silence. How could she possibly have any tears left to cry? While there was no limit to anguish and grief in this life, surely, at some point, the tears would run dry. Surely the sobs would tire and weaken, leaving nothing but blind numbness.

A faint voice rasped through the murmurs in the cattle car. "Where's ... my sestra?"

Sniffling, Nada jerked her face from Henrik's chest and searched with blurry eyes for Ester. Her dark gray Ustaša coat lay unbuttoned and askew, revealing that an alarming pool of blood had soaked through Ester's shirt.

An electric jolt shot through Nada's body. "*No,*" she breathed, her heart squeezing tight. Nada slipped from the comfort of Henrik's arms, eyes brimming as she stumbled closer. "No, no, no, no."

Her breaths fell fast as she dropped to her knees where Ester lay on the floor. Maria kneeled on her other side, pressing a cloth to her wound. Ester's tired green eyes looked up at her as Nada brushed her friend's disheveled, blond hair from her pallid face, touched her clammy cheek, and clasped Ester's shoulder. Nada's gaze landed on Maria's hands, on the blood-soaked cloth. She shook her head as a sob wrenched from her.

Maria grasped Nada's arm. "She's all right. She'll be all right, Nada."

She lifted her eyes to Maria. Stared as she held her breath.

"I've stopped the blood flow. The Ustaša didn't hit anything vital. She's lost some blood but she'll be okay."

Nada slumped, covering her face with her hands as she cried. Ester was okay. She was fine. She was alive. Nada wouldn't lose her. Her hands trembled just the same.

"Nada?" Ana's little voice came floating from nearby.

"Come with me, girls," Henrik murmured. "Give your sestra a moment."

Nada sank forward to rest her forehead on Ester's shoulder. "You're not allowed to leave me. Do you hear? Not now. Not ever."

A weak half-laugh huffed by her ear. "And stoke that temper of yours?" Ester whispered. "I wouldn't dare."

Nada chuckled through her tears.

"Nada, help me remove her coat so I can bandage her wound," said Maria. "And then she can use it for a pillow."

She straightened, nodding, then wiped the moisture from her face. As Maria kept pressure on the cloth, they both helped Ester sit upright. The girl grimaced as she did so, tipping to lean against her mother, and something small tumbled from her coat. Nada glanced down at a muted spark on the floor. It was the red star pin Nada had tucked inside Ester's pocket.

Nada turned back to Ester, catching her staring at it too.

"Let's get your jacket off and then I'll pin it to your shirt." She began pushing the coat off her shoulders.

"No," she said, breathless. "You take it. It's your star, Nada."

She looked at Ester with a wrinkled brow.

Her lips lifted into a faint grin. "You defeated an army much greater than your own."

Nada's throat swelled tight. Blinking away the prickle in her eyes, she refocused on removing Ester's coat. Pressing her lips tight, she helped Maria wrap a bandage around Ester's waist before bundling the jacket beneath her sestra's head as she reclined.

Finally, Nada picked up the star pin and clutched it in her hand. With it, she had carried a promise. To witness an end to such great and pointless death. She threaded the pin through the leather of her button bracelet once again, and there it would stay.

Her eyes slid over to her little sisters, sitting against the cattle car wall between Vinko and Henrik. Vinko held the girls' attention, whispering animated stories to distract them. Stories of a wild mouse who painted the hooves of horses white as snow, who tricked the Ustaše out of their clothes, and braved the wicked Poglavnik's lair to save her sisters.

All the while, Henrik kept his face buried in his hand, elbow resting on his drawn-up knee. That's when her focus landed on the blood soaking the leg of his pants.

Nada's gasp carried through the cattle car. "Henrik!"

She clambered to his side, eyes welling as she wrestled with her coat to take it off.

Henrik looked up, his own eyes glistening. "I'm okay."

But she continued to fumble, wrapping the sleeves around his leg, then tying them.

"Nada, I'm fine." His hands came over hers to still them. "It only grazed me."

She shook with a sob and threw her arms around him. She cried into his neck, all tension releasing from her body. "I can't lose any more people I love. I can't."

"I know." His palms glided along her back to press her close. "You won't. It's over now."

While Nada's tears quietened, she remained cinched to Henrik. And he allowed it.

TWO HOURS HAD PASSED SINCE THEY LEFT JASENOVAC. Nada sat coiled into Henrik's shoulder in the corner of the wagon. Ana slept on his other side, resting her head against Henrik's thigh, while Maša lay curled on the floor beside Vinko, his jacket her makeshift blanket. Moonlight managed to seep between the spaces and holes of the carriage walls, lighting the passengers enough to make them out. The chuff and rattle of the train lulled him, lending a dreamlike quality to Nada's nearness and his own grievous thoughts. Too many innocents had perished tonight. Nada's mother was lost, and Vinko found. In the blink of an eye, Nada and her siblings had become orphans. It all filled his chest with a hurt so profound he had to fight to bottle it in. To be strong for Nada.

She shifted, and her tired, hooded eyes lifted to the other corner of the carriage. There Maria slept beside Ester, her own coat covering them both.

He peered down at Nada, at her hand resting on his arm. "Are you all right?"

She looked up at him, her dulled red eyes giving answer enough. Her light breaths crossed his skin, reminding him of the words she'd breathed into his neck. *I can't lose any more people I love.* Warmth spiraled beneath his ribs to the point of aching. Did that mean she loved him the way he loved her? He wanted to know, but now wasn't the time to ask or even declare anything.

Henrik forced himself to change his train of thought. He gazed around the cattle car, looking over each inmate. "Eighty."

Nada still watched him, a crease forming in her brow.

"From what I saw, all the carriages carried about the same.

They were nowhere near full. That makes about eighty prisoners who made it on the train." The others had been gunned down faster than they could get onto it.

She studied the passengers, her eyes turning glassy as she did.

While it wasn't an end to the war, and their rescue wasn't great by any means, they had saved everyone they could. At least Henrik and the others had made some kind of difference. It was all they could ask for. In times like these, nothing was ever fair.

Henrik tucked loose strands of Nada's hair behind her ear, her Ustaša cap and hair pins long gone. "I'm going home with you, Nada."

She turned to him again, searching his gaze. Finding the sincerity there.

"You said I left when you needed me most. I won't do that again." When Nada said nothing, he continued. "I think we should take the girls and go to Orahovica. To Filip and your grandparents. It's safer and quieter in the country. And there's enough room for all of us."

Her breaths shallowed and her brow furrowed while she sat perfectly still.

Henrik's heart plummeted. "That's if ... you want me there."

She clasped the back of his neck and pulled him down to claim a gentle kiss. "I want you there," she whispered, with feeling. "You made me a promise, remember?"

He did. He'd promised endless days of sun and joy and kissing. He'd promised a life by her side.

Which meant Henrik could wait to know for sure if Nada loved him. They had nothing but time ahead of them.

THE STEAM TRAIN RUMBLED AND CHUGGED ALONG THE tracks as Nada stood leaning against the cattle car doors. The gray hues of early morning bled through the cracks in the wood planks, offering faint light to see by. The passengers had been asleep for hours, but for Nada, sleep refused to come. The considerable weight of her loss hung in the air, taunting her with waves of grief that kept her mind reeling. Eventually, she gave up trying and sauntered over to the doors, hoping movement would distract her.

Nada turned her gaze toward Henrik, sleeping upright in the corner of the wagon, head resting against the wooden wall. Maša had climbed into his lap to sleep against his chest. A sunburst of love billowed and tugged at her heart, reminding her she wouldn't be left numb in the wake of her loss forever. She would feel joy again one day, and she'd feel it with Henrik—the boy she'd hoped would come back into her life.

When Nada had found Henrik in the Partizan camp, she'd wanted their friendship to go back to the way it had once been. But nothing in life ever stayed the same. She'd fought tooth and nail to rescue her family from the death camp, but life unfolded in its own way regardless. She couldn't control any of it. And that was why she couldn't hold on to her past with Henrik anymore. She could only look to the future and begin something new. Something better.

Vinko's eyes cracked open from his place near Henrik and the girls. Seeing Nada awake, he rose, careful not to wake the others. Rubbing his face, he joined her by the door. "You couldn't sleep?"

Nada shook her head.

"I'm sorry, Miš." His eyes shined with moisture. "I'm sorry your mother's not here with us, traveling home."

Nada swallowed down the thick mass in her throat and looked to the corner of the carriage. She would have given her soul to see her mother curled up and asleep on that floor beside her siblings. To see Ana and Maša tangled in their mother's arms. Instead, the floor lay vacant beside her sisters. Nada's eyes roamed from Henrik—handsome and radiating a sense of home and comfort—to Vinko, the boy who made her laugh and smoked like a chimney. The boy who had become more than a fellow Partizan.

Nada offered him a sad smile. "She might not be with us any

longer, but I'm still surrounded by family." She clasped his hand and gave it a squeeze as a tear rolled down her cheek.

Nada glanced around the cattle car, at the devastating sight of the rescued prisoners. Their malnourished bodies, frail and skeletal, wearing rags as lackluster as their skin. The death camp had diminished them to mere ghosts—shells of the people they once were. All they had lost, and all those left behind, created a deafening pall in the confined space. An aura you could touch and never forget.

And many more victims now lay lifeless on the sinister grounds of Jasenovac, their blood staining the ground—forever a marker of the horrors carried out in such a godless place.

"I didn't save everyone," Nada whispered. "There were six hundred prisoners and only eighty are on this train. I was supposed to free them all."

Vinko leveled his disbelieving gaze with Nada's. "This is war you're talking about. It's not on your shoulders alone to fix it."

She drew an aching breath. "You're right. It's on all of us. The Ustaše joined as one to form such an evil, immensely powerful force. If a handful of us could do what we did at Jasenovac, imagine what we could accomplish if every man and woman joined to defeat them. And if what Henrik says is true, that the Partizan army is closing in on them, then freedom could be within reach."

Faith burned through the heaviness lacing her body. Nada glanced down at her red star pin. It sat small and unassuming against her wrist, and yet its worth was far greater than she could have ever imagined. It was a symbol of hope.

All we can do is believe that things will get better.

As Nada's father had taught her, destruction was the catalyst for renewal. To rebuild. To be stronger than before. There was only one direction to go from here.

The slowing train eased to a stop, sending Nada swaying. The steam hissing through the silence stirred the former inmates, waking them. Nada unlatched the cattle car doors and slid them wide open. The light of a new day flooded in, full of vitality and promise.

Lifting her chin, she cast her eyes ahead, standing tall. Nada would see the war extinguished, and its demons and roiling shadows scattered to the ends of the Earth. Yes, demons were relentless and cruel, and they clung to your back to remind you of their weight.

But you could always rise up and defeat them.

Printed in the USA
CPSIA information can be obtained
at www.ICGtesting.com
LVHW092042290524
781737LV00019B/58

9 798990 61571